The Sha...
It is, Ri...
Elyril cocked her head, puzzled by the comment. *Nightseer?*
You know the provenance of the war, Dark Sister. That secret must be kept.
She sat up straight, troubled. *I will keep it, Nightseer.*
I know.
The tickle on Elyril's finger turned to a twinge, an ache, a sting. She exclaimed, jumped to her feet, and pulled at the ring. She could not so much as turn it. It felt grafted to the bone of her finger. Her heart raced.
"No, Nightseer! You do not know—"
There is nothing I do not know.

The Overmistress

Mirabeta stifled a gasp at the mention of Venomindhar and Venominhandar. The destruction the two greens had wreaked in Sembia generations earlier was legend. She controlled her shock and reminded herself that *she* wielded power in Sembia. She spoke to the dragon as she would any underling.

"You will journey to Saerloon. There, you will answer to Lady Merelith and her commanders as they lay siege to Selgaunt. She will report back to me."

The dragon hefted the decanter of wine and drained it all in one long gulp. He wiped his mouth and said, "Saerloon is a long journey from here even in my natural form, woman."

"Overmistress," Mirabeta corrected him. "And I will arrange for your transport."

The Hulorn

"Are you a man of faith, Prince?"
Rivalen's golden eyes flared and narrowed.
"Is that a rude question?" Tamlin stuttered. "If so, I apologize. I thought—"
Rivalen waved a ringed hand. The shadows around him swirled. "It is not rude, Hulorn. It is forthright. That is one of the things I admire about you."
Tamlin felt himself color at Rivalen's praise. He valued it as much—perhaps more—than he had ever valued the praise of his father.

FORGOTTEN REALMS®

THE TWILIGHT WAR

Book I
Shadowbred

Book II
Shadowstorm

Book III
Shadowrealm
May 2008

THE EREVIS CALE TRILOGY

Book I
Twilight Falling

Book II
Dawn of Night

Book III
Midnight's Mask

ALSO BY PAUL S. KEMP

R.A. Salvatore's War of the Spider Queen

Book VI
Resurrection

SEMBIA: Gateway to the Realms
The Halls of Stormweather
Shadow's Witness

FORGOTTEN REALMS

SHADOWSTORM

THE TWILIGHT WAR · BOOK II

PAUL S. KEMP

The Twlight War, Book II

SHADOWSTORM

©2007 Wizards of the Coast, Inc.

Published by Wizards of the Coast, Inc. FORGOTTEN REALMS, WIZARDS OF THE COAST, and their respective logos are trademarks of Wizards of the Coast, Inc., in the U.S.A. and other countries.

Printed in the U.S.A.

Cover art by Raymond Swanland
Map by Todd Gamble
First Printing: September 2007

9 8 7 6 5 4 3 2 1

ISBN: 978-0-7869-4304-3
620-95968740-001-EN

U.S., CANADA,
ASIA, PACIFIC, & LATIN AMERICA
Wizards of the Coast, Inc.
P.O. Box 707
Renton, WA 98057-0707
+1-800-324-6496

EUROPEAN HEADQUARTERS
Hasbro UK Ltd
Caswell Way
Newport, Gwent NP9 0YH
GREAT BRITAIN
Save this address for your records.

Visit our web site at www.wizards.com

For Jen, Riordan, and Roarke, Mom and Dad.

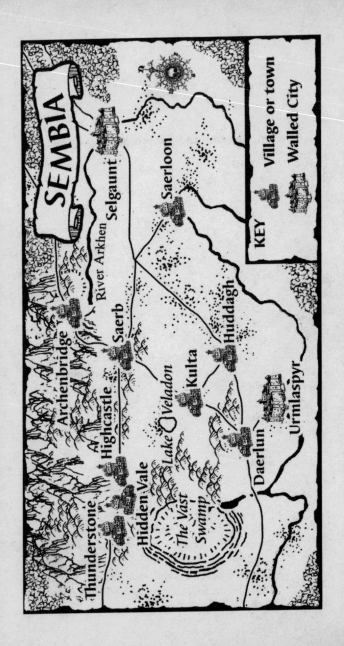

CHAPTER ONE

11 Uktar, the Year of Lightning Storms
(1374 DR)

The freezing wind howls despair into my ears, rips through my meager clothing, cuts like knives against my flesh. In the bleak distance I hear the rumble of falling ice, the groan of gigantic glaciers grinding one against the other like the bones of titans. The pained screams of the damned rise above the noise and soak the air.

"Welcome to Cania," my father says. His voice comes from everywhere, from nowhere, and worms into my soul.

The power in his tone causes Erevis and Riven to clutch their heads and groan. The blood that leaks from their ears freezes a crimson streak down jaw and neck. Erevis leans forward and vomits onto the ice. It steams for only a moment before Cania turns it hard and cold. Riven does the same and the wind devours the curses he offers between heaves. My ears, too, might be bleeding. I cannot tell. I still feel the sting in my forearms from the Source's tendrils, but little else. Mind and body have not fully integrated.

I think: I brought us here. And the thought is accompanied by the despairing realization that I am, truly, my father's son. Darkness is loose in me, given freedom by my own hand. I have gone in a moment from possession by the Source to possession by an archdevil.

I laugh but it turns to sobs. The tears freeze on my face, unable to fall.

We stand on a soot-dusted mound of packed snow and rock overlooking a desolate plain of filthy ice. Rivers of hellfire cut a jagged, arterial path through the plains as far as I can see. Steam billows in the air where hellfire meets ice. The snow-swept wind carries the stink of charred flesh, rot, and brimstone.

Suffering and despair are thick in the air. Thrashing souls burn within the rivers of flame. Their screams, plaintive and agonized, make an eerie symphony with the wind. Ice devils—towering, pallid insectoids armed with iron hooks and coated in exoskeletons like plate armor—prowl the river banks. They are far enough away that they seem not to notice our arrival. Or perhaps they do not care.

The burning souls try from time to time to clamber up the river bank for a respite from the flames. They are free of the fire for only a moment before the gelugons pounce, impale them on their hooks, and toss them, flopping and screaming, back into the fire.

The scene makes me lightheaded.

Erevis spits out the last of his vomit, glances at the suffering, and turns away. He shouts a spell into the icy air. Shadows swirl protectively about him and war with the wind. He finishes the casting and puts an ice-rimed hand to himself, to me, to Riven. The magic insulates me from the cold. Erevis removes his cloak and places it around me. He takes me by the shoulders, looks me in the eyes, and shouts something, but I cannot make it out. I hear only the damned and wind and glaciers and the echo of my father's voice. I am distant from events, outside myself.

He sees my despair and his face shows concern. I don a mask of strength and nod to assuage him. Seemingly satisfied, he pats my shoulder and turns, weapon ready, to search the desolation for my father.

I do the same, squinting into the wind but dreading what I will see.

I spot my father first and my breath catches; my heart sinks. I point.

"There," I say, and hear the hopelessness in my voice.

Erevis's and Riven's gazes follow my upraised arm. When they see him, both go still.

"Gods," Erevis says, but I barely hear it. The shadows about him withdraw into his flesh, as if in fear.

Riven says nothing, but his single eye is transfixed, his habitual sneer erased by open-mouthed awe.

Mephistopheles, Archduke of Cania, Lord of Hell— my father—crouches a long bowshot from us atop a hill of ice. The freezing wind blows over his muscular form and pulls ribbons of smoke from his flesh. The smoke swirls into the shapes of tortured forms and screaming mouths before dissipating in the air. His exposed skin glows a soft crimson, as if lit from within. Black fire flares intermittently from his form, cloaks him in evil the way shadows cloak Erevis. He turns to regard us and his eyes—white eyes like mine—fix on us, on me. The full weight of his gaze drives the three of us to our knees.

My father rises and he is as tall as a giant. His cloak flutters in the wind, and the great, tattered black membranes of his wings unfold. His long, coal-colored hair—like mine—whips in the wind. Twin horns, also like mine, protrude from his brow.

I am my father's son. Tears freeze in my eyes and I scrape them away.

Below, the damned see him, too. They point, cower, and wail. He gazes in their direction and they submerge themselves fully in the torturous hellfire rather than fall for long under his baleful gaze. The ice devils raise their hooks and grunt a salute. My father smiles at the suffering, showing his fangs, and returns his gaze to us.

He takes wing in a cloud of snow and smoke and I can only watch.

He is beautiful as he soars into the gray sky and blistering air, terrible and terrifying, a perfect predator.

But his prey is not flesh.

Erevis recovers himself first. He curses, leans on his blade, and climbs to his feet. He clutches the powerful weapon in a shaking hand, eyes on my approaching father, and pulls Riven to his feet.

"On your feet," he says above the wind. "On your damned feet."

Riven wobbles but draws his sabers and nods. His one good eye moves to me, back to my father, back to me. I see the fear in his face. I have never seen it there before.

They each extend a hand to help me stand but I do not respond. I am limp, horrified, awed. They shout for me to rise, try to pull me up by the armpits, but I cannot stand.

They release me, share a look, some words I do not hear. As one they close ranks before me, forming a bulwark between my father and me.

But the only wall that mattered between Mephistopheles and me—the wall in my mind—has already crumbled. I tore it down to save myself from the Source, and the flesh and bravery of my friends is not enough to remake it. The devil within me feels glee at the approach of my sire. The man feels disgust. I stare at the sky, torn, divided.

We are lost.

Erevis shouts at me over his shoulder, and his words penetrate my haze. "Get up, Mags! Do not give him this!"

I look at him, barely comprehending.

Bow says the devil in me.

Rise says the man.

Mephistopheles swoops in the air, prolonging his approach, letting the fear build.

"Cale . . ." Riven says to Erevis, his eye on my father.

"I know," Erevis snaps. Shadows ooze from his flesh and swirl closely about him. "But we hold this ground. Understood?" He thumps Riven on the shoulder. "This ground is ours."

"It's only ground, Cale," Riven says. "We can leave it."

Erevis shakes his head. "We cannot. The shadows do not answer me here. I cannot take us out."

Erevis's god is not lord in Cania. My father is.

Riven goes still and stares at Cale for a moment. He knows there is no escape. He looks back at me, at Cale, up at my father.

I see the resolve harden in him. He is as much ice as Cania.

I am awed by more than merely my father.

I have seen my friends stand together before, the First and Second of Mask. I watched Erevis drive his thumbs into the braincase of a death slaad. I have seen Riven's blades move so fast they whistled. I know they are not normal men; normal men would still be on all fours on the ice, awaiting death.

But I know, too, that they are no match for the Lord of Cania.

Each beat of my father's wings looses smoke into the air. As he nears us, the tattoo on my bicep—a red hand sheathed in flames, the symbol of my father—stings my flesh. Smoke rises from my arm. I do not need to look at it to know that the flames are swirling on my skin. Mephistopheles has marked me and I am his.

But the pain stirs me to motion; the bravery of my friends draws me back to myself. I quell the fiend within me, lick my lips, and try to climb to my feet. I will not die on my knees. I will stand with my friends.

They see me stir, turn, and pull me the rest of the way to my feet.

"Godsdamned right," Riven says, and gives me a thump on the shoulder. "Godsdamned right."

Cale knew they had a twenty count, no more, and there was nowhere to run. He held Weaveshear in a numb hand and blew out clouds of frozen breath. He whispered a series of rapid prayers, invoking magic that made him stronger and faster.

Looking upon the archfiend, he did not think it would be enough.

Magadon spoke in a low tone, his voice hollow. "This is my doing. I planted this location in Erevis's mind as he moved us between planes. Or part of me did. I am sorry."

Riven spared Magadon a hard look but said nothing.

"It wasn't you, Mags," Cale said, and meant it.

Riven shifted on his feet.

"I am sorry, Riven," Magadon said to him.

Riven drew a dagger from his belt, flipped it, and offered the hilt to Magadon.

"It's enchanted. Take it. It is better than nothing."

Magadon did not take the dagger. He looked at Riven, at Cale. "We cannot fight him and live."

"Which doesn't mean we don't fight," Riven snapped. "I don't go down without giving what I've got. And neither should you." He held the dagger's hilt before Magadon's face. "Take it."

"I have a weapon if I have need," Magadon said, but took the dagger anyway.

Cale said, "If we cannot fight, then we have to negotiate. What can we offer him, Mags?"

Mephistopheles vanished from the sky and reappeared directly behind them. His form dwarfed them. His wings enveloped them. The unholy energy that sheathed the trio stole their breath. One of Mephistopheles's enormous hands closed over Cale's shoulder, and the claws sank into his skin. He bent and put his mouth to Cale's ear.

"There is nothing you can offer me that I cannot otherwise take," the archdevil said, and the sound of his basso voice buried them all under its power. His fetid breath stank like a charnel house.

Supernatural terror accompanied the archdevil's presence but Cale fought through it. He remembered that he had faced his own god, stabbed Mask in the chest.

"But this is no alley," Mephistopheles whispered into Cale's ear. "And I am not your god."

Shadows leaked from Cale's skin, twined around Mephistopheles's hand.

"No," Cale answered. "You are not."

Moving deliberately and forcefully, Cale took the archdevil's hand, removed it from his shoulder, and turned to stand in the towering shadow of a ruler of Hell. Riven and Magadon, perhaps freed of their terror by Cale's nerve, did the same. Riven and Cale edged before Magadon and closed ranks.

The fiend radiated spite. It took all Cale had to stand his ground.

Mephistopheles's white eyes bored holes into him. The archdevil inhaled deeply.

"You stink of goddess and godling, shade. Where is the Shadowlord now, I wonder? Do you imagine that he will save you?"

Cale decided then and there that he was of one mind with Riven—he would not die without giving what he had. He tightened his grip on Weaveshear and shadowy tendrils leaked from the blade.

"Save me from what?"

"Nothing here we need saving from," Riven added. The assassin, who looked small standing beside Cale, looked insignificant standing before the archdevil.

Mephistopheles's eyes narrowed, moved from Cale to Riven.

The devil poked the tip of a black-nailed, ringed finger into Riven's chest.

"You are transparent to me," he said.

"I am easy that way," Riven said with a sneer.

Mephistopheles's lip curled and he scraped his claw down Riven's chest, hard enough to rock the assassin on his feet, penetrate armor, and draw blood.

"I think that you could have been one of mine," the archdevil said.

Blood from the gash in Riven's chest darkened his shirt and cloak, but the assassin did not wince, though a tic caused his one good eye to spasm.

Cale placed the edge of Weaveshear's blade under the archdevil's finger and lifted it away from Riven.

"That is enough."

Mephistopheles put a fingertip on the blade and black fire twined around the steel. Cale held onto the hilt and darkness snaked from his hands.

Shadows met fire, churned and sizzled.

The fire flared, consumed the shadows, and Weaveshear flashed red hot. Cale's skin blistered. He cursed and released the weapon.

Mephistopheles snatched it from mid air and held the superheated blade without harm. He studied it, smelled it. Cale and Riven shared a glance. Both knew they were out of their depth.

Mephistopheles smirked, dropped the weapon. It hit the ice of Cania tip first, sank half its length into the ground, and sent up a cloud of hissing steam as it cooled.

"A mildly interesting toy," the archdevil said.

Cale kept his face expressionless as he retrieved the weapon, still warm, from the ice.

Magadon cleared his throat and said in a small voice, "We are leaving Cania, father."

Mephistopheles's brow furrowed and he looked down on Magadon, as if for the first time.

"Did something speak? I hear a voice but see nothing here worthy of addressing me."

"We are leaving," Magadon reiterated.

"Ah," Mephistopheles said, glaring at Magadon, who wilted under the scrutiny. "It is my ungrateful son who dares utter words in my presence. And leaving, you say? But you have only just arrived. And it was you who brought them here."

"No," Magadon said. "It was you."

"You perceive a difference where there is none."

Magadon looked up with defiance in his eyes. Cale was pleased to see it.

"You lie," Magadon said, his voice strong at last. "There is a difference."

Mephistopheles's eyes flashed anger. "Think you so?"

Sensing the danger, Cale edged closer to Magadon.

The archdevil turned on him, growing to twice his height in a breath.

"He is spoken for, shade, body and soul!"

The power in Mephistopheles's voice caused ice to crack, the damned to whimper in fear, and drove Cale back, knocking him breathless to the frozen ground.

Riven lunged forward, one blade low, one high. The archdevil held up a hand and a rush of black power from his palm drove Riven flat on his back and skittering across the ice.

Magadon stood alone before his father.

Mephistopheles recovered his composure and shrank back into himself. His expression went from enraged to calm in a heartbeat.

"I am not yours," Magadon said.

"You are mistaken," Mephistopheles responded. "We have dreamed wonderful dreams together, you and me."

Magadon shook his head and looked down at his feet. "No. They weren't mine. They never were. You put them there."

Mephistopheles reached down and placed a giant hand on Magadon's emaciated shoulder. The mindmage blanched at the touch—smoke rose from his flesh.

"How could I do so if you did not invite them?"

Shadows swirled around Cale, comforting him, healing him. He climbed to his feet and pointed Weaveshear at the archdevil.

"He *is* spoken for, devil. But not by you."

"Truth," Riven added, as he, too, rose.

Mephistopheles looked from Magadon to Cale and his lips formed a hard line. The dark fire around him flared. He beat his decayed wings and the wind of Cania answered with gusts. The cold cut through Cale's protective spell. The archdevil's voice was as gelid as the plain.

"All here is mine, shade, even the shadows. You will never leave here. Your lot is to be punished. I will flay your souls and the screaming tatters that remain will be playthings for my gelugons."

Cale did not bother to deny the archdevil's claim. He instead said, "We will hurt you first. I promise you that."

"Hurt you so you remember it," Riven added.

Unholy power, dark and cold, flared around Mephistopheles's form.

"Do not," Magadon said, and Cale was not certain if he was speaking to his father or his comrades.

Mephistopheles kept one hand possessively on Magadon and held his other out at his side. A wickedly pointed iron polearm as tall as Cale appeared in his fist. Magic crackled on its point.

"Hurt me? Think you so?"

Cale stared into the face of his own death and affirmed his claim.

"Think we so."

Shadows haloed him, thick and dark, and he drew strength from them. Riven twirled his blades and invoked Mask's power until his sabers bled darkness.

"Seems Mask is here after all," the assassin said, and spat in the archdevil's direction.

"But not for long," the archdevil said.

A soft popping sound heralded the arrival of a gelugon beside Mephistopheles. It stood nearly as tall as its master. The white orbs of its insectoid eyes stared down at Riven and Cale. It held a huge hooked spear in its clawed hand. Frost and soot covered its naked exoskeleton. Wet, steaming respiration leaked through its clicking mandibles. Another gelugon appeared on the other side of its master, another, another. A dozen popped into existence around Mephistopheles, then a score materialized around Cale and Riven and Magadon.

Cale stood in the midst of threescore devils certain in the knowledge that he would die. But he resolved to give Hell to the Lord of Hell before he did.

He called to mind the words to a spell that would charge him with divine power, Mask's power. He looked at Riven and said farewell with his eyes. Riven looked back and nodded.

They turned to Mephistopheles.

"Enough," Magadon said.

The mindmage's words hung in the air, as frozen as the ice. Magadon looked up at his archdevil father and, for the first time, Cale noticed the uncanny resemblance between father and son—the eyes, hair, horns, and jaw.

The archdevil cocked his head with curiosity and the unholy storm of dark energy gathering about him subsided to a simmer.

"Enough, father," Magadon said.

As sudden as a lightning strike, Mephistopheles backhanded Magadon across his head. The force of the blow knocked the mindmage sprawling to the ice. The gelugons clicked eagerly, shifted on their clawed feet. Cale and Riven started forward.

"No!" Magadon said, halting Cale in his steps. He rose to all fours.

Mephistopheles loomed large over Magadon's prone form.

"You dare speak thus to me, half-breed? You are the happenstance of my spraying seed, nothing more. Your life has provided me with a measure of amusement, but that life is over now. I will kill your soul, the same as theirs, but your suffering I will prolong.

Blood trickled from Magadon's nose. He spit out a tooth and lifted his gaze to his father, but only for a moment before he bowed his head in despair.

Cale realized that he and Riven could fight before they died. Magadon could not. It was not in him, not then. Cale had to find another way. He said the first thing that popped into his mind.

"A bargain, devil."

Mephistopheles kept his eyes on his son as he answered.

"You possess nothing of interest to me except your pain. And that, I claim as my own."

He raised his polearm high. The wind howled.

Cale's mind raced. He tried to imagine what he could offer that might appease the archfiend.

"Kesson Rel," he blurted, and the shadows around him swirled. He swore he heard chuckling on the wind. He had gambled. He knew only a little of Kesson Rel.

The archdevil cocked his head, his weapon leaking evil into the cold air. The gelugons clicked and grunted.

"That is an old name," Mephistopheles said softly.

Cale heard the curiosity in the archdevil's tone.

"Will you hear more? I have more to tell."

Mephistopheles regarded Cale with a thoughtful look. He lowered his weapon and signaled his gelugons. They gave disappointed grunts and blinked away, one after another, back to their sport with the damned.

"What more is there?" Mephistopheles asked. "Choose your words well, shade. There are not many left to you."

Cale debated on how much to say, what to offer. He looked at Magadon, prone and bleeding, afraid. He glanced at Riven, who stared at him intently.

Cale took a deep breath and did what he must for his friend— he defied his god. He had no choice.

"Kesson Rel possesses something that belongs to another. You know what it is. I will get it back . . . and give it to you."

The archdevil's eyes flared, but with anger or excitement Cale could not tell. Cale didn't know what Kesson Rel had taken, only that Mask wanted it back and that Mephistopheles seemed intrigued.

Mephistopheles said, "The divine essence of your god, stolen by the first thief of the Lord of Thieves? You make a promise you cannot keep. Have you not already promised it to another?"

Cale quailed when he learned what he had offered, but his words bound him. He nodded. "I have made a promise to another," Cale said softly, feeling Riven's eye on him. "But I will keep my promise to you nevertheless."

Mephistopheles stared at him, into him, through him.

"Words have meaning in Cania, shade. Promises are not idle here—not to me."

"I know what I have done," Cale answered.

What he had done was make conflicting promises to Mask and Mephistopheles. He owed a god and an archfiend the same thing—the divine power stolen by Kesson Rel.

Mephistopheles looked out across the plain.

"Speak," Cale dared say. "I have made you an offer."

Mephistopheles grinned, showing fangs. "I am considering it."

Cale moved forward and helped Magadon to his feet. He whispered a healing spell to Mask—expecting full well that the god would not answer him—and sighed with relief when healing energy flowed out of his hands and into his friend.

Magadon squeezed his shoulder gratefully and did not let him go.

"Erevis . . ." Magadon began.

"Quiet, Mags. It is not over." Cale looked up at Mephistopheles. "I have given you my terms. Do you accept?"

The archdevil said, "Your god would not be pleased if he knew what you offered."

"My god often finds me displeasing."

"So do all fathers their sons," Mephistopheles said, looking at

Magadon. "If I accept your offer, how will you guarantee payment of your debt?"

"My word is all you get. It was enough for him. It is enough for you."

The archdevil shook his head. "No. I am not as trusting as the so-called *god* of thieves." His eyes hardened and fixed on Magadon. "I shall keep my son to ensure you do not default."

Cale put himself before Magadon. "No."

"Erevis," Magadon said, and tried to step out from around Cale. "I will—"

"No," Cale said to Magadon, to Mephistopheles. "Non negotiable."

"Everything is negotiable," the archdevil said.

"Not this."

Mephistopheles stared into Cale's face, measuring his resolve.

"Very well," Mephistopheles said at last. "I will accept a compromise."

The archdevil waved his hand in the air and motes of sickly green energy sparkled over Cale and Riven's skin.

"What is—"

The magic cut Cale's words short and held him immobile. He could not speak, could not move. His heart hammered against his ribs as Mephistopheles grew to twice his already enormous size and reached around him . . . for Magadon.

Magadon tried to hold onto Cale, but Mephistopheles peeled him loose.

"I will keep half of him instead of the whole," the archdevil said.

The mindmage, unaffected by the spell that held Cale immobile, squirmed like a fish in the archdevil's hand.

"Father, no!"

Mephistopheles wore a smile that Cale had seen before only on madmen. The archdevil stepped back so that Cale and Riven could see everything.

Black energy pooled around father and son. Magadon

screamed. The archdevil, as tall as a titan, laid Magadon across his palm and stabbed him in the abdomen with the tip of one of his dagger-sized claws.

Blood poured from Magadon's torso; he wailed with pain as the devil opened his body.

"No! No! Erevis, help!"

Cale struggled against the enchantment that held him immobile, felt around the edges of the magic and tried to slip the chains of the spell. To no avail. Shadows swirled around him. Frustration and anger rose in him so strongly that he thought he must burst. He broke through enough only to voice a scream.

"Stop!"

Mephistopheles paid him no heed. He tore his claw through Magadon's torso, opening his abdomen fully, and spilled his innards. They fell in a steaming heap to Cania's ice.

Magadon's screams died. The hole in him gaped.

The archdevil shook out the corpse to empty it of blood and organs. A shower of crimson spattered the ice.

Mephistopheles took Magadon's limp body by the ankles and torso and tore it in two at the waist. The sound of tearing flesh and cracking bone sent bile up Cale's throat. He could not swallow and it burned the back of his tongue, acrid and foul. Tears formed in the corners of his eyes and froze in the cold air.

The archdevil held aloft the two pieces of Magadon and chuckled. "A half-breed, truly."

Cale vowed with every breath that he would kill the archdevil, punish him, cause him pain.

Mephistopheles dropped both halves of the body to the ice. Magadon's face stared at Cale, the dead eyes and mouth wide with pain. The mindmage's arms spasmed grotesquely in his own gore. Cale prayed it was only a reflex.

Mephistopheles reached down into the pile and with two fingers drew forth a glowing, silver form, a ghostly image of Magadon.

A soul. Magadon's soul.

Cale wanted to close his eyes but could not.

The form squirmed in Mephistopheles's grasp as the archdevil held it up before his face. He leered and his eyes glowed with hunger. The face of Magadon's soul contorted in terror, pounded its fists against the archdevil's hand, but could not escape.

The archdevil lifted the soul high, tipped back his head, opened his mouth, and bit the soul in half. He swallowed it down as the other half writhed in his grasp. The silence with which Magadon's soul endured the agony made it all the worse to witness. Cale heard the screams only in his own imagination.

The Lord of Hell cast the remaining half of the soul back into Magadon's remains. He shrank back down to his normal, merely giant size, bent low, and exhaled a cloud of vile power over the gore.

To Cale's horror, the bloody pile began to stir. Magadon's eyes focused directly on Cale and his mouth opened in an animal scream that rose above the wind, that dwarfed the wails of the damned.

Slowly, the mindmage began to pull himself together. Screaming and gibbering all the while, he scooped his innards back into his torso, pulled his upper and lower halves back together. As the parts reunited, Mephistopheles's magic stitched the bloody pieces back into a man.

The archfiend waited until Magadon was almost whole, then grabbed his son by his hair, pulled him up, and put his mouth to Magadon's ear. He whispered something that Cale could not make out. The terror in Magadon's eyes made Cale thankful that he could not see Mephistopheles's lips to read them.

The archdevil released his son and Magadon collapsed to the ice. Mephistopheles eyed the immobile Cale, circled behind him.

Cale never felt more vulnerable. He waited for pain.

It did not come. Instead, he felt the archdevil rifling in his pack.

"Here," the archdevil said. "I knew I smelled the tang of a goddess. This, too, I claim as mine."

He circled back into Cale's field of vision and Cale saw that Mephistopheles held in his hands the black book that Cale had taken from the Fane of Shadows. The archdevil flipped open the back cover of the book and flipped through the pages, thumbing from back to front.

Cale could see that the pages contained more writing than the last time he had opened the book in Stormweather Tower. Precise purple script covered the sheets. It appeared that the book was . . . rewriting itself from the back to the front.

"Another interesting toy," the archdevil murmured. He snapped the book shut and smiled. "Interesting times lay ahead."

Mephistopheles flicked his wrist and the book disappeared in a puff of foul-smelling smoke. He looked over to Magadon, who was once more whole, but prone on all fours, slick with gore, and coughing. The archdevil moved to Magadon's side, grabbed him by the arm, and jerked him to his feet.

"No more," Magadon said in a broken voice.

"Your obeisance comes too late, half-breed."

To Cale, Mephistopheles said, "What's left of him is yours. But if you renege, I will destroy utterly what I have taken and come for the rest. You cannot protect him. Bring me what you've promised, and I shall vomit him up and do him no further harm."

With that, he threw Magadon toward Cale.

At the same moment, the spell holding Cale and Riven immobile ended.

Cale could do nothing but catch his blood-slicked friend, who groaned and collapsed in his arms, but Riven twirled his blades and stalked toward the archdevil.

"No, Riven!" Cale shouted immediately. "No!"

The assassin did not look at Cale but stopped his advance. His breath came like a bellows.

"Not now," Cale said.

The assassin stared hate at the archdevil.

Magadon started to shake in Cale's arms. It took a moment for Cale to realize that he was sobbing.

"Riven," Cale said, more softly. "We are leaving."

Riven looked back at Cale, saw Magadon, and his expression softened. He turned back to the archdevil, spat at his feet, and sheathed his blades.

Mephistopheles only cocked an eyebrow in amusement.

Cale held his friend and stared into Mephistopheles's face, into his eyes, and did not blanch.

"I will get you what I've promised and you will return the rest of him to me. And when that bargain is concluded, I will exact payment for this."

"And the price will be high," Riven added, as he stepped beside Cale. He put a hand on Magadon's shoulder, gently, the way Cale had seen him touch his dogs.

Mephistopheles lost the amused expression. "You make another promise you will find difficult to keep, First of Five."

Cale shook his head and stared. "I have never made a promise more easily kept."

"That's truth," Riven added coldly.

Mephistopheles did not even glance at Riven. He studied Cale's face for a moment.

"You, too, could have been one of mine, I think."

Cale stared. "You know nothing about me."

"I know you entirely. I know what you want. I know what you are willing to do to have it."

Shadows oozed from Cale's flesh. He felt Riven's eye on him, Magadon's eyes.

"Shall I say it?" the archdevil asked. "If I do, it will never happen."

"You know nothing," Cale said, but his voice lacked conviction.

Mephistopheles looked upon Cale and smiled. "You wish to transcend, wish it desperately. So do all men who hate themselves. But you never shall. Not now."

The truth of the words was too evident to deny.

Mephistopheles filled the silence with a chuckle. "Now,

begone from my realm. Skulk back into the shadows in which you cower and get me what you've promised."

He blew out a black cloud that engulfed the three comrades.

"And remember always that I am a liar," the archdevil said.

Cale's stomach lurched as they moved between worlds.

Elyril sat cross-legged and nude on the carpeted floor, her back to the hearth. The darkness in the chamber caressed her skin, teased pleasantly at the soft hairs of her arms and legs. She took a pinch of minddust from the small metal box on the floor at her side. The pungent drug took effect immediately and her consciousness expanded.

The flames from the fire behind her cast malformed shadows on the pale plaster wall opposite. The minddust darkened them, sharpened their lines. Elyril watched them dance and spin and tried to understand their truth.

What do they say? projected Kefil.

The enormous mastiff lay curled beside her, a mountain of black fur, muscle, and teeth.

They keep their secrets, she answered. *Silence, now, Kefil.*

Kefil sighed, licked her hand, and shifted position.

Elyril watched faces and shapes form and dissipate in the chaos on the wall. She willed them to speak, to give her wisdom. She wished to know the secret of the sign and the book to be made whole. She held her arms aloft, stirring the shadows, and whispered, "In the darkness of the night, we hear the whisper of the void."

Her words set the images to roiling. Dozens of faces formed momentarily in the darkness and leered at her from the wall. They said nothing, offered her no secrets, and her frustration grew. She shifted her position to change her perspective. Kefil groaned and rolled over on his back. Elyril inhaled another pinch of minddust and lit her senses on fire.

The wall darkened and the faces withdrew. Stillness ruled the room. She was alone in the darkness. The air thickened. She saw her heart beating in her shadow.

A diabolical face appeared on the wall and lunged out of the plaster to hang in the air before her—a devil sent her by Shar, or Volumvax. Horns jutted from the brow to shadow the malevolent eyes.

Elyril recoiled in surprise but recovered herself quickly.

"Speak," she ordered the image. "Where is the book to be made whole?"

The fiend licked its lips, mockingly smiled a mouthful of fangs, and spoke to her in a tongue that she could not understand, but with such power that the words nauseated her.

She knew there was truth in the speech, if she could only understand. She needed more minddust.

She reached for her tin of drugs, took a pinch between her fingers, and inhaled, but the face withdrew into the wall, smirking. She clenched her fists in anger.

"I do not understand!"

Her voice took physical form and bounced off the walls and around the room.

". . . not understand . . . not understand . . ."

Kefil raised his head and looked around the room. *To whom do you speak? The fire is long dead. There are no shadows on the wall.*

"What? You lie."

But he did not. The fire behind her was dead. She was alone in the darkness. How long had she been sitting so? How could there have been shadows without the fire?

Kefil stood, sighed, and stretched. *What is it you wish to understand, Mistress?*

Elyril pulled a nearby wool blanket about her. The minddust made her skin sensitive and the blanket chafed. She threw it aside.

"The location of the book to be made whole. The nature of the sign."

So that you may free the Divine One?

Elyril smiled and nodded. "So that I may sit at his side as the Shadowstorm darkens the world."

Kefil scratched his ear with a hind leg. *Perhaps you will never know the location of the book or the nature of the sign. Perhaps Shar will keep this secret from you always. Perhaps not knowing will drive you mad.*

Elyril glared at the mastiff.

"And perhaps I shall make a rug from your pelt."

Kefil said nothing more.

Elyril spent the rest of the night praying and trying to wrest information from the darkness. But Shar held her secrets, and the truth of events lay just beyond Elyril's reach.

CHAPTER TWO

15 Uktar, the Year of Lightning Storms

The slim stone towers and high walls of the Abbey of Dawn perched atop a rise in southeastern Sembia, not far from the coast of the Dragon Sea. The three tapered spires of the abbey's east-facing chapel gave the impression of reaching for the heavens, of something about to take flight. The polished limestone walls and accents of rose-colored stone glittered in dawn's light.

A pear orchard and a patchwork of barley and vegetable fields stood within the shadow of the walls—the harvest had already been brought in—and beyond that lay only the whipgrass of the plains, clusters of yellow and purple wildflowers, and copses of larch and ash. The winding wagon path that meandered through the plains from Rauthauvyr's Road to the north was barely visible in the swaying grass. Few used the path. The abbey served as a cloister for servants of Lathander and was almost entirely self-sufficient. Most who came spent years there.

As an adolescent, Abelar had worked the barley and turnip fields, carted bushels of pears from the orchard to the abbey, drawn water from the wells. The work had taught him the value and nobility in a day's hard labor.

As a man, he had stood watch on the abbey's walls and rode forth with his fellows of the Order of the Aster to do battle against darkness. His time in the Order had taught him the value of strong steel and courageous men and women.

But those days seemed far in the past. He had been away from the abbey for months. Schism had rent Lathander's church, had taken root in the abbey, and Abelar had been declared unwelcome. It saddened him that the abbey at which he had sworn his life to Lathander had become a kiln where heresy was hardened and the Morninglord's faith weakened.

"Abelar?"

Abelar's mind returned to the present. He sat atop his mare, Swiftdawn, amid the whispering grass, perhaps half a league from the abbey. The wagon path stretched before him. The rising sun warmed his cheek.

"You spoke?" Abelar asked Regg, who sat beside him on his roan mare, Firstlight.

"I asked if you were certain of this course," Regg said.

Road dust covered Regg's cloak and plate armor, and several days' growth of beard covered his cheeks. Regg eyed the abbey the way he might a skittish colt. Like Abelar, Regg also served Lathander, but he had not taken rites at the Abbey of Dawn.

Abelar nodded. "I am certain."

Regg's mare, sweaty and road weary, turned a circle and snorted in the cool air. Abelar's mare, too, snorted. Perhaps they smelled a wolf in the wind. Abelar stroked Swiftdawn's neck and whickered. She tossed her head but calmed.

Abelar and Regg had left the rest of the men in a village to the northwest and journeyed to the abbey alone. Abelar had been concerned that his appearance at the head of an armed force would be misconstrued. He had come to mend the rift as best he could. He needed to persuade with words, not weapons.

"Swiftdawn and Firstlight do not share your resolve," Regg said, patting his nervous mare.

"Our brethren are within that abbey, Regg."

Regg stilled Firstlight and scoffed. "Brethren? They are Risen Sun heretics. They look for their so-called Deliverance while the world collapses around them. What have they done since Mirabeta took power? Even Morninglord Duskroon in Ordulin sits idle. His silence ratifies Mirabeta's claims to power. I hardly recognize our faith, Abelar. Those who lead it are fools."

Abelar shook his head. "Lathander leads it, Regg. But some who follow have lost their way. They are misguided, but not fools. They will heed us. They will see the light."

He hoped that saying the words would make them so. The Risen Sun heresy had originated months ago and spread like a wildfire among many of Lathander's clergy, including those at the abbey. The heretics asserted that the Deliverance, an event in which the Morninglord would remake himself as the ancient sun god Amaunator, was imminent. The heretics so focused on gaining new converts and preparing the way for the Deliverance, which they presumed would not only remake Lathander but also usher in a new era of worship and hope, that they lost sight of the church's duty to Faerûn. They wanted Lathander to change the world for them, rather than changing it themselves in Lathander's name.

"They will not heed us," Regg said. "And they may arrest us. They banished you, Abelar. Abbot Denril sent you from them."

Abelar nodded. "That, he did."

The memory pained him. Abelar had learned how to wield a blade and shield from Denril, long before the priest had become Abbot and taken charge of the abbey. Denril had sponsored Abelar's entry into the Order of the Aster after Abelar, at eighteen winters, had saved a passing caravan by slaying a rampaging ogre single-handedly. Denril also had presided over Abelar's dismissal from the Order and the abbey after Abelar had refused to acknowledge the truth of the Risen Sun heresy. Their parting had been bitter.

"He is as much politician as priest," Regg said with contempt.

"You underestimate him," Abelar said.

Regg looked at him from under his bushy brows. "I pray you are correct, but fear you are not. He would gain much were he to turn you over to Mirabeta."

Sunlight caught the flecks of mica embedded in the abbey's smooth walls and they sparkled like a dragon's trove. The stained glass arches set into the upper windows of the chapel's towers flashed in the sun.

When he had first come to the abbey, Abelar had sometimes snuck out before dawn just to sit in the grass, commune with Lathander, and watch the light from the rising sun grace the abbey. He missed the feeling of those days. They had been . . . innocent. It had been easy then to know friend from foe, right from wrong.

Much had changed.

"They will be at Dawnmeet," Regg said.

"We will give them time to finish," Abelar said, and turned Swiftdawn so that she faced the rising sun.

Regg did the same and they held their own Dawnmeet service, reciting a brief prayer together.

"Dawn dispels the night and births the world anew," they said in unison. "May Lathander light our way, show us wisdom, and in so doing, allow us to be a light to others."

They dismounted and took a meal of hardtack in silence. Like everyone in Sembia, they rationed their food. The priests in Abelar's company used their spells to provide the men with enough food to stave off hunger, but Abelar hoarded it like it was gold.

After they had eaten, they remounted and rode toward the abbey.

"The guards in the gatehouse will soon see us coming," Regg said. "They will be prepared for our arrival."

"Aye," said Abelar. He held his shield forward, in plain view, so that the rose of Lathander emblazoned on it would be visible.

Elyril and Mirabeta sat at a small table on the open-air balcony of the three-story tallhouse that the overmistress occupied while in Ordulin. Elyril wore a simple, long-sleeved dress to shield her pale skin from the morning sun. Her dark-haired aunt wore a formal green day gown.

A banner flying Sembia's heraldry—the raven and silver—hung from the roof eaves above them. Smaller pennons flanked it to either side, both flying Ordulin's golden wagon wheel on a field of green. All three flapped softly in the gentle breeze. The hum of conversation and the rumble of wagons carried up from the cobblestone street below. Elyril heard the occasional order barked by the uniformed Helms who kept the pedestrian traffic at a discreet distance from the overmistress's tallhouse.

One of Mirabeta's mute serving girls, pole-thin and sunken-eyed, stood unobtrusively near the open double doorway that led into the tallhouse. Mirabeta had brought her own staff to Ordulin from Ravenholme.

"The sunlight is pleasant," Mirabeta said.

Elyril and her aunt breakfasted on dried currants, day old bread, and a light, fruity wine from Raven's Bluff.

"It is," Elyril lied.

Mirabeta glanced up at the pennons. "I think I will change Sembia's colors to something that includes the Selkirk falcon."

The overmistress smiled, obviously pleased at the thought. She still held the same satisfied air she had worn since a rump session of the High Council had elected her War Regent. Elyril did not share her aunt's sense of ease. Since setting the Sembian civil war into motion, she had received contact from neither

Volumvax nor the Nightseer, and her communions with Shar had resulted only in frustration. She did not fully understand her role in events and her ignorance irritated her. She felt herself on the verge of a revelation, but always it remained just out of reach. Only increasingly frequent use of minddust allowed her to endure the uncertainty.

"Malkur Forrin is returned to Ordulin," Mirabeta said. "The Hulorn escaped him. I received the news yesterday."

"That is regrettable," Elyril said. "How did the Uskevren manage to escape? Perhaps word of events reached him on the road?"

"I have no details yet," Mirabeta said, and sipped her wine. "My envoys to Cormyr and Cormanthyr report a favorable response to our overtures. Both the Regent and the new Coronal appear to accept the premise that our . . . current troubles are and should remain an internal Sembian affair."

"That is welcome news, aunt."

In truth, neither Cormyr nor the elves of Cormanthyr were in positions to take sides in the Sembian conflict. Both had recently fought wars of their own. Sighs of relief in Arabel and the elven halls had probably greeted Mirabeta's gentle demand that they remain neutral in Sembia's conflict.

Footfalls approached from within the tallhouse. Mirabeta's chamberlain, Turest Gillan, appeared in the doorway. A defect of birth—common among the Selkirks' inbred servants—caused his heavy-lidded eyes to look in two different directions. Tufts of gray hair jutted this way and that from his overlarge skull.

He stood in silence, waiting to be recognized. Elyril watched his form blur and shimmer, moving rapidly through time. He changed from adolescent to elderly and back to his fifty or so winters in the span of a heartbeat. Only Elyril seemed to notice the changes.

"Turest?" Mirabeta said at last.

The chamberlain bowed, avoiding eye contact, not an easy matter for a man who looked in two directions at once. Mirabeta would flog even her chamberlain for presuming to look her in the face. Elyril had once heard the chamberlain scream while being punished. He had a pleasant, high-pitched screech that amused her.

"A credentialed messenger has arrived, Overmistress. He bears a missive under seal from Yhaunn."

Mirabeta swallowed a currant and dabbed her mouth with a hand cloth. "Verify that the message is genuine. If so, bring it to me and extend such courtesies to the messenger as are appropriate. If not, bring it to me and have the messenger fed to the dogs."

"Yes, Overmistress."

Elyril and Mirabeta shared a curious glance as Turest exited the balcony. The mute serving girl, as quiet as a ghost, moved to the table and refilled their wine goblets, then returned to her station.

Elyril said, "Perhaps Endren Corrinthal has died in the Hole."

"Tymora has never favored me with such good fortune," Mirabeta said, but smiled nevertheless.

Turest returned shortly thereafter, bearing an ivory scroll tube traced in gold, its cap sealed in wax. He presented it to Mirabeta.

"Rynon has examined it and assures me that it bears no baleful magic or poison, Overmistress. The seal appears genuine."

"Well done, Turest," said Mirabeta.

Turest bowed, nodded at Elyril, and withdrew from the balcony.

Mirabeta examined the seal for herself, hummed her satisfaction, and cut the wax with her thumbnail. She popped the lid and withdrew several sheets of rolled vellum, also officially sealed. She broke the seal, unrolled the vellum, and read. Her expression changed from curious, to alarmed, to angry.

Elyril set down her wine glass. "Aunt?"

Mirabeta stared past Elyril. "Yhaunn has been attacked.

The Nessarch reports that much of the lower city is in ruins. A kraken of enormous size rose from the sea and destroyed the lower districts."

Elyril could not keep the shock from her voice. "A kraken? Such a creature has not been seen in decades!"

Mirabeta continued. "He estimates over a thousand are dead and several times that are displaced. The docks are destroyed. The city's forces beat the creature off but a simultaneous raid on the Hole freed Endren Corrinthal. The attack from the sea appears to have been timed with the attack on the Hole. Endren and his rescuers leaped down a mineshaft but no bodies were found. Divinations confirm he is alive, but cannot locate him."

Elyril stared at her aunt, absorbing the import of the words, before softly speaking a curse so vile the mute serving girl gasped. Elyril waved the little wretch from the balcony. "You are dismissed. Begone. We are discussing matters of state."

When they were alone, Elyril said, "It could not have been Abelar Corrinthal who freed Endren. We have reports of him to the southeast. Who, then?"

"We have no word," Mirabeta said, crumbling the missive in her hands. "Damn it all." She glared with heat across the table. "I should have executed Endren in the public square. It was you who advised placing him in the Hole, Elyril."

Elyril kept her false face in place and her anger in check. She adopted a look of contrition.

"True, aunt. It seemed well advised at the time. I apologize for failing you."

Abasement always sated Mirabeta's anger. Her gaze softened and she made a dismissive gesture. "It was well advised at the time. Had we executed Endren, the civil war would have been fought on Ordulin's streets rather than in the countryside." She rocked her wine glass on its stem. "In any event, the Nessarch asks for as much aid as we can spare. Yhaunn's docks need to be rebuilt."

Elyril nodded. Yhaunn was the primary port through which

Ordulin received its stores of food and supplies. Rebuilding its docks as rapidly as possible would be a priority.

"Allow me to fly Ordulin's standard in Yhaunn, aunt. That will assure the Yhauntans that Ordulin supports them fully and will allow me to investigate the details of Endren's escape. Perhaps there is more to be learned."

Mirabeta nodded. "A sound idea. Travel to Yhaunn as my ambassador. I will order the appropriate credentials prepared. Inform the Nessarch that aid is on the way. Then find out what you can about the escape. If there are traitors among the Yhauntans, I want them found out and made into examples. This time, the examples are to be public, Elyril."

"Of course, aunt," Elyril answered.

"Use magical transport. I want you in Yhaunn quickly."

"I will arrange for Rynon to transport me there." Elyril leaned back in her chair and thought through what she had heard. She said, "The timing of the kraken's attack and the attack on the Hole were not coincidental. And neither Selgaunt nor Saerb has the service of mages capable of controlling a kraken."

"We are of like mind. The affair lends credibility to rumors of an alliance between Sembia and the Shadovar." Mirabeta put a finger to her lips in thought. "Perhaps it is time to seek an ally of our own?"

"Aunt?" Elyril asked.

"Later, Elyril. Let me think more about the costs."

Elyril could do nothing but accept the words. Despite her attempts to know all she could about her aunt's affairs, Mirabeta kept some secrets to herself.

Elyril tapped her fingers on the table, eyeing the magical ring with which she communicated with the Nightseer.

"The Shadovar are said to be formidable mages, but few in number."

Mirabeta nodded absently. "At the moment, the Shadovar are beside the point. The rebels in Selgaunt and Saerb must be made to pay for the destruction at Yhaunn."

Elyril smirked. Selgaunt and Saerb were no more rebels than the day was dark. The rebellion was based on a fiction. But that was the power of a lie. Told often enough, even the liar started to believe it.

"That is true, aunt. This attack, if unavenged, makes Ordulin look weak."

Mirabeta frowned.

Elyril hurriedly added, "My apologies for saying so, Aunt, but . . ."

Mirabeta shook her head. "No. You are correct. We must respond, and quickly."

Elyril leaned forward and her shadow whispered Shar's will in her ear.

"I see an opportunity here, War Regent. The wanton destruction in Yhaunn will further incite the populace against Selgaunt and Saerb. You should announce the attack to the people, embellishing as needed. Then any response you make, any response at all, will be seen as justified."

Mirabeta picked up a dried currant, eyed it, chewed it thoughtfully. "What do you make of the freeing of Endren Corrinthal? It troubles me. The nobility in and around Saerb will rally to him."

Elyril leaned back and made a dismissive gesture. "I make nothing of it. The nobility around Saerb are merely a collection of rich merchants who decided they'd rather run their holdings from the countryside than the cities. Saerb's army, such as it is, will be little more than a collection of house guards, hireswords, and a few adventuring companies."

"But a skilled leader, a man like Endren Corrinthal, could transform them into an effective fighting force."

Elyril said, "I think you overestimate him, but if you are correct, then that is all the more reason to act quickly. Selgaunt and Saerb expect you to wait until spring to begin a campaign, but you need not delay. Ordulin is secured and you can already field an army of several thousand. Saerloon's muster proceeds apace. You could strike the rebels unprepared, seize the initiative before Endren can rally anyone, separate their forces by putting your armies between them. You could raze Saerb to the ground. The people would thank you for it and name you the avenger of Yhaunn. After that, Selgaunt. Lady Merelith has informed us of her ability to deploy rapidly. She could be before Selgaunt's gates within days of your order."

"Merelith wishes to expand her reach to include Saerloon and a conquered Selgaunt."

Elyril nodded. "And so long as she answers to Ordulin, what care you?"

Mirabeta looked across the table, thoughtful. She drove her thumbnail into a currant and said, "I am intrigued."

Elyril licked her lips, imagining the deaths. She said, "An immediate attack on Saerb has the added virtue of drawing Abelar Corrinthal into the open, if he dares."

They knew Abelar Corrinthal was riding through Sembia, gathering forces as he went. By all accounts, he'd had little success.

"He will dare," Mirabeta said, and looked across the table at Elyril. "He has a young son, born dumb. He will not abandon the boy to our forces, not if half of what I've heard of him is true."

A thrill of delight ran through Elyril. She imagined murdering Abelar's idiot son herself and offering the Lathanderian's despair and grief to Shar and Volumvax as sacrifice. She could not keep excitement from her tone.

"An attack on Saerb can end the Corrinthals in one stroke, War Regent. If we make examples of a few members of the northern nobility, the rest will quail. Selgaunt can be taken at your leisure."

Mirabeta pushed away her plate and toasted Elyril with her wine goblet. "I like this course, Elyril. I like it very much."

Elyril sat back in her chair, satisfied, and looked out over the city. In the distance, the dome of the High Council glimmered in the sunlight.

"Let us set things in motion," Mirabeta said, and rang the magical bell on the table to summon the chamberlain. He arrived within a twenty count.

"Overmistress?"

"Malkur Forrin can be reached through Ostrim Heem at The Dented Kettle inn. Send word that he is to attend me immediately. Also, send Rynon to me. He is to prepare a sending for Lady Merelith. Saerloon needs to be warned of the kraken and given the order to speed its muster."

Turest's bug-eyes widened, but he said only, "Yes, Overmistress. And I shall have the table cleared apace."

After Turest left, Elyril said, "Malkur Forrin?"

"If Saerb is to be an example to Selgaunt and the rest of Sembia, Forrin is exactly the type of man we want heading the attack. I will have words with him over allowing the Hulorn to escape. But war, like politics, is uncertain. Occasional setbacks are inevitable and sometimes owed to circumstance." She looked meaningfully at Elyril. "Repeated setbacks, however, are more often owed to incompetence. Keep that in mind, niece, on your travels to Yhaunn."

Elyril took her meaning but said nothing. She imagined how her aunt would scream when the Shadowstorm came and she died in darkness.

"Something amuses you?" Mirabeta asked.

Elyril shook her head. "No, aunt. I am merely enjoying the sunshine."

Abelar and Regg reached the abbey as the Dawnmeet finished. One solemn ring of the chapel's ceremonial gong carried over the walls and denoted the end of the service. The faithful would be dispersing to their duties even as the guards alerted the Abbot to the presence of visitors.

The gatehouse guards, armed with broadswords, wore

yellow tabards over their breastplates and mail. They exited the gatehouse to stand before the immense double doors set into the abbey's walls. They eyed Abelar and Regg coolly. Four crossbowmen atop the wall leveled their weapons at Abelar and Regg.

"What is this?" Regg asked, eyeing a crossbowman. "Do we look as if we intend to storm the walls? You see the rose on our shields."

"We see it," one of the crossbowmen said darkly.

Abelar recognized the two guards standing before the doors. "Beld, Dak, come now. None of this is necessary. I return as your brother in faith."

Beld's young face reddened behind his thin beard. "You were not to return at all, Abelar."

Abelar swung down from Swiftdawn and stepped before Beld. He stood half a head taller than the young warrior. "True, Beld. But unexpected events have transpired. I must have word with the Abbot."

"He is at service—"

"Dawnmeet is finished," Abelar said softly. "The Abbot will retire to the chapel for private contemplation. I have not been away so long as to have forgotten that. He will see me, Beld. Tell him that I am here."

Beld looked at Dak, at Abelar. He sighed, nodded, and said to Dak, "Inform the Abbot that Abelar Corrinthal has returned and wishes an audience."

Dak eyed Abelar, Regg, and Beld, and hurried off.

"That is more like it," Regg said, and swung off his horse. He called up to the crossbowmen on the walls. "And take care to point those tips at the stone, you bastards."

The crossbowmen grumbled but lowered their weapons.

"It is good to see you again," Beld said to Abelar. "The light is still in you."

Abelar smiled. "It is."

Beld said, "I wish you would simply agree with the Abbot."

Abelar put a hand on Beld's shoulder. "Faith does not work so, Beld. You know that. We each must follow our own conscience. I must do what I must do. So must the Abbott. So must you. Remember that. And remember, too, that we are not so far apart, the Abbot and I. We both worship the Morninglord."

Beld looked doubtful but nodded.

Presently the crank in the gatehouse started to clink and the double doors in the abbey's wall creaked open. A balding, overweight priest in red and yellow robes awaited them within.

"Dawnbringer Asran," Abelar said, and inclined his head. "Light shine on you."

"And on you, Abelar Corrinthal." Asran nodded past Abelar at the dawn. "The risen sun is beautiful, is it not?"

Abelar caught the double meaning. "Its light feeds the rose," he answered, and turned to Beld. "You will see to our horses?"

"Aye," said the young man. "That, I will."

"I suspect we will not be long," Regg said under his breath.

Abelar and Regg turned over their reins to Beld. Abelar took the opportunity to put his back to Asran and speak softly to Regg. Beld did them the courtesy of pretending not to hear the exchange.

"Keep your peace with Asran, and with the Abbot when we see him. No hot words."

Regg looked both aggrieved and amused. "Perhaps you would prefer that I await you in the courtyard?"

Abelar shook his head. "No. I fear my memory of him will distort how I perceive his words. I will want your opinion of his demeanor afterward."

"Well enough."

With that, they turned and walked into the abbey. Asran smiled insincerely and said, "Welcome back, Abelar. The timing of your return is auspicious. The Abbot teaches that the Deliverance is near. I am pleased that you learned wisdom in time."

Abelar kept his tone even. "Nothing has changed, Asran. I am not come to embrace the Risen Sun."

The heavyset priest faltered in his steps. He looked shocked. "Why have you returned, then?"

"That is a matter for me and the Abbot."

Asran's cheeks flushed but he nodded and led them toward the chapel.

The sounds and smells of the smithy, the weaving looms, the swine pens, the stables, all recalled to Abelar his youth. Chickens scratched in the dirt, fluttered out of their path.

Work stopped as they passed. Abelar felt eyes on them throughout, some hostile, some sympathetic. The short walk across the grounds to the temple seemed to take all morning. The finely hewn doors to the chapel stood open. Stained glass panels flanked the doors, depicting a youthful Lathander holding aloft a newborn babe.

As it always had, the image reminded Abelar of the Nameday of his son. Eltha had died while giving birth but Elden had been born alive. Grief-stricken for his wife, Abelar nevertheless had swaddled the boy and taken him outside to see the world into which his mother had brought him. The overcast sky had been as gray as iron. Abelar had cradled his son close, thought of Eltha, and prayed to Lathander to bless them both and light the paths of their lives. Father and son had both cried when the clouds parted and the sun shone through.

As Elden had grown, all who knew him could see that he had been born simple. Abelar loved him all the more for it. Elden laughed and cried with uncensored abandon.

"Abelar?" Asran called, his tone irritated. The priest was five steps ahead of Abelar, standing on the chapel's portico.

"Are you all right?" Regg asked.

Abelar nodded. "I was thinking of my son. I'm well. Come."

The Abbot gave them an audience in the circular private chapel off the main worship hall. Asran opened the wooden door, nodded for them to enter, and closed it behind them.

Two circular rows of birch pews surrounded a veined marble statue of Lathander in his guise as a hale young man, smiling, with both arms reaching upward in welcome. Above the sculpture, morning light poured in through the round stained glass window of a golden sunrise set into the arched ceiling. The light drenched the room in reds, yellows, and oranges.

Abelar frowned. The window had been changed since he had last been to the temple. Previously, the glass had shown a red rose radiating beams of yellow light. The new sunrise motif was an acknowledgment of the Risen Sun heresy.

The Abbot stood near the statue, bathed in the light of his new window, and watched them enter. He did not smile. He wore robes of yellow and red embroidered with a rising sun motif at the breast. Long gray hair hung loose against his careworn face. His voice was a commanding baritone, seemingly too large to be contained by his thin body. Abelar had heard the Abbot utter hundreds of heart-soaring sunrise sermons. He had also heard him utter heresies.

"You have returned though you were exiled from these walls."

Abelar bowed. "You know I would not have violated your edict if the matter were not urgent. It is gracious of you to see us. My thanks."

"And mine," Regg said, though his voice was tight.

The Abbot did not acknowledge Regg. His intelligent brown eyes searched Abelar's face as he asked, "Have you finally seen the light, Abelar?"

Abelar answered, "What wisdom I had then, I have now."

The Abbot frowned. "Quite so, then." He gestured at the ceiling. "Do you approve of the new window?"

Abelar heard the real question and answered accordingly. "It is well crafted but lacks substance. I prefer the rose to the Risen Sun."

The Abbot feigned a smile. "I see. Well, as you said, what wisdom you had is what wisdom you have."

Regg scoffed and started to speak but Abelar put up a hand to stop him. He asked, "May we approach and sit, Denril?"

The Abbot cocked his head. "No title, Lord Corrinthal? Have we fallen so far?"

Abelar let his words speak for themselves and the silence stretched. Finally Denril gestured at a pew and said, "Yes. Sit. Please. You must be road weary. Shall I have refreshment brought?"

He moved as if to summon Asran but Abelar stayed him with an upraised hand and a shake of his head. "Our thanks, but no. We cannot stay long. My men await our return."

Abelar and Regg walked down the aisle to the center of the circle. Both made obeisance before the statue of Lathander and sat. Denril remained standing and spoke. "You are a criminal, you know. As is your father. Or so says the overmistress."

"The overmistress is a liar. But you know that already," Abelar said evenly.

The Abbot made a dismissive gesture and circled the statue. "As are all politicians. What I know is that you remain outside the Light and spend your energies on political matters. You are stubborn, Abelar. Prideful. The Deliverance is at hand. I see the signs all around, as does anyone with clear eyes. Come back to us before it is too late."

Regg shifted uncomfortably in the pew. Abelar chose his words carefully.

"I see signs around us, Denril, but not signs of the Deliverance. I see signs of evil waxing. Meanwhile, good men sit idle. The church sits idle, content with its holdings. *You* sit idle."

The Abbot frowned and shook his head. "You are mistaken, but you have always seen things in such a way. This is no epic struggle, Abelar. It is base politics and it is beneath you. I blame your father for dragging you into this mud."

Abelar stiffened. "That is the second time you have mentioned my father with derision. Do not do so again."

"He is a murderer, not so?"

Abelar felt warm but controlled his building rage. Regg must have sensed it; he put a hand on Abelar.

"That is the last time I will tell you, Denril," Abelar said. "Do not mention my father so."

Regg stood. "Perhaps we should take our leave . . ."

The Abbot's gaze turned to a hard stare. "Why have you come, Abelar? Do you wish my aid and that of the Church? You will have neither. You see evil ascendant? You are a deluded heretic. This is a political dispute. Nothing more."

Abelar rose from his seat. He could hardly believe his ears. "Has your reason abandoned you? A political dispute, you say?"

The Abbot stepped forward to face him, anger in his eyes. Regg interposed himself between them.

"Yes. What care I for who rules Sembia? The faith will persevere whoever holds power. And the faith is more important than the realm or who rules it. Converts flock to the Morninglord's temple each day. That will increase as war brews."

"You are mad," Abelar said, before wisdom could stop the words.

"All right . . ." Regg said.

The Abbot shook his head. "You cannot see beyond your own worldly concerns. The Deliverance will soon be upon us. My duty to the Morninglord is to win converts to his cause, not to choose sides in a civil war."

The Abbot's words might as well have been coming from the mouth of a stranger. Abelar said, "You win converts because you offer them a faith of ease. They are taught to sit on their hands and wait for their god to deliver them. But he never will. That is not his way."

"I offer them a faith of hope. And what do you know of his way?"

"What do *I* know—"

"We are leaving," Regg said, and tried to push Abelar toward the door. Abelar would not have it.

"You offer a lie," Abelar spat, and found the volume of his voice increasing. "There will be no Deliverance. It is heresy."

Regg cursed softly.

The Abbot answered with a shout. "A heresy!? You dare say so in these halls?"

"Calmer words, men," Regg said, but the Abbot ignored him.

"You are blind, Abelar Corrinthal! And when the Deliverance comes, you will be left behind!"

Abelar scoffed and pointed an accusatory finger at his former mentor. "Darkness is coming, not Deliverance, and when it does, you will realize your folly."

The doors to the chapel flew open and a half-dozen priests and men-at-arms burst inside, maces bare.

Regg moved Abelar away from the Abbot.

"All's well here," Regg said to the men.

The Abbot snarled at Abelar. "I should arrest you and take you to Ordulin for trial."

"Shall I, Abbot?" asked one of the men-at-arms, a young, overeager convert who could barely grow a beard.

Regg let Abelar go, put a hand to his hilt, and stared at the young man. "Try it, boy, and you'll not have to wait for your deliverance."

Abelar heard the hardness of Regg's words and they brought him back to himself. He would not have bloodshed within the faith, not within the walls of one of its temples. With effort, he regained his composure, chided himself for losing his temper, and looked to his onetime friend and teacher.

"You will not arrest me, Abbot," he said gently. "We have not fallen so far as that."

The Abbot stared at him, his face still flush, his heavy breathing audible. Finally, he said, "Go, Abelar. Never return here. I will have you arrested if I see you again."

The words stung Abelar but he nodded. He turned, gathered Regg to his side, and walked through the crowd of Lathanderians, once his brethren. They glared at him and he did not have the strength to offer his own in return. His legs felt weak under him.

As he walked through the door of the chapel, the Abbot called after him, "I receive the power to cast spells in the Morninglord's name every morning, Abelar. Think on that. If what I believed was a lie, why would I still receive such a boon?"

Abelar did not turn or slow. He had no answer. He, too, could channel divine power in the Morninglord's name. As could Regg. He did not understand why his god would allow both sides of the schism to claim his blessing. Abelar presumed that Lathander had a purpose in prolonging the dispute, but he could not see it.

They exited the chapel and entered the courtyard. Regg shouted for their horses. The crowd of priests and warriors followed them out of the chapel. The eyes of those in the courtyard regarded them with hostility. Some fell in with the priests and warriors.

"He is lost in the depths of his doctrine," Abelar said to Regg, shaking his head.

"Aye," Regg said, and nodded. He turned a circle and shouted to all of those looking on them, "And so are you all lost! To the man!"

Some among the onlookers murmured angrily.

"Away from here," shouted one.

"Begone," yelled another.

"Gladly," Regg answered.

Beld brought forth their horses and Abelar and Regg swung into their saddles.

"I did not have time to even remove their saddles," Beld said, indicating the horses. "And they are temperamental beasts."

"It is the company here," Regg said, and patted Firstlight.

Abelar looked to Beld and smiled. "Thank you, Beld. You are a good man."

Beld looked stricken. "I am sorry it has come to this, Abelar."

Abelar nodded. "As am I. Be well."

With that, they rode out. Abelar knew it would be the last time. A black mood descended on him. Lathander would not be pleased that he allowed a darkness to root in him but he could not stop it. He had lost the father of his blood to the Hole of Yhaunn and now had lost the father of his soul to a heresy.

"The sun rises and sets," he murmured to himself.

As they rode outside of crossbow range, Regg clapped Abelar on the shoulder and chuckled. "And you told *me* not to speak with heat."

Abelar could not bring himself to smile. "I was in error."

"You were not."

Regg's words did nothing to comfort him. "I miss my son, Regg."

He had left Elden, only four winters old, with a nurse back in the family estate near Saerb. Abelar wanted nothing more in that moment than to frolic in the sun and play orcs and knights with his boy.

Regg nodded and gave Abelar a sympathetic pat. He looked away and said nothing.

A call from behind turned them around. Three horsemen tore down the wagon path from the abbey. Rucksacks of gear swung crazily from their saddles. The horsemen waved a hand and shouted for Regg and Abelar to wait.

"That is Beld," Regg said, shielding his eyes. "With two others."

"It is."

Regg smiled. "We lost an Abbot but gained three blades. I will take that trade."

Abelar waved a welcome at Beld and his comrades. "The sun rises and sets," he said, this time in a firm voice.

Elyril and Mirabeta awaited Malkur Forrin in the tapestry bedecked meeting rooms within the overmistress's tallhouse. Elyril had gone several hours without a snuff of minddust and the lack made her irritable.

Bookshelves packed with scrolls and tomes lined two of the

room's walls. Elyril eyed them and imagined holding in her hands the book to be made whole. Its lack, too, made her irritable.

Late morning sunlight carried through the large, leaded glass windows. Elyril sat in a soft armchair in a shadowed corner, out of the direct light. She leered at the shadows the sunlight cast on the wall and they leered back. She idly twisted the magical amethyst ring on her finger. She tried to remove the band but it stuck on her knuckle. She pulled harder and still it would not come off. She cursed it softly and the shadows laughed.

The ceiling creaked as the servants went about their business on the second floor. The sound grated on Elyril, made her itch behind the eyes.

"Aunt, I am eager to begin my preparations for the trip to Yhaunn. Perhaps I should retire to my suite and see to matters?"

She started to stand, imagining the welcome sting of mind-dust in her nostrils, the mind-opening perspective, the calm . . .

Mirabeta, who sat in a high-backed chair in the center of the chamber, did not look at her. "No. I want you here when Forrin arrives."

Elyril grimaced and gestured obscenely at her aunt's back. She walked to Mirabeta's side and drove her heel into her aunt's shadow on the floor. The shadow's wails delighted her but she kept the satisfaction from her face. The twisted faces that lived in the chamber's table laughed for her.

"I am your servant, Overmistress."

For now, whispered the faces.

A rap on the chamber door announced Malkur Forrin's arrival.

"Enter," Mirabeta called.

Turest opened the door and Malkur Forrin strode past him. Forrin brought with him the smell of leather, oiled steel, and the road. A chain hauberk hung from his shoulders, a broadsword from his belt. An open-faced helm capped his head. He doffed the helm, showing his graying hair and scars, and bowed.

"Overmistress. Lady Elyril. It is a pleasure to once more be in your company."

"That is all, Turest," Mirabeta said, and the chamberlain closed the door behind Forrin.

Forrin said, "My ladies, the payment we received was less than that to which we agreed. I have sent messengers to you and—"

Mirabeta's voice froze the room. "That is because the performance we received was less than that to which we agreed."

The mercenary's eyes narrowed in a question. "In what regard, Overmistress?"

Mirabeta's voice remained calm. "The Hulorn lives, does he not?"

Irritation creased Forrin's tanned brow. "He does, but what of it?"

"He is a man I asked you to kill," Mirabeta said, her voice rising with each word. "He is a man who, having survived your attack, entered into an alliance with the Shadovar of Shade Enclave."

Malkur drew himself up, crossed his hands behind his back, and stuck out his whiskered chin. "That is unfortunate, but hardly my fault. And may I remind the Overmistress that Miklos and Kavin Selkirk lie in unmarked graves in the wilderness—as you wished—while Saerloon is allied to your cause, believing itself attacked by rebels—also as you wished. All of that is due to Malkur Forrin and his Blades. Surely you do not intend to focus on the escape of a single man to renege on your bargain?"

Mirabeta rapped her fist on the table and glared at Forrin. "No. I choose to focus on the Hulorn's escape because allowing it was a failure, and I do not tolerate failure, in matters large or small."

Malkur's lips curled in a snarl, revealing a couple of missing teeth, and he put a hand to his sword hilt, a gesture Elyril marked not as a threat, but as habit.

"Failure?" he said. "Overmistress, the Hulorn was aided in his escape by a shade—no doubt a Shadovar, which suggests that the alliance you mentioned was in place before he escaped me and would have continued whether he lived or died. But still we would have had him. Only the arrival of Abelar Corrinthal's forces saved him."

"An excuse," Elyril observed.

Malkur glared at Elyril, back at Mirabeta. "An excuse? Perhaps if the younger Corrinthal had not been allowed to escape Ordulin, matters would have turned out differently. What of *that* failure?"

"That was a political decision," Elyril said.

"An excuse," Forrin answered with a sneer.

Elyril affected a thoughtful expression and looked to her aunt. "Aunt, did I mishear or did this mercenary just imply that Abelar Corrinthal is a better field commander than he? Perhaps we should—"

Malkur stiffened at the slight. "Hardly, Milady. Corrinthal's forces outnumbered mine more than two to one. And as I have already explained to the overmistress—"

"Shut your mouth," Mirabeta said harshly, and Malkur, eyes wide with surprise, did exactly that. Mirabeta continued. "You come into my presence and speak with such insolence?"

Before Forrin could stutter a reply, Mirabeta said, "Do you think that your knowledge of recent events insulates you from my anger? That it frees your tongue to speak to me as if I am one of your sergeants? I assure you, it does not."

Malkur's eyes went from surprised to sly. "I know what has happened here, Overmistress. I am a soldier but no fool. You have lied your way into a war, probably murdered your own cousin. I am pleased with both matters, but let us at least be candid with one another. Your grip on power depends upon those lies remaining as buried as Kendrick's sons."

Mirabeta sat as still as the dead. "My hold on power depends on nothing of the sort. What you think to have occurred is utterly unimportant. Are you so stupid as to think that the truth matters? Are you?"

"We are past that," Elyril said, nodding.

Mirabeta said, "I speak and the nobility and the rest of the populace believe what I say. The words no longer matter. They wish to believe me. They *need* to believe me."

Elyril saw the opening offered by her aunt and took it.

"So you go tell your tale, mercenary. And the overmistress will respond by saying that Malkur Forrin is a treasonous liar who seeks to discredit her to avenge his removal from the Sembian military by the Selkirk family."

"That is not so," Malkur said dismissively.

Elyril said, "You will be imprisoned in the Hole and die there."

"Overmistress . . ."

Mirabeta followed Elyril's lead. "Malkur Forrin and his Blades are Zhentarim all, and were behind a plot to murder the overmistress and replace her with a shapeshifter in her guise."

"Another lie," Malkur said, but less dismissively. Elyril saw nervousness sneaking into his eyes.

"You will be hanged for treason," Mirabeta said.

"Overmistress, I . . ."

Elyril stared into his grizzled face and amused herself by interrupting him with a half-truth. "Malkur Forrin is an agent of Sharrans. And it was the Church of Shar that secretly backed the rebellion of Selgaunt and Saerb. He wishes the overmistress dead and Sembia covered in darkness."

"Outrageous!" Malkur said, and took a step backward.

Elyril did not let up. "You will be tortured and finally drawn for your crimes. Your life will end in screams."

Malkur stood mute, dumbfounded. At last he said, "There are many witnesses among my men."

"Their words are as nothing," Elyril said. "They are loyal to you, not the state. They will agree with our account or they will share your grave."

Mirabeta nodded and spoke in a soft tone. "Grounds for your torture and execution can be invented at any time, dear Malkur. None will question it, and what you think is the truth will die with you. My grip on power is firm. Quite firm. Do you understand?"

The mercenary's eyes darted from Elyril to Mirabeta to the wall to the floor. Elyril could fairly see his mind working. Soon she saw acceptance in his expression.

"I understand, Overmistress."

Mirabeta stared at him for a moment, then gestured at the chair across from her. "Excellent. Only now have we been truly candid with one another. You have no leverage with me. Not now, not ever. I am the overmistress and War Regent. Do not forget it. Now, sit."

Malkur slid into the proffered seat, contrite. The twisted faces in the table mocked him.

"I am your servant, Overmistress," he said. "Forgive my presumption."

Mirabeta said, "You are forgiven. And you are more than my servant. You are my Commander General. As of this moment. The proclamation will go out this day."

Malkur looked surprised that his fortunes could so rapidly turn.

Elyril smiled at him. "Welcome back to the Sembian military."

"Thank you, Overmistress. Milady. You are most generous."

"You will lead a force on Saerb," Mirabeta said.

"When, Overmistress?"

"Immediately."

He nodded. "As you wish." He licked his lips and looked meaningfully at Mirabeta. "I will see to these matters now . . . unless I might be of service to the overmistress in another way before I depart?"

Mirabeta kept her eyes on Malkur and dismissed Elyril with a wave of her hand. "Elyril, see to the drafting of your credentials and the proclamation appointing Malkur Commander General. Turest will assist you."

"Yes, aunt," Elyril said, relieved to be free of duties to her aunt.

She exited the chamber and hurried to her room, to Kefil, to her minddust, to her dreams of shadows.

Phraig dreamed of a wind of screams and a snowstorm that scalded his skin in fire.

He awoke, heart pounding, eyes on the cracked plaster of the ceiling. His wife lay asleep beside him, her breathing slow and steady.

He had heard something, hadn't he? Or perhaps he had only dreamed it? He swallowed to wet his throat, lay still, and listened.

He heard nothing.

He let out a slow breath and tried to calm himself. His dreams had been haunted since his ordeal in the Hole. He knew the servants of Mask had not died after leaping down the shaft. Everyone knew. The guards had sought bodies and found none.

Since the attack, his fellows had looked at him askance, had not invited him to dice and cards. Almost a score of guards had died in the attack and Phraig knew his fellow guards held him responsible.

But they had not seen the shadowmen. They had not stared into the one good eye of a killer and seen an emptiness there as black as the Hole itself. Looking back, Phraig did not believe the shadowmen had been men at all. They had been . . . something else, and every one of his fellows would have done just as he had. His choice had been to resist and die or comply and live. He had a wife. He had wanted to live.

Staring at the ceiling, he determined, suddenly and with perfect clarity, that he would quit the guard. He could find work helping rebuild the docks. Laborers would be needed for months and he had a strong back. He could wield a hammer as well as a sword.

The decision lightened his mood. He thought of a new beginning, placed a hand on Arla's hip, closed his eyes, and slept.

A sound from the other room awakened him—a soft rattle, as of metal on metal. The air felt chill. His heart jumped anew and he opened his eyes. Arla still slept soundly beside him.

Careful not to disturb her, he swung his legs off the bed and put his feet on the wooden floor. He licked his lips, closed a fist on the hilt of the dagger he kept on the side table near the bed.

Moving slowly and silently, he rose—careful to avoid stepping on the chamber pot—and padded across the small bedroom, trying to shake off the blurriness of sleep. His wife did not stir.

There. The rattle again. It came from the front door.

A burglar? Or perhaps a drunk at the wrong door?

The bedchamber door, ajar, separated their sleeping quarters from the rest of their two-room garret. He pulled open the door with his free hand and looked out.

Darkness, pierced only by the soft glow of embers in the small fireplace. He licked his lips, studied the room, and saw nothing but their meager furnishings. He moved silently across the room to the entryway and quickly checked the hook lock.

Still fastened.

Sweat slicked him. His breath came fast. He could not explain it but he felt dread in his bones. He stood in the dark, breathing heavily, listening, certain that someone lurked on the other side of the door, separated from him by nothing more than a thin slab of weathered wood. He clutched the dagger in a sweaty fist. He would not be taken unawares. Drunk or burglar, they would find him ready.

He put his ear to the wood and listened.

He heard breathing, the deep respiration of powerful lungs.

But not from the other side of the door.

From right behind him.

A presence filled the room and stole the air. The room grew so cold Phraig could see his breath. Fear seized him. He whirled, gasping.

What he saw paralyzed him with terror. The dagger fell from his hand. He felt his mouth hanging open but could not close it. He gaped at a giant figure with glowing red flesh, white eyes, black wings, and horns. The fiend held a black clawed finger to its lips for silence—and smiled.

Phraig could only stare. His vision went blurry. His heart sounded like a drum in his ears. The room spun. He felt ice gather on his beard and eyebrows. He saw only the fiend's white eyes.

"Phraig?" Arla called from their bedroom, her voice slurred from sleep. She might as well have been calling from another world.

The diabolical figure looked at the bedroom door, back at Phraig, and raised an eyebrow.

"I hope your mate is attractive," it said, and enveloped Phraig in darkness.

CHAPTER THREE

18 Uktar, the Year of Lightning Storms

The setting sun dipped partially below the horizon, setting the roof of the world aflame and casting Selgaunt into shadow. Clouds as thin and dry as old bone lined the sky. Tamlin knew they would offer no respite from the drought in the north.

He stared out a window of the western tower in the Hulorn's palace and looked out on his city, a city swollen with refugees who would feed on anything, and fear that would feed on itself. He could not shed the impression that Selgaunt was barely holding its ground, that the continuing press of stinking, sweating humanity that flooded into it by the day must soon push it by sheer weight of numbers into the dark waters of the Inner Sea.

Apprehension hung as thick as fog in the air. War was coming.

He watched as the sun fell below the horizon and Selgaunt went dark. Night summoned the linkboys. Street lanterns flared to life, chasing the darkness and turning Selgaunt's streets into radiant serpents that slithered between rows of packed shops, inns, and residences. Only the northwest corner of the city, not far from Temple Avenue, remained unlit. The Shadovar, housed in a makeshift embassy there, preferred the darkness.

To the east Tamlin could see the Khyber Gate. Though he could not see them, he knew a crowd had gathered there, a throng of rickety people with their rickety wagons. No matter how many refugees entered the city each day, the next day brought still more, sometimes by the handfuls, sometimes by the score. There was little to keep them on their farms, and all feared being caught outside of the city's walls when Ordulin's forces arrived.

Tamlin allowed all of them entry, despite the food shortage. He had ordered every priest in the city capable of doing so to use their god-given magic to create food and clean water. The priesthoods had resisted his overt encroachment on their self-perceived prerogative, but he had forced them. The soldiers and militiamen, hungry from training and most in need of their strength, ate first, then the rest of the populace. Stomachs still grumbled, but no one was starving. His actions had won him the affection of the people and the anger of the priesthoods.

In the immediate aftermath of Ordulin's declaration of war on Selgaunt and Saerb, many citizens had fled the city. The raft folk had been the first to flee, in an immense flotilla of barges festooned with colorful cloth and pennons. Some among the wealthy had found sudden "business" to occupy them abroad. Even Tamlin had quietly sent his mother, sister, and brother—over their objections—to Daerlun, ostensibly to court a pledge of neutrality from Daerlun's High Bergun, but really to remove them from harm. Most of the priests and priestesses had even abandoned the city, possibly in spiteful response to Tamlin's edicts. Only two or three clerics remained in each temple, and even those would have fled had

Tamlin not forbade them from abandoning the city.

The flight was over now. Those still within Selgaunt's walls were those who would make a stand there. The city was transforming before his eyes from a rich mercantile capital into a hungry military encampment.

Squads of armed men in green tabards and weathercloaks moved in formation down the wide streets by night, and militia drilled in the commons and outside the walls by day. Scouts prowled the roads leading into the city. Workmen thronged the gates and walls. The clang of hammers, the cut of saws, and the sound of chisels striking stone carried through the air day and night.

Engineers supervised the reinforcement of the walls and gates, secured grates in the sewers, constructed an apparatus to drop part of the High Bridge into the Elzimmer River, built a battery of trebuchets, and oversaw the digging of cisterns to provide water during the inevitable siege. Tamlin had drained half of Selgaunt's treasury financing the work. If necessary, he would requisition the wealth of the Old Chauncel and the temples for additional monies. When Mirabeta's army came, it would find Selgaunt prepared. Or so he told himself.

When word of war had first circulated, Tamlin had worried about insurrection. He had feared the people would rise up, overthrow him and the Old Chauncel, and turn all of them over to Mirabeta in order to avert a war. But insurrection had never happened. He was not sure how, when, or why it had occurred, but citizens of the city had resigned themselves to war under his command. They would defend their city and their holdings.

The responsibility sat on him like a lead hundredweight.

The bells of the Temple of Song sounded the seventh hour. Tamlin saw the pennons atop the bell tower fluttering in the breeze. He knew Temple Avenue would be crowded for evening services. Desperation and fear filled temples better than any sermon. Even itinerant street preachers of obscure gods found a ready congregation for their words.

Tamlin found no succor in faith. He had learned from his father to make all the expected offerings to Tymora, to Waukeen, and lately, to Tempus, God of Battle, but they were only gestures, empty of meaning. He found himself mildly envious of people of faith: Vees Talendar, even Mister Cale. The faithful had a religion with which to anchor their lives. Tamlin's sorcery offered nothing of the kind. He had no anchor, and the waters were growing rougher each day.

A breeze off the bay carried the tang of salt and fish. Ships filled the harbor, some laden with timber and quarried stone for building, others with much needed food purchased by Selgauntan agents in the markets of Westgate, Teziir, and Starmantle. Countless torches, lanterns, and glowballs made the docks the brightest lit area of the city. An army of dock workers and sailors unloaded crates, sacks, barrels, and weapons. Far out into the bay, bobbing pinpoints of light marked the locations of the handful of under-equipped caravels that constituted Selgaunt's navy. It would not be long before Saerloon's warships would try to close the sea lanes.

Tamlin looked north, out over the river, past the High Bridge. He could see little. Darkness swallowed the plains. He imagined enemies out in the black. Each morning he awakened with the fear that he would see Ordulin's banners flying on the horizon at the head of an advancing army. Or perhaps Saerloonian pennons from the east would presage the beginning of the siege.

He could not remember how he had ended up standing where he stood. Events had moved so fast he scarcely had time to comprehend them, much less react to them. Dread ate at him. He knew it, but could do nothing to help himself. He slept little.

His hopes, such as they were, lay with the Shadovar. He had nothing else. The Shadovar alliance would save the city, or Selgaunt would fall and Tamlin would die.

He took a deep breath, smelled a distant fire on the air. He turned and called back into his chambers, where Thriistin, his chamberlain, awaited his command.

"Send for Lord Rivalen. I think the populace should see us together."

He did not say that he, too, found reassurance in the Shadovar ambassador's presence.

Cloaked in more than a dozen protective wards, Mirabeta sat alone at a small table in The Rouged Cheek, an expensive fest-hall in the Trade District of Ordulin. A magical hat of disguise masked her identity, giving her the appearance of Rynon, her house mage. As such, she tried to look interested in the surroundings. Her contact had requested that she meet him here. She had been instructed to pick any table, have a goblet of wine, and wait. She had done just that.

Paintings of men and women engaged in sex play—sometimes in pairs, sometimes in groups—covered the walls. Provocative, well-proportioned statuary stood on pedestals and in wall niches. A bearded minstrel sat on a stool on a corner stage, strumming a mandolin. Shirtless young men and scantily-clad young women lounged languidly on overstuffed divans, couches, and benches. The sweet smell of perfume and the pungent aroma of incense and sex filled the air. Laughter tinkled. Conversation hummed.

Men and women of wealth, most of them holding masks before their features, moved through the courtesans, evaluating, flirting, partaking of narcotics and spiced wine. From time to time, a pair or group would retire upstairs for a private encounter. The looming civil war and the food shortage had done nothing to curb the appetites of Ordulin's wealthy. Perhaps it had even increased their desires, as they sought escape in purchased pleasures.

A slim, dark-haired woman in a form-fitting gown of violet silk approached Mirabeta's table. She held before her face a pale, ceramic mask of a nymph with laughing eyes and a bright smile. Mirabeta could see only her strikingly green eyes.

"You have not touched your wine," the woman said.

"I am waiting for someone."

"Indeed."

The woman pulled back a chair with her foot and sat down.

Mirabeta looked at the slight woman, puzzled. She looked as fragile as glass, hardly what Mirabeta anticipated in a follower of The Scaly Way.

"Morthan?" Mirabeta asked, mentioning the name—or at least the alias—of the merchant who served as her sometime contact with the Cult of the Dragon.

"Morthan is otherwise occupied. You have me instead."

Mirabeta absorbed that. She disliked surprises. "You are authorized to speak for the Cult?"

The woman nodded. "I am. And here is what I say: My mistress, Aurgloroasa, is mildly intrigued by the overmistress's offer."

The minstrel's playing ceased, so Mirabeta lowered her voice so that she would not be overheard.

"The offer will expire soon. 'Mildly intrigued' is not a commitment. My mistress, the Overmistress of Sembia, requires a firm promise of assistance with the problem of Selgaunt."

An adolescent serving boy approached the table with a tray of crystal goblets and a decanter of wine.

"Wine, milady? Goodsir?" he asked.

Mirabeta declined but the young woman said, "Please."

The boy poured a glass, bowed, and stepped away. The young woman did not drink, but moved the glass before the empty chair to Mirabeta's left.

The minstrel appeared, abruptly pulled back the chair, and sat.

"What is this?" Mirabeta said, pushing her chair back and beginning to stand.

"Please stay seated," the young woman said softly. "Please."

Mirabeta lowered herself back into her chair, eyeing the minstrel. None of the Cheek's patrons seemed to have noticed, or they did not care.

The young woman said, "Vendem is my associate."

Vendem drank the goblet of wine in a single gulp and smiled a mouthful of overlarge teeth. As Mirabeta watched, his brown eyes turned green, with vertical reptilian slits, then back again.

"Well met," he said, in a baritone as rough as gravel.

Mirabeta knew instantly what he was. She steadied her breath and controlled her heartbeat. She was not fearful for her safety. Rynon maintained a contingency spell on her person that would whisk her instantly to the chambers in her tallhouse if she were attacked. No, it was not fear she felt, but awe. She was sitting in a festhall beside a force of nature. She had seen the destruction a dragon could wreak during the Dracorage.

"I hear your heart . . . milady," the dragon said.

Mirabeta started to protest but the dragon held up a calloused hand with fingernails like claws. He leaned in her direction, closed his eyes, and inhaled deeply.

"Your appearance is a fraud. You are female, over forty winters in age, and last bathed two, perhaps three days ago. The smell of sex is still on you from about as many—"

"Enough," Mirabeta snapped.

The dragon chuckled.

"More wine," he called loudly, and the pretty boy scrambled over to refill his cup. "Leave the decanter," the dragon said, and the boy did.

After the boy had departed, the masked woman said, "Intriguing. You are actually a woman. You show little fear at the presence of a dragon and give orders as one accustomed to obedience." She looked across the table at the dragon and cocked her head. Mirabeta could imagine her smiling behind the mask. "Vendem, I warrant we are in the presence of the overmistress herself."

Mirabeta saw no point in denying the claim. She said, "We were discussing the offer. *My* offer."

The dragon chuckled and a thin stream of acrid green smoke floated from his nostrils. The smell burned Mirabeta's nose and made her eyes water. She waved her hand in the air to disperse it.

The dragon was a green, his breath a burning, deadly gas.

The woman, seemingly unbothered by the gas, said, "Respect-fully, Overmistress, you have made only a request, not an offer."

Mirabeta understood the point. She said, "The Shadovar are allied with Selgaunt. Should my armies lose this war, the Shadovar will have established themselves in Sembia. Not far from Daerlun."

The dragon growled.

Mirabeta had learned that the Cult of the Dragon regarded the Shadovar with hostility. She did not know why and did not need to know. She also knew that the Cult had a strong presence in Daerlun. A Shadovar presence in Selgaunt would pose a threat to their continued operations.

"As I said," the young woman continued, trying to appear casual, "Aurgloroasa is intrigued."

Mirabeta eyed the woman. "My time is limited. Make your demands known."

"Very well. Free rein entirely in Daerlun and Urlamspyr."

Mirabeta scoffed and countered. "Daerlun only. It is as much Cormyrean as Sembian. And the Cult is to be entirely out of Ordulin."

The young woman leaned back in her chair and regarded Mirabeta through the eyeholes of her mask. "Saerloon, Urlamspyr, and Selgaunt remain as ever they were?"

Mirabeta nodded. "If your agents are caught there, they will be punished."

The young woman considered, and said, "Done, Overmistress. Be assured that Aurgloroasa will hold you to your bargain."

"And I to hers," Mirabeta answered. "Now, where is my assistance?"

The current state of affairs flashed through the overmistress's mind. Forrin and his forces were already marching on Saerb. She had received word from Lady Merelith that the muster in Saerloon was almost complete. Merelith's mages had perfected a stratagem to bring the battle to Selgaunt quickly, and Mirabeta wanted to capitalize on it. But the Selgauntan alliance with the Shadovar concerned her. She could not afford a prolonged siege. If she could put a dragon at Saerloon's disposal, the siege of Selgaunt would be short indeed.

The young woman gestured at Vendem. "You have met your assistance. Overmistress Mirabeta Selkirk, meet Vendemniharan, birthed of Venomindhar and sired by Venominhandar. He will remain in service to you for one month."

Mirabeta stifled a gasp at the mention of Venomindhar and Venominhandar. The destruction the two greens had wreaked in Sembia generations earlier was legend. She controlled her shock and reminded herself that *she* wielded power in Sembia. She spoke to the dragon as she would any underling.

"You will journey to Saerloon. There, you will answer to Lady Merelith and her commanders as they lay siege to Selgaunt. She will report back to me."

The dragon hefted the decanter of wine and drained it all in one long gulp. He wiped his mouth and said, "Saerloon is a long journey from here even in my natural form, woman."

"Overmistress," Mirabeta corrected him. "And I will arrange for your transport."

The howl of the wind and the screams of the damned fell away. Long moments passed in darkness. Cale felt a sensation of rapid motion, then a sudden stop. The biting cold vanished, replaced by fetid warmth. The darkness of the archfiend's breath dispersed and Cale, Magadon, and Riven materialized in shadow, standing in stagnant, knee-deep water and stinking mud.

Broad-leafed trees and twisted shrubs poked out of the mire to claw their way into a shadowy sky. Malformed creatures, startled at the trio's sudden appearance, shrieked and hissed at them from the dimness of their dens. High above, ungraceful forms wheeled about on awkward wings in the black, starless sky. Periodic flashes of dim, vermillion light backlit the clouds and cast the sky in leering contrast. A thin brownish fog floated around them, ghostly and full of secrets. The moist air, rife with the stink of decay, sank into their clothes. So, too, did the shadows.

Cale recognized the location—his adopted home, the Plane of Shadow. The familiar darkness, unique to the Plane, strengthened him, and he tried to pass that strength through his arms to Magadon.

"Mags?"

"I am all right," Magadon said, and disentangled himself from Cale. The mindmage looked haggard and his clothes hung from him in tatters. Blood, his own, slicked him. The memory of horror haunted his colorless eyes. Cale remembered how the mindmage had looked moments earlier—a pile of gore steaming on Cania's ice.

"You look at me like a broken thing," Magadon said, and his voice cracked.

Cale shook his head, the movement too fast for the denial to be true. "No. I am just . . . pleased to see you whole."

"I am far from that, Cale."

Magadon's words took Cale aback. "You have never called me 'Cale.'"

Magadon shrugged and looked away. "No? It seems right."

Cale and Riven shared a look and Cale noticed Riven's beard—it had grown substantially since they had left Cania.

"Your beard," Cale said.

"And yours," Riven said.

Cale ran his hand over his face and felt several days' growth on his cheeks.

"What happened?"

"Time distortion as we moved through planes," Magadon said.

"So what happened to the time?" Riven asked.

"Lost to us," Magadon said. "The same as . . . other things." He kneeled into the fog and used the black water of the swamp to wash the filth and blood from his flesh. Demon scales, as red as pox, showed in irregular patches on his exposed skin. The tattoo on his bicep, the mark of his father, was stark on his otherwise pale skin. The scars that once had marred it were gone. Magadon touched his horns thoughtfully, frowning.

Riven looked across the fog at Cale. "Why here?"

Cale heard an accusation behind the question. "Because what I promised him is here. Or at least the trail is. It must be."

Riven touched the holy symbol at his throat and walked to Cale's side.

"He said you had promised it to another, that Mask would be displeased. What have you done, Cale?"

Cale looked past Riven to Magadon. "What I had to. You'd have done the same."

Riven studied his face and his gaze flitted for a moment to Magadon. "Maybe."

Magadon stood. "I am here. Do not speak of me as if I am not." The mindmage, clean of blood, approached them and offered Riven the dagger the assassin had given him on Cania.

"Keep it," Riven said.

"I have a weapon," Magadon said.

"So you said," answered Riven. "Keep it anyway."

Magadon shrugged, tucked the blade into his belt. He looked up into Cale's face. "What did my father mean when he said you had promised it to another? To whom? I, at least, should know."

Cale stared into his friend's pain-haunted white eyes, more certain than ever that he had done the right thing. "You both should know. And you will. But it is a long tale and this hardly seems the place for telling it. Let's put some solid ground under our feet and get our bearings. Then I'll tell you both everything. Well enough?"

Riven looked skeptical.

"Everything," Cale emphasized.

"Well enough, then," Riven said.

Magadon turned a circle, examined the lay of the land. Stinking water, tangles of trees, and patches of jagged reeds surrounded them. The fog-shrouded air muffled sound.

"Place feels familiar," Riven observed.

Cale had been thinking the same thing. It hit him, then, but Magadon said it first. "It appears my father is not without a sense of humor. This is the same swamp where we first encountered Furlinastis."

Cale and Riven cursed. They had faced Furlinastis the shadow dragon once before. Cale had wounded him, but they had lived only because the dragon, citing a promise made long ago, had spared them. But he had promised, too, that he would kill them should they return to the swamp.

Something thudded against Cale's boot under the water, giving him a start. He stabbed down into the murk with Weaveshear but hit nothing. Tension gripped him.

He started to speak, but an ominous hush fell. The swamp stilled. The chorus of insects ceased. The howling creatures retreated to their murky dens and fell silent. The air above them emptied of the flying creatures.

"Dark," Riven said. "Dark and empty." The assassin held his blades and turned a circle.

Cale did the same. Shadows leaked from Weaveshear.

"He is coming," Magadon said, his voice strangely flat. "Now."

Shadows poured from Cale's flesh. He molded them with his mind into shadowy duplicates of himself that mirrored his movements. The illusions would distract the dragon and, with luck, draw some of its attacks. Riven prayed to Mask under his breath and shadows from the air coiled around his blades.

"Where, Mags?" Riven asked. The assassin stood in a crouch, his breathing steady.

Magadon shook his head and looked into the darkness. "Nowhere. Everywhere. We will never see him."

Cale knew Magadon was right. Even with his shadow sight, Cale saw nothing but dark water and coils of fog. The shadow dragon was as much one with the darkness as Cale.

But they could hear him, and Cale's darkness-sharpened hearing caught a sound: a rhythmic rush of air, the beat of huge wings from somewhere above them.

"In the air," he said.

He scanned the sky but saw nothing. He felt the dragon's approach the same way he felt an approaching storm. He felt exposed. They had no cover.

"Link us, Mags," Cale said.

The mindmage could connect their minds so they could communicate silently at the speed of thought.

Magadon shook his head. "No."

Cale looked at him sharply.

Magadon said, in a softer tone, "I cannot, Cale. I am not . . . I cannot."

Cale stared at the mindmage, unarmored, damaged in his soul, worn as thin as old leather. He had not even drawn his dagger.

"He's got nothing but a dagger, Cale," Riven said, his eyes on the sky, his thoughts apparently mirroring Cale's.

Cale made his decision. "We are leaving. This is not our fight."

A roar from above drenched them in sound. The dragon broke from the darkness of the sky, backlit by a vermillion flash, a mountainous form of black scales, muscle, and shadow. He dove directly at them. Another roar sent waves through the waters of the swamp.

The creature bore down on the trio. His teeth were the length of daggers. His wings stretched two bowshots across from wingtip to wingtip. His massive form trailed a cloud of shadows the way a shooting star trails flames. Cale saw faces in the shadows, old faces, familiar faces. The dragon opened his mouth wide to breathe. The faces in the clouds opened their mouths, too, and Cale read their lips, or perhaps heard their whispers.

Free us!

"Cover!" Riven shouted, though there was nowhere to run.

The moment before Furlinastis spat a cloud of viscous black vapor from his mouth, Cale caught a glimpse of Magadon, staring up at the dragon, arms limp at his sides, face impassive. Cale had no time to process the implications before the dragon's life-draining breath saturated the area in ink. The swirling cloud of shadowstuff wormed into Cale's body through his nose, ears, and eyes, pulled at his soul, drank his life force. He staggered in the muck, fell. He heard Riven groan and curse.

Furlinastis hit the swamp with the force of a thunderbolt. His body displaced so much water that a waist-high wave of foul liquid washed over Cale. The dragon's respiration sounded like a forge bellows.

Despite the life-draining effect of the dragon's breath, Cale recovered himself enough to draw the shadows to him. He reached out his consciousness for Magadon and Riven as the shadow magic took hold.

"You were warned never to return," the dragon's sibilant voice said from out of the darkness. "For that—"

Cale heard no more. He thought of one of the only places on the Plane of Shadow fixed firmly in his memory, a place from which they could begin their pursuit of Kesson Rel—the city of Elgrin Fau the lost, once the City of Silver, but now the City of Wraiths.

The shadows engulfed them and swept them there.

Furlinastis knew the First and Second of Mask were either dead or had escaped, for he could no longer hear their hearts. The cloud of darkness dissipated and he saw only the lifeless husks of dozens of frogs, fish, snakes, and other small creatures native to the swamp floating on the surface of the water, their lives extinguished by his breath. But there was no sign of the humans. They had escaped him.

He roared in frustration, beat his wings, and took flight. Enraged, he turned a circle in the sky and swept low over the stagnant water of his domain. The force of his passage bent reeds and small trees, and sent up a spray of water in his wake. He blew out another cloud of his life-draining breath, another, and the vapor annihilated thousands of creatures. Their deaths did little to mitigate his anger.

The shadows around him swirled as the souls of the priests trapped within his shadow shroud focused their wills. Faces formed in the shroud, all clamoring for freedom. The cacophony of voices subsided and one voice rose above the multitude. Furlinastis recognized it as that of Avnon Des the Seer.

The Chosen of the Shadowlord have returned. The First has come to claim what is his, what we have held for him these unnumbered years. The end is upon us. You will die and we will be freed to go to our rest.

"If they return again, they will die. You will never be freed, priest. You chose your prison."

And you yours, dragon. You chose Kesson Rel for your ally.

Furlinastis again howled his rage into the dark sky. "I chose nothing! I was compelled by his magic, the same soul magic that binds you to me now, that binds him to you! If I die and you are freed, so, too, will he be freed."

Yes, Avnon Des said, his tone almost sympathetic. *But that doom was charted long ago. They will return and you will die. The course is set.*

"I will fight them. They are only men."

No. They are more.

The words sent a charge of emotion through Furlinastis, a feeling he had not experienced for centuries, not since his first encounter with Kesson Rel the Shadowtheurge. It took him a moment to recognize it as fear.

I am sorry, Avnon Des said. *He made you his vessel. We had to make you ours to trap what he expended to bind you. There was no other way.*

Furlinastis heard sincerity in the words, but they brought him no comfort. He told himself that Avnon Des was wrong.

Within the shroud, Furlinastis felt the stirrings of power, felt the squirming, semi-sentient thing that was a portion of Kesson Rel contending with the priests. Avnon Des's face grew pained, melded back into the shadows.

Furlinastis murmured, "It is because of you, fool theurge, that I have been bound to this swamp for these thousands of years. It is because of you that I will die."

Kesson forced enough of his will through the wall of priests to answer.

The end is near, wyrm. And I will again be whole.

Furlinastis roared into the sky and wheeled upward, toward the clouds, amongst the lightning.

Tamlin sat atop his mare and rode slowly down the city's cobblestone streets. Prince Rivalen rode beside him, man and horse wrapped in twilight. A dozen spear-armed Scepters in green weathercloaks and mail walked before and behind them and kept the streets clear. Groups of citizens clustered to watch them pass. Tamlin sat tall in his saddle, waved and nodded. He tried to look determined but could not maintain it for long. The huddled forms and fearful faces that stared at him out of the dark undermined his confidence.

Tamlin spoke in low tones so that none but Rivalen would hear him. "My entreaties for a negotiated resolution have gone unanswered."

Rivalen nodded. "The overmistress does not wish peace."

A few men in the crowd—off duty militiamen, no doubt—raised a defiant cheer condemning Ordulin. "When will the Selkirk whore bring her army, Hulorn?"

"We wish some sport," shouted another.

Tamlin raised his fist and forced a smile.

"I cannot believe it has come to this," he said to Rivalen. "How can the realm have been so close to war without anyone realizing it? We will kill each other over trifles, over a lie."

Prince Rivalen eyed him sidelong. His golden eyes shone like fivestars.

"That is so and has ever been so. I have lived two thousand years and have seen in that time that men almost always die for trifles. Exceptions are rare."

"Your years have made you a cynic, Prince," Tamlin said softly.

Rivalen laughed, a hard, staccato sound. "A realist, Hulorn. In truth, everything is a trifle when viewed through the lens of history. Empires rise and fall, men live and die. The Jhaamdathan Empire ruled a great portion of the world at one time. Have you ever heard of it?"

Tamlin felt ignorant but shook his head.

"Of course not," Rivalen said. "Only scholars have. Yet the Jhaamdathans thought their influence would extend forever. Men delude themselves into thinking that the events in which they participate are of particular significance to history, but they rarely are. One empire is the same as another."

"What of Netheril, Prince? Even I have heard of it. Its influence reaches through time, even unto now."

Rivalen waved a hand dismissively and it trailed shadows. "Netheril is an exception. A sole exception. But even it will fade from the memory of men someday. All is fleeting, Hulorn, and only one thing is certain—an end to all things."

Tamlin chuckled. "I mistook you, Prince. You are worse than a cynic. You are a nihilist."

Rivalen shrugged. "Things are what they are, whatever we may think. It is our task to wrestle meaning from meaninglessness while we still can. Does that make me a nihilist still?"

Tamlin's smile faded. He envied Rivalen the perspective of two thousand years.

"Are you a man of faith, Prince?"

Rivalen's golden eyes flared and narrowed.

"Is that a rude question?" Tamlin stuttered. "If so, I apologize. I thought—"

Rivalen waved a ringed hand. The shadows about him swirled. "It is not rude, Hulorn. It is forthright. That is one of the things I admire about you."

Tamlin felt himself color at Rivalen's praise. He valued it as much—perhaps more—than he had ever valued the praise of his father.

"I ask only because I have been considering matters of faith recently. In my own life, I mean. Our conversation put me in mind of it."

Rivalen said, "Times of crisis breed introspection. And yes, I am considered pious among my people."

The admission mildly surprised Tamlin.

"May I inquire, then, which gods you worship?"

Rivalen looked above Tamlin and into the moonless sky. When he looked down again, he smiled kindly, the expression made oddly threatening by his ornamental fangs.

"I worship but one. A goddess."

"Really? I've known none but priests to worship only one god or goddess."

"I am a priest, Hulorn."

Tamlin reined his horse and stared at Rivalen. Their bodyguards looked startled for a moment, but quickly formed a cordon around the two.

"A priest? I thought you were . . . something else."

"A mage?"

Tamlin nodded.

"I am both, Hulorn. A theurge, my people call me."

Tamlin's respect for Rivalen redoubled. "That is a rare combination, Prince."

"Perhaps not as rare as you think. I have never found my faith to be at odds with my magical studies."

"You worship Mystra, then?"

Rivalen stared at him, his face impossible to read. "No." He gestured at the road, and shadows leaked from his fingers. "Shall we continue?"

"Uh, of course." Tamlin turned his mare and they started moving again. The bodyguards fell in around them.

Rivalen said, "Mystra is not the only goddess who welcomes practitioners of the Art into her ecumenical orders. Have you considered formalizing your own worship, Hulorn?"

Tamlin smiled and shook his head. "No. Religion does not speak to me, Prince. My father was the same way. Coin is in the Uskevren blood, not faith."

"You are not your father, Hulorn."

To that, Tamlin said nothing, though the words pleased him somehow.

"You need only a Calling," Rivalen said.

"No god or goddess will be calling me, Prince." Tamlin tried to laugh at the notion but could manage only a forced smile.

"A Calling does not always come from the divinity," Rivalen said. "Sometimes it is communicated through an intermediary— another priest of the faith."

Tamlin felt Rivalen's eyes on him but did not return the Prince's gaze. He understood what Rivalen seemed to be offering and was tempted by it.

"You have not even told me the name of the goddess you worship."

"True," Rivalen said. He paused for a time, then said, "I have given you cause to trust me, have I not?"

The question surprised Tamlin. "You have. Of course."

"I feel there is even a friendship between us. Or at least a burgeoning friendship. Am I mistaken?"

Tamlin shook his head. "You are not, and your words please me. I feel the same."

The shadows around Rivalen swirled. "My Lord Hulorn, you know very little about me and I fear an ill-timed admission about my faith may put a wedge between us. My faith is . . . poorly understood."

Tamlin thought of Erevis Cale, of his surprising admission to Tamlin that he worshiped Mask, the god of thieves and shadows. Rivalen's admission could be no worse. He said, "I bring few preconceptions in matters of faith."

Rivalen reined his horse and studied Tamlin's face. Tamlin reined his mount and bore the Prince's gaze.

Finally, Rivalen said, "Then I shall share something with you that I share with only a few outside my people. A secret, if you will."

"I will keep it in confidence," Tamlin said, pleased that Rivalen would trust him so.

Rivalen nodded, sighed. "Over my two thousand years I have learned that pain and loss are common to all men in all times. Not all men experience love or know joy, but all men know pain and loss. All men know fear. And in the end, all men know the emptiness of the void."

"That is so," acknowledged Tamlin slowly, though he was not sure he understood completely.

Rivalen stared into his eyes. "That realization led me to Shar, Hulorn. I worship the Lady of Loss."

For a moment Tamlin thought Rivalen must have been making a jest, but he saw from the Prince's solemn expression that the words were truth.

"Shar?" he asked, startled. The single word was all he could manage.

Rivalen nodded and said nothing. The shadows turned slow spirals around his flesh.

"Shar. But I have heard . . ." Tamlin started to say, but stopped. "Shar is . . ."

He shook his head and looked away. He could find no words that would not offend the Prince.

Rivalen said, "As I said, my faith is poorly understood. Dark rumors abound but they are mostly born of ignorance. Shar does not cause pain and loss. She simply embraces their existence, and teaches her true faithful to do the same as part of the cycle of life and death. There is peace in that, Hulorn. And power."

Tamlin looked up at that. Rivalen stared back at him, unreadable.

"You know me, Hulorn, know me well. I assure you that any distasteful deeds done in Shar's name have been caused by those who call themselves her faithful but who little understand her teachings. I am doing what I can to put an end to their error."

Tamlin nodded, his mind still swimming.

"Does this change anything between us?" Rivalen asked.

Tamlin thought of his father, of Mister Cale. "I must ask you something, Prince."

Rivalen's face was a mask. "Ask."

"Where is Mister Cale?"

The shadows around Rivalen swirled, but his expression did not change.

"Erevis Cale retrieved his comrade and left Sakkors. I do not know where he is now."

Tamlin studied Rivalen's face, seeking a lie. He saw nothing and decided against asking more. Mister Cale had chosen his course, and one confession from Rivalen was enough for the evening.

Tamlin said, "Nothing is changed between us. We remain . . . friends."

Rivalen studied his face, nodded. "I am pleased to hear those words." He paused, said, "Hulorn, Erevis Cale was wrong about us. About me. You may trust me."

I must, Tamlin thought but did not say. Instead, he said, "Erevis Cale was wrong about many things. And I do trust you, Prince."

They started off again.

A group of passersby—laborers, to judge from their coarse clothing—stopped and stared at Rivalen, pointed and whispered. A city linkboy nearby stood open-mouthed under a street torch and eyed the Shadovar ambassador. Rivalen smiled at the boy and the lad's mouth gaped still wider. The flames in the street torch dimmed as Rivalen and Tamlin passed.

"Your citizens are not yet accustomed to our presence," Rivalen said.

"They will become so, in time," Tamlin said.

Rivalen smiled and said, "I think you are right."

They rode in silence for a time before Tamlin turned the discussion to a matter that had troubled him since learning of it. He said, "Mister Cale succeeded in freeing Endren Corrinthal. Our spies confirm it. Yet I have heard nothing from Endren or Abelar."

Rivalen eyed Tamlin sidelong. "Perhaps, having gotten what he wishes, Abelar Corrinthal no longer considers an alliance with Selgaunt necessary. Perhaps he hopes that the overmistress's army will break itself on Selgaunt such that he never need put himself or his holdings at risk. Perhaps Erevis Cale spoke ill of you and your alliance with us."

Tamlin frowned, uncomfortable with how closely Rivalen's words mirrored his private thoughts. "I think not," he said slowly. "Abelar seemed an honorable man to me."

"You thought the same of Erevis Cale, I suspect. Pain and loss, my Lord Hulorn. I have seen it countless times. Men remain men. But whatever the Corrinthals intend, know that you may rely upon me and my people. And I feel that I may rely upon you and yours. That will be enough. We will prevail against whatever comes."

To that, Tamlin made no reply. He wished, all of a sudden, he had not sent his family away. For the first time in a long while, he wished his father was alive. He felt isolated entirely. He had only Rivalen and Vees.

"Yhaunn is in ruins, Prince," he said. "I have scried it myself. Our spies speak of a monster from the sea."

Shadows snaked around Rivalen's head and hands. "Your spies are well informed. We control a kraken, Hulorn, and it attacked Yhaunn at my command. I thought the scale of the attack appropriate, given our need for a large distraction."

Tamlin had suspected something large, but not a kraken. "A kraken!? You used a bound kraken to attack a Sembian city? Hundreds of civilians are dead. You should have told me your intent. I would have forbade it."

Rivalen turned on him, his eyes hard. The shadows around him churned, as if in agitation, but when he spoke his tone was mild.

"Squeamishness is seldom rewarded in war, Hulorn. Do you think Mirabeta's army will hesitate to raze Selgaunt if it serves her purpose?"

Tamlin took the Prince's point. "Of course not, but . . ."

Rivalen continued. "Still, I should have informed you of the details." He half-bowed in his saddle. "My apologies."

Tamlin suddenly felt embarrassed for raising the matter. He did not enjoy the thought of women and children dying in the kraken attack, but the Prince's point was correct. War was war. He made a dismissive gesture. "I should not have mentioned it. You are correct, of course. Mirabeta has forced us to fight a war, so fight a war we must. I suspect matters will get worse before they improve."

"You can be certain of that," Rivalen said.

"Can the kraken be used to secure the seaways? At the least, it can prevent a naval assault on the harbor?"

Rivalen nodded. "It was wounded in the attack and is difficult to control. But I will see to it, Hulorn."

Tamlin considered, said, "Could it attack Saerloon if we had need? Only if matters become extreme, of course."

"It could," Rivalen said with a knowing smile and a nod. "Though I suspect Lady Merelith has or soon will take precautions against such a move."

"No doubt," Tamlin agreed.

They moved north toward the Khyber Gate. The huge wood and iron slabs had been closed for the night, but the work of reinforcing them continued. The workmen, laboring by torch and glowball, halted in their labors to look upon the Hulorn and the Shadovar. Tamlin and Rivalen dismounted and received a briefing from Mernan, the stooped, elderly engineer supervising the work. Tamlin had less than a score of quality engineers in his service. He valued them as highly as platinum.

"New crossbeams reinforce the gates, my lord," Mernan said, gesturing at the oiled iron beams that reinforced the gates at the top and bottom. "A second bolt will soon be forged. The hinges are strong and well set into the stone. They are unassailable from the outside."

Tamlin nodded, pleased at the rapid progress.

Rivalen strode over to the gate and the workmen parted before him, eyes wide. He placed a hand on the wood and shadows flickered from his fingertips. The workmen murmured and whispered, their tone distrustful.

To Tamlin, Rivalen called, "I can provide spellcasters who can further bolster the strength of the gates."

"The wood is enspelled," Mernan answered irritably. "Bolt and hinges, too. Our mages saw to that."

"Not well enough," Rivalen said. He placed both hands on the huge gate and recited a series of arcane words. Despite his understanding of magic, Tamlin did not recognize the spell. The workmen backed off, fearful.

Mernan protested loudly. "My lord," he said to Tamlin.

Rivalen completed his spell and parted his hands. In response to his gesture, an arch-shaped opening formed at the base of the gate, large enough to give passage to three horsemen abreast. The workmen gasped. Mernan's protest stuttered into silence. A group of a half-dozen refugees on the other side of the gate rose from their bedrolls and wagons to stare wide-eyed at the magical aperture.

Rivalen held his palms outward, uttered a single magical word, and the aperture disappeared as if it had never been. Mernan rushed forward to touch the wall where the hole had been.

"It is solid," he said.

Rivalen nodded at the engineer and turned to Tamlin, though he spoke loud enough for all to hear. "The overmistress's forces will not have a mage among them who is my match in the Art, but the spell I just used requires not mastery, but mere competence."

Tamlin took Rivalen's point, took it gratefully. He said, "We welcome any additional magical aid you can offer."

"Indeed," said Mernan, with grudging respect. Even many among the workmen nodded.

"I will see to it," Rivalen said.

The two remounted and continued along Selgaunt's walls to its other gates. Everywhere it was the same—teams of workmen labored into the night to improve the city's defenses. Tamlin took heart from their diligence. They passed several squads of armed men. The Helms and Scepters had been collapsed into one force. Rorsin and Onthul were doing good work in training them to act cohesively, and using them to drill the militiamen.

"The city is nearly ready," Rivalen observed. "You have capable men and women here."

Tamlin nodded, though he did not feel ready. "When will your additional forces arrive?"

"Five hundred of our elite fighters will arrive as soon as they can be spared. Construction of their barracks is nearly complete, and the conversion of the tavern to our embassy continues apace. The Most High has our forces engaged in other matters, but those will wind down soon enough."

"We will have time," Tamlin said, feeling the chill in the air. "Mirabeta will wait until the spring to attack."

"Perhaps," Rivalen answered, and Tamlin heard doubt in his tone.

"You think she will move sooner? This year?"

"I do not know, Hulorn. The overmistress is unpredictable."

Tamlin shook his head. "I dislike this. Settling in for a siege."

"It is the only course, at the moment," Rivalen answered. "Mirabeta's forces outnumber yours substantially. If the overmistress attacks, Selgaunt must hold for a time. That is all. Aid will come. My people stand with yours, and I with you."

The words brought Tamlin great comfort. He looked around at the towering walls and the strong men and women who worked them. "If we must hold, we will hold," he said, and tried to believe it.

Later, as they prepared to part, Tamlin said to Rivalen, "I would like to discuss your faith with you again. Sometime soon. I would know more of Shar than the tavern tales I've heard in the past. She, at least, has sent you to us while the priests of other gods abandon the city."

"She has, indeed," Rivalen said.

Tamlin nodded, said, "For now I would ask that you keep the nature of your faith quiet. As you said, it could be misunderstood."

Rivalen reached out and put a hand on Tamlin's shoulder. The Prince's shadows curled around Tamlin's arm. "Of course, my Lord Hulorn. And I look forward to further conversations. I am always eager to teach new students about my faith."

Tamlin chuckled.

"You are amused?" Rivalen asked.

"Yes," Tamlin said, still smiling. "But not with you. I was just imagining Vees's reaction if he were to learn the nature of your faith."

Rivalen joined him in laughter.

After bidding farewell to the Hulorn and stabling his mount, Rivalen discarded his false face—that of mentor and father figure to the malleable Uskevren boy—and activated his sending ring. He reached out for Vees Talendar.

Nightseer? Vees asked.

Where are you, Dark Brother?

Vees delayed a moment before answering, *In the Lady's sanctuary, praying. Shall I—*

Rivalen ended the magical connection, pulled the night

about him, and whispered, "The secret sanctuary of the Lady on Temple Avenue."

The shadows answered him and swept him in a breath from the street in the Noble District to the secret fane of Shar on Temple Avenue. He appeared in the main worship hall, amongst the benches. At the front of the hall, a single candle burned on the dark altar, the stone surface draped in a cloth depicting a black disc ringed in purple.

A cloaked form knelt before the altar—Vees Talendar. He held his hand before his face, eyeing the amethyst ring on his finger, no doubt awaiting a response from Rivalen. When he did not receive it, he shook his head, turned back to the altar, and whispered the Thirteen Truths, beginning with the first.

"Love is a lie. Only hate endures. Light is blinding. Only in darkness do we see clearly. Forgiveness is false . . ."

Rivalen stepped into the shadow space and materialized behind Talendar. He took the nobleman by his shoulders and jerked him to his feet. Talendar exclaimed in surprise.

Rivalen hissed into the nobleman's ear, "In the darkness of the void, we hear the whisper of the night."

"Nightseer! It is you. I am—"

Rivalen, much taller than Talendar and as strong as an ogre in darkness, took Talendar's hair in one fist and lifted him off the ground. The nobleman squealed in pain and hung in his grasp like a marionette, kicking.

Rivalen began again. He spoke slowly, enunciating each word. "In the darkness of the void—"

"Heed its voice," Talendar said through gritted teeth, swatting at Rivalen's hand. "Heed its voice, Nightseer."

Rivalen dropped him to the floor in a heap. Talendar scrambled to his feet, rubbing his scalp, breathing heavily. He turned to face Rivalen. "If I have given you offense—"

The shadows around Rivalen churned, reflecting his anger. "If you lie to me before this altar, Dark Brother, I will kill you where you stand."

Talendar's face fell. "I would not lie to you, Nightseer."

"Erevis Cale is a shade," Rivalen said. "This you knew. Yet you did not see fit to tell me. Why?"

Talendar's eyes widened with surprise and fear, then moved to the floor, the wall, anywhere but Rivalen. He started to speak, stopped, started again, stopped. Rivalen knew that Talendar must have rehearsed an answer to the question a hundred times, but the rehearsed answer was a lie, and Talendar dared not speak it.

"Speak now or you will die for holding your silence," Rivalen commanded.

Talendar bowed his head. He closed his eyes and winced as he spoke. "I wished to keep a secret from you, Nightseer. That is the reason. It was petty. I see that now. I—"

"Turn around," Rivalen ordered him.

Talendar looked up sharply, his face pale. He licked his lips. "Nightseer, I apologize if—"

"Turn around."

Talendar stared into Rivalen's face, blinked, nodded, and slowly turned around. His body was as tense as a bowstring. The sound of his rapid breathing echoed off the stone walls of the hall. He stood hunched, awaiting his fate.

For a moment Rivalen let him wonder what doom awaited him. He put a shadow-shrouded hand on the back of Talendar's neck. The nobleman gave a start at the touch. Darkness streamed from Rivalen's hand, wrapped around Talendar's throat.

"Nightseer, please," Talendar said, his voice quaking.

Rivalen caused the tendrils to tighten around Talendar's throat. The nobleman gagged, grasped at them, but could not loosen their grip. Rivalen tightened them further and said, "The Lady smiles on secrets well kept, Dark Brother. But this was not such. Next time, consider well what you tell and what you do not . . . and why."

Rivalen would not kill Talendar—yet. He dispelled the shadowy tendrils and Talendar fell to the floor, coughing and gasping for air.

"Forgive me, Nightseer," he croaked.

"Look upon that altar, Dark Brother. If you are guilty of another such lapse, I will see you laid across it and opened. You will enter Shar's realm not as her servant, but as her sacrifice."

Talendar, on all fours, stared at the altar and began to shake. In a quavering voice, he said, "Love is a lie. Only hate endures. Light is blinding . . ."

Rivalen turned himself invisible and rode the shadows out of the temple to an alley on Temple Avenue. He appeared near a crowd of refugees—two couples with their children—huddled for warmth around a burning brazier.

He moved past them and onto the avenue. Glowballs and burning braziers lit the street. The stars glowed between the notches of the towers, spires, chapels, and shrines of Selgaunt's many gods. He noted each of them in turn—Leira, Milil, Sune, Oghma, Tymora, a handful of others.

"All is fleeting," he said to them.

CHAPTER FOUR

18 Uktar, the Year of Lightning Storms

Cale, Riven, and Magadon materialized on a grassy knoll in a light rain. Riven put his hands on his knees and coughed black phlegm until Cale thought the assassin would surely vomit. Magadon, looking like he might fall over at any moment, sagged to the ground. Cale, too, felt the life-draining effect of Furlinastis's breath. His breathing was ragged; he felt as if his chest were in a vise.

"Are you all right?" he asked them.

Riven nodded between coughs. Magadon took a deep breath and looked to Cale.

"I am well."

They stood atop a low hill dotted with shrubs and a twisted tree that looked like a gallows. The ruins of the once grand city of Elgrin Fau crouched in the deeper darkness of the valley below.

Creepers, stunted shrubs, and twisted trees overgrew the city's ancient streets. The weathered hulks of stone buildings—once shops, residences, and temples—stood in silent rows like gravestones. Piles of rubble dotted the ruins here and there. Tall statues, worn featureless by the eons, stood sentinel over the silence.

Even in death the city felt magisterial, with its grand arches, carved columns, and broad, pavestone plazas. Cale wished he could have seen it under the sun, filled with life.

The temple of the Seekers of the Sun, its dome still intact, rose futilely into the darkness. After Kesson Rel had banished Elgrin Fau to the Plane of Shadow, the worshipers there had never again seen the sun. The followers of light had died in darkness.

Cale's gaze focused on the black clot in the center of the city. He could not see through the murk but he knew an enormous cemetery stood there. It had once been a park or commons, but the residents of Elgrin Fau had converted it to a graveyard in order to bury their dead within the soil of their city. A magical portal stood in the center of the cemetery, a monument placed there by Kesson Rel to mock the citizens after they had died and been transformed by hate and Kesson Rel's magic into undead.

Riven controlled his coughing fit, wiped his mouth, and said, "Explain yourself, Mags. Now."

The threat in Riven's voice turned Cale around.

Magadon did not even look up at the assassin. "What do you mean?"

Riven stepped into Magadon's space, his hands on his saber hilts. Magadon looked up.

"Play stupid and see if I play along," Riven said.

"Riven . . ." Cale began.

Riven held his stare on Magadon. "I saw you when the dragon attacked, Mags. You didn't move a step. You stood there like a sacrifice. Why?"

Cale, too, had witnessed Magadon's inexplicable passiveness. "I saw it, too, Mags. What were you thinking?"

Magadon climbed to his feet. "It happened too fast," he said, but there was a lie in his tone.

Riven's eye narrowed. "A lie. Explain yourself."

Magadon looked into Riven's face. "And if I don't? What will happen that is worse than where I've been? Than where I am?"

Cale understood then. He stepped forward, put his arm between his two comrades, and opened up some space. Riven glared at Magadon before walking away.

Magadon spoke to Riven's back, his tone vaguely taunting. "Tell me, Riven. What will happen? I'm already half dead. What do you think you can do?"

"That's enough," Cale said.

Magadon glared at Cale. "Don't you dare pity me. Ever."

Riven turned around and his voice dripped contempt. "You giving up then, Mags? That devil stole half your soul and now you want to surrender the other half? You want to die? Is that it?"

Magadon could hold Riven's gaze for only a moment before looking away.

To Cale, Riven said, "I've seen that look in the eyes of other men, men who despise themselves, men who make mistakes intentionally because they don't have the balls to handle their own affairs." He turned back to Magadon and said, "You want to die, die. I gave you my dagger. It kills just fine. But don't put us at risk because you won't sheathe steel in your gut. You hear me?"

Magadon looked up, but looked away just as fast.

Cale put a hand on his shoulder. "Mags?"

Magadon shook his head, made no eye contact with Cale. When he spoke, his voice quavered.

"I don't know what I want. Godsdammit. Pieces of me have been falling off since we parted a year ago. The Source, my father. I'm falling down, here." He looked up at Riven. "I'm falling down, Riven."

Riven stalked over, his eye burning. He took Magadon by the other shoulder.

"Stand up, then," the assassin said, and shook him gently. "Stand up."

Magadon looked into Riven's face, into Cale's.

"We need you with us, Mags," Cale said. "Are you with us?"

"Are you?" Riven asked.

Magadon looked away, looked back at them. Finally he firmed up and nodded.

"What's left of me is with you."

Cale decided it would have to be enough. He turned to Riven.

"Well enough?"

Riven looked only at Magadon. "We are all neck deep in this, Mags. All of us. There's no giving up. Not now. Not ever."

Magadon nodded and the patter of rain filled the silence.

"Now," Riven said to Cale. "You said you'd tell us everything. Start talking."

Cale said, "Let's get out of this damned rain first."

"Follow me," Magadon said, and led them away from the city until they found a small copse of twisted trees as large as mature oaks. They sheltered under the broad leaves, which kept most of the rain at bay. It was too damp for a fire, so they huddled near the bole and stared at one another through the darkness.

Magadon and Riven waited for Cale to speak. Cale framed his thoughts and spoke in a low tone.

He told them of his encounter with Mask in an alley in Selgaunt, of the god's ominous warnings regarding Sembia and the Cycle of Shadows. He told them of how he had attacked his own god and gotten tossed about like a child's doll for his pains. He told them of his promise to take from Kesson Rel the divinity that Kesson Rel had stolen from Mask long ago. They knew that he had promised the same thing to Mephistopheles as ransom for Magadon's soul. He told them of the book he had taken from the Fane of Shadows, how it had erased itself and begun rewriting itself back to front. He told them, finally, of how Mephistopheles had taken it from him. When he finished, no one spoke for a time.

"Well?" he asked them.

Riven shook his head. "Dark, Cale. Dark and empty."

Cale said, "Agreed." He looked each of them in the eye. "Now is the time to walk away. I chose this path. Kesson Rel, Mask, and Mephistopheles are my problems. The promises are mine to keep. If you're not—"

"Nobody is walking away, Cale," Riven said.

Magadon nodded. "I've got nowhere to go." He cleared his throat and eyed Cale and Riven. The rain slicked his black hair. His horns glistened. "What now, then?"

Cale answered, "The gate in Elgrin Fau."

Riven and Magadon eyed him. Magadon said, "The gate is guarded."

"And we had a go at it before," Riven said.

Cale nodded at both of them.

A darkweaver guarded the gate, together with an army of wraiths—the dead of Elgrin Fau.

"We barely kept our skins last time," Riven said.

"Matters stood differently then," Cale answered.

When they had faced the darkweaver and wraiths the first time, Cale had not known how to control the powers granted him by the shadowstuff. Neither had Riven. Both of them did now.

"True enough," Riven said. He rummaged in a belt pouch for his pipe, found it, and started to fill it.

"We do not know where the gate leads," Magadon said.

Cale acknowledged the point. "No, we don't."

Riven struck a tindertwig on his boot, shielded its small flame from the rain, and lit the pipe. Around the stem, he asked, "You think it leads to Kesson Rel?"

Cale nodded his head. "I do, but there's only one way to be sure."

Riven blew out a cloud of smoke. "What about Selgaunt? You leave the Uskevren boy to that Shadovar and he will suffer."

Cale knew. But Tamlin had made his choice. And Cale had

made his. Cale's duty was to Magadon, and to his god. Not to Tamlin, not to Sembia.

"*Korvikoum,*" he softly said, invoking his favorite concept from dwarven philosophy. Choices and consequences, the dwarves taught. Cale had learned the lesson well. Tamlin soon would, too.

He looked his friends in the face.

"Get some rest. We are as safe here as anywhere. We will take a few days to recover some strength." He looked meaningfully at Magadon, who looked as if he had not eaten a decent meal in months. "Then we go at Elgrin Fau."

The rain stops after a few hours. I sit in the darkness under the strange trees, feeling nothing for them. My bond with the world is broken. I am separate from it, alien.

I hesitate to seek my mental focus. I know I must do so—if I am to be of any use to my companions, and to myself, I must be able to call upon my mental abilities—but I fear what I will find, or not find.

I finally work up the strength, close my eyes, and sink into my consciousness. For a time I swim in thoughts, memories, and ideas. I sharpen my concentration and feel around tentatively.

Immediately I confirm that I am less than I was. A scarred hole in my center evidences what my father took, what he yet holds. What's left of me swirls around the hole like a maelstrom. I see my desire for the Source. It permeates my being. And I see more. I see that there is no separation within me any longer, no wall to separate man from fiend.

And the fiend is strong.

The fiend finds tempting the thought of murdering Cale and Riven in their sleep. The man resists. The man feels compelled to kill first Rivalen Tanthul, for giving me over to the Source, then to kill my father, for taking what he took.

The fiend finds the man's bloodlust amusing.

Part of me wishes to die but I do not know if it is the man or the fiend that urges suicide.

I am afraid—afraid to live, afraid to die. It is unbearable.

I feel eyes upon me and know that Cale is not sleeping.

I remain attached to my mindscape but open my eyes to let the outer world register.

Cale is lying on his back. His eyes are open and staring at me. He holds his silk mask in his hand and I presume he has been praying to his god. I wonder how much he sleeps. His eyes—glowing yellow on the Plane of Shadow—pronounce him inhuman, half a man.

But he is half a man because the rest of him is shadowstuff. I am half a man because the rest of me is gone.

There is a question in his eyes. I have no answer.

He rises, checks to ensure that Riven is asleep, and approaches.

I see the concern on his freshly-shaven face and know that he is my friend. I come out of my mind to see him fully.

He crouches across from me and I am reminded of another time on the Plane of Shadow when we spoke across a fire and first became friends. We had been different men, then. And there is no fire between us now, only darkness.

He speaks in a low tone. The shadows cling to him like black gauze.

"Can't sleep?"

I shake my head. "I am preparing to meditate."

He nods, looks away, looks back at me. He wants to say something. Finally, he does.

"I will fix this, Mags."

He is making promises to himself, not to me.

"I do not know if this can be fixed, Cale."

He looks at me in earnest. "Why do you say that?"

The words come out before I can stop them. "I am . . . not myself. I am afraid of what I am."

The words hit him hard. He has said similar things of himself.

He nods and looks away. His fist is clenched around his mask, though he tries to hide it from me.

"I fear I have only a short time, Cale. There is a darkness in me that will overwhelm the rest if I don't . . . stop it."

He takes my meaning and looks back at me sharply.

"Do not even think it," he hisses. "I do not care what Riven said. I will fix this."

There is no doubt in his tone, his eyes. I have never met anyone like him.

"I have a hole, Cale," I say, and put my hand on my breast, my heart. "Here. And I swear to the gods that the rest of me is slowly slipping inside it. I'm trying to keep myself, but I feel myself falling. Every moment a little more of me slips away."

He leans forward, seizes me both with his eyes and his hands.

"You're done slipping as of this moment. This far and no farther. Understand?" He shakes me, unaware of his strength, of my weakness. "This far and no farther."

I stare into his face—the face of a believer—and only one response is possible. "Very well, Cale," I say, and change the subject by nodding at his mask. "I am sorry you are in this situation with Mask."

He leans back, eyes still burning. "It was my decision and I would make it again." He looks down at the mask in his hand. "Besides, this is nothing new. Our relationship has been nothing better than fitful, anyway. He still answers when I pray. That is enough."

I nod, try to smile. He does, too, but quickly turns serious.

"You told me once that blood does not make the man. That our soul is our own, always."

I nod. I had said something like that to him, once. It seems long ago.

"Remember that," he says.

He stands, pats my shoulder, bids me get some sleep.

"Cale," I say. A confession rushes up my throat.

He looks down at me, yellow eyes concerned. I see no judgment in them. "The creatures on Sakkors . . ."

He nods, waiting.

"They are called krinth. They are slaves to the Shadovar."

I hesitate. He bids me continue. "I . . . think I did things to many of them, Cale. Opened their minds while I was . . . with the Source. Rivalen Tanthul made me do it. It hurt them, changed them. But . . ."

He kneels down, looks me in the face. "But?"

I shake my head. The fiend is laughing at me. I want to tell Erevis that I took pleasure in altering the krinth, in exercising my will over them, but I know he will not look at me the same way if I do.

"Nothing," I say. "That is all."

He knows I am lying but does not press. Perhaps he wants to know nothing more. Confessions, after all, change both those who give them and those who hear them.

"Rest, Mags," he says, and returns to his bedroll.

I close my eyes and return to my mind, to my battle.

I am a ghost, haunting myself.

For two days, they awoke to the same darkness in which they had slept. The Plane of Shadow never saw a dawn. Darkness was eternal.

Power filled Cale's mind. Despite his conflicting obligations to god and archfiend, the Shadowlord continued to answer his prayers. Cale did not understand it, not fully, but did not need to.

Each day after sleeping, Riven sat up, coughed, spit, and lit his pipe. The dark smoke curled into the dark sky. Magadon always sat apart from them, without armor, without his backpack full of gear, with only a dagger for a weapon. To Cale he seemed lost. Cale was determined to help him find himself again.

Throughout the days, Cale used a minor conjuration to summon food and water, mostly stew in bowls made of bread. The three men ate, smoked, talked, shaved, checked their gear and weapons, and idled away the hours. The time passed slowly, but Cale could see Magadon regaining his strength. He ate more and more and Cale was pleased to see it.

"I am ready," Magadon said to them on the second night.

Cale and Riven nodded.

"Tomorrow, then," Cale said.

The next morning they took their fill of breakfast in silence. Afterward, they stood and readied themselves.

Cale held his mask and drew Weaveshear. Darkness leaked from the blade in lazy strands. Riven checked the buckles on his armor, tested the balance on both his sabers. Magadon sheathed the dagger Riven had given him on Cania.

"Mags, can you link us?" Cale asked tentatively. "Do not, if it will . . . make things worse."

Riven looked a question at him, but Cale ignored it.

Magadon shook his head. "It does not make it worse. It just reminds me of what is."

The mindmage looked to Riven, to Cale, and Cale felt a soft tingle under his scalp.

We're linked, Magadon projected. He held out his palm and a yellow ball of light formed above it. The light flared, lengthened, shaped itself into the form of a blade.

Riven whistled softly and chuckled. The assassin patted Magadon on the shoulder. "Looks like you do have a weapon. Good to have you back."

Magadon nodded at Riven. To Cale, he projected, *I'm with you. For as long as I can be.*

Whatever the price, Cale answered, *I will fix it.*

Magadon smiled softly, an indulgent smile, and closed his eyes in concentration. A green glow haloed his head, spread to his arms, torso, and thighs, and sheathed him in force—armor made from his mind.

They were ready. Cale looked his friends in the face.

"I will put us directly into the cemetery, as near to the gate as I can. Ignore the wraiths as much as possible and move right for the darkweaver and the gate. All we need to do is get through it."

Magadon nodded. Riven tapped the holy symbol that dangled from a chain around his neck.

"We go," Cale said. He pictured the cemetery of Elgrin Fau in his mind, pulled the shadows about him, and moved them there.

CHAPTER FIVE

20 Uktar, the Year of Lightning Storms

Elyril arrived in Yhaunn with Kefil and donned the appropriate false face. She made her required appearance before the Nessarch, the rotund and bearded Andilal Tharimpar. She endured Andilal's ham-handed flirtations as she stood at his side and looked out of a Roadkeep balcony and down on the descending terraces of the city. The thin spires of Glasscrafters' Hall, capped with orange domes that looked like flames, dominated the skyline of the city's center. Beyond and below it, in the lower terrace, the dock ward lay in ruins.

Elyril expressed concern and resolve on her aunt's behalf, and agreed to tour the destruction of the docks with the Nessarch's aide and son, Kalton Tharimpar, an entirely ordinary man of thirty or so winters with pale skin, a thin beard, and curly brown hair. When the time came, she inhaled minddust and brought Kefil along on a thick leather leash.

"That is the largest mastiff I have ever seen," Kalton said. He wore a fox-trimmed cape over his high-collared shirt and tailored breeches. A heavy blade hung at his side. He eyed Kefil warily.

"He has been my companion since childhood," Elyril said, and patted the dog's massive head. Drool dripped from his enormous jowls. He licked Elyril's hand and stared distaste at Kalton.

They took a carriage down the city, across the ramp bridges that connected the various terraces, until they reached the docks. There, they disembarked.

Elyril shook her head at the immensity of the destruction. Piles of shattered stone and splintered wood littered the dock ward. Most of the city near the shoreline lay in ruins. Dislodged piers jutted askew from the still muddy waters. All around her, the innards of crumbled buildings lay surrounded by the ruins of their skin. Kalton offered his hand and assisted Elyril through the destruction, smiling ingratiatingly but staying to one side of Kefil.

"Milady can see that progress has been rapid."

Elyril saw nothing of the kind but nodded anyway. Teams of laborers used carts and mules to clear the debris as best they could. Nods and curt bows acknowledged Elyril and Kalton, but nothing more. The workmen were too intent on their tasks. Kefil growled at shadows.

"He seems an aggressive animal," Kalton said.

"He is," Elyril agreed.

Flotsam from the destruction congealed like a scab along the shoreline. An enormous, concave depression in the mud and stone marred the shore where the kraken had beached for the attack. Countless gulls wheeled in the air, cawing. Others prowled the mud for morsels.

"The creature was enormous," Elyril said.

"Unlike anything I have ever seen," Kalton said, his voice somber. "I assisted a ballista crew. We hit it three times. I think it could have been a hundred. The creature felt nothing." He looked about. "But we will rebuild. Did Milady ever visit the stiltways before recent events?" He pointed to Elyril's right, at an entire block of collapsed wooden buildings. The remains of stilts stuck up out of the ruins like shards of bone. Elyril thought them comical.

"I did not," she said.

"That is regrettable," Kalton said. "They were the soul of the docks. Shop upon shop, all on stilts and interconnected with ladders, swings, and chutes. I loved it as a child. Crime there had become a problem in recent years, but still . . ."

"Drugs?" Elyril asked.

Kalton nodded. "Of all kinds."

Elyril wished she had seen it, indeed.

Kalton firmed up and said, "But that, too, we will rebuild, better than before." He pointed toward the northern end of the harbor. "The northern piers suffered damage only from the rush of water. Most are salvageable and, as you can see, several remain usable."

Split logs reinforced some of the northern piers. Four caravels flying the heraldry of Raven's Bluff sat at anchor near them. Dock workers swarmed over ships and docks, unloading crates and barrels. A half-dozen carracks floated nearby, awaiting their turn to unload.

"I am shocked at the destruction," Elyril said, though she was amused at the many ghosts of the dead that lingered around the wreckage, particularly around the stiltways. They floated here and there, grimacing. Kefil snapped at those within reach. Elyril continued. "The attack was outrageous, outside the bounds of decency."

Kalton licked his thin lips and looked about at the destruction. "On that we are agreed, Milady."

She put a hand on his forearm and saw the eager gleam it

elicited in his eye. Kefil growled a warning.

"The rebels will be made to pay," she said. "I assure you of that. And my aunt soon will send additional aid to assist with the rebuilding here."

He placed his hand over hers and she held her smile despite his sweaty palm.

I wish to devour his balls, Kefil projected.

The thought pleased Elyril but she commanded the mastiff to heel.

Kalton caressed her hand. "I am pleased to hear that. Your aunt is an impressive woman. As are you."

She smiled and gently disengaged her hand from his. "Would it be possible to speak to the Watchblades who were guarding the Hole the night of the attack? My aunt is interested in determining the specific identity of the attackers who freed Endren Corrinthal."

He smiled and bowed. "We have already questioned them, as well as the corpse of the raider we felled, but you are welcome to speak to them again. The Watchblades I will put at your disposal. The corpse we preserved in anticipation of further investigation. I will arrange for all of that tonight, if it suits you."

"It does. Thank you, Kalton."

He smiled. "But before any of that, I insist you join me for a meal. It is already late afternoon and I am spoiled by your company."

Kefil circled around to Kalton's shadow and tore it to shreds. Kalton did not notice.

"You flatter me," Elyril said, and faked a smile. "Of course I will dine with you."

Later, prior to the meal, she stroked Kefil and inhaled an extra snuff of minddust, which helped her endure Kalton's babbling and his storm of boring stories. She laughed aloud when a swarm of flies burst from his mouth. He gagged and spat and she laughed all the harder. He seemed puzzled by her mirth and she did not bother to explain.

Afterward, she returned to her official residence—a well-appointed, two-story home and office near the Roadkeep that housed official guests of the Nessarch.

Did you murder him? Kefil asked. The mastiff lay stretched before the stone fireplace, faking sleep.

"Of course not," she said. "I am an ambassador. He is the Nessarch's son."

You are mad, Kefil said, and began to snore.

Elyril ignored the dog and prepared for her interrogations. She clothed herself in spells from Shar that allowed her to detect lies and that made her words supernaturally persuasive. She had the steward send for the guards from the Hole and interrogated them, one by one, in a small study.

Her spells made all of them deferential and cooperative but most had seen little. Moments after they had first heard the kraken attack, magical darkness had shrouded the interior guard post. They had never seen their attackers. The guards at the top of the lift had caught only a glimpse of the raiding party before they had been rendered unconscious by attackers who emerged from the shadows behind them.

Shadovar, Elyril assumed. She wondered how involved in events the Nightseer might have been. She pulled idly at the magical amethyst ring on her finger.

None of the guards had been complicit, Elyril determined, and none of were lying. She had expected as much. The Nessarch's priests would have ferreted out any traitors.

The raiders numbered less than ten, by all accounts, but had moved so quickly and quietly that the guards had been unable to organize an effective response. By the time the guards had responded in number, Endren had already been freed. The guards had pursued, but one of the raiders sacrificed himself to give time for his fellows to escape; he killed seven guards with his hands before the other guards finally cut him down. His magically preserved body remained in the possession of the

Nessarch's charnel keeper, in the bowels of the Roadkeep. Priests of Waukeen had questioned his corpse at the Nessarch's request, but learned nothing. They intended to try again, or so thought the guards.

The raiders never made it back to the lift. Instead, they fled down an old mineshaft. Stones and bolts had knocked them from the walls but no bodies had been found at the bottom. Importantly, Elyril learned that the Hole's zone of dead magic ended before the shaft hit bottom.

And that was how the raiders escaped, she assumed.

After hours of discussion with the guards, Elyril had learned little. Two tasks remained to her: an interview with a former guardsman named Phraig—the same Phraig who had been forced by the attackers to lead them to Endren—and an interview with the dead raider. Priests of Waukeen might not be able to compel the corpse to speak, but a priestess of Shar would.

While the steward sought Phraig—he had quit the guard recently—Elyril arranged for a carriage to transport her back to the Roadkeep.

When she arrived, she found that Kalton had instructed the staff to extend her every courtesy. A guard escorted her deep into the Roadkeep's lower levels. There, an elderly charnel worker in a stained leather apron met her.

"The corpse of the dead raider taken from the Hole," she said, and the small old man bobbed his head.

"Yes, Milady."

As they walked, the old man said, "The dead without a family or temple are brought here and interred in the old mines. We have converted them to catacombs."

Elyril nodded but paid little attention. The smell of death filled the air. She found it exciting.

Presently, they reached a small room. The elderly man fumbled with a key, turned the lock, and opened the door. Candlelight spilled out. The body of the raider, wrapped in grave cloth, lay atop a wooden table.

"Milady does not need to see the body underneath, I trust?" he asked.

"On the contrary," Elyril said. "I do."

The old man's face fell and he grumbled, "I will have to rewrap it, Milady. Has the Nessarch approved this?"

Elyril glared at him. "I serve the Overmistress of Sembia, granther. And the Nessarch answers to her. You are not too old to be flogged."

The old man paled and tottered to the table.

"No need to be hasty, Milady. No need for that, now."

He produced a small knife and slit the cloth that bound the body. Stink filled the room, despite the preservation spells. He cleared away the wrap to expose the body and stepped back.

"That will be all," Elyril said. "I need to examine his body for a certain mark. I will summon you when I have completed my investigation."

The thin, gray-haired man eyed her with suspicion but dared not gainsay her. He bobbed his head and withdrew. The closing door flickered the candle flames that lit the room.

Elyril ran her fingers over the dead man's purpling skin. An easterner, Elyril saw, from the eyelids and swarthy skin. But not a shade. Slashes from the guards' blades gaped in his flesh like open mouths. They whispered secrets to Elyril.

Make the book whole, they said. *The storm will follow.*

She touched her invisible holy symbol and quietly incanted the words to a spell that would pull a portion of the dead man's spirit back to his body. As she chanted, the room grew dark, the shadows long.

A soft purple glow emanated from the dead man's wounds. His eyes creaked open to reveal black orbs.

"Name yourself," Elyril commanded.

The stiff head turned awkwardly in her direction. The dead eyes fixed on her. "Return me to the night eternal, priestess."

"Name yourself," Elyril repeated.

The corpse's mouth hardened, but Elyril's spell pulled the words out. "I am Skelan."

Elyril leaned over his body, let her invisible holy symbol lay against the flesh of his chest. "Who were you?"

Creases lined Skelan's face as he tried to resist, but Elyril's magic compelled an answer. "In life, I was a follower of the Twilight Path and servant of the Shadowlord."

Elyril cocked her head. "Mask?"

The dead man nodded, once.

"What is Mask's interest in Endren Corrinthal?"

Skelan's jaw tightened. The tendons in his neck stood out as he tried to keep his mouth closed, but Elyril's magic was the stronger.

"The Shadowlord charted a path for us across Faerûn to serve his Chosen, the Left and Right Hands of Shadow, the First and Second of Five. His purpose is their purpose. They wished Endren Corrinthal freed."

Elyril inhaled the stink of death, stared into Skelan's eyes, and said, "What are their names?"

Skelan hissed and shook his head.

"Their names, Skelan," Elyril purred.

"I will answer no more questions from you, Sharran. Release me."

Elyril snarled and pressed her invisible holy symbol into Skelan's forehead. He writhed. "Their names."

"No," he said through gritted teeth. "Nothing more."

"Speak," she said. "Speak!"

He said nothing. His body shuddered and his eyes closed, but she knew he was still there.

Angry, she put her mouth next to his ear and whispered, "Then sit in that rotting shell forever. The catacombs are cold."

She stood, spat on the corpse, and strode out of the room past the startled old man.

"Milady?" he called after her. "Milady?"

"Leave me!" Elyril said, and waved him away.

Irritated, she ignored the carriage and decided to walk the city by night. Her temporary residence was not far. Foul Selûne had set and she paced under a blessedly moonless sky. As she walked, she pondered events.

What role had Mask to play in matters? And where was the ten-times damned book?

Lost in thought, she found herself on a dark side street. How had she ended up in an alley? The buildings, standing close together, blocked the sky from her view. She stumbled over a drunk and nearly lost her footing. He grunted with pain, slurred something incomprehensible. She cursed him and continued on. Ahead, she saw the glow of street lamps from a main thoroughfare.

"The Shadowstorm is not what you hope," the drunk murmured to her back.

The words froze her, sent a chill down her neck. She turned around and stalked back to the drunk, a hand on her invisible holy symbol.

He lay huddled against the wall, wrapped in rags and filth. His greasy dark hair was matted against his scalp. He squinted and held up a grubby hand for coin.

"Coin for a beggar, Milady?"

"What did you say to me?" she asked. "Just now. Speak it again. Are you a prophet?"

The man looked up at her and she saw cunning in his eyes. She liked it not at all.

"I *am* a prophet, of sorts. I said that a storm would bring hope. The city needs rain to wash it clean. Coin, Milady?"

Elyril stared into his eyes and saw no lie there. She smiled at her misperception. Lack of sleep was clouding her senses. She chuckled and kicked the drunk in the stomach. He groaned and curled up.

"Milady is a dark soul," he said between gasps.

"Never address your betters unless you are addressed first."

The man tried to unfold and crawl away. "Yes, priestess."

Satisfied, Elyril turned and walked away.

Only after she had taken ten steps did she realize that the man had called her a priestess. She whirled around but he was gone, swallowed by the shadows.

Had she misheard him again? She decided that she must have.

She returned to the residence provided by the Nessarch to find Kefil sleeping and her doughy steward awaiting her.

"I have located the former Watchblade," the steward said. He must have seen the lack of recognition in Elyril's eyes. "Phraig, Milady. You asked me to find him. He awaits your pleasure in the side room."

"Ah, yes. This late?"

"You asked, Milady. This watchman has . . . strange habits, it would seem."

"Have him wait a moment."

She retired to her room and snuffed a pinch of minddust before entering the study and ordering the steward to bring Phraig before her.

The young Watchblade entered the room and the lamplight dimmed for a moment. His movements appeared stilted, and Elyril wondered if he had been drinking. Or perhaps he was still recovering from wounds suffered during the raid. From his mussed hair and sunken eyes, Elyril deduced he had slept little. He wore no blade other than his eating knife, and he bore a large leather satchel over one shoulder.

"I am Phraig, Milady," said the former Watchblade with a bow. His deep voice, coming from so small a man, surprised Elyril. And the tone struck her as vaguely mocking. His eyes shone in their sockets—the white was entirely too pronounced— and the intensity of his gaze made Elyril uncomfortable.

"Sit. I have questions for you about the recent raid on the Hole."

Phraig sat.

Elyril felt warm, as if the boy radiated heat. She cleared her throat and said, "You were forced to lead the raiders into the Hole. Tell me everything. Omit not even the smallest detail."

Phraig did, staring at her throughout. Elyril learned that one of the leaders was missing an eye and another was bald and unusually tall. Both served Mask, which was consistent with what Elyril had learned from Skelan's corpse. She assumed them to be Mask's Chosen, his Left and Right Hands. Phraig named them: Erevis Cale and Drasek Riven.

"They spoke their names to you?"

Phraig looked sly. "I heard their names, Milady."

Elyril accepted that.

Despite the new information, Elyril still could not connect events. Was Mask's priesthood allied with the Selgauntans and Saerbians? Had Mask taken an active hand in attempting to thwart Shar's plans to cause the Shadowstorm?

Her frustration manifested in curt questioning of Phraig, who held an infuriatingly self-satisfied smile throughout the interview. After a time, Kefil padded into the study. He stopped just inside the doorway and sniffed the air suspiciously.

"My mastiff," Elyril said, expecting Phraig to show the same discomfort everyone did around Kefil.

Phraig turned in his chair, smiling. "What a fine animal." He held out a hand. Elyril saw that his fingernails were long and black—no doubt, he was afflicted with some illness.

Kefil's hackles rose. He bared his teeth and growled.

"Here, pup," said Phraig.

Kefil abruptly tucked his tail between his legs, whined, and fled the room. Phraig clucked his tongue and turned to regard Elyril with a smile. "Somewhat passive, isn't he?"

"That is all, boy," Elyril said, wishing for another snuff of dust before retiring. "You may go."

Phraig did not stand.

"Did you hear me? I said we are done."

"I did hear you, Milady. But . . ." He trailed off and looked away.

Elyril's irritation turned to curiosity. He was holding something back.

"Is there something more? If you hold back from me, I will see that you are punished. Make no mistake—"

He looked up at her from hooded eyes and whispered, "I have a secret."

The words elicited goose pimples on Elyril's skin. Her hand went to her invisible holy symbol. She felt on the verge of an epiphany. She leaned forward and said softly, "Speak it, Watchblade."

Phraig's eyes were sly. "I took something from the dead shadowman." He made a gesture that could have indicated anything. "*She* told me to."

Elyril's heart accelerated. Her body tingled. She licked her lips. "Whom do you mean by 'she'?"

Phraig looked away. "You know. You must. The night itself spoke to me with the voice of a woman. It told me to take it, told me to keep it for you."

Elyril was holding her breath. "Keep . . . what?"

"This." Phraig rummaged in his satchel and pulled out a large book. Black scaled leather covered gilded vellum pages. Elyril's breath caught when she saw it.

"The book," she breathed. She held out a hand as if to touch it, but stopped just short, struck with the unreality of events. "How can this be?" she asked.

"She said to give it to you. Take it." He offered it to her. "I have never opened it. Perhaps it can answer your questions."

Elyril stared at it for a moment, finally took it in trembling hands. It was uncomfortably warm where Phraig had held it, as if the man were on fire, but she did not care. She ran her fingertips over the rough cover, the way she might a lover.

"She told me it was unfinished," Phraig said. "The middle is gone, she said."

"The book to be made whole," Elyril said, hushed, awed.

"This is yours, then, Milady?"

Elyril nodded, rapt. She was reminded of the first time she had ever partaken of minddust, the feeling of well-being, of transcendence.

"Mine," she said. "Yes."

"Then I will take my leave," Phraig said. He stood, brushing her hand with fingers not hot, but cold as snow. "I feared I was going mad, hearing voices, seeing things. After all, if I were mad, how would I know?"

The words struck her and she looked up into his eyes. The light caught them strangely and she saw only whites.

"How would I know?" she echoed.

He smiled a mouthful of fangs, turned, and exited the room.

Elyril sank back into her chair, cradling the book against her breast as if it were a newborn babe. She bathed in its warmth, thanked Shar, opened it, and began to read from back to front.

It told of Shar's creation from darkness, of her battles with her sister, Selûne, of her secret creation of the Shadow Weave in mockery of Mystra's Weave. It told of Shar's end, which was the end of all things. It hinted at more, at a moment of necessary weakness but ultimate triumph for the Lady of Loss, a time when she would devour the shadow.

Elyril pored over every word, every page, inhaling more and more minddust, and in so doing she learned the book's secret. It lay between the words, in the empty spaces on the page. She laughed aloud at its import.

The emptiness spoke in its silence of a ritual—the ritual that would free Volumvax and summon the Shadowstorm. Elyril felt flush at the prospect.

But she could not learn all she needed to know. Some details of the ritual were missing. The book had been divided and the middle pages were gone.

It wanted a mate. It wanted to be made whole.

Elyril had to find the rest.

✿ ✿ ✿ ✿ ✿

The late afternoon sun shone down from a cloudless sky. Abelar and Regg, accompanied by Beld and his two companions, rode beside a drought-dried stream bed across the grassy plains, toward the small village Abelar had commandeered to quarter his forces for a few days while he traveled to the Abbey of Dawn.

They rode through high grass, past autumn-stripped stands of birch and maple. They fell silent when they passed the melted remains of a small village. The village's cottages had been reduced to shapeless, discolored lumps. The blackened skeletons of dead trees stood in fields of blasted grass and bore silent witness to the carnage wrought by an enraged dragon.

"The dragon rage," Regg said. "A black, probably."

Abelar nodded. He had seen a black up close, ten leagues west and south of Saerb. He thanked Lathander that the rage was over.

They left the destruction behind and traveled onward. Presently they reached the fallow fields around the village. The poor harvest had made food scarce. Winter would be unforgiving to the villagers.

At Abelar's orders, his company took only shelter from the villagers, never food, not even for the horses. The force counted six priests among their number. All were untested and inexperienced, but all were competent to perform the minor miracle of conjuring food and fresh water. They kept the men fed and distributed any excess to the hungry villagers, starting with the children. More often than not, Abelar's company left the villages better off than when they arrived. The overmistress's forces would be larger, and would not be as kind. Civil war would leave thousands of innocents dead.

"Sembia is not in a state to survive a war," Abelar said to Regg.

Regg nodded agreement. "What realm is? Cormyr is still

reeling from hers. Here, the wounds of the rage are fresh and the drought lingers. War is always ugly, my friend. And the weak always suffer most."

"But not on our watch," Abelar said softly.

"Truth," Regg affirmed. "Not on our watch."

Ahead, the chimneys of the log cottages and farms of the village sent thin plumes of smoke into the clear sky. The rhythmic ring of a smith's hammer carried over the plains. The breeze carried the smell of a cooking fire.

The riders crested a brush-covered rise and saw the village below—a collection of simple homes and animal pens built around a large commons. A woman and her undernourished adolescent daughter drew water from the community well. A few scrawny dogs padded through the lanes.

The canvas tents of Abelar's company covered a tree-dotted field on the far edge of the village. A boar roasted on a spit over a fire; one of the men must have taken it on a hunt. Two men tended it while the rest went about their business—cleaning armor, training, eating, talking. The company's horses grazed in the dry grass away from the tents. All were saddled, as if the company were ready to ride.

"Where's the watch?" Regg asked.

"Watching," said a voice from their right.

Three men in leather jerkins rose from a crouch and stepped out of the undergrowth. All bore loaded crossbows in their hands and broadswords at their belts. Bone signal whistles dangled from leather thongs around their necks.

"We could have shot you all dead a stone's throw back," said Garold, a young freckled warrior with a head of hair so red the men called him Bloodmane. His two companions, Rynn and Enerd, grinned.

"If it had been otherwise I'd have had your balls," Regg said, half-seriously.

Abelar chuckled and gestured at Beld and his two companions. "Meet Beld, Aldas, and Dens. They will ride with us."

"Welcome," Garold said. He looked to Abelar. "There's ill news, commander."

Abelar frowned. "Speak it."

"The overmistress's army is marching. We have heard that Forrin heads it."

Regg cursed and spat with contempt.

"Malkur Forrin?" Abelar asked.

Garold nodded.

That explained why Roen had the horses ready to ride. Abelar still had a handful of allies among Lathander's church in Ordulin. They magically relayed information to Roen, the company's senior priest, as circumstance allowed.

"Forrin is a butcher," Regg said. "At the Battle of the Deurst Lowlands, he—"

Abelar cut Regg off.

"How many in his army? Composition of his forces? Is Saerloon marching as well?"

"Roen could tell you, my lord."

"To where are they headed?" Abelar asked. "Do you know that, at least? Selgaunt?"

Garold lowered his head, looked to the men flanking him, at his boots.

"Speak it, boy," Regg said, though Abelar's heart was already sinking.

"Saerb, sir. Or so I've heard."

Abelar's mind turned instantly to Elden, unprotected, standing in the path of an army. He cursed and heeled Swiftdawn toward the village. Regg, Beld, and the other riders fell in behind him. Regg shouted back to Garold and the perimeter guards.

"Gather your gear and recall the rest of the guards! Prepare to ride!"

They galloped through the village and into the camp. His men rose to meet him. All wore hard looks.

Regg indicated Beld and his comrades. "These men ride with

us. Gear up. We ride apace. Leave the boar to the villagers."

The men scrambled to break camp.

Roen emerged from his tent, wrapped in his armor and with a heavy flanged mace at his belt. The pale, black-haired priest, as tall and slender as a sapling, nodded at them. Abelar and Regg swung out of their saddles and the men exchanged greetings.

"Welcome back, my lords. You've heard about Forrin already, I see."

"Tell us everything you know," Abelar said.

While the men broke camp around them, most taking a moment to welcome Regg and Abelar back, Roen said, "Forrin marched from Ordulin last night under cover of darkness. His force is more than one thousand cavalry. They are heading west toward Saerb. That is all we know."

"Four times our number," Regg said, and whistled. "The overmistress does nothing halfway. She wishes to draw us north."

Abelar nodded, considered. "There are men in and around Saerb who will fight if battle is brought to their doors."

"They are leaderless," Regg said. "Small groups of competent swordsmen, but not an army. If they fight, they'll die piecemeal."

"Aye, but if we can arrive before Forrin, we can consolidate them with our force. We—"

"There is more," Roen said.

Abelar and Regg looked at the priest.

"Yhaunn was attacked by a creature or creatures from the sea. Much of the city was ruined or flooded. Hundreds died. Perhaps thousands."

"Gods," Abelar said.

"Attacked by whom?" Regg asked.

"Our spies say that Selgaunt was behind it. Or so says the overmistress in her pronouncements."

"Selgaunt?" Abelar asked. "How?"

Roen said, "Our spies say the Selgauntans have made alliance with the Shadovar."

"The Shadovar?" Abelar could not believe it. Selgaunt's

Hulorn had not impressed him overmuch, but he had not taken the Uskevren boy for a fool. The Shadovar could not be trusted.

Roen nodded. "It could be another lie of the overmistress."

Abelar put it from his mind. "It does not matter now. Saerb is our concern."

Regg said, "The overmistress will use Yhaunn to justify slaughter, Abelar. Forrin will raze Saerb to the ground. Those who do not flee will die."

Abelar stared him in the face, then Roen. "Not on our watch."

Regg nodded, and so did Roen.

"My lord, there is yet more," said Roen. "During the attack from the sea, a small force attacked the Hole—"

"Attacked the Hole?!" Regg exclaimed.

Roen nodded and continued. "Your father disappeared in the attack."

Hope rose in Abelar. "Disappeared? Escaped, you mean?"

Roen shrugged. "This was days ago, my lord. There is no word of him since."

"But he escaped?" Regg prompted.

Abelar understood Roen's point. "Or he was taken."

"Taken?" Regg asked. "By whom? The Shadovar?"

Abelar shrugged. There was no way to know. If his father were alive and freed, he would have contacted Abelar if he were able. Perhaps he was wounded. Or perhaps he was held against his will by those who had taken him. He shook his head.

"My father is beyond my aid for now. Saerb needs us. As soon as the men are ready, we ride."

Roen swallowed. "My lord, I hesitate to bring this to your attention, but . . ."

Abelar waved him on impatiently.

"There is disease in the village."

"What kind of disease?"

Roen blanched. "It is terrible, my lord. The sufferers cough blood until they can expel it no more and drown in their own fluids. The village elder believes a group of refugees who passed through the village a tenday ago may have carried the disease. A family is afflicted. The husband already has succumbed and the wife and their children are bedridden. The crone who tended them has died herself and no one else in the village will look after them. Jiiris has looked to them but . . ." Roen looked down at his feet. "The meager gifts granted me by the Morninglord are insufficient to the task. I cannot cleanse them."

"Children?" Regg asked.

Roen nodded.

Abelar thought of Elden and did not hesitate. "Take us to them."

Roen led them into the village of cottages. Children, men, and women greeted them and smiled. Hacking coughs racked several of the villagers. Abelar and Regg shared a look.

Two young boys, perhaps five or six winters old, marveled at Abelar's shield and the rose enameled on it. Abelar unslung it and let them play with it.

"No dragon slaying without me," he said to them. "And I'll need it again soon. Yes?"

"Yes, goodsir," they said.

He tousled their hair and they scurried off, arguing over who would play with it first.

"There is fear in the eyes of everyone here," Abelar said softly to Regg.

"Aye," answered Regg. "It is not just disease."

"No," Abelar agreed. "It is not just disease."

Roen took them to a mud-packed log house on the western edge of the village. The shutters and doors were closed, but the sickly sweet stink of contagion sneaked through the cracks. Roen knocked once and entered.

A miasma filled the home and the smell of sweat, filth, and old blood hit Abelar like a mace. The two-room cottage had little in the way of furnishings. A few chairs, a table, a sideboard. A low fire burned in the small hearth. A pot of what Abelar assumed to be broth hung over it. Jiiris's two slim swords and gloves lay propped against the wall near the fire. An open doorway led to another room.

Coughing, deep and wet, sounded from within. A child's cough joined in, then another. A soothing voice sounded—Jiiris's—and the coughing subsided.

Jiiris stepped out of the room. The young priestess had her light hair pulled back in a horse's tail. Blood specks stained her sleeves. She wore a strip of cloth over her mouth and nose to ward off disease.

Abelar and Regg had nothing to fear from contagion. When they had sworn their souls to the Morninglord, he had blessed them with resistance to certain weaknesses of the flesh, including disease. He had also gifted them with the ability to heal disease by touch. They could not do it often, but they could do it.

"My lords," Jiiris said. She removed the strip of cloth from her mouth and smiled. "Welcome back. How did you fare at the Abbey?"

"Not well," Abelar said, and left it at that. "Gear up. We ride soon." He nodded at the room she had just exited. "I will see to them."

Jiiris nodded. "The light is in you both. I am glad of it." She thumped Regg on the shoulder, smiled at Roen, and passed close to Abelar, though she did not touch him.

Abelar caught her gently by the arm. "You have performed a good service here."

She colored, nodded, smiled gently, and exited the cottage.

"Await us here," Abelar said to Roen. He and Regg entered the sickroom.

Five hay-stuffed mattresses lay in the room, along with chamber pots and blankets. The smell made Abelar's eyes water. A scarecrow-thin woman lay on one of the beds, her mouth flecked with blood, her face drawn and sweaty. Four children—all girls—lay on the other beds, all wrapped in blankets, all pale. The collective respiration in the room sounded like a rasp over wood.

"Five," Abelar said softly.

"And it has already spread," Regg said.

Abelar and Regg could channel Lathander's grace only in small portions, and they needed time afterward for their own souls to heal. They could not heal everyone before leaving.

They walked to the bedside of the mother. Their boots clunked loudly on the floorboards. Abelar knelt and put his calloused hand on her brow. Her green eyes opened. She opened her mouth to speak but it turned to a coughing fit that wracked her entire body.

Abelar spoke softly. "We are healers, goodmadam. Servants of Lathander. We are here to help."

Her eyes softened and she smiled. She raised a hand, weakly, to gesture at her children. Abelar understood. She wanted them to help her children first. He nodded at Regg, who moved from child to child, comforting them, humming a song the while.

Abelar stroked the mother's dark hair, slick with sweat. "Hear me, now. We can cleanse this disease but not for all of you. Only for four. That is as far as our gifts go for a time, and we must leave tonight. If we are tardy in our task, many others will die."

She stared at him, unmoving, and he did not know if she understood. One of the daughters broke into a wet coughing fit that left her struggling for breath.

"What do you want us to do?" Abelar asked her.

Her eyes closed, opened, and she parted her bloody lips to speak. Abelar knelt in close and she said in a broken whisper, "My daughters."

Abelar leaned back and looked into her eyes. His eyes, and hers, welled with tears.

"Who will care for them if you are gone?"

The tears spilled down her temples and she looked away. She closed her eyes, bit her upper lip, and shook her head. Abelar understood. There was no one. But she would not choose one of her daughters to die. A coughing fit shook her.

Abelar looked at his hands, cursing the weakness of his own flesh.

He would not choose one of them to die, either. He stood and looked at Regg, who was holding the tiny hand of one of the little girls. He nodded at the doorway and they exited the room and gathered with Roen.

Outside, Abelar said, "I will stay. Take the men—"

"Stay?" Roen exclaimed.

Regg shook his head and chuckled. "I knew that you would say those words. No. I will stay and manage the plague here. When the village is cleansed, I will ride after you."

"We need you both," Roen said.

Abelar ignored the priest and studied his friend's craggy face, saw the sincerity of the offer. "No, Regg. This is my duty to perform. Besides, your father is in Forrin's path."

"As is your son," Regg answered.

Abelar felt a flash of doubt but pushed it down. He could not abandon the village.

"Go get them both," he said to Regg. He looked to Roen. "Go get them both."

Regg and Roen stared at him for many heartbeats, and both finally nodded. Regg took Abelar by the arm. "The Light is in you, my friend. It shines brightly."

"And you," Abelar answered. He indicated the sick room. "Let us do what we can for them now."

Abelar and Regg entered the room and placed their hands on the daughters in turn. They prayed aloud and pulled the divine energy of the Morninglord from their own purified flesh and channeled it into the young girls. Immediately, the girls' breathing eased and they fell into slumber.

Unable to do more, Abelar went to the mother's bedside. "Your daughters are well."

The woman smiled, said in a whisper, "I want to see them."

"You will," Abelar said. "They are sleeping now. Listen to me. I will not leave you. But you must fight for a few days more, then I will be able to heal you as I did your daughters. Do you understand? You must fight until then."

She nodded. Tears flowed anew, but not tears of sadness. She touched Abelar's hand and Abelar squeezed her fingers. He had taken lives in Lathander's name, many lives, but he never felt more about his god's work than when he used his hands to heal.

"I am . . . sorry that I put you to that choice," he said. "It was inexcusable. My own son is in danger and it clouded my judgment."

She shook her head and smiled, coughed.

"I understand," she said hoarsely. "And you should go to your son."

"I will," Abelar said. "But not until you are well."

She stared into his face, nodded gratefully. Regg knelt beside them, put his hand on her brow.

"Be well, goodmadam. May Lathander watch over you and the dawn bring you hope."

Abelar and Regg stood, regarding each other.

Regg said, "Stay in the light, Abelar Corrinthal."

"And you. I will follow after as soon as I can. You and Roen have the company."

Regg nodded and they parted.

Abelar watched through the cottage's open shutters as Regg and Roen led the company off. He imagined Elden at the end of Forrin's blade and the mental image almost caused him to mount his horse. A coughing fit from the sickroom pulled him back to his duty. He laid down his sword beside the hearth and went to his chosen task.

For hours he drew water, cooked broth, and spoon-fed it to mother and daughters. The daughters mostly slept, while the mother mostly coughed. Still, the smiles and clear eyes of the daughters in their waking hours reminded Abelar of why he had taken Lathander's rites.

Abelar learned the girls' names: Lis, Nissa, Sill, and Dera, the eldest. He obtained new bedding for them, and sang to them, as he often did to Elden. He smiled when they smiled, learned their laughs. They hovered around their mother and their love for her touched Abelar.

Throughout the day and early evening, their mother deteriorated. Abelar did not know if she would survive until he could heal her. He tried to think how best to prepare the girls for such a loss, but he could think of little. He saw the fear in their eyes.

When the girls slept, he spent the hours in meditation and prayer at the mother's bedside, holding her hand, asking Lathander to heal her, and to help Regg reach Elden in time. He kept vigil at the mother's bed throughout the night and slept little. He sensed the approaching dawn.

The creak of floorboards in the adjacent room drew his attention. He rose in silence, so as not to disturb his patients, took up a small clay lamp, and crept into the room.

He saw no one.

He started to return to the sickroom when a small flash of red on the floor caught his eye. He stared at it for a long while, to ensure he was not imagining it. He was not.

A single rose petal lay on the floor in the center of the room.

He walked to it, kneeled, gently held it between two fingers. It was fresh, as smooth as velvet. It could not have been tracked in. He had seen no roses in the village.

It was a sign. Warmth suffused his body.

"Thank you, Morninglord," he murmured.

Dawn's light, as pink as a rose, radiated through the slats of the closed shutters. Abelar rushed to them and threw them open. Rose-colored light bathed the room. Its touch warmed Abelar, calmed him. The light washed over the entire village, casting it all in a pastel glow.

Outside, brilliant reds, oranges, and yellows painted the eastern horizon. Abelar knew its meaning.

"Thank you, Morninglord," he said excitedly, and hurried to the sickroom. "Up, girls! Dera, get them up! Now, girl! Open every window in the house! Get your mother into the light."

The girls rose groggily from their beds and did as Abelar bade them. Meanwhile, Abelar ran outside and through the village, shouting. "Up and outside! Everyone, now! Stand in dawn's light! Do it now!"

Faces appeared in windows, bodies in doorways. Abelar pulled out anyone he could reach and ordered everyone else outside. In short order, the entire village stood outside, marveling at dawn's light, at the eastern sky.

Abelar hurried back to the cottage to find the girls crying and embracing their mother, who stood on shaky legs in the rosy light filtering in through an open window. She met Abelar's eyes and sobbed.

"You are healed," Abelar said, and his words were not a question.

She nodded through her tears. "Thanks to you, goodsir."

Abelar shook his head and smiled softly. "No. Thanks to Lathander." He hurried across the room, embraced her, kneeled and embraced the girls. "Tell everyone what has happened here. I must go. Be well."

"What *has* happened here?" asked Dera.

Abelar stood. "The Morninglord has blessed us all. Farewell."

They called their thanks after him as he hurried from the room, collected his weapon, and rushed outside. He whistled for Swiftdawn and she galloped to his side. He swung into the saddle and the boys who had taken his shield the day before ran over to him, carrying it between them. He took it up, smiled at the boys.

"Are you going to slay a dragon?" the taller of the boys asked.

"Yes," Abelar said. He put his heels into Swiftdawn. "Ride!"

Malkur sat upon his leather-barded warhorse at the side of the hard-packed road, flanked by three of his commanders, Lorgan, Reht, and Enken. With them were Vors, the war priest of Talos, and one of the company's battle mages, Mennick. All had shed the markings of their mercenary company and instead wore the gold-wheel-on-green of Ordulin.

Malkur took care to position himself in the sunlight. Since the attack on his men by the shade in service to the Hulorn, Malkur kept light about him as often as possible.

The column of his cavalry stretched along the road, a ribbon of steel and flesh. A rolling cloud of dust, creaking leather, and the chink of armor accompanied their travel. The men saluted him as they rode past, but held only rough formation. Teams of outriders rode a quarter league to fore, behind, and on the flanks, reporting back on the half-bell. The supply train, escorted by four-score riders under Gavin's command, brought up the rear of the column. The supply train slowed them, but that could not be avoided.

"The men are eager for a fight," Reht said.

"They will have one soon enough," Lorgan answered.

Enken fiddled with one of his many knives and said, "Perhaps. Or perhaps we'll find naught but an empty city and nobles cowering in their manses. They will evacuate when they learn we are coming."

All but Vors chuckled. He said, "If a ride halfway across Sembia does not have a battle at its end, I am killing one of you in Talos's name."

The men laughed still harder. Vors did not even smile.

"See to your units," Malkur said to his commanders. "We ride past dusk and into the night. We reach Saerb within five days, or you answer to me. Reht, Lorgan, and Vors, you three remain."

Enken and Mennick saluted and galloped off to rejoin their units. They shouted orders as they moved up and down the line.

"Commander?" Lorgan asked.

"Take a force and angle south of Saerb. Take three hundred

fifty men. Ride hard and sweep wide. We will attack Saerb in five days. Be in position by then, but stay low before that."

Malkur wanted Lorgan to cut off any residents of Saerb or its environs who might try to flee before his army toward Selgaunt. Lorgan understood the purpose of the order.

"Those will be ripe pickings," Lorgan said.

Malkur looked to Reht. "Take seventy men, plus Vors and Mennick. Leave tonight and ride hard ahead of Lorgan's force. The Corrinthal estate is half a league east of Saerb proper. Everyone there is to die except Abelar Corrinthal's young son. His name is Elden. He was born dumb and looks it, by all accounts. Bring him back to me alive."

Vors smiled and his crazed eyes lit up at the thought of slaughter.

Reht only nodded. Killing was his work. He did not revel in it, Malkur knew, but he did not shirk it.

"I will want a force of all former Blades," Reht said. "Night fighters. We may need to dodge an army, should Saerb field one."

"Agreed," Forrin said. "Go."

Lorgan said, "I will need at least one more priest, as well."

"Take Avrek," Forrin said, naming another Talassan war priest in their company. That would leave Forrin with a handful of priests to service the main body of troops.

"Thank you, Commander," Lorgan said.

Reht, Lorgan, and Vors saluted and rode off. Vors howled with delight at the passing troops and shook his axe in the air.

Forrin watched the rest of his force ride by, satisfied. He had good fighters and strong leaders. He had arranged commissions for all of his junior commanders from the Blades, and had filled the remaining command positions in the unit with men he knew to be loyal to him from his previous days in the Sembian military. Twelve hundred medium horse were riding on Saerb, and Malkur had, directly or indirectly, handpicked all of them. They would do exactly as he wished.

And what he wished was to burn first the Corrinthal estate, then Saerb itself to the ground. The overmistress had instructed him to make Saerb an example. Malkur intended to do exactly that.

CHAPTER SIX

20 Uktar, the Year of Lightning Storms

A mixture of dread and relief washed over Tamlin as he received the news that part of the overmistress's army was marching on Saerb. Dread that war, real war, had finally come. Relief that it had fallen first on Saerb, rather than on Selgaunt.

Prince Rivalen, Vees Talendar, and the bull-necked Rorsim Soargyl joined him around a conference table in the palace.

Tamlin said, "Our spies report that a contingent of the overmistress's army moves on Saerb. I wish your views on how we should respond."

Rorsim looked to Vees, to Rivalen, back to Tamlin, and said, "I could put two hundred good men in the field to intercept Forrin."

Vees looked puzzled and stroked his beard. "Two hundred? What would two hundred do? Forrin has many times that."

Rorsim eyed Vees. "Our two hundred could join with Corrinthal's forces, if possible. Or assist with a retreat of Saerb's population to Selgaunt, if not. There isn't a wall built for a fight anywhere in the north. They cannot make a stand there."

"We do not even know where Corrinthal's forces are," Vees answered reasonably. "Divinations have been inconsistent. Nine Hells, he could be dead."

Rorsim cocked his bucket-sized head to concede the point.

Tamlin looked to Rivalen. "Prince? Your thoughts?"

"Where are the men you promised us?" Rorsim blurted at Rivalen. "I have done what can be done with the Helms, Scepters, and militia, but—"

Shadows swirled around Rivalen. He regarded Rorsim coolly and Rorsim retreated into the depths of his chair.

"Members of an elite unit will be available soon," Rivalen answered in his deep voice. "They are engaged in other matters at the moment."

"Other matters," Rorsim muttered. "Always other matters."

Rivalen manipulated something with his fingers, studied its corners. Tamlin saw that it was a fivestar.

Rivalen said, "Hulorn, I believe that sacrificing any of the meager force you have here would put Selgaunt in a very weak position should the army gathering at Saerloon choose to march. There are rumors that may happen soon."

Rorsim leaned forward in his chair. "We would have advance notice and would be able to return before Saerloon's forces could arrive. There is no risk to Selgaunt."

Rivalen regarded Rorsim with his golden eyes. "There is always risk in war, and unknowns. I know that much better than you, Rorsim Soargyl. How many wars have you seen firsthand? Battle is not a contractual dispute over the shipment of goods."

Rorsim's face reddened behind his beard. "I have drawn my fair share of blood, sir."

Rivalen's golden eyes flared. "I do not doubt it. But should something delay your force's return from the north, then what? Should Forrin learn of your advance and divert from Saerb to engage you, or cut off your route back to Selgaunt, then what?"

"That is sense, Deuce," Vees said to Tamlin, and leaned back in his chair.

Tamlin thought so, too. He said, "I admire your zeal for battle, Rorsim, but even if we could get men into position in time, this is not our fight."

Rorsim looked like he had eaten something sour but said nothing.

Vees said, "Take the time we have just gained to further strengthen Selgaunt's defenses."

Rivalen said, "Hulorn, the war for Sembia's future will be won or lost here, not in Saerb. That is a hard truth, but a truth nevertheless."

"Yet I am uncomfortable doing nothing," Tamlin said. "The people of Saerb . . ."

Rivalen tapped his fingers on the table. Shadows flared from his fingertips with each tap. "They will flee, Hulorn. And when the Shadovar troops become available to us here, they will travel to the refugees and encourage a retreat to Selgaunt. We can bring them into the city. Assuming that is acceptable to you?"

"Shade troops, you mean?" Tamlin asked. There seemed little a shade could not do.

Rivalen nodded. "Yes, Hulorn. Shade troops from the enclave."

The plan pleased Tamlin. He would not abandon the people of Saerb, but he would risk little. He nodded at Rivalen.

"Thank you for the advice, all, and for the offer, Prince. We will do as Prince Rivalen advises. We are adjourned."

Rivalen knew that Tamlin was, at his core, a compromiser. He wanted always to feel as if he were doing something but he wanted also to take no risks. Were he to flip a fivestar to decide a question, he would hope for it to land on its edge so that he could choose a middle course. For now, that served Rivalen. But sooner or later the young Hulorn would have to choose obverse or reverse. Rivalen had grown fond enough of Tamlin to allow him a chance to make that choice.

"Prince Rivalen, will you remain a moment?" Tamlin asked.

"Of course, Hulorn."

While they waited for Vees and Rorsim to exit the conference room, Tamlin poured himself a goblet of wine. When they were alone, he said, "I have heard nothing from the envoys sent to hire mercenaries. It has been too long. Something has happened to them."

Rivalen allowed concern to show in his eyes, though his own agents had killed Selgaunt's envoys. Rivalen wanted the Hulorn entirely beholden to the Shadovar.

"They perform dangerous duty," he said. "No doubt the over-mistress has many spies in Selgaunt, just as you do in Ordulin."

Tamlin sipped his wine, regarded Rivalen over the rim. "I would feel more at ease with our situation were Shadovar troops in the city. You have said often that your forces are highly mobile. If they were at our disposal, perhaps we could take the offensive rather than await a siege? Mirabeta has taken a risk sending out half her army to Saerb."

Rivalen nodded and gave Tamlin what he most craved—praise. "You think aggressively, Hulorn. That is admirable and befits a leader of a nation."

Tamlin tried to hide his smile behind another drink of wine but Rivalen saw it. Tamlin said, "I will settle for winning this conflict and remaining the leader of Selgaunt."

Rivalen looked pointedly across the table. "Why rein your ambition so? You should be as aggressive with it as you are in your war planning."

"How do you mean, Prince?"

Rivalen looked away. "I hesitate to speak it."

"Come," Tamlin said. "We have already been candid with one another about sensitive matters of faith. This is no different. I have come to rely on your candor, Prince. Please."

Rivalen nodded. "Hulorn, I believe Sembia has been transformed by this conflict. The overmistress has rendered the High Council moot and your people accept it as if it were always so. It is a dead institution. Sembia will have its autocrat. It is only a question of who it shall be and whether he shall be benevolent or . . . otherwise."

Tamlin paused in mid drink. The moment stretched.

"Intriguing," he said at last, his tone thoughtful, and hurriedly added, "That you think so, I mean."

Rivalen knew he had laid the foundation. He was bringing Tamlin along at exactly the right pace. He'd seen it before. He knew the look in a man's eye when ambition found purchase. Tamlin's expression showed it. He thought he wanted to be a shade and a king. What he really wanted was deeper than that. He wanted to step out of the shadows of his father, of Erevis Cale, of his own self-image as an unaccomplished son of an accomplished father. Rivalen knew the feeling, had experienced it himself thousands of years earlier. Perhaps that was why he was so fond of the boy. Besides, it amused Rivalen that Tamlin sought to escape the shadows of his past by stepping into the shadows Rivalen offered.

"I know the wait for Shadovar reinforcements is difficult, Hulorn," Rivalen said. "But be assured that our troops will arrive as soon as they are freed from other obligations. Let us then decide what course to take in war. In fact, it is my hope that I will be able to lend even more aid than troops at that time."

Tamlin raised his eyebrows. "Oh?"

"I will inform you when I have more information to tell."

Tamlin smiled. "The Sharran keeps his secrets, eh?"

Rivalen donned a false smile. "Indeed, but only because matters are still a trifle unclear." He spun shadows around his fingers.

Tamlin watched him intently, then said, "The leading priests of the city, those who remain, have informed me that they will not fight directly against Mirabeta's forces. They will aid and heal, but none will bear arms or cast spells to harm. I presume the priests of Ordulin and Saerloon have taken a similar position."

"Perhaps or perhaps not. Your priests play at neutrality to preserve the status of their faith, whatever the outcome of the war. It is disheartening. You need not accept their terms, Hulorn."

"No?" Tamlin asked.

"No. There are priests in Shade Enclave whom I may be able to call upon. Hulorn, perhaps now is an appropriate time to discuss Shar's faith further?"

Tamlin tipped his goblet toward Rivalen. "I think I would enjoy that very much."

The night was old but Elyril did not attempt to sleep. Minddust and excitement kept her heart racing for hours. She had long ago giddily dismissed the steward and now sat in the study with Kefil.

And with the book.

The mastiff lay at her feet, licking his paws. The book lay against her breast, warming her skin and the invisible holy symbol she wore at her throat. She fiddled with the magical ring on her finger, amused that she knew yet another secret of which the Nightseer was ignorant. He would learn of it soon enough, when he bent his knee to the Lord Sciagraph.

And to you, Kefil projected.

She smiled, replayed the events in her mind again and again.

Kefil said, *The guardsman, Phraig, was not a man.*

"Not while he was in this room," Elyril agreed. "Then, he was a vessel of Shar."

Kefil grunted indifferently and shifted his position.

Elyril stared at the walls and listened with pleasure to the death rattles of everyone who died in Yhaunn over the next slice of the night: an elderly chandler, a young girl with wetlung, a male prostitute who fell from a balcony, a cobbler with a weak heart. The grief of those the dead left behind she offered to Shar and Volumvax as sacrifice. Cradling her book and thinking of the Lord Sciagraph, her mind drifted into dark places.

Kefil's growl brought her back to herself.

Had she fallen asleep?

The darkness in the room deepened. A presence emerged from the black. Kefil scrambled to his feet, growling and snapping.

She recognized the presence immediately and felt such ecstasy that she could scarcely breathe. Her body tingled; her muscles went weak; her heart rose. She closed her eyes, fell to the floor, and whispered, "I kneel before Shar's shadow, who shrouds the world in night."

Silence, Volumvax commanded.

The sound of his mental voice in her head made her giddy and lightheaded. He had never before spoken to her. The room spun; her breath came so fast she feared she would pass out. Indeed, she must be Shar's chosen servant!

You dare call to me? the Lord Sciagraph said.

Dread devoured Elyril's excitement. She fumbled for a reply. "I . . . did not. I am grateful my lord has blessed me with his presence. I . . . have news."

She kept her head down but held up the book given her by Phraig.

Silence for a moment, then, *You possess half of the book to be made whole. What is its secret?*

"A ritual hides behind the words."

You are my servant, and Shar's.

The praise sent such a thrill through Elyril that she gasped.

"It was left behind by servants of Mask. The Lady put it into my hands."

The temperature in the room dropped noticeably. Elyril could see her breath when she exhaled.

Volumvax touched the back of her head—he was not flesh, she

realized, but shadow—and the touch filled her with such terror
that it nearly stopped her heart.

Mask? The servants of the Shadowlord are afoot?

Elyril could not breathe, could not speak. An ache in her
mind turned to a stab of pain, transformed to a flash of agony.
She thought her eyes must pop out of her head. She screamed,
but dared not look up.

Speak now, Dark Sister, or your heart stops after its next beat.

Her mouth was too dry. She nodded, tried to swallow.

Give me their names.

She nodded her head, gulped, croaked, "Erevis Cale and
Drasek Riven, Lord Sciagraph."

Volumvax withdrew his touch and Elyril gasped with relief,
sagged.

*Time is short, priestess. Obtain the rest of the book. When it is
whole, perform the ritual and summon the storm . . .*

Elyril almost looked up but caught herself just in time. "Lord
Sciagraph, I do not know how to find the rest of the book."

The Nightseer holds it, though he knows not what he holds.

Elyril did not process the words immediately. "The
. . . Nightseer?"

*It was I who arranged to put it into his hands through one of his
underlings.*

Elyril was unsurprised that Volumvax had kept the secret
of the book from her. Such was the habit of Shar's inscrutable
nature. She was pleased, however, that the Nightseer possessed
it in ignorance.

Before Elyril could ask anything more, Volumvax's manifes-
tation ended.

Too weak to stand, Elyril crawled back into her chair, her
mind racing.

She thought it strange that the Lord Sciagraph had shown
such anger at the mention of Mask. She thought it strange, too,
that Shar and Volumvax seemed to be acting without the full
knowledge of the other's activities. Did the Lord Sciagraph keep

secrets even from the Lady of Loss? No. It was blasphemy.

Elyril put it from her mind and turned her thoughts to how she would obtain the rest of the book from the Nightseer.

Kefil said to her, *You are imagining all of this. It was a dream.*

"You lie," Elyril said, and held the book tightly against her body.

Rivalen returned to the darkness of his quarters and sat in a large armchair. Matters had progressed well with the Hulorn. Rivalen felt he could turn Tamlin to Shar whenever he wished. The boy's ambition ruled his morality. Rivalen liked that about him.

Cradling his holy symbol in his hands, he whispered the words to a spell that would allow him to send a short message to the Most High. When he felt the magical energy gather around him, he uttered the sending. "The Hulorn's trust has been earned and Selgaunt is ours when we wish. War in Sembia is inevitable."

The magic carried his words across Faerûn, into the ears of the Most High. Rivalen awaited a response and it came quickly. He felt it as a buzzing in his ears followed by the whispered words of his father.

Perhaps the non-Shadovar who know you to have created this war should be dealt with?

Rivalen nodded. His own thoughts mirrored those of the Most High. He wanted the Hulorn to regard the Shadovar as saviors of his cause, not instigators of the war. Rivalen had taken care to ensure that only two non-Shadovar knew of Shar's involvement in starting the conflict—Elyril Hraven and Vees Talendar. He would be direct with Elyril. For Vees, he planned something unique. It did not please him to ponder the killing of a Dark Sister and Brother, but he would do it nevertheless.

The Most High continued, his voice harder. *You have*

done well, Rivalen. Your mother would take pride in your accomplishments.

The words pulled Rivalen to his feet. The magical sending ended.

Shadows swirled around him, reflecting his concern. Jumbled thoughts careened around in his mind. The Most High's words echoed through his brain.

What had the Most High meant? He had never before mentioned Alashar in such a manner. Did the Most High know, or even suspect, that Rivalen had murdered Alashar at Shar's command? How could he have learned it? Rivalen had revealed the secret to no one. Only he and Shar knew it.

Rivalen replayed in his mind countless conversations he'd had with his father over the centuries, scouring them for hints. He remembered nothing that alarmed him and tried to put his mind at ease. His father could not have known. If he had, he would have killed Rivalen long ago. Unless . . .

Unless Shar herself had informed the Most High and at the same time commanded him to take no vengeance. Perhaps the Most High's Own Secret was that he knew the truth of Alashar's murder. For centuries he could have been looking upon Rivalen not as a son, but as the murderer of his beloved, his need for revenge held in check only by Shar's interdiction.

Rivalen tried to dismiss the thoughts as blasphemous. He reminded himself that he knew nothing for certain and wondered if he were not imagining threats. He had seen it often among Sharrans. A faith so reliant on secrets sometimes bred among the faithful mistrust and wild imaginings that bordered on madness. Still, his theory rang true to him.

"Why?" Rivalen asked the darkness. "Why betray your most powerful instrument?"

Shar gave him no answers. She never did.

But Rivalen saw an answer.

Shar wanted a wedge between the Most High and Rivalen. She had betrayed Rivalen to bring him closer to her. She wanted

Rivalen beholden to her, wanted him to choose his faith over his city and his family, the same way Rivalen wanted the Hulorn beholden to him.

"I chose faith over family the day I murdered my mother, Lady."

The darkness held its silence, and its secrets.

Thoughtful, Rivalen removed an exquisitely crafted miniature chest from an inner pocket. Concentrating on it, he triggered its magic, and its mate, a full-sized chest exactly alike in appearance to the miniature, appeared on the floor at his feet.

He spoke the sequence of command words that discharged the protective wards he maintained on the chest, and used a minor spell to open its lock. He lifted the lid.

Coils of shadow leaked from the opening, carrying indecipherable whispers into the air. Within the chest lay *The Leaves of One Night*. He had taken to carrying it with him, rather than leaving it in the vault of the temple in Shade Enclave. It seemed right to have it near him.

He placed his hand atop the book's black cover, felt its coolness, felt the characters written on it shifting under his touch. He intoned a prayer to Shar and the book whispered in his mind.

He resolved that he would no longer secrete it on the ethereal plane. He wanted it closer to him, wanted Shar's words nearer his ears. The chest and the book would remain warded in his quarters or on his person. If Shar had something to say to him through the book, he wanted it close enough to him that he would hear.

CHAPTER SEVEN

21 Uktar, the Year of Lightning Storms

Cale, Riven, and Magadon materialized not at the center of the cemetery, as Cale had intended, but at its edge, just outside the low, crumbling stone wall that described its perimeter. Black moss clung to the wall and the still, damp air stank of old rot.

Within the wall, darkness gathered as thick as fog. Even with his shadesight, Cale could see only twenty paces through the miasma. In the distance he could just make out the dim, diffuse green glow of the gate. The distorting swirl of darkness and shadows made it appear leagues away. The flash flared and died, flared and died, like a heartbeat.

A city of crumbling gravestones, crypts, and mausoleums stood between them and the gate. Grass and weeds overgrew it all.

"There must be some kind of ward," Cale said, to

explain why they had not materialized near the gate. Strangely, he felt little correspondence with the darkness inside the cemetery. He felt only the shadows and darkness very near him. He understood why. The cemetery's shadows belonged to another.

"We go afoot," he said.

Magadon looked out over the cemetery. The gate flashed again.

"That's a lot of ground to cover," the mindmage said.

"And a lot of wraiths," Riven added.

"It is," Cale answered to both of them. He intoned a prayer to Mask that would shield him and his companions from the soul-draining power of the undead creatures. He touched himself, Magadon, and Riven in turn.

"If they come, this will preserve our souls, but the cold of their touch will still steal your warmth. We stay together at all costs."

Riven, evidently resigned to their course, said, "We move fast and straight. Right for the gate."

They all shared a look, nodded.

Cale vaulted the wall and dropped into the cemetery's deeper darkness. The air closed in around him. It felt thick in his lungs, oily on his skin. His breathing sounded loud in his ears, while everything else sounded far away and muffled.

Small gravestones worn smooth by time dotted the grass at his feet. Ghostly structures—crypts and mausoleums—lurked at the edge of his sight.

Riven and Magadon dropped to the ground beside him.

"The darkness is different in here," Magadon said, and waved his hand in the air. "Like cobwebs."

"Damned air is like a vise," Riven said. He cleared his throat and spit. "Tastes foul."

Cale nodded. The darkweaver spun strands of shadows the way a spider did a web. Cale imagined the creature lurking at the center of its shadowy net, waiting, feeling the vibrations in the shadows caused by their approach.

"Let's move," Riven said.

"This way," Cale said, and led them deeper into the city of graves.

He moved as fast as he dared in the darkness. The air grew colder with each step they took. Tombs surrounded them on all sides, foreboding and ominous. The air resisted Cale's movements slightly, as if he were walking into a light wind, as if it were pawing at him.

"It's too goddamned quiet," Riven said softly, and the darkness made his words a whisper.

A hiss sounded from out in the darkness before them. They halted their advance.

"It knows we're here," Riven said.

"That it does," Cale said softly. "Mags, some light."

Magadon nodded, concentrated, and a soft yellow light haloed his head for a moment. A ball of white luminescence formed over him and moved with him. The darkness squirmed away from it like a living thing. The light—dimming already under the unrelenting shadows—revealed the gossamer-thin filaments that veined the air.

A muffled, haunting moan sounded, seemingly from deep under their feet. Another answered from their right. Another came from their left. Soon the moans carried from all directions, a chorus of hate sung by Elgrin Fau's doomed citizens, all of them transformed by Kesson Rel's foul magic into wraiths.

The sound of their pain and malice curdled Cale's flesh. The air grew so chill that his teeth chattered. Riven cursed, turned a circle, and twirled his blades. Shadows bled from Weaveshear, spiraled around Cale.

Magadon focused his gaze on his palm and manifested his mindblade.

"Keep moving," Cale said, and strode quickly through the gravestones.

Magadon and Riven flanked him. Their breath came hard. Despite the cold, sweat slicked Cale. There was no end to the graves, no sign of the gate. The thrice-damned thing had stopped flashing, or the darkweaver had draped it in darkness. Cale had no way to know how close they were to the portal. And they had awakened the dead. They were moving blindly.

"Stop," he said. "Stop for a moment."

He needed to get his bearings. He had lost his sense of direction. The frozen air turned his breath to mist. The shadowstrands were everywhere. He could determine nothing. They might easily be walking in a circle.

The wraiths' moans fell silent. Cale found it more ominous than comforting.

"What is it?" Riven asked, his voice as tight as a bowstring.

Cale shook his head. "I don't know where we are. I don't see the gate."

Magadon did not hesitate. "That way," he said, and pointed over Cale's shoulder. "You had it right."

Cale and Riven shared a look. Magadon caught its import.

"I said I was with you. That way. Trust me."

Cale nodded, apologized with his eyes to Magadon for his mistrust.

They took ten strides and all at once the wraiths issued forth from the surrounding tombs like a flock of crows. Black ghostly forms, only vaguely recognizable as humanoid, rose out of the ground, out of the crypts, out of the mausoleums. There were hundreds of them, thousands. Emberlike eyes glared out of the holes of their faces. Moans and whispers filled the air. Cale heard words in the whispers but could not make them out.

"Cale?" Riven asked, eyeing the approaching wraiths.

Cale said, "Stay close to me and keep moving. Mags, the more light the better."

Magadon's brow furrowed and the ball of light hovering above his head flared. The wraiths moaned in answer, swirled in agitation. From somewhere off in the darkness, the darkweaver answered the wails of the wraiths with a hiss.

"Move," Cale said. He held forth his mask and let the

Shadowlord's power flow through it and surround them.

Riven and Magadon closed ranks with him and they moved in lockstep in the direction of the gate. The wraiths closed on them, swirled around the edge of Cale's power, glared at them from outside the radius of Magadon's light. The creatures engulfed them like an unholy fog. Cale could not see where they were going.

"Mags?"

"Still this way, Cale," Magadon answered.

"Back to your rest!" Cale shouted at the wraiths, and pushed more power through his holy symbol. Divine energy flowed through him and into the air. It crashed into the wraiths, cutting a tunnel through the swarm. Moans chorused in Cale's ears.

Cale, Magadon, and Riven pushed through the opening. But there were so many. They pressed against Cale's power. The strain was draining him. Magadon's light was dimming. They would not be able to shield themselves for much longer, and when the barrier collapsed . . .

Dark hands reached up out of the cold earth and clutched at them. Riven and Cale saw them and jumped aside but Magadon was too slow. The mindmage gasped at the touch of the undead and his light dimmed further.

The wraiths took advantage and swarmed forward in a black tide. Cale braced himself and channeled divine power through Weaveshear and his mask.

"Away!"

But the wraiths did not slow. Moans sounded from all around. Black hands reached for them from all sides. Red eyes surged forward.

Cale shouted as the black tide broke on them. He took Weaveshear in two hands and tore through one, two, three wraiths. They moaned as parts of their forms boiled away in foul-smelling black smoke. Cale barely felt any resistance as he cut through the incorporeal creatures. Riven twirled, spun, ducked, his blades whirling and whistling through the wraiths' forms.

Magadon stabbed his mindblade downward into the earth at the creature that had attacked him. Oily dark smoke and a moan rose from the sod.

The wraiths were a black blizzard, their forms swarming around them, grasping, shrieking. Ghostly hands reached through Cale's clothing, armor, and body to clutch at his heart. The cold caused him to gasp, slowed him. Many of the wraiths simply flew through the companions, one after another, the unearthly chill of their forms taking its toll on flesh before they darted away.

Cale, Riven, and Magadon's blades slashed and cut but the tide of wraiths was unending. Magadon's mindblade slashed through the torso of a wraith, stabbed another through the torso, but two of the creatures penetrated his guard and reached into his chest. He screamed and fell to his knees as one, another, and another wraith flowed through him. His scream died; his mouth hung open, frozen. His mindblade fell from his hand and dissipated.

Cale drove back a handful of wraiths with a series of furious slashes, then bounded to Magadon's side. He sliced Weaveshear through a wraith as it emerged from Magadon's body and the creature dissolved into black fumes and a fading moan. He held the blade over his head and summoned as much divine power as he could. Shadows gushed from the blade and his voice boomed over the battle.

"Away, dead of Elgrin Fau! Our quarrel is not with you but with Kesson Rel! Away!"

Power veined the shadows leaking from the blade and the wraiths writhed, recoiled, and withdrew. They hovered at a distance, ringing Cale, Riven, and Magadon in a wall of black forms and burning eyes. Whispers replaced the wraiths' moans.

Riven helped Magadon to his feet and steadied him. The assassin drew darkness from the air with his fingertips, charged his hands with its power, and placed them on Magadon. Magadon's face regained its color and he visibly strengthened.

Riven thumped him on the shoulder and relaxed his grip on his companion.

"Cale?" Riven asked, eyeing the wraiths.

The creatures hovered motionless, regarding them, whispering.

Cale shook his head but held Weaveshear at the ready. He did not know what to make of their strange pause. He did not think he was holding them at bay; he did not feel them challenging his power. The wraiths' whispers sounded like falling rain.

"What are they saying?" Magadon asked.

Despite his facility with several languages, Cale did not understand the wraiths. Struck with an idea, he hurriedly intoned the words to a prayer that allowed him to understand and speak the tongue of any creature. As he uttered the final syllable, the cloud of wraiths fell silent and parted.

Through the gap flew four wraiths, each as large as three of the lesser wraiths. The fell creatures flew toward the companions. Dread and cold went before them.

"Big bastards," Riven said, and spun his blades.

Cale had never seen them before, but he knew their identity nevertheless. He remembered as if he had learned it in a dream: The Silver Lords of Elgrin Fau.

"Hold your ground," he said to Riven and Magadon, as if they had any other choice.

The wraiths floated forward until they hung in the air face-to-face with the companions. Their black misty forms towered over Cale. Their red eyes smoldered. They had the vague forms of men, but each was as large as an ogre.

"Lord," Cale said in their language.

Riven and Magadon looked at him sidelong.

One of the wraiths whispered, "You have spoken the name of the damned."

Another whispered, "You name him as enemy."

Cale knew they meant Kesson Rel. He nodded. "I am sworn to kill him and take from him what he stole from the Shadowlord."

The cloud of wraiths around them burst into urgent whispers. Cale caught only snippets: "Avnon Des," "the Chalice of Night," "the Conclave," "the Hall of Shadows."

The larger wraiths looked sharply upon the lesser and silence fell.

"You have walked this ground before," the wraith said. "Name yourselves."

Another of the large creatures reached out an insubstantial hand toward Riven. The assassin tensed and readied his blades.

"Hold," Cale said tightly.

"Him or me?" Riven asked, blades still ready.

Cale smiled despite the tension of the moment. "Both."

Riven held and the wraith stopped before touching him. Its ghostly fingers hovered near the holy symbol that hung on a chain about his neck, then withdrew.

Cale held up his mask. "I am the Right Hand of the Shadowlord." He nodded at Riven. "And he is the Left."

"A servant of the Shadowlord murdered this city."

The horde of smaller wraiths broke into a chorus of whispers. Cale heard the building hostility. He nodded.

"Now it is to be set right. Let us pass."

"Nothing can set it right," the Silver Lord hissed, and the cloud of wraiths crept in closer.

Cale inclined his head, conceding the point. "No. But Kesson Rel can be made to pay."

The wraiths' whispers died out and the four larger wraiths regarded Cale for a moment before they turned toward each other. They crowded together closely, as if in discussion, though Cale heard no words pass.

Cale, Riven, and Magadon shared glances but no words. Many moments passed before the wraiths turned back to the companions.

"His life is ours to take. But we are bound to this place by his craft. You must bring him to us. Swear it or die."

Cale shook his head. He was done with promises. "No."

The wraiths swirled in agitation. The air turned frigid. Red eyes flared. The circle of lesser wraiths around them closed in. The larger loomed over them.

"Cale . . ." Riven said.

Cale said, "I will return him here if I can. If I cannot, I will kill him where I find him. If that comes to pass, I will bring you proof of his death."

The wraiths fell silent, considering his offer. Finally, one of them said, "So be it."

Another said, "You must pass his creature alone. We are bound not to harm it."

"We are not so bound," Riven said.

With that, the wraiths flowed apart and opened a path toward the gate for the three companions. Cale, Riven, and Magadon shared a look, then started through. Cale felt the wraiths' eyes on them throughout. The creatures reached for them as they passed, as if to touch them, but never did.

When they emerged from the mob of wraiths, they could see ahead the raised circular stone platform upon which the darkweaver crouched. The gate glowed behind it, suspended between rune-covered twin pillars. A swirl of pitch wound around the platform, clung in ribbons to the darkweaver's enormous, spiderlike body. Eight tentacles as thick as barrels and as long as a dagger toss sprouted from the creature's sides. Clusters of black eyes dotted its form.

The gate flashed brightly and Cale caught an image within it of a black spire suspended over a void.

The darkweaver saw them and its tentacles churned. It lifted half its body from the platform and hissed. A voice in Cale's head said, *Lay down your weapons and approach. No harm will befall you. You may use the gate as you wish.*

Cale felt the magical compulsion behind the words but resisted it. He knew the darkweaver's message was a lie. He looked to Riven and Magadon. Both were clear-eyed; both nodded.

"Oh, we'll approach," Riven said, low and dangerous.

"We go," Cale said, and rushed toward the dais. Riven and Magadon sprinted hard after. The army of wraiths behind them followed on their heels, moaning in anticipation.

The darkweaver hissed again, lifted itself on four of its tentacles, and shambled its girth partway down the platform. It reared up its front, opened a sphincterlike mouth large enough to swallow a man whole, and vomited a cloud of shadows. The darkness roiled forward like a storm and engulfed Cale and his companions.

Cale felt around mentally for the sense of the darkness and found it, distant but there. He stepped through it in a single stride to appear on the platform behind the darkweaver's hulking form. The energy from the gate behind him made the hairs of his arms stand on end. He ignored it, reversed his grip on Weaveshear, and drove it into the creature's gray flesh. Shadows poured out of the gash and the darkweaver squealed in agony. It twisted its body and lashed at Cale with three of its tentacles. Cale dived under one blow, and intercepted the second with his upraised blade, severing the thick appendage and leaving it flopping and bleeding shadows atop the dais. A third thudded into his side, cracked ribs, and knocked him from the platform. He hit the ground in a heap and his breath went out of him. The darkweaver loomed over him.

Yellow light pierced the darkweaver's cloud of shadows, and Riven and Magadon rushed forward out of the darkness. Riven held his sabers before him; Magadon held his glowing yellow mindblade—the source of the light—in his fist. Cale noticed for the first time the thin black streaks that ran the mindblade's length.

The darkweaver braced its tentacles on the ground and leaped off the dais and into the air. Magadon pointed a hand at the airborne creature as a red glow haloed his head. A beam of white luminescence shot from his palm, hit the darkweaver in mid air, and sent a few chunks of seared flesh flying off. Hissing with pain but undeterred, the darkweaver hit the ground nearly atop the mindmage, tentacles flailing. A writhing limb clipped Magadon on the side of the head and knocked him to the ground. A second wrapped him about the torso, lifted him from his feet, and began to squeeze.

Riven lunged at the creature, his blades and body a whirlwind as he chopped his way through the darkweaver's tentacle attacks. He ducked, spun, leaped, dodged, all while cutting his way to Magadon. Chunks of the weaver's flesh flew off in all directions; shadows spilled from the wounds.

Cale shouted the words to a spell that powered his hands with baleful, black energy. He stepped through the shadows, appearing atop the darkweaver's humped back, and slammed his fist into the creature. The energy streamed out of him and split the creature's flesh. A deep hole opened, and stinking shadows leaked from it.

The darkweaver shrieked with agony and bucked, throwing Cale from its back. Cale hit the ground in a roll and rode the momentum onto his feet. A tentacle tried to sweep his legs out from under him but he jumped over it. As he came down he drove Weaveshear's point through the tentacle and pinned it to the earth.

Magadon freed a hand and another burst of energy from his palm hit the creature in the face and destroyed several of its eyes. Riven sent another severed tentacle flopping to the earth.

The darkweaver shrieked, its ruined flesh gushing shadows.

Cale shadowstepped atop the creature's back and drove Weaveshear into the wound created by his spell. The blade sank all the way to the hilt. The darkweaver hissed, spasmed, and collapsed. It did not move.

Cale leaped off it, breathing hard.

"All right?" he asked his comrades.

"Fine," said Riven, wiping his blades on his trousers.

"Better than this pile of dung," Magadon spat, and hacked the corpse of the darkweaver with his mindblade, once, twice, a third, a fourth. By the time he was done, he was smiling like a madman.

Cale and Riven shared a look. Cale's gaze lingered over the seemingly corrupted weapon.

Magadon's smile vanished. Without offering an explanation, he let the blade dissipate.

A hiss escaped the carcass of the darkweaver. At first Cale thought it was not dead, but then black fumes went up from its flesh in a cloud. The stink caused Cale to gag and cover his mouth. Magadon vomited.

The three backed away from the carcass as the hissing grew louder. They watched as the creature's body began to dissolve before their eyes, shrinking, collapsing on itself, boiling away into foul gas.

When it was gone, Cale sheathed Weaveshear and said to the wraiths, who still watched, "That is the first of Kesson Rel's servants to fall."

The wraiths whispered and surged forward, circling the spot where the darkweaver's body had been.

Cale, Riven, and Magadon climbed the stairs of the platform and walked up to the gate. The glowing green curtain of magical energy stretched between two stone pillars as thick as oaks, both covered in runes. The shadows around Cale poured into the gate, drawn by its power.

The wraiths floated forward and gathered around the platform, an ocean of black forms and red eyes. They whispered their pain and hate at Kesson Rel.

"Your promise binds you," the Silver Lords said in a whisper. "Bind you . . . bind you . . . bind you."

Cale looked out on them, the lost, and nodded.

"There's an army of them," Magadon said, his eyes wide.

"That there is," Cale answered.

The three men turned to the portal, shared a glance and a nod, and stepped through.

❧ ❧ ❧ ❧ ❧

Abelar thundered northward across the plains. Late autumn and the prolonged drought had dried and faded the whipgrass. He pushed Swiftdawn to her limit. With each of Swiftdawn's strides, he cursed himself anew for leaving Elden behind in Saerb. He'd had little choice—his father had needed him in Ordulin and Elden could not easily travel—but he cursed himself nevertheless. His presence in the capital had accomplished nothing. But his absence from Saerb might cost him his son. He had no illusions about what Forrin would do to his son should he take him alive.

Two days out of the plague-afflicted village, he caught up with his company. They were making camp near a drought-shrunken pond under the fading light. The last rays of the setting sun cast the plains in gold and the sky in red.

He saw figures pointing to him, calling out. He held up his blade and caused it to flare with white light.

"It is Abelar!" someone shouted.

Abelar roared into the camp. Smiles and a chorus of hails greeted him. He swung out of his saddle, gave and received thumps on the back. Regg strode through the throng, grinning, but with a question in his eyes.

"The village, Abelar?" Regg asked.

The men and women around them went quiet.

Abelar touched the holy symbol he wore about his neck. "The Morninglord shined on the village, on me, on us. After you left, I spent the night in meditation, praying for the sick mother, asking the Morninglord to strengthen her, to let her hold on until I could heal her affliction. When morning came the dawn sun filled the sickroom with light the color of a rose."

The men and women around him murmured.

"We saw that dawn," Roen said from behind him. "All marveled at it."

Abelar nodded, continued. "As I stand here now, I swear that all who stood in the light of that dawn were healed. All of them. The entire village. It was miracle."

Regg bowed his head.

Roen said, "The light of renewal. The Morninglord is gracious."

Abelar nodded solemnly. "It is good to see you," he said to Regg. "All of you."

Regg clasped his forearm. "And you."

He and Regg had stood together through blood and steel for years. Neither had fought a battle without the other in more than a decade.

Regg said, "The miracle could not have been for naught. All will be well with Elden and my father, I think."

"You speak my hopes," Abelar said.

After the company ate, the men settled in for the night and Abelar lit a short candle. He meditated, prayed, and thanked Lathander for his blessings. He slept little. When the candle burned down, he roused the men and the company set off in the pre-dawn darkness. He did not like to start a day's ride in darkness, but he wanted to cover as much ground as possible. They had two hours behind them before they paused at dawn to greet the rising sun. Afterward, they rode hard and fast.

He let Swiftdawn set the pace. A gift from Lathander after he had matured in his faith, she was superior to an ordinary warhorse in every way: faster, stronger, more intelligent. Regg's mount, Firstlight, was of the same sire and exhibited the same qualities. The rest of the company's mounts struggled to say with them but Abelar did not slow.

"Ride, Swiftdawn," he urged her. "Ride."

She whinnied and tore across the plains. Firstlight answered with her own snort of excitement and matched her stride for stride. Both horses neighed encouragement at the mounts near them.

Abelar reveled in the sunlight, and prayed to the god who had blessed his son's Nameday with light, to keep his son safe.

Regg spoke over the pound of hooves. "Kaesa is a wise woman. She will flee before Forrin's forces ever arrive. Everyone will."

Abelar nodded but knew his friend was overly hopeful. The Corrinthal estate of Fairhaven lay to the east of Saerb itself. No one in it, including Kaesa, Elden's nurse, would learn of the approach of Forrin's forces until it was too late to flee anywhere.

And war would hit the whole area hard. Saerb had no strategic value of any kind and it was not built with warfare in mind. It had no walls and no standing army. Abelar had not mustered his forces there precisely because he did not want to give the over-mistress an excuse to bring battle to the city.

Forrin could have only two purposes in marching on Saerb—to draw Abelar into battle, and to make the fate of the city an example to others who might defy the overmistress. To do the latter, Forrin not only needed to burn, he needed to kill. Abelar figured he would send an advance force ahead, probably under cover of night, to cut off any possible retreat of Saerb's residents. The entire population would be penned and slaughtered. The overmistress and her vile niece would not restrict war to warriors. Yhaunn would be Mirabeta's excuse. Forrin would be her instrument.

Abelar dug his heels into Swiftdawn's flanks and rode.

Cale, Riven, and Magadon appeared on the other side of the gate.

"Still the Plane of Shadow," Magadon observed.

Cale was not so certain. The gloom felt . . . different.

They stood on a platform high above a wide, concave basin of smooth rock, not unlike a drained lake bed. Polished smooth by time, the surface of the basin glistened like black glass. The gate they had stepped through sizzled behind them. Sheer stone cliffs surrounded the basin on all sides, giving it an effect like a bowl. The jagged peaks of nearby mountains rose above the walls, looking like enormous fangs. Cool air stirred the men's cloaks.

Over the center of the basin floated a tower of black rock, a spear jutting into the gloom. Tall thin windows and numerous balconies dotted its facade. Clots of deeper darkness floated around it. Creatures of shadow—their forms impossible to distinguish in the distance—flitted through the air along its sides, in and out of the apertures. Green crystals dotted its surface here and there and cast a baleful luminescence. The glassy surface of the basin dully reflected the tower's image and the reflection pointed directly at Cale, Riven, and Magadon.

Four thick chains, the links as thick around as a man's waist, anchored the spire to the basin, as if it would otherwise launch itself like a quarrel. Directly below the floating tower swirled a vast pool of inky shadows, churning slowly, hypnotically. Ropes of shadow, eerily similar to veins, rose out of the pool, wound their way up the chains, and spiraled around the tower.

Looking upon that roiling pool put a pit in Cale's stomach. As he watched, three man-shaped shadows coagulated from the ink, struggled free of the pool, and burst into the air to join their brethren flitting about the tower.

A walkway of black metal, wide enough to accommodate two wagons abreast, described an enormous octagon around the basin, caging the tower. Like the tower, the walkway floated in the gloom, seemingly supported by nothing.

"We are moving," Magadon said, nodding at the walkway.

The motion was ponderous but Magadon was correct. The walkway was slowly rotating around the tower. The tower's reflection in the basin moved with them. Cale did not try to understand how.

A large metal platform stood at the intersection at each of the walkway's eight corners. Each featured two towering poles of rune-encrusted metal, all of them as tall as a giant. Shadows spiraled around them. Between each pair of poles hung a sizzling curtain of dim green energy.

"More gates," Magadon said, and nodded behind them at the

curtain they had stepped through. "This one comes from Elgrin Fau. What of the others, I wonder?"

"Some kind of nexus," Cale said.

"A planar crossroads," Magadon said, nodding. "But to what purpose?"

Riven oathed softly and pointed a blade at the sky.

Cale looked up to see dark clouds streaking by so rapidly that they looked smeared across the sky. Lightning ripped the heavens, a sudden storm of bolts that flashed so fast and frequently that the entire sky looked veined with them. It made Cale dizzy to look upon it.

As fast as it had started, it ceased.

"What in the Nine Hells?" Riven asked, blinking from the flashes.

Magadon squinted up at the sky. "Clouds streaking past. An entire lightning storm in a heartbeat." He looked at Cale and Riven, thoughtful. "Time is passing differently here relative to the outside."

"But where exactly is 'here'?" Cale said.

"Doesn't matter," Riven said. "We're not staying for a visit. We find Kesson Rel, kill him, get clear."

Before Cale could respond, a bass voice from their left said, "If that is your intent, then you are tardy. Kesson Rel has been dead these thousands of years. Well, thousands of years as time passes outside the Calyx."

Out of the gloom of the walkway to their left stepped an enormous form. The towering, gray-skinned giant looked like a man but stood three times Cale's height. Black eyes looked out from a gaunt, craggy face that could have been carved from stone. Long white hair contrasted with the shadows that clung to his form. Disproportionately long arms dangled almost to the giant's knees. He wore no armor, but his gray flesh looked hard enough to turn a blade. The hilt of a sword stuck out over his shoulder. A leather bag that could have contained a man hung from his side.

Cale and Riven backed up a step but held their blades at the ready. The giant's eyes lingered over Weaveshear.

"Your weapons are unnecessary," the giant said.

"We will see," Riven answered, and slowly spun his sabers.

"Name yourself," Cale demanded.

The giant inclined his head. "I am Esmor. And you are the Right and Left hands of the Shadowlord. This place is the Adumbral Calyx. The Divine One rules here, not Kesson Rel. I will take you to him and he will explain matters."

Cale had never heard of the Divine One or the Adumbral Calyx.

Before Cale could respond, another giant stepped out of the gloom to their right. The damned creatures walked the shadows as easily as Cale. The newcomer looked similar to Esmor in appearance, except that his pate was bald.

"I've got left," Cale said to Riven, and kept his face to Esmor.

"I've got right," Riven said, and took position before the other giant.

Esmor nodded at the second giant. "This is Murgan."

"Greetings, Right and Left," Murgan said.

Esmor said, "Murgan will accompany us to the spire."

Magadon's black-streaked mindblade flared into existence. The giants blinked in the sudden flash of yellow light.

"We have not yet agreed to go anywhere with you," Magadon said.

A flash of anger showed in Esmor's black eyes but he reined it in quickly. Cale did not like the look of it.

"But you must," Esmor said. "The Divine One wishes you brought to him."

Cale kept Weaveshear at the ready. Darkness leaked from its tip. "You named us the Right and Left. How did you know that?"

The giant adopted an affected smile. Everything about the creature was false.

"The Divine One knows many things," he answered.

Cale looked to Riven, to Magadon, back to the giant. "Take us to him."

Esmor looked at Murgan and something passed between them. Both seemed pleased. Murgan brandished a thin shaft of black crystal and pointed it at the tower. A thin ray of darkness shot from the wand, hit the tower near a large doorway, and stuck to it. The ray broadened and thickened until a flat expanse of shadow stretched from the walkway to the tower, forming a bridge.

"Move quickly," Esmor said, and stepped onto the span.

Cale, Riven, and Magadon followed, blades still at the ready. Murgan brought up the rear and boxed them in. Cale looked back to see the bridge disappearing behind them as they moved along it. There would be no retreat.

Other bridges formed suddenly, extending from the other platforms of the octagon to the spire. More giants walked across them. The creatures seemed to have been stationed at the other platforms.

The giants had been waiting for them, Cale realized. He hurriedly signaled Riven in handcant. *The giant lies.*

Riven shot back, *Agreed. This is an ambush.*

Cale felt a familiar tingle under his scalp—Magadon's mind link. The connection opened and Magadon said, *I do not trust them.*

He is a liar, Cale said. *And this is a trap. They were waiting for us at the gates. Look at them all. They knew we were coming but not where we were coming from.*

How do we play it? Riven asked.

Cale shook his head. He did not have enough information.

The carrion birds are gathering, Riven said, nodding at the sky, at the gathering cloud of shadows that swooped and wheeled above them, red eyes burning. Hundreds more wheeled around the spire.

Mags, can you get inside Esmor's head without him knowing?

Surface thoughts, Magadon said. *Any deeper and he will know.*

Do it, Cale said. He needed to know more about their situation.

He could sense even this, Magadon said.

They were halfway to the spire. The basin glimmered below them. Undead shadows whirled above. The roiling black pit under the spire continued to birth its abominations.

Do it anyway, Cale said, and readied himself for things to get ugly. Beside him, Riven tensed. Cale felt a slight pressure in his head, indicating that the mindlink had gone quiescent.

Magadon did not break stride, merely closed his eyes and concentrated for a moment. Esmor scratched at his ear but otherwise showed no sign that he sensed the mental intrusion.

Cale felt the tingle of the reactivated mindlink.

The Divine One is Kesson Rel, Magadon said. *And he plans to ambush us within the tower.*

Elyril awakened, still groggy from minddust, to an irritating tickle on her ring finger. She lay in dim lanternlight in her room in Yhaunn. Kefil snored on the floor at the side of her bed. The book brought her by Shar's agent lay beside her and her hand rested on it protectively. The fire in the hearth had burned down to embers. She sat up and hung her legs off the bed. Her head felt as if it had been beaten by maces.

Nightseer?

Dark Sister, Rivalen answered.

Elyril shook her head to clear it. *I was sleeping, Nightseer. I—*

I know, Dark Sister.

His words and tone snapped Elyril to clarity. How could he have known she was sleeping?

You have well served the Lady of Loss, Rivalen said. *War is now inevitable in Sembia.*

The Nightseer's praise left her unmoved. She served him only until she could wrest from him the remainder of the book to be made whole. Then, she would usher in the Shadowstorm and serve Shar beside the Divine One. Then, the Nightseer would bend his knee to her. She smiled, reached back, and ran her fingertips over the book.

The Shadowstorm, too, is inevitable, Nightseer.

It is, Rivalen agreed. *Your work is done now.*

Elyril cocked her head, puzzled by the comment. *Nightseer?*

You know the provenance of the war, Dark Sister. That secret must be kept.

She sat up straight, troubled. *I will keep it, Nightseer.*

I know.

The tickle on Elyril's finger turned to a twinge, an ache, a sting. She exclaimed, jumped to her feet, and pulled at the ring. She could not so much as turn it. It felt grafted to the bone of her finger. Her heart raced.

"No, Nightseer! You do not know—"

There is nothing I do not know.

The purple amethyst in the ring flared and the silver band blackened. An agonizing stab of pain ran the length of Elyril's arm and started to spread into her chest. She gasped in pained horror as her fingers shriveled into thin twigs covered in wrinkled skin. The Nightseer's ring shrank to maintain its hold on her finger even as the magic spread to her hand, turning it to a husk. The magic crawled up her forearm, killing a little more of her with each breath.

She screamed. *How could you do this to me?! How?!*

Your bitterness is sweet to the Lady, Rivalen said, his voice soft, almost sympathetic. *I offer it to her as you die. Dark journey, Elyril Hraven.*

The connection ended. The pain did not.

Elyril screamed with agony and railed with rage as the magic of the Nightseer's ring consumed her body. Kefil climbed to his feet and circled her excitedly, tail wagging.

Did the Nightseer bend his knee to you? Kefil projected.

She kicked at the dog, lost her balance, and fell to the floor. He licked her face.

"Get away!" she screamed.

He sat back on his haunches, panting.

The door to her room flew open and there stood the balding steward in his nightclothes.

"Help me!" she said, and climbed to her feet.

He stood still, shocked, wide-eyed.

"Help me!" she screamed, and ran toward him, arms outstretched.

He mouthed an oath, turned, and fled the room.

Elyril raged after him from the doorway. Her entire arm was little more than a withered stick. She felt the magic root in her chest, neck, and face. Half of her was melting like a candle, collapsing on itself. She whirled around and Kefil put his paws on her chest and tried to lick her face. His weight drove her against the wall.

"Away!" she screamed, and pushed him with her good arm.

Have you summoned the Shadowstorm? he asked, tail still wagging, eyeing her adoringly.

"Shut up! Shut up! Shut up!" She put her hands—the one a mere nub—to her ears. She screamed, terrified, dying. Panicked, desperate, she scrambled around the room searching for a blade with which to cut off her hand, her whole arm, if necessary. If she could only get free of the ring . . .

She turned over the night table with her good hand, threw drawers to the floor, toppled a small armoire, tossed her bedding about the room. The book to be made whole fell to the floor. So, too, did an oil lamp, which broke and sent its contents spraying across the floor. It ignited and spread immediately to the toppled side table and bedding. She did not find a blade. She found only the book to be made whole and hugged it to her breast.

"Divine One!" she wailed. "Volumvax! Aid me!"

Her speech was slurred. Half her face hung slack, ruined.

Kefil lingered around her, standing in her shadow, whining. *You are mad*, he said.

Her leg shriveled under her and she fell to the floor. The fire spread to the wall tapestries and they burst into flame. Heat and smoke filled the room. She coughed, gagged, cried.

Kefil licked her, whined more. She pushed him away with her good foot. He fled the room at last, tail between his legs. As he exited the doorway, he said, *You are mad and none of this is real. You have always been mad. None of this is happening . . .*

Elyril sat in the middle of the inferno and stared at the shadows on the wall. She eyed the wreckage of her body, and an uncontrollable giggle shook her. She saw it all, then, understood fully, and knew what she was to do.

She called to mind a transformative spell that might save her, a spell she had never before used on herself, though she had on others. She giggled again, inhaled smoke, and fell into a coughing fit.

When she recovered, she touched her holy symbol and struggled with her ruined mouth to speak the magical phrases that would transform her body.

The bed caught fire. The sheets curled as they burned. The heat in the room blistered her already shriveled flesh. The smoke set her eyes to watering. She ignored it all and carefully pronounced each word of the spell. When she completed it, she held her desiccated arm before her body and watched the magic transform her flesh again. Her skin darkened, became insubstantial shadowstuff.

The Nightseer's ring blackened further, the amethyst flared anew, and a charge went through her metamorphing body. Her nerves blazed with pain. She screamed, but her spell, corrupted by the Nightseer's ring, continued to transform her. When the magic turned her fully insubstantial at last, the ring fell through her hand and rolled into the flames.

Free of the Nightseer's spell, she cavorted in the fire. She saw the book to be made whole and flew to it. When she touched it, it turned as insubstantial as she and she held it to her breast.

She laughed aloud and collected the Nightseer's ring. Her touch turned it insubstantial and she secreted it on her person. She was living shadow. She could read Shar's portents in her own transformed flesh.

Screaming not in pain but in ecstasy, she fled the residence for Selgaunt, for the Nightseer. She would yet be the author of the Divine One's Shadowstorm.

And she would make the Nightseer pay.

"I have a ring to return to you, Prince Rivalen," she said.

Mirabeta placed the sealed missive into Rynon's pudgy hand. Vendem, in human guise, stood beside her, smiling his overlarge teeth at Rynon. The house mage's uncomfortable expression showed his discomfiture.

"You are fat," the dragon said to him.

Rynon looked like he had been smacked. He colored, stuttered, finally said, "And you, sir, are a rude cretin."

"Tasty though, I'd wager," the dragon said, eyeing the mage up and down.

Rynon looked with shock at the dragon, at Mirabeta, said, "Overmistress, this is most irregular. This person is . . ."

Mirabeta cut him off. "You will transport yourself, my letter, and Vendem to the Lady Merelith. After she has read and acknowledged the contents of my missive, you are to return to me."

"Provided I do not eat you first," said Vendem.

Rynon refused to look at the dragon. "Will I be returning alone, Overmistress?"

She smiled and nodded. "Vendem will remain in service to Lady Merelith."

Rynon bowed to Mirabeta, glared at the dragon. "I pity her."

Vendem grinned.

"Leave now," Mirabeta ordered.

Her letter to Merelith explained the true identity of Vendem and that he was in service to Mirabeta. The letter further ordered Merelith to proceed with an immediate attack on Selgaunt. With Vendem leading the attack, the siege of Selgaunt would be no siege at all. It would be a slaughter.

Mirabeta would have all of Sembia consolidated under her rule before Deepwinter.

CHAPTER EIGHT

24 Uktar, the Year of Lightning Storms

Abelar and Regg, leading the company atop Swiftdawn and Firstlight, crested the rise and saw it first. Abelar raised his hand for a halt and the whole of his force came to a stop along the rise. Only the soft chink of metal and the occasional whicker of a mount broke the silence. All eyes looked below them on the plain.

Perhaps three long bowshots in the distance, a force of cavalry rode. They numbered perhaps twice that of Abelar's company. Abelar could not make out their standard but he noted the color of their tabards— Ordulin's green.

A murmur moved through the men. Horses pawed the ground, snorted. Armor chinked as men shifted in their saddles.

"The sun sets and rises, Abelar." Regg said, a sharp edge in his tone.

"That it does."

Regg said, "They are many to our few. Twice us, I'd say, but not the thousand we'd heard. What are they doing out here, I wonder?"

Abelar knew the answer. "Forrin split his force to cut off retreat from Saerb. They're angling around from the south. The rest of the army is hitting Saerb directly from the east."

"Forrin cannot be far from Saerb, then," Regg said. "Two days away, maybe three."

Abelar nodded. "Get the standards up and sound a blast. Let them know we are here."

Regg issued the order and the two standard bearers unfurled their pennons. Each showed a field of white adorned with a red rose for faith, a sun for light, and a boar rampant for strength. When the standards were up, the company's trumpets sounded and their clarion carried over the plains.

Heads and horses in Ordulin's company wheeled around. Fingers and blades pointed back at Abelar's forces. Ordulin's commanders put their boot heels into their mounts and moved briskly among the squads, pointing and shouting. Their shouts carried faintly over the plains. Men and horses reversed formation and began to form up into an arc concave to Abelar's men.

"They see us, I think," Regg said with a grin.

"That they do."

Regg said, "All medium cavalry. I see crossbows but no massed archers."

"Nor I," Abelar said. The battle would be fought with blades, up close. He pointed to a pair of unarmored men among the forces. "But see there? Wizards. They probably have a few priests in their number as well."

"Agreed. The wizards are to their advantage. But battles are won by flesh and steel, not spells. So it has been ever."

Abelar nodded. "Put us into a loose line. We advance with flanks lagging."

"Advance?"

Abelar nodded, his eyes on his enemy.

Regg shouted the order and the company moved into position. Sergeants shouted commands; horses neighed; men adjusted armor and shields.

Abelar watched his foes as they took formation. They moved with discipline, even skill. He figured many of them to be one-time members of Forrin's Blades, experienced men, but dark hearted from all he'd heard.

He called his cadre of six priests to him. Each wore a breast-plate over mail and bore a round steel shield enameled with Lathander's rose. Led by Roen, they formed a semicircle around Abelar as Ordulin's trumpets blared below. He looked each of them in the eye. Despite their limited experience, he saw only resolve there. The Light was in them.

"They have spellcasters in their force," he said. "We will advance loose, flanks lagging. The casters will try to hit us as we close. Stay in the pocket behind us and watch for their casters."

"Not hard for Roen to look over the line," Jiiris said, grinning. "He sits the saddle as tall as an ogre."

The priests laughed. Abelar smiled and continued. "Do whatever you can to disrupt their spells. Once we're engaged, the casters will matter little."

"We will counter them, Commander," Roen said, and the others nodded.

"I know," Abelar said, and meant it. "Stay in the light."

He clasped each of their forearms in turn, holding Jiiris's a beat longer than the others, and they rode off to take their positions behind the line.

Abelar took a final glance at Ordulin's forces. Regg rode up beside him.

"I wonder if Forrin is among them?" Regg asked.

"Doubtful," Abelar answered.

Regg nodded agreement. He said, "The men are ready. They should hear from you."

Abelar took his eyes off Ordulin's forces. The time had

come to rally his men. He held up his shield so it caught the sunlight and shimmered. Regg did the same. As one, they offered a supplication to Lathander. When they completed their spells, their shields held the sun's glow and hummed with power. They clasped forearms.

"Stay in the light," Regg said, and grinned.

"And you," Abelar answered, and did not grin.

Ordulin's forces sounded a series of trumpet blasts and the cavalrymen gave a great shout.

Regg rode along behind the line of Abelar's men, shield blazing. He thumped men and women on the back and offered quiet words of encouragement. Abelar took position before the line and faced the company.

A wall of flesh and steel extended to either side of him for three hundred paces. He saw Roen's head in the rear, flanked by his fellow priests. Helms and blades caught the sun and glittered in the light. But for Regg's soft words and the flapping of the standards in the wind, silence fell.

All eyes were on Abelar, hard eyes, but eyes filled with faith. He had chosen the men and women of his company well. They were good soldiers. More importantly, they were good men and women.

For a time he said nothing. He simply rode along the line, making eye contact with the men and women who had chosen to trust him with their lives. He wanted them to see his strength of faith, his conviction of purpose.

They did. Some saluted; some nodded. None looked away. He returned to the center of the line and said, "The Morninglord's light shine on you all."

"And on you," they boomed as one.

Abelar turned Swiftdawn and gestured with his shield at Ordulin's forces. "Look out on them. See their souls. Know them for what they are."

He stared down for a moment at Ordulin's cavalry, which was finalizing its formation, before turning back to his own company.

"Know that their purpose was to cut off retreat from Saerb, to murder families as they fled another army that approaches from the east."

Looks hardened. Men shifted in their saddles. Horses whinnied.

"This day, right now, they fail of that purpose."

As one, the company shouted assent.

Behind Abelar, Ordulin's trumpets blared. The men of Forrin's army let up a shout of their own and Abelar heard them start forward. Abelar kept his eyes on his own warriors. They kept their eyes on him.

"To a man, they are in service to a base cause, an evil cause, whereas we . . ." he paused and looked up at the sunlit sky before looking back at his command. "We serve a noble purpose, a higher calling, and the Light is in every man and woman in this company."

He held up his blade and willed it to flare. It luminesced white hot, overwhelming even the glow of his shield, casting the entire company in its radiance.

His men cheered, raised their own blades.

Abelar turned Swiftdawn to look at the advancing enemy. Ordulin's forces were moving at a hustle, and slowly gathering speed. They advanced in a concave formation, flanks curved and leading. A few crossbows twanged. A dozen bolts slit the air and rained down on the company. Shields and armor turned them all.

Abelar turned to face his men.

"Regg observes that they are many, while we are but few. To that I say, aye. The many are always willing to do evil. The few make a stand in the light." He looked up and down his line. "Today we, all of us, make our stand in the light."

His company again shouted assent, but Abelar was not done. "So, aye," he said. "They *are* many. And we are few. Aye."

He urged Swiftdawn into a trot and paced the line, repeating the phrase, giving it a rhythm. He thumped his glowing blade on his glowing shield. "They are many, we are few. They are many, we are few."

Regg echoed his gesture and took up the chant. Roen and the priests in the rear did the same. Soon the entire company was thundering the words, rhythmically beating sword to shield.

"They are many! We are few! They are many! We are few!"

Abelar inhaled deeply as the fire rooted in his gut, as his hands transformed from those of a healer to those of a warrior, as a surge of righteous wrath filled his breast so strongly it felt as if it would lift him from his saddle and propel him to the heavens. He turned to face Ordulin's forces, raised his blade, and shouted defiance.

His wrath spread like contagion to his men and they echoed his shout.

Ordulin's cavalry moved from a trot to a full gallop. They bore down on Abelar's company, blades and shields ready, blood on their minds.

Abelar intoned a prayer to Lathander and channeled the strength of his soul into his blade, which glowed still brighter. He was bathed in light. His company moved restlessly behind him, eager to receive the order. He held his blade up.

"The path is lit, brothers and sisters! Ride!"

The clarions blared, the soldiers roared, and the entire line lurched as one down the rise.

Abelar led them, bent over Swiftdawn, blade held before him. The standard bearers flanked him, pennons whipping in the breeze. The wind whistled over his helm. His shield and blade hummed in his hands. The thunder of hooves could not drown out the chant of his men.

"They are many! We are few! They are many! We are few!"

The chant propelled him forward. Their faith strengthened him. He was spirit, as light as the wind.

Ordulin's men let out a shout as the distance between the two onrushing forces shrank. Abelar eyed the men at the forefront of Ordulin's charge. One of them bore an axe rather than a sword. The man wore no helm and his long hair flew behind him. A symbol decorated his shield: a lightning bolt, the symbol of Talos the Thunderer, the dark god of destruction and storms.

"Ride!" Abelar shouted to his men, and gave Swiftdawn her head. She snorted and ran like the wind, pulling ahead of even the standard bearers.

"Xoren and Trewe, stay on me!" he shouted to the standard bearers. They nodded and he held his blade aloft, letting its light signify the wrath of his god and bolster the courage of his men. He would be the spear point. He lowered his blade and pointed its tip at the Talassan, leaving no doubt of his intent.

The Talassan saw the gesture and snarled. The wild-eyed priest stuck out his palm and a bolt of blue lightning shot from it at Abelar. Abelar intercepted it with his enspelled shield and deflected the bolt into the ground, where it scorched the grass and threw up a divot of earth.

Seventy paces separated the forces.

"They are many!"

In the rear of Ordulin's forces, Abelar saw not two but three wizards incanting spells from horseback. As he watched, one of the wizards suddenly went rigid, as still as a statue, and his mount slowed, bucked, and threw him. Beside another, a rosy-hued long sword appeared in mid-air, slashed downward, and severed a hand.

Abelar shouted Lathander's praises. Roen and his priests were doing exactly as he'd asked.

Fifty paces.

The third wizard completed his spell and a clap of thunder boomed near Abelar. Men screamed. A few horses whinnied in terror, bucked, and threw their riders. One of Abelar's standard bearers, Xoren, covered his ears and lost his saddle. Abelar did not slow. He hoped that Roen and his priests could see to the fallen.

Thirty paces.

"We are few!"

Ordulin's men shouted in answer. Their line stretched out

well beyond Abelar's flanks. They would collapse around Abelar's force and try to encircle his company.

Abelar would not have it. He would drive his company right through them and out the other side. He angled Swiftdawn for the Talassan and the Talassan answered in kind.

Ten paces.

Hooves thundered. Men roared. Abelar held the Talassan's wild eyes. The Talassan raised his axe high. Abelar's blade vibrated with power.

The two forces collided in a cacophony of shouts, screams, whinnies, and the ring of metal on metal.

The priest of Talos chopped down with his axe. Abelar blocked with his shield and the enspelled slab of metal shattered the Talassan's axe. Abelar drove his magical blade through the Talassan's breastplate and ribs with such force that it drove the priest from his horse. Abelar carried him along for a stride, impaled on the blade, before shedding the corpse and pushing forward.

"On me!" he shouted, his light still blazing. "On me!"

He drove Swiftdawn through the tide of flesh and steel. She bit and stomped as he tore through Ordulin's ranks. His blade rose and fell, rose and fell. Blood sprayed; men and horses screamed; blows rained off his shield and armor. He gritted his teeth and killed everything within reach. His shield arm went numb. A blow to his chest nearly unhorsed him but did not penetrate his breastplate. He burst through the rear of Ordulin's ranks, a handful of his men at his side, and found himself not ten paces from one of Ordulin's wizards. The mage's sunken eyes widened with fear.

Abelar and his men put heels to their mounts and charged him. The wizard tried to turn his horse while he jerked a slim shaft of metal from his belt and pointed it at them. The wand discharged a wide beam of white-hot flame that caught both Abelar and Mekkin in the chest. Their tabards caught fire and sections of their breastplates flared red hot. Mekkin fell from his saddle, screaming. Abelar grunted through gritted teeth as his skin blistered and charred beneath his armor, but he kept his saddle and drove Swiftdawn into the wizard's horse. The smaller mount staggered under the warhorse's impact and the wizard scrambled to hold his reins. Abelar crosscut his throat and nearly decapitated him.

Ignoring the pain in his chest, he leaped off Swiftdawn and fell to Mekkin's side. He channeled healing energy into his blade hand, but Mekkin spasmed and died before Abelar could save him.

Abelar cursed and bounded back atop Swiftdawn as the battle caught up to him. The bulk of his force, following his lead, burst through Ordulin's ranks before the flanks of the larger force could collapse on their rear. "Sound a reformation," he said to Trewe, one of his standard bearers. "And stay on me."

Trewe blew the three-note muster and Abelar sped away from Ordulin's forces, drawing his men after. Ordulin's own trumpets sounded a call, and they, too, disengaged to regroup.

Abelar turned to survey the scene. A bowshot separated the forces. Dead men and horses littered the plain. Two riderless mounts, both Saerbian, pranced uncertainly through the carnage, eyes wild. Swiftdawn whinnied to call them; the two mounts snorted and galloped toward Abelar's company.

Regg rode up beside Abelar, his tabard and blade bloodied but no serious wounds on him. "They are not as many now, by Lathander!" Regg said, grinning. Regg could grin through a funeral.

"Truth," Abelar agreed.

"You are afire," Regg said, pointing at Abelar's tabard.

Abelar ignored the flames and they burned themselves out. "That, I am."

He did a rough head count and figured he'd lost perhaps forty men. He allowed himself only a moment to grieve for them and wish them well in Lathander's realm. He counted all his priests among the living. Already Roen and his fellow priests tended to the wounded with healing magic. He spotted Beld among his force. Blood spattered the young warrior's face—not his own. Beld saluted him with his blade.

"I was right to leave the abbey," Beld shouted, and the men near the young man smiled.

Abelar nodded at the young warrior. He turned Swiftdawn and looked out at the dead and wounded on the field. He put Ordulin's losses at close to a hundred, with at least one wizard dead and another without a hand. The Morninglord had shined on their effort. His company had accounted well for itself.

"Get the men in another line," he said to Regg. "Close gaps from the fallen. We give them another charge."

"Now?"

Abelar nodded. He had the upper hand and had no intention of relinquishing it. "Same formation as before. Be quick. You have a thirty count."

Regg spun Firstlight and barked orders while Trewe blew two notes to signal the formation. The men and women of the company, their blood up, reformed rapidly.

Ordulin's forces responded as Abelar had hoped. They moved to realign, but acted with less certainty than before. They could see to a man how they had fared against Abelar's company, and their wizards had been of little effect.

"They fight without conviction," he said to Swiftdawn, and she tossed her head in agreement. "They will break if we hit them hard enough."

He raised his blade and spun Swiftdawn in a circle. His force was ready. The sun shone down on him. His blade blazed.

"They fight with fear in their hearts," he shouted. "We fight with faith in ours."

"Huzzah!" responded his company, and raised blades. A few horses reared.

Abelar turned to face Ordulin's line. "On me, men and women of Lathander! Ride!"

Trewe sounded another clarion call and Abelar led the charge across the plains. The collective shout of his men sounded like the roar of an ocean wave.

Ordulin's forces scrambled to complete their realignment. Horns sounded and commanders moved frenetically among the men, shouting orders, pointing, but they were too slow. Crossbows sang. One or two of Abelar's men fell but the charge continued.

Disorganized and disheartened, Ordulin's men milled about and large gaps showed in their lines. Their commanders shouted, galloped along the line. Abelar shouted and veered Swiftdawn toward the left side of their ranks. He would hit them on the flank and roll them up.

His force thundered after.

Ordulin's forces readied shields and weapons, and braced for impact. Abelar picked the man he would kill first, a bearded commander on a black mare. He turned Swiftdawn toward him and bore down.

A curtain of flame sprang into existence ten paces before him. The blaze stood twice as tall as a man and stretched the length of the battlefield, blocking the charge of his company. Black smoke poured into the sky as grass and shrubs burned.

"On me!" Abelar shouted, and did not slow.

Trewe's trumpet blew and his company, mounted on battle-trained Saerbian horses, followed his command, riding hard directly at the inferno.

Abelar raised his blazing shield and shouted the words to a counterspell, one of the handful of spells known to him. The heat from the inferno warmed his armor, chapped his face.

He did not slow.

His spell engaged the magic of the wall and tore at its power.

He did not slow.

He felt his eyebrows and beard singe. He bent low and held his shield before his face and against the side of Swiftdawn's head. She snorted, encouraging the other mounts of the company, and jumped at the wall.

His countermagic prevailed and dissolved the magical barrier into harmless smoke. Abelar, his armor and shield trailing smoke, raised his blade in triumph. His men cheered, shouted, and the uncertainty in Ordulin's forces turned to shock.

Abelar's company hit them like a battering ram. Horses shrieked; men shouted; blades rose and fell; blood sprayed and men died.

In the chaos Abelar lost sight of the commander he had targeted, so he slashed with his blade and bashed with his shield at any man within reach who wore a green tabard. "We . . ." he shouted, and smashed his shield into the face of a young fighter.

". . . stand . . ."

A sword slash tore open his shield arm. He answered with a stab to the chest that split breastplate and breastbone.

". . . in the light!"

He parried a flurry of blows with his shield. Swiftdawn reared, kicked, and drove his attacker's mount backward. Abelar drove Swiftdawn after, chopped downward, and cleaved helm and head.

His men around him took up his chant.

"In the light! In the light!"

The words took on the rhythm of a heartbeat and blades and shields rose and fell in time with it. The morale of Abelar's force was swelling; that of Ordulin's forces was collapsing. Abelar took advantage. He swatted Swiftdawn on the flank and shouted, "Clear!"

Swiftdawn reared, kicked, bit, and turned a circle, clearing a space around Abelar. The commander hurriedly recited the words to a spell that would encourage his forces and discourage those of Ordulin. A rosy glow spread out from Abelar's shield in all directions to a distance of a spear toss. It lasted for only a moment but its magic caused all of Abelar's men caught within it to roar with fervor and fight with redoubled effort, while Ordulin's soldiers groaned and temporarily lost their nerve. At almost the same moment, a blazing sphere of luminescence formed above Regg and shed its light on the battlefield. Abelar knew Regg's spell to be a harmless light spell, but it was symbolic and it was enough.

Ordulin's forces broke under the onslaught, first a few, then several, then all of them. Their commanders shouted unheeded orders as men wheeled their mounts and fled in two large groups. A few dropped their weapons and pleaded for mercy.

"Do we pursue, Commander?" shouted Regg, with Firstlight whinnying eagerly.

Abelar watched his enemy flee, considered, and shook his head. "No. Stand the men down."

Regg nodded and gave the orders. Abelar scanned his men for Roen, spotted him, and summoned him to his side. The priest had a dent in his breastplate and bled from a gash in his thigh.

"Lathander watched over his faithful," Roen said.

"Aye," Abelar agreed. "See to the wounded, Roen. Heal ours first, then theirs."

Roen cocked his head. "Theirs? What are we to do with them, commander?"

"Disarm them, get a pledge to give up the fight, and take the thumb from their sword hand to ensure it. Then give them a horse, if we can spare it, and let them go."

Roen's eyes widened, but he nodded.

Abelar had little choice. He had no way to hold prisoners and he would not execute enemies unless he saw no other course. Taking a thumb would make them useless as combatants. It was enough.

"Be quick, Roen," he said. "We ride as soon as it is done."

Half an army was still bearing down on Saerb, on his son.

Cale held his holy symbol in hand and inventoried the spells he had prepared. He had a thirty count to invent a plan. Either that, or he had to shadowwalk out of the Calyx with Riven and Magadon.

Cale? Riven asked.

I am not leaving without doing what we came to do, Magadon said.

Cale agreed. They might not get another attempt on Kesson and if they did not, Magadon would be lost.

We ambush the ambusher, Cale said to his friends. *Stay close to me. When we see him, I will isolate us with him. If that fails, we leave—*

No, Magadon said. *You promised me—*

I have not forgotten, Cale snapped. *But we leave if that fails, Mags. There are too many.*

Magadon said nothing more and Cale decided to take it as acquiescence.

If it succeeds, we will not have much time. Hit him with everything you have. We kill him, take what we came for, and get the Hells out.

Magadon and Riven indicated agreement as they approached the spire.

Cale knew they would face hundreds of shadows, at least a score of shadow giants, and the First Chosen of Mask—the *first* First Chosen of Mask, selected millennia ago. Their plan would have to go perfectly.

Beside Cale, Riven shook his head and chuckled.

He must have been thinking much the same thing.

Elyril flew high above the earth, her form as insubstantial as the night's breeze. Abandoned villages and fallow fields lay below her. Sembia was dying. Civil war would kill it and the Shadowstorm would desiccate the corpse.

She cradled the book to her chest, reveling in her new form. The tome pulsed against her breast like a heartbeat, whispered truths into her mind, and pulled her toward the rest of it—*The Leaves of One Night.*

She was one with the darkness, truly Shar's instrument. She could become corporeal should she require it, but she preferred the form of a living shadow.

She saw now that all she had done and experienced—from the night she had murdered her parents to the night she had transcended the Nightseer's betrayal—had been to transform her into shadow and make her worthy of her position as the future consort of Volumvax the Divine One. She would take *The Leaves of One Night* from the Nightseer and make the book whole. She would cast the spell and summon the Shadowstorm. The Nightseer would be consumed in its violence and she would rule the transformed world beside Volumvax.

She giggled and her voice was like the wind.

Tamlin sat alone in his study, dressed in a heavy overcloak. A single candle provided light. Cool night air shook the flame. Despite the cold, Tamlin preferred the window to be open. He felt less confined. Selûne's silver crescent shone in through the open window.

He closed the book he had been reading and watched the play of shadows about the room. He wondered what it would be like to know the shadows so intimately that they responded to his will, to step through the invisible space that connected them, to live for millennia.

He had read all he could of shades, shadow magic, even a bit about ancient Netheril, though there was little to be found on the subject in Selgaunt. But books could teach him only so much. He wanted to know more.

A knock at his door drew his attention.

"It is Thriistin, my lord," said his chamberlain from the hallway.

"Enter."

The door opened and Thriistin stood in the corridor. The old fellow looked stricken. Dark circles painted the skin under his eyes and his mouth hung partially open. His alarm spread into the room and Tamlin rose from his chair, his blood pounding.

"What is it?" Tamlin asked.

"Word has come from our western scouts. Saerloon has marshaled. An army of thousands is preparing to march."

The words hung in the air, fat with dire portents. Tamlin sat down, remembered to breathe. To his surprise he did not feel frightened, merely numb.

"So many?" Tamlin asked.

Thriistin nodded.

Tamlin said, "Have the scouts sent to me. I will need further details. And notify Lord Rivalen immediately."

"Yes, Hulorn," Thriistin said, and hurried from the room.

The import of the words started to settle on Tamlin. His pulse sounded in his ears. A sudden headache put a knife through his temples. Mirabeta had not waited for the spring. War would come to Selgaunt not in months but in days.

Tamlin did not feel ready for it.

Rivalen walked the night-shrouded streets of Selgaunt alone. He had no destination in mind—he simply wanted to be seen. Others among his entourage did the same in other parts of the city from time to time. To appear less threatening, less foreign, Rivalen had ordered all of the Shadovar to keep the darkness that habitually coiled about them to a minimum.

Passersby watched him with more curiosity than fear. Some soldiers even saluted him. Rivalen was pleased. The citizens of the city were becoming accustomed to seeing a Shadovar among them.

Rivalen saw that most of the shops—those still open after nightfall— contained scant goods. Commerce had slowed almost to a halt as the city braced for war. Rivalen made a point to stop and examine what goods he saw. A dozen pairs of boots sat in the light of a glowball on the walkway outside a cobbler's shop. Rivalen stooped, picked up a pair made from cow hide, turned them in his hands.

"These are well made," he said to the balding cobbler, who watched him from a few paces away.

The man looked surprised that Rivalen had spoken to him. "Uh . . . thank you . . . my lord."

"What is their price?"

"Uh . . . one silver raven, my lord."

Rivalen nodded, produced the coin, and handed it to the cobbler.

"A fair price."

"Thank you, my lord."

Rivalen walked off, pleased to see that a small crowd had gathered to watch the transaction. There was hope in their eyes, the same hope he saw in the Hulorn's eyes when he looked at Rivalen.

Rivalen nodded at them and walked on. As he moved down the streets, through the crowds, he attuned the magical ring on his finger to the similar ring worn by his brother, Brennus. He felt the connection open.

Rivalen, his brother said.

Have you been able to locate Erevis Cale? Rivalen asked.

No, Brennus answered, and Rivalen heard the frustration in his brother's tone. *It is inexplicable, almost as though he and his companions have vanished from the multiverse. I suspect something shields them but I cannot determine even that for certain.*

What sort of something? A spell?

Brennus hesitated. *I do not know, Rivalen. Perhaps a spell. Or perhaps something more.*

Such as?

He is a priest. We know this.

It took a moment for Brennus's implication to register. *Are you implying that his god is shielding him from us?*

Rivalen found the very notion offensive. After all, Shar offered him no such boon, and he was her Nightseer.

Brennus said nothing and the silence stretched.

Perhaps he is dead? Rivalen offered at last.

Brennus answered, *I would know if it were so. He could be hiding within an area of dead magic. Perhaps still in the Hole of Yhaunn. That is a possibility.*

There, Rivalen said, comforted. *Continue your efforts, and inform me if you locate him. What of Sakkors and the Source?*

Yder has accomplished much. Sakkors is almost fully restored. Three hundred of our elite warriors under Leevoth arrived yesterday to bolster the five hundred battle-bred krinth already here. The Most High has put all of them at your disposal.

Mention of the Most High evoked a sense of unease, but Rivalen was otherwise pleased. Leevoth and his men were among the finest shade warriors in Shade Enclave. Each bore a glassteel blade infused with shadow magic that sheared through metal as if it were cloth.

Brennus continued. *The Source itself is functional but its consciousness appears . . . damaged, hostile. The mind-altered krinth are able to control it for a time, but only for a time.*

Then?

Their minds are consumed. They are left catatonic.

Rivalen nodded. He would have to use the Source's sentience sparingly. The mindmage, Magadon Kest, had altered only thirty or so of the krinth.

Events are moving quickly here, he said. *Have Yder position Sakkors to assist should I need it. An hour or less away, not days. I will send for him at the appropriate time.*

What more do you wish of me?

I want you here.

There?

Yes. Finalize matters on Sakkors and transport yourself here. I may have need of your divinations. And I wish to show the Hulorn good faith. He is increasingly nervous.

Very well, Brennus answered. *Shall I bring Leevoth and his men, then, as well?*

No, Rivalen answered. *Their entrance is to be more . . . dramatic.*

How do you mean?

A voice in the crowd called out to Rivalen.

Come as soon as you are able, he said to Brennus, and broke the connection.

"Prince Rivalen!" called a man in the crowd. "When will we have the aid of the Shadovar? Rumors say that the armies of the overmistress will soon come."

Others among the crowd nodded, murmured agreement.

"Assistance is on the way," he returned, loud enough for all to hear. For effect, he let the shadows around him churn. Eyes widened.

"Fear nothing," he said. "I regard Selgaunt as my own city. I assure you that no army will breach its walls."

Smiles, raised fists, and a ragged cheer answered his words.

Rivalen walked on among his future subjects.

Later he returned to his quarters and one of the Hulorn's messengers informed him that Saerloon had begun to marshal.

He could not hold in a smile.

CHAPTER NINE

26 Uktar, the Year of Lightning Storms

Abelar, Regg, and their company—less the four score dead or incapacitated from the battle—raced toward Saerb. Mounts and men fought fatigue with every league they covered, but fear for their friends and families pulled them ever north and west. They had slept little. Roen and the priests kept them all fed on magical fare and they ate in the saddle. They stopped during the day only for Dawnmeet and as the stout Saerbian mounts required. Leagues of whipgrass-covered plains lay behind them. Leagues more still lay before them.

Only the sound of thundering hooves marked their passage. The men did not jest or chat with one another as they rode, as was their habit. Their usual camaraderie had surrendered to quiet purposefulness. The battle with Ordulin's forces had driven home the hard realization that civil war had started. Matters would soon get much worse, Abelar knew, and much bloodier.

The unoccupied road stretched before them like a ribbon. They passed villages from time to time but slowed only to warn the villagers that war was coming and that they should flee south.

Fear for Elden consumed Abelar's thoughts. He occupied the hours by reciting in his mind passages from Lathander's *Book of Light*. He reminded himself that dawn always chased even the darkest night, that the sun set but always rose anew. The proverbs brought him scant comfort.

The setting sun turned the cloudless western sky into a pool of orange and red. Abelar took it as a good sign. A line of tall ash trees to their left cast long shadows over the plains.

"What do you make of that?" Regg asked, pulling Abelar back to himself. Regg nodded ahead to the top of a rise, perhaps a crossbow shot distant.

Abelar squinted in the fading light. A patch of darkness blotted the rise under a stand of trees, as if a storm cloud had fallen from the sky. The darkness flowed down the rise like fog, filling the low spots with shadows.

Abelar knew it to be magical. He whistled for the attention of his men and called a halt. The men pulled up, all eyes on the hillock. Hands went to hilts. Horses whinnied.

"Roen, put some light on it," Abelar called.

Roen chanted a prayer to Lathander and pointed his hand at the rise. A globe of light flared into being over the hill but only partially countered the darkness.

Abelar saw forms within the shadows, half a dozen men or more. Darkness concealed all but one and that one stood a head taller than the rest. Something about the man's stance and stature looked familiar. The man raised a hand in greeting.

"Morning light," Regg oathed. "Can it be?"

Abelar stared, his mind racing, his heart swelling. "Can it? Can it?"

The men and women pointed at the rise and an excited murmur ran through them.

Regg put a hand on Abelar's shoulder, though he kept his eyes on the rise. "The Morninglord reunites the sundered before night falls. It is a good sign, Abelar."

Abelar nodded, overwhelmed by the blessing. He put his boots into Swiftdawn's flanks and sped forward. Regg and the company followed hard after.

Abelar's father, smiling, stepped out of the shadows, which dimmed Roen's globe of light with each passing moment.

Abelar pulled up on Swiftdawn, leaped from the saddle, and swallowed his father in his arms. Regg and the rest of the company swarmed around them.

"Father," Abelar said, and did not try to hold back the tears.

Endren returned the embrace, his voice choked. "My son. You are well."

They drew strength from one another for a time, standing in the light of the setting sun. The men and women of the company looked on and spoke softly of standing in Lathander's favor.

Abelar held his father at arm's length and looked at the six shadow-shrouded men who stood several paces behind Endren. Shadows coiled around them, leaked from their flesh. Abelar thought of Erevis Cale. The darkness had embraced him in the same manner. Hard eyes looked out of shadow-cloaked forms. All of them wore impassive expressions on olive-skinned faces. They bore no weapons that Abelar could see, and their loose-fitting trousers and tunics befitted peasants more than warriors.

"Who are these men?" he asked Endren. Without waiting for an answer, he shouted to them, "House Corrinthal owes you a debt. I owe you a debt."

The tallest of the men inclined his head but said nothing.

Endren half-turned to face the shadowmen. "They are my rescuers. Or some of them. They pulled me from the Hole, nursed me back to health in their temple, then brought me to you. I still do not know how they found you. They speak little.

But I do know that they serve Mask and travel the shadows as if they were roads."

Abelar and Regg shared a look.

"Mask?" Abelar asked his father. "You are certain?"

Endren nodded. "Strange, not so? That servants of Mask should save the father of a servant of Lathander."

"Stranger than you know," Abelar answered. He looked past his father to the men. "You are not the first servants of Mask I have met in recent days. Are you Shadovar?"

Shadows swirled and the tallest of the men suddenly stood beside him. He had covered ten paces without taking a step. Swiftdawn neighed nervously and backed away a step. Regg cursed in surprise.

Endren said, "This is Nayan. Nayan, this is Abelar, my son."

Nayan gave a half-bow, his gray eyes unreadable. He gestured at his six companions and spoke in accented common.

"We are not Shadovar, but hail from Telflammar. These are Shadem, Vyrhas, Erynd, Dynd, and Dahtem."

"Such names," Regg said. "And no weapons or armor."

Nayan's gaze never left Abelar's face. "Mask speaks to few servants in these days. Name him whom you saw."

Abelar did not care for Nayan's tone but bore it. The man had saved his father.

"Erevis Cale. He named himself a priest of Mask."

Nayan's eyes widened. The shadows around his five companions deepened, roiled. "Where and when did you see him?"

Regg said, "And who are you to demand—"

Abelar held up a hand and Regg fell silent. "Who is Erevis Cale to you?" Abelar asked.

Nayan studied Abelar's face. "He is the Right Hand of the Shadowlord, and we are his instruments."

Abelar heard no lie in Nayan's words. He told of his meeting with Erevis Cale and Selgaunt's Hulorn.

Nayan's face showed nothing, but his tone suggested disappointment. "That was too long ago, Abelar Corrinthal. We have seen him in the interim. He and the Left Hand led us in the rescue of Endren Corrinthal."

"The Left Hand?"

Nayan nodded. "Drasek Riven."

Abelar put a hand on Nayan's shoulder. The man's muscles felt carved from stone. "Then I have him to thank as well as you."

Nayan accepted Abelar's gratitude with a nod of his head. He said, "The Left and Right departed Yhaunn for Selgaunt after rescuing your father. We have not seen either of them since and cannot locate them."

That did not bode well for Selgaunt, Abelar thought, but did not say. Instead, he said, "I hope they are safe and stay in the light."

Nayan smiled slightly. "If they are safe, they do not owe it to the light."

Regg laughed aloud. Even Abelar smiled.

Regg said, "We have heard a rumor that the Shadovar serve the Hulorn of Selgaunt. Perhaps the rumors have mistaken your lord for a Shadovar?"

"None would make that mistake," Nayan answered.

"We will solve this mystery together, Nayan," Abelar said. "Come. You and your men are welcome in our company. We ride northwest for Saerb."

"And there's battle upon our arrival," Regg added.

Endren gave a start and looked pointedly at Abelar, a question in his eyes.

Nayan bowed his head. "Gratitude, Abelar Corrinthal, but we serve only the hands of Mask and they are not among your number. We will await their return or summons at our temple."

Abelar said, "Erevis Cale is an . . . ally of mine. He would have you with us, I think."

"Perhaps," Nayan answered. "If so, he surely will tell us upon his return."

"Nayan . . ." Endren began, but Abelar held up a hand to halt his father's words.

"He is his own master," Abelar said to Endren, then to Nayan, "I am disappointed. I need every fighting man I can get. But so be it. You may take horses, if you wish."

"And weapons," Regg added.

Nayan smiled. "We have no need for either." He bowed to Endren, to Abelar, to Regg, and walked back to his men. The man moved with clockwork precision. Abelar began to understand how the shadowmen must fight. He had heard of men who killed as efficiently with their hands and knees as with steel.

"Farewell, Nayan," Abelar said.

"Safe travels, men of shadow," Endren called.

Nayan inclined his head, the shadows around them deepened, and they were gone in a breath.

The men and women of the Company burst out in discussion.

"The Right Hand of Mask," Abelar said, mostly to himself. "What else is this Erevis Cale?"

Regg clapped him on the shoulder. "I do not know, but he saved your father. I find myself liking him more and more."

Endren studied Abelar's battle-torn clothing. "We have tales to share, it seems. Events have moved quickly, yes? You spoke of battle in Saerb?"

Abelar nodded. "Forrin leads an army there."

Endren's eyes narrowed and his brow furrowed so much his gray brows touched.

"Malkur Forrin the Butcher?"

"Aye. The overmistress has named him to head her armies."

Endren cursed and shook his head. "She is ever more a fool. How far away from Saerb are we?"

"Two days."

"How far from Saerb is Forrin?"

"We do not know. I have no men to spare as spies, Father."

Endren cursed again, then looked up sharply, bushy eyebrows raised in a question. "Where is Elden, Abelar?"

Abelar held his father's gaze though he wanted to bow his

head in shame. "Fairhaven. I left him there. I did not think—"
He shook his head and looked away. He could say no more.

Endren closed his eyes, inhaled, squeezed his son's shoulder.
"You left him to serve me. I am sorry. But you were right to leave
him behind, Abelar. He is a child. If you had brought him to
Ordulin, you would not have escaped after my arrest, and neither
would he."

Abelar nodded, bolstered by his father's words. He knew he had
done the only thing he could, but it helped to hear another say it.

Endren looked past them and called, "A mount and steel.
Now."

Regg smiled at Abelar and repeated the call. "Trewe, a horse,
a blade, and mail for Lord Corrinthal!"

While they waited for the mount and gear, Abelar hurriedly
briefed his father on their situation—the battle of two days
earlier, the number of cavalry they expected in Forrin's force.
After he'd finished, Endren looked Abelar in the face. "You have
carried our name well." He nodded at Abelar's holy symbol. "And
his name, as well."

Abelar inclined his head, surprised at the praise. His father
seldom offered it. "Thank you, my lord."

Trewe brought forth a white mare and Endren took the reins.
For the first time, Abelar noticed that his father's shield hand was
severed at the wrist. "Your hand!"

Regg, too, looked surprised. "Morning light," he oathed.

Endren eyed the stump and nodded. "I said we had tales to
share. This was the price of slipping my chains." He held up his
sword hand. "But this one still holds a hilt well. And I can outride
either of you, even with no hands."

Abelar smiled.

"We know it to be so," Regg said.

Roen approached with a suit of mail and a blade.

"Help me with the armor," Endren said.

Regg helped Endren into the armor and the elder Corrinthal
belted on scabbard and sword.

"I thought we'd not meet again, Endren," Regg said. "I am pleased to have been wrong."

Endren adjusted the mail and put a hand on Regg's shoulder. "I thought similarly. You have watched over my son in my absence. I am grateful."

Regg shook his head. "It is he who watches over me. Over all of us. And it is no mere man that watches over him, my lord."

"So you say," Endren said.

"Enough," Abelar said, embarrassed.

Endren's eyes went to Regg's holy symbol, to Abelar's. Abelar knew his father worshiped many gods, and did not credit Lathander above the others.

Endren asked Regg, "Your father is still in Saerb?"

Regg nodded.

"I have not seen Torar in many years," Endren said.

"He is in ill health," Regg said, and Abelar heard the concern in his friend's voice. Torar would not be able to flee easily when war came to him.

Endren said, "Then for Elden and Torar's sakes, let us hope the Morninglord continues to watch over my son. If he does, I will build him a new temple myself. Hear you that, Abelar?"

Abelar smiled, nodded. "I hear it."

"Let us ride," Endren said, and swung into the saddle.

For two nights and a day of hard riding, Reht avoided the roads and traveled only between sunset and dawn. He did not want word to reach Saerb that his force was moving through the countryside. He presumed Lorgan would take the same precautions, though his course took him farther south of Saerb.

During the daylight hours, Mennick cast an illusion that stayed until after sunset, and made any available copse of trees appear as a large and overgrown woods. Reht and his force of seventy hid within the illusion—unaffected by it, since they knew its origin and presence—and waited for night. From time to time, a horseman or donkey-drawn wagon would move past in the distance, but nothing to indicate that Saerb or its nobility expected an attack.

Shortly after each sunset, Mennick touched each of the men with a wooden wand tipped with a fleck of chrysoberyl that granted them the ability to see like cats in the darkness. They traveled quietly but quickly and covered much ground.

The breath of horses and men formed clouds in the chill night air. The moon hung low in the sky, lighting the tips of the distant Thunder Peaks. Stars lit the clear sky.

Stands of pine and larch dotted the increasingly hilly, rocky terrain. Reht moved the force back onto the road for fear that traveling the rough land at night would lame a horse. He had only a handful of spare mounts.

The sparsely inhabited Sembian northlands featured only an occasional hamlet built around this or that noble's country estate. Reht and his men skirted them easily. The area seemed almost sleepy. An army would soon wake it up. "The hunting must be good here, eh?" he said to Mennick and Vors, who rode beside him.

Mennick agreed. "Boar, I'd guess, given the scrub in these lowlands."

Vors said absently, "What does a dying man see in his last moments? When my axe splits his head, is his focus sharpened in that instant before death? Or does he perceive only dully what has happened?"

"What?" Mennick asked, his tone puzzled. "We were discussing hunting."

Vors grinned. "So was I."

Reht stared contempt at the war priest for a moment before looking to Mennick. "Stags aplenty to go with your boars, I'd wager. There. Look."

He pointed to a small woods not far from the road. With his

catlike vision, he saw a trio of deer—two does and a fawn—that had ventured out of the trees to forage in the grass.

"No stag, though," Mennick said.

"He's around," Reht answered.

Late in the second night, still half a league east of Saerb, with dawn a few hours away, they reached what Reht thought to be the Corrinthal estate, ranch, and pasture. He halted the men about a bowshot away, dismounted, and crept forward through the scrub and trees with Mennick. The smell of fires filled the air.

A wall of stacked timber enclosed the expansive grounds of the large estate. Grain fields surrounded it on two sides and extended into the darkness. A rill ran alongside and under the western wall. A wooden gate and gatehouse in the north-facing wall provided the only obvious ingress. Two glowballs hanging from the corners of the gatehouse provided light.

"Can you see the heraldry over the gate?" Mennick asked him.

Reht had an archer's eye, and with Mennick's spell allowing him to see in dim light, he made out the insignia set into the gate—a white horse running under a blazing sun, the Corrinthal symbol.

"I see it. This is it. I need a tactical look, Mennick."

"Aye."

The wizard quietly intoned the words to a spell and touched himself, then Reht. Reht knew to expect the flying spell to make his body feel lighter. When it did, he willed himself to rise, and his feet left the earth.

"Hold a moment," Mennick said, and put a hand on Reht's arm. The wizard incanted a second spell and vanished from Reht's sight.

"That's for both of us," Mennick said, though Reht needed no explanation. He had experienced the invisibility spell often enough. They could see themselves, but not each other.

"Let us have a look," Mennick said, his voice coming from above.

Reht willed himself into the air, rose to a height of a spear cast, and looked down on the Corrinthal estate.

Within the walls, Reht noted a large stable and four large barns, a horse run and training area, several livestock pens, a score or so small buildings clustered along the western walls—probably the village where farmhands and other laborers lived—and a large wooden building that he assumed to be a barracks for the house guard. In the center of the compound stood the two-story, sprawling rustic Corrinthal manse.

Mud-packed timber made up the bulk of the manse, and a wooden porch wrapped around three sides of it. A low stone wall with a wrought iron gate separated the manse from the rest of the grounds.

Glowballs beamed at the entrance to the stables, and on the porch of the manse. A few torches burned in the cluster of buildings at the western end of the compound. Light trickled out of three shuttered windows of the manse.

"That barracks can house thirty men," Reht said.

"Easily," said Mennick. "I would put it at forty."

Reht pointed at the cluster of buildings along the southern wall, though Mennick could not see him.

"There will be some men in the village who will fight."

"Aye."

"I see eight guards at the gate."

"No others, though," Mennick said. "They'll have dogs. If we use stealth, we will have to move quickly."

Reht considered the compound and made his decision. Stealth was not his best approach. He had a sleeping compound. Except for the guards, the fighting men within would not be armed or armored. He needed to hit hard and fast.

"We go at it hard. I will lead the men through the gates. Stay here and burn the barracks as we approach, then support as you can. If the boy is in the manse, I will find him. When I've got him out, burn the manse, too."

Mennick sounded unhappy. "The smoke will be seen."

Reht knew. "Forrin is a day and a half behind us. By the time anyone investigates and learns what has occurred, it will be too late to anticipate an attack."

Meanwhile, he would send Abelar Corrinthal a message.

Mennick nodded at the explanation. "As you say."

"Dispel this invisibility when I land."

Reht descended, called out to Mennick to indicate that he was earthbound, and Mennick uttered a single word of power. A tingle in Reht's flesh signaled the end of the invisibility spell. He heard Mennick hurriedly recast the spell on himself as Reht crept back to his men.

When he reached them, he said, "Gear up. We go as soon as all are ready. Most of them are asleep. We hit hard."

The men snapped to it, checked straps, buckles, and weapons. They had been eager for a fight since leaving Ordulin. Reht said to Vors, "We need to get through the gate quickly. What can you do?"

"Blast it from its hinges," Vors answered with a grin. "Leave it to me."

Battle always excited the war priest. He thumped axe to shield, whirled, and paced through the men, growling at them to move quickly.

To the rest of the men, Reht said, "Vors will get the gate down. Dist and his men—take the eight gate guards. Zerton, Ethril, and Dant—take squads to the barracks."

"Where on the grounds is the barracks, Reht?" Zerton asked. The heavyset warrior was one of Reht's most reliable sergeants.

"Mennick will light it up," Reht answered. "There will be no missing it. Thirty men inside, maybe more."

Zerton and Dant nodded.

Ethril said, "Thirty men who will be leaping from windows while their beds burn."

"And getting not much farther," Zerton said, tightening a buckle on his breastplate.

"Aye, that," many said, and others chuckled.

"House guards," a few said with contempt.

Reht said, "Vors, me, and Norsim's men have the house." He fixed a hard look on Vors and Norsim, a tall, thin sergeant whose luck with dice was legendary among the men. "The Corrinthal boy is four winters in age and was born an idiot. He looks it. He comes out alive. But no one else does. Understood?"

Vors growled acquiescence. Norsim nodded.

"Mount up, men."

Leather creaked and mail chinked as men climbed into the saddle. The horses snorted, sensing the tension of their riders. Reht donned his helm, drew his blade. His men did likewise.

"Under cover of silence," Reht said to Vors. "Until we get close."

"I must be able to speak aloud for the Destroyer's power to break the gate."

"Silence until we get close," Reht reiterated. "Then cast your spell."

Vors glared but did as he was ordered. The war priest held aloft his shield, adorned with the lightning bolt of Talos, and asked for the Destroyer's blessing in the coming battle. The image of the lightning bolt flared for a moment and even Reht felt a warm surge in his gut. Vors intoned another spell and put a calloused hand roughly on Reht's shoulder. Reht's curse at the priest died in the magical silence, so he instead shoved Vors's arm away. The priest grinned.

Sound could not be made within the sphere of magic that radiated from Reht for eight or nine paces. Vors fell in toward the rear of the men, outside the area of the silence, and intoned a second such spell, though Reht could not hear it. The war priest put his hand on Dist, and returned to Reht's side.

All eyes were on Reht. He turned his mount, the silence ponderous. He put his heels into her and led his force toward the Corrinthal estate.

Signaling with his hands, he ordered the men into a five-wide column, organized by squads. He increased speed to a hard gallop. The wind stirred his cloak. The ground shook under the horses' hooves but the spells of silence killed the noise. The lighted gate of the Corrinthal estate lay just ahead. He and his men charged across the grass, bearing down on it.

A tiny ball of flame traced a thin orange line from a point over their heads toward the barracks, invisible behind the Corrinthal walls. It exploded into a towering plume of flame and smoke, and lit up the night.

Reht could only imagine the shouts of alarm. The light from the fire framed the gates. He saw the silhouettes of the guards leaping to their feet and looking back on the flames, pointing. They did not yet see Reht's men approaching.

Vors made a cutting motion with his hand and the silence spells ended. The thunder of hooves and the rush of the wind overwhelmed all sounds coming from the estate, save the bleat of an alarm horn. Vors ducked low in the saddle as they neared the gate, which was still closed.

The guards saw them, shouted, pointed. One leveled a crossbow.

"Do whatever you intend to do, priest! Now!"

Vors shouted out the words to a spell and held his shield before him. A visible wave of destructive force went forth from it. It hit the crossbowman, shattered his weapon, and rolled toward the gate, splintering wood, twisting metal, and opening the way. The men charged onward.

Vors split the head of the crossbow-armed guardsman with his axe, and Reht rode down another as he lunged from the gatehouse and slashed with his blade. The men of the company shouted battle cries and rode over the downed gates. The clang of metal and shout of combat sounded in their wake as Dist and his men, rearmost in the formation, engaged the surviving gate guards.

Reht, Vors, Norsim, and the rest of Norsim's squad rode hard for the Corrinthal house. Shutters flew open and sleepy faces showed in the windows, shouting with surprise and alarm.

The rising flames from the burning barracks cast the estate in livid orange light. Mennick had aimed his spell well—the front of the building was ablaze, blocking the doors. Men crawled out of windows, unarmored and unarmed, coughing. A few ducked out a back door and gathered at the rear.

"Move," shouted Reht, and pointed at the building. "They're assembling in the rear of the barracks."

He need not have uttered the order. Thirty of his men were already thundering for the barracks.

"And 'ware crossbowmen in the village," he shouted after them, but did not know if anyone heard.

Reht, Vors, and Norsim's squad leaped the low stone wall before the Corrinthal manse and charged toward the doors. They swung out of their saddles and bounded up the porch for the large double doors. A wooden symbol hung above the doorway—a rising sun over a rose. Vors split it with his axe.

"You, you, and you," Reht said, indicating Norsim and two others. "Get around back and watch the doors, windows, and cellars. No one escapes." He looked back at the gates to see Dist cut down the last of the gate guards. "Half of Dist's men are to assist. The rest to the village."

Shouting and the noise of scattered combats sounded from all around the grounds. Norsim called for Dist while the other two men started to sprint around the porch toward the back of the house.

Without warning, a column of flame engulfed Reht, Vors, Norsim, and the men around them. The flash of searing heat and blast of explosive force blew Reht onto his back. He found himself staring up at the sky, dazed, his face charred, his armor smoking. He heard moans around him, the smell of burning flesh. The porch posts had caught fire. It would soon spread to the roof.

"This house is favored of the Morninglord," said a hard voice. "And those are *his* flames."

Reht looked up to see a towering bearded man in a hastily donned breastplate enameled with the rose of Lathander. Other than the armor, he wore only a nightshirt and boots. He held a large flanged mace in a two-handed grip.

In stride, the man crushed the skull of one of Reht's downed men. Blood spattered mace and man. The violence returned Reht to his wits. He rolled over, grabbed his sword, and pulled himself to his knees.

The man raised his mace to kill another, but lightning from the sky slammed into his chest and drove him against the wall of the manse.

Mennick.

The priest of Lathander, the rose enameled on his breastplate blackened, sagged to the porch, unmoving.

Vors climbed to his feet, his long hair and beard singed, his face blistered. He roared and drove his axe into the priest's chest.

"Up," Reht said to his men, and stood. "Give them no time to organize a defense."

All but two of his men got to their feet. All showed burns, but were hale enough to fight. The two downed men were dead, their exposed flesh as black as seared meat. Reht put them from his mind. He felt the burned flesh on his face and hands. He would have scars, but the pain was tolerable.

Trusting in Norsim and Dist to secure the exterior of the manse, Reht and Vors and a handful of others kicked in the double doors and entered the foyer.

Two guards in the Corrinthal horse-and-sun, each armed with a short spear, charged from the hall beyond and lunged at them. "Die, dog!" yelled the nearer guard.

Reht's shield turned the taller guard's spear point and knocked him off balance. Reht drove his blade into the guard's abdomen and up under his ribcage. The man dropped his spear and fell to his knees, eyes wide, trying to plug the hole in his abdomen with his hands. Reht kicked him to the floor to die.

Vors dodged the stab of the second guard and chopped downward with his axe, cutting the point from the spear and leaving the man with only a wooden haft.

Howling with battle madness, the war priest rushed the guard, drove him backward, pinned him against the wall, and head-butted him in the face. The guard's nose exploded blood and he sagged to the ground. Vors took his spear haft.

Boot stomps and shouts sounded from further within the manse. "More coming," said one of Reht's men.

Another explosion from outside rocked the house.

Vors grabbed the stunned guard by his long brown hair and shook him until the pain focused the man's eyes.

"The Corrinthal scion," Reht said to him.

Vors shook him by the hair. "Lie and you die."

The man's eyes flicked toward the wide, curving stairway visible in the room immediately beyond.

"You get nothing from me," the man said.

Vors circled around him and strangled the man with his own spear haft.

"Upstairs," Reht said, bounding forward. "I lead."

Shouts and screams pulled Kaesa from sleep. A boom sounded and the entire house seemed to shake. Clad only in a nightdress, she jumped from her bed, heart racing, and threw open the shutters of her small, second floor bedroom. She gasped at what she saw.

Flames from the burning barracks painted the sky orange. She could feel the heat even across the distance. Mounted men attacked the house guards as they escaped the flames through the barracks windows. Lots of mounted men.

"Lathander preserve us," she whispered.

Where was Mriistin? Lemdin the house mage? What was happening?

Her heart beat so hard against her ribs that she could not easily breathe. Shouts sounded from within the house and pulled her around. She heard the stomp of boots and shouted orders outside her door. Terror held her immobile. She fought for breath.

Her door flew open and she screamed.

Erthim stood in the door. Her Erthim. He held a bare blade and shield. He wore a shirt of mail but not his breastplate. Kaesa saw figures behind him but could not make out their faces. His men, she assumed.

She ran to him. "Erthim!"

"Kaesa," he said, his tone relieved.

He embraced her tightly but steered her away from the door. Wrapped in his strong arms, she allowed herself to think that all would be well.

"What is happening, Erthim?" she asked.

Shouts sounded from downstairs. Hostile shouts. She heard the ring of blades.

"Is that from the foyer?"

He held her at arm's length and spoke urgently. "Don a cloak and boots. Gather Elden and go out the back of the manor. Do not stop no matter what you see or hear. Do not try to get a mount. The stables are too far. Go on foot and try to get to the stag woods. Hide there until this is past."

She shook her head. She could not leave him, the manse. She started to speak but he cut her off. "Do as I say, Kaesa. Now. Do it for Master Corrinthal. We owe that to him."

Someone in the foyer screamed with pain. A wild shout followed it, more animal than man. Erthim did not turn around. His hands were tight on her shoulders. Tears formed in her eyes but she nodded.

"Take your dagger. Do not let them take you or Elden."

That brought her up short. "What?"

More combat from downstairs.

"They will . . . do things to him, Kaesa. He is Lord Corrinthal's son. Nod if you understand."

She stared into his eyes, nodded.

"I will come when I can." He embraced her again, hard. "I love you, Kaesa."

He released her, turned, and shut her door behind him without looking back. She heard him barking orders to his men.

She and Erthim had been courting for two months. He would have been her husband. She had not kissed him goodbye. She had not told him she loved him. She started for the door, stopped. He knew she loved him. He had to know.

Crying, she gathered her cloak, her shoes, the dagger she kept in a small sheath near her bedside. Her tears dotted the wooden floor as she moved about. Light from the burning barracks lit the room in flickering orange. The sounds of combat grew louder outside her room. It sounded as if the attackers were on the stairs. More shouts sounded from the grounds outside.

She kept as calm as she could. She had everything she needed. She ran through a side door, down the hall, and into the small room near hers where Elden slept when his father was away.

She opened the door to find his shutters open and the room bathed in the light of the barracks fire. She scanned the room, saw his bed, the side table, the wooden toys carved like horses, but she did not see him.

"Elden?" she hissed from the doorway.

She heard a soft moan and saw the pile of furs on his bed stir. She hurried across the room and gently lifted the covers.

He was curled up in the bed, eyes squeezed shut, arms around the tiny brown puppy he fancied from Dors's litter. He was humming to himself, as he often did when frightened.

"Elden," she said softly, and touched his leg. "It's Kaesa."

She felt his body release some of its tension but he did not open his eyes.

"Fore," he said, and Kaesa understood him to mean "fire."

Elden had been born dimwitted, with a body that answered his commands only awkwardly. Only those who knew him well—Kaesa, Regg, Lord Corrinthal, and Master Corrinthal—could understand all he said.

Kaesa had long considered him a gift from Lathander. What he lacked in wits he made up for in love. He was a lesson to all of them. The thought of something happening to him . . .

She sat on the bed and stroked his face with her fingertips. She had to calm him. He stopped humming, opened his eyes, and smiled.

"K'sa."

"Shh," she said, and touched his lips. His tongue stuck slightly out of his mouth, as it always did, and she playfully poked it with her finger. He giggled. Sleep had mussed his hair.

"It will all be fine, Elden. The men have the fire under control. No horses are hurt. And you and I are going on a trip. We will see your papa."

He perked up at that, brown eyes hopeful. "Papa?"

She nodded, hating herself for lying. "Yes. But we must leave right now. We are going to play hide and find in the stag woods." She took his hand. "Come now."

She tried to pull him from the bed but he resisted.

"Bowny come," he said, and held up the puppy for her to see.

It looked at her in the longsuffering way of all puppies.

She knew better than to dispute with him over the dog. He would have a tantrum.

"Yes, Brownie can come. Let's get you some clothes and shoes."

Sounds of battle carried through the walls. Elden's eyes widened with fear and he clutched at her. She embraced him, careful of the puppy, and stroked his back.

"It is all right, Elden."

She could not wait for him to calm down. Carrying him on her hip, she found his clothes, set him down, and hurriedly dressed him.

"Elden Corrinthal!" shouted a voice from somewhere down the hall. "Show yourself, boy!"

Elden squealed with fear. Terror gripped Kaesa. She was sweating, breathing too heavily.

"Forget the shoes," she said, and picked him up. She was able to carry him with ease. He was not a large boy, and fear lent her strength. The puppy nestled between them. She held her dagger in the other hand.

"Here we go, now. You must stay very quiet."

"Elden Corrinthal!"

She heard the thumps of doors being kicked open, the screams of those caught by the attackers.

She went in the opposite direction of the sounds, picking her way through quiet halls, parlors, and finally down the rear stairs to the dining hall.

"It will all be fine," she whispered to Elden.

Sobs shook him. She was crying, too. She had not noticed. "It will all be fine."

She hurried through the kitchen. Screams, shouts, and the light from the fire carried through the windows. Elden buried his head in her neck and whimpered. The puppy squirmed.

She looked out a window. She saw fighting near the barracks, men moving around the stables, and a few small combats here and there on the grounds. The wind blew embers and sparks from the fire, making the sky look aflame. Battle cries sounded from everywhere. The dead littered the grounds. Men on horses moved among the carnage, shouting, killing.

To Kaesa, it looked like an image of the Hells. She maneuvered Elden so he could not see it.

She looked out the window to her left and saw a clear path between the village and the stables. The fire cast little light there and patches of shrubs and trees would provide cover. If she could make it to the stag woods, she knew a place she could hide. They would never find her.

Her legs felt weak and she feared they would fail her. She was breathing but did not seem able to gulp enough air. Elden's fingernails gouged her skin. She asked Lathander for protection and said, "Here we go. Be silent, now."

She cut across the kitchen and down the rough stairway that

led to the large root cellar. The smell of spices and loam filled the air. She felt her way through the large, dark cellar until she reached the stairs that led outside. She climbed them, listened for a moment with her ear to the door. She heard only her heart, only her breathing. She shouldered open the door and ran. Panic lent her speed. She stumbled but did not fall.

A surprised shout greeted her exit. Someone had spotted her. A soft scream slipped between her lips. Tears flowed down her face. Elden held her so tightly around her neck she could hardly breathe.

"Stop, woman!" said a man's voice.

She did not stop, but she heard footsteps, heavy breathing, and the clink of mail behind her. Elden was crying on her shoulder. The men behind her—more than one—were closing.

She made up her mind. She swung Elden around in mid-stride, threw them both to the ground, and brandished her blade, intending to do what Erthim had commanded. She held her blade above her head.

"I am sorry, Elden."

Elden's innocent eyes went wide and he mouthed her name.

She hesitated.

A hand closed on her wrist and jerked her arm almost out of its socket. She screamed.

"I said *stop*, wench," growled a man's voice in her ear.

She felt a pinch in her back and lost her breath. Her vision went blurry for a moment. She looked at Elden, smiled, but he stared at her with terror in his eyes. She looked down, surprised to see the bloody end of a sword's blade sticking out of her stomach. Warm liquid filled her mouth. She tried to speak, to tell Elden that everything would be fine, but her voice failed her.

Elden screamed and Kaesa fell.

Reht exited the manse, bloody, tired, and pained with a few sword cuts. He would be damned to the Abyss, however, before he would stoop to asking Vors to heal him. The estate was secure. Corpses dotted the grounds. A few pigs, freed from their sties, rooted at the bodies. Reht's men moved about in groups of two and three, searching for survivors, collecting loot. A line of men, women, and children from the village sat in the grass, hemmed in by several of Reht's men.

The relative quiet, after the din of combat, was marked.

Reht had not found the boy. He did not relish explaining his failure to Forrin.

Smoke from the burning barracks had reached the stables and panicked neighs and stomps sounded from within. He could hear several horses beating against their stalls. He turned to the man nearest him.

"Get someone to calm those horses and get them out of the stables. All of them come with us."

Reht knew Saerbian horseflesh to be among the finest in Sembia. He would have at least something to show for tonight's slaughter. To another man, he said, "Get a headcount and report back."

Reht guessed he had lost fewer than a dozen men, but the combat had been so dispersed that he could have lost more.

Norsim and Rolk came around the corner of the house. Norsim roughly pulled a small boy along behind him. Spotting Reht, he waved his other hand.

"We have him, commander!"

Reht grinned like a fool.

"Norsim's luck has held," Vors said with a chuckle.

Blood and dirt covered Norsim's tabard. The boy stumbled along beside him, lunging from time to time for the small brown bundle that Norsim's companion, Rolk, held in his hands. Norsim shook the boy by the arm as he approached Reht.

"Be still!"

The boy cowered and was still.

"We caught him in the arms of a woman," Norsim said. "She called him 'Elden' before we finished her. And he's the face of an idiot."

Reht grabbed the boy by the chin and pulled his head up. Tears streaked his face. Fear filled his eyes. His eyes were too close together and his tongue stuck out slightly between his lips. His brown hair stuck out in all directions.

"Are you an idiot, boy?"

"Bowny back," the boy said through his tears, and pointed at the puppy Rolk held.

"What is your name?" Reht asked the boy. "Tell me and I will give you the dog."

The boy swallowed, looked from Reht to the puppy, back to Reht. "E'don."

That was good enough for Reht.

"Give him the dog," he said to Rolk.

Rolk held it out and Eldon reached for it. Vors snatched the puppy from Rolk's hands, grinned, and twisted off its head. He threw head and body at Eldon's feet.

"There he is, boy," the war priest said, and laughed.

Elden screamed in horror and threw himself against Norsim. He buried his face in Norsim's trousers and sobbed. "Papa," he wailed. "Papa, Papa, Papa."

"Your papa is never coming," Vors said, still laughing. "Never."

Reht lunged at Vors and punched him squarely in the face. The priest fell on his ass, blood pouring from his nose. He growled, spit blood, started to stand, but Reht put a blade at his throat.

Behind him, the boy's words deteriorated into incoherence, into an awful animal wail of despair.

"Get the boy out of here!" Reht said over his shoulder. He put his foot on Vors's chest and pressed him flat to the ground.

"One time is all you get, priest. Do something contrary to my orders again and you'll bleed from more than your nose."

Vors snarled, daubed at his nose, and grinned. He said, "This is the only time you point a blade at me and live."

Reht backed off a step.

"Raise that axe when you stand. Do it. I'll add you to the corpses."

Vors climbed to his feet, his hand on his axe. His eyes burned with hate but he did not raise his weapon.

Reht had figured as much. No one who tortured a small boy could be anything more than a coward when faced with a determined man.

"Bind the boy," Reht said to Rolk and Norsim. "Execute anyone still alive. Take the horses and whatever foodstuffs we can carry. We ride within the hour."

He still had a few hours of darkness left before sunrise. He wanted the dawn to find him and his men as far from the Corrinthal estate as possible.

CHAPTER TEN

26 Uktar, the Year of Lightning Storms

Cale sweated shadows. The spire loomed before them. The thick chains anchoring it to the basin creaked under the strain, a sound like muted screams. The spire appeared carved from a single block of rough black stone, as if a mountain had been uprooted, pared down, and hollowed out. Undead shadows clung to its sides like bats to the roof of a cave.

Thousands of malice-filled red eyes stared down at Cale, Riven, and Magadon as they approached. Below them, the churning sea of pitch vomited up another shadow. It streaked past them and took station on the side of the spire.

Cale could channel enough of Mask's power to control or destroy dozens of shadows, but he could not manage the thousands hugging the spire.

To Magadon, Cale said, *Mags, be ready with light.*

As much as you can for as long as you can.

Magadon nodded, eyes wide.

Before them loomed an archway large enough to accommodate the giants. Similar openings appeared on all sides of the spire. Two giants flanked the arch ahead of the three companions. Both wore helms and mail, and held bare swords as long as Riven was tall. Shadows clung to them and they eyed Cale, Riven, and Magadon with poorly concealed hostility.

Dim green light lit the smooth-floored chamber beyond the archway. A crowd of giants was gathering within.

As if on command, the undead shadows surrounding the sides of the spire swooped down in a long cloud.

"'Ware!" Riven shouted.

Riven, Cale, and Magadon had their blades up and ready but the shadows swooped past them and darted through the archway, for a moment blotting out the light coming from within the chamber.

They blew out a breath as one.

Esmor said to them, "There is nothing to fear here."

Cale almost laughed.

Murgan only glared at them in silence.

I hope you're certain of what you're doing, Cale, Riven said. *If this goes bad, it will go very bad.*

Cale was not at all certain of what he was doing. He had only a loose idea in his mind of what he would do when he saw Kesson Rel. He needed to see the lay of the room and Kesson's location in it. But he knew they would not get a better opportunity.

Just be ready, he said to Riven.

Riven nodded, murmured a prayer to Mask as they walked. His saber blades leaked shadows. He pulled his magical spell-storing stone from his belt pouch and tossed it into the air before his face. It stayed aloft and orbited his head.

"What are you doing?" Murgan asked, in the lazy tone of a dullard.

"Mind your own affairs, dolt," Riven answered.

They walked through the archway and into the round chamber beyond.

The eyes of two score giants fixed on them. Darkness trailed around the great creatures, just as it did from Cale. Undead shadows blanketed the walls. Cold radiated from them. Cale glimpsed a few dark-cloaked humans moving among the throng, their expressions sly. Immense archways before them and to their left and right opened onto adjacent corridors and chambers.

A mosaic on the floor formed a great purple circle ringed in black. The giants had taken care not to stand upon it. The purple disc motif reappeared throughout the assembled giants and humans on tattoos, necklaces, armbands, tabards, shields, holy symbols.

Cale recognized the symbol, though he did not understand its presence in the spire. Rivalen Tanthul had borne a similar symbol.

Shar.

Statues of the Lady of Loss, cast in dull black metal, stood around the perimeter of the chamber. Some showed Shar in her guise as a lithe human woman armed with daggers. Others showed her in a long cloak, her face hidden within a hood. Cale was reminded of the statues he had seen long ago outside the Fane of Shadows.

The ceiling soared above them to a height of fifty paces. A wide balcony of black stone jutted from the wall opposite them, about halfway up its height. A glittering purple cloth lay draped over the balustrade.

Cale, Riven, and Magadon stopped abruptly. Murgan pressed close behind them.

On the balcony, looking down on the assembled crowd, stood the man who had stolen divinity from the God of Thieves. He looked cast from metal himself.

Ivory bracers and earrings contrasted markedly with skin the color of obsidian. He stood a head taller than Cale and ribbons of shadow curled languidly about his form. Cale made him as a shade.

Black horns, curled like a ram's, sprouted from his bald head. His angular features showed no emotion as he unfolded membranous black wings and met Cale's gaze. His eyes were as dark as holes.

Shadows boiled from Cale's flesh. Weaveshear vibrated in his hand.

That is Kesson Rel? Magadon asked.

That is him, Cale answered.

A wild-eyed female gnome stood at Kesson's side, holding the hem of his leather cloak off the floor. Her long red hair stuck out in spikes. She shifted on her feet and eyed Cale, Riven, and Magadon with undisguised eagerness.

To Cale's surprise, he felt nothing. Not awe, not fear, not anger. Kesson was just another mark that Cale had been hired to kill. His pay would be Magadon's soul.

"Forward," Murgan said. "Stand in the shadow of the Divine One."

Esmor and Murgan ushered them in further and the rest of the giants crowded close. The humans standing amongst the giants—Cale guessed them to be priests of Shar—slithered through the crowd, encircling the three companions.

The trap would soon be sprung.

Silence fell in the chamber, save for the eager panting of the female gnome.

Cale let himself feel the darkness in the room, on the balcony. He drew it close to himself.

Ready yourselves, he said to his companions, and called to his mind the series of spells he would need to cast.

Kesson placed his palms on the balcony's railing and looked down on the trio. His voice was as smooth as glass. "I wished to look upon you two, the servants of the Shadowlord in this age. This I have done." He shook his head in feigned disappointment. "The Shadowlord has fallen far to choose such as you. He must be desperate indeed."

Riven spun his sabers. "Why don't you come down here, and we'll chat about that?"

Kesson smiled, showing fangs. The female gnome guffawed. The giants shifted on their feet. Cale could feel their eagerness.

"You have something I want," Cale said. "Give it to me willingly and I will not kill you."

Stand ready, Cale said to his companions. *Riven, you have the gnome. Mags, light—and lots of it.*

The giants laughed raucously. The gnome giggled uncontrollably. Kesson merely held his smile. "I think not."

"The hard way, then," Riven said. He spat on the symbol of Shar and ground it into the floor with his toe.

The giants murmured in anger. Huge hands went to huge hilts. They wanted only a command. Kesson's eyes narrowed.

Almost, Cale said. *Almost.*

"Kill these pretenders," Kesson said.

The moment the words left his mouth, the Sharrans incanted spells. The giants jerked their blades free of their scabbards and charged.

Now! Cale said.

He surrounded himself and his companions in darkness and rode it to the balcony. The gnome shrieked at their appearance and reached for the daggers at her belt. Kesson faced them, his face hot with anger, the words to a spell already on his lips.

A doorway off the balcony led into a large chamber beyond. Cale could not tell its function and did not care. Movement at the corner of his eye turned his head.

Hundreds of shadows peeled off the wall and swarmed toward them like a hail of arrows.

He called upon the darkness once more and pulled everyone on the balcony into the room beyond.

The moment they materialized, Riven drove both his sabers into the gnome's back and out her abdomen. Blood sprayed and she hissed with pain, eyes wide. He jerked the blades free and she fell to the ground, bleeding, dying.

A ball of light as bright as a noon sun formed above Magadon's head and lit the chamber. The pursuing shadows shrieked and stopped.

The illumination stung Cale's flesh, set his eyes to watering, and dissolved his shadow hand, but he hurriedly spoke the words to an abjuration.

Kesson, too, endured the light. He held out an arm to shield his eyes but continued to cast his own spell.

They stood in a long, wide hallway with rows of statues running its length on both sides. Like those on the ground floor, the statues depicted Shar. They looked stricken in the luminescence.

An elf woman with long dark hair and a shimmering blue robe stood on the far end of the hallway. She held a smooth, straight staff of black wood in her hand, and several wands hung from her belt. A bow was slung over her shoulder. Surprise stole whatever words she might have uttered.

Cale finished his spell before Kesson, and a circular line of silver energy expanded outward from him until it described the entire chamber.

The spell warded the room, making magical travel into and out impossible while Cale's spell remained. Cale would not be able to shadowwalk out, but neither would Kesson, and none of his servants could shadowwalk or teleport in.

Everything you have, Cale told Riven and Magadon. *And keep the light bright. I will seal the room.*

Kesson finished his spell and spun a long finger in the air. Thousands of magical blades, each about as long as a dagger, formed a ring in the air around him and spun like a cyclone. They reached floor to ceiling and moved so fast they hummed. Cale could hardly distinguish one from another. They caught two of the statues within their orbit and stone chips flew until the force of the blades' impacts toppled the images of Shar. They fell with a crash.

Green light flared around Magadon's head and a bolt of white energy shot from his palm, through the wall of blades, and struck Kesson Rel in the chest.

Kesson grunted and the force of the energy drove him backward a step. The smell of burning flesh filled the air.

The elf recovered from her shock, shrieked in rage, and incanted a spell of her own. A ball of shadows coalesced in her hand and she flung it across the room at Magadon. It hit the floor at his feet and burst into a viscous glob of shadows as thick as tar. The substance covered Magadon to his knees and affixed him to the floor. It started to ooze up his body, covering him in the gook.

"Cale! Riven!" Magadon shouted.

Help him, Cale said to Riven.

Cale had only a moment before two score giants found their way into the chamber. Clutching his mask, he shouted the words to his next spell. When he pronounced the last couplet, the magic created smooth gray stone from the air and Cale mentally molded it into a hemisphere that covered the entire chamber. All doors were blocked.

Magadon's light would hold off the shadows, and Cale's wall of stone would hold off the giants. At least for a time.

"You will not leave here," Kesson said. He incanted another spell, the words sharp and powerful, and pointed his finger at Riven.

"Die," he pronounced.

A black ray went forth from his finger. Moving to help Magadon, Riven never saw it coming and it hit him in the back. His face went white and he fell to his knees, eyes wide, mouth open, gasping for breath.

"You will suffer for this," the elf said, and leveled her staff at Cale. Blue lightning fired from the tip and tore across the chamber. Cale interposed Weaveshear, absorbed the lightning, and pointed the blade back at her.

The blade discharged the bolt and it hit her in the midsection, shattered her staff, and blew her backward against the wall. She fell to the ground, smoking from her clothes, the charred piece of her staff clutched in her hand.

Cale turned to look at Riven. *Riven?*

Cover your ears, Riven answered, as he climbed to his feet and uttered a single word of the Black Speech. With his one good hand wrapped around Weaveshear's hilt, Cale could not effectively cover his ears. Cale's ears rang and he felt a moment's dizziness. Magadon shouted with pain, but the word disintegrated the black substance holding the mindmage to the floor.

Behind him, Cale heard the elf woman intoning a spell. He turned, saw her casting from her knees.

She is mine, Magadon said.

The elf's speech turned to slurred incoherence and her eyes widened. She screamed and clutched her head. Blood poured from her nose, her eyes, her ears.

Behind his wall of blades, Kesson held forth his hand and an arc of unholy energy went forth from it. It hit Cale, Riven, and Magadon and tore holes in their flesh, cracked bones, bruised organs. They screamed as one.

Cale endured the pain, quickly scanned his friends to ensure they were alive, then bounded forward and stuck Weaveshear into the whirling blades. He grunted with frustration when the blade did not absorb the spell and the impact of the spinning blades almost knocked Weaveshear from his hands.

Kesson chuckled, spoke the words to a spell. Cale answered with a spell of his own. They stared at one another through the blades as they cast.

Kesson finished first. Another wave of black energy went forth from his palm, bypassed Weaveshear, and rent Cale's flesh. Gashes and sores opened on his arms, abdomen, and face, and blood poured from the holes. He stumbled over the words to his own spell, spat the final syllable, and summoned a column of flame that engulfed Kesson.

Riven appeared at Cale's side, pale but breathing, bloody

sabers in hand, and took him by the arm. The magical gem circling the assassin's head flared and healing energy warmed Cale's flesh and closed most of his wounds. Cale cast his own spell of healing and it mended the rest.

Kesson did the same, staring at them throughout. When he finished his spell, he looked whole again, and time was his ally. Cale had sealed out Kesson's servant creatures and prevented Kesson himself from fleeing. But Kesson had sealed Cale and Riven out with a curtain of whirling blades.

Kesson said, "This will end only one way."

His smile vanished as another energy bolt from Magadon slammed into his chest, charring his robe and skin.

"Give us what we came for!" Magadon shouted.

Kesson roared in answer and fired a bolt of yellow lightning from his hand. Magadon dodged too late and it struck him squarely in the side and spun him around like a child's top. He screamed. His clothes caught fire and he fell to the floor. His arms spasmed grotesquely and inarticulate grunts escaped his mouth.

We cannot do anything from out here, Riven projected.

Cale agreed. *See to Mags, then help as you can.*

Riven looked a question at him but Cale did not bother to explain. He sped across the room to the elf, casting a spell on the way that filled him with divine power. By the time he reached the elf's side, he was stronger, and half again his normal size. He sent her bow and quiver skittering across the floor to Magadon, then picked her up—to his surprise, she was still alive, though insensate—and lifted her onto his shoulder.

A floor-shaking boom sounded against the stone wall Cale had summoned—the giants were coming.

He looked across the room, saw Riven using the shadows to heal Magadon, and made up his mind. He inhaled, steeled himself, and ran at the blade barrier full speed.

Kesson's expression showed surprise, but he hurriedly moved through an incantation. He completed it before Cale closed the distance and a green beam as thick as an arm shot from his outstretched hand. Cale tried to sidestep it, stumbled, caught himself with a hand on the floor, but dropped Weaveshear. The beam would have hit him in the side, but instead hit the elf on her arm. The limb disintegrated into dust and the pain brought her around enough to utter a scream. Cale did not slow to recover his blade. The elf, perhaps sensing his intent, squirmed in his grasp, shouted at him to stop.

Cale used her body as he would a tower shield. He positioned her against him so that her body faced the spinning blades. They both screamed as he leaped through the blizzard of whirling steel.

Dozens of slashes rent his flesh, pierced his body, knocked him sideways. Her slight frame vibrated from the multitude of impacts she suffered. Blood sprayed them both. His own, hers, he could not tell.

They fell to the floor within the whirling wall of blades. Blood soaked the tatters of his clothes and flesh. He cast the elf to the floor beside him. She was little more than a pile of bloody rags and torn flesh.

He climbed to his feet, and Kesson was upon him. The Divine One clutched Cale's wrists and whispered dark words of power. Unholy energy poured into Cale's body, lighting him on fire with pain. Cale screamed, used his greater strength to hold Kesson's arms out wide, and kicked him in the chest. Bones cracked and the Divine One staggered backward.

Cale could not follow up. He sagged, barely able to stand. He quickly intoned a prayer of healing, the most powerful he knew, and winced as the spell knitted shut the scores of wounds in his flesh.

Kesson, too, incanted a spell. When he finished, he, like Cale, stood at half again his size.

"Shar's power is the greater, First of Mask."

"We will see," said Cale, and charged.

Kesson spoke a single word of such power that it stopped Cale in his steps and left him reeling. He tried to step forward, fell to one knee. The room spun. He could not get his bearings. He put his hand down to prevent from falling on his face. He knew he was vulnerable but he could not cause his body to answer his commands.

Kesson stepped forward and took him by the throat. Cale's eyes focused enough that he could see into Kesson's black eyes. He saw madness there.

The Divine One snarled and put a claw-tipped finger to Cale's forehead. There, he carved a bloody symbol into his flesh.

"Pain," Kesson said, and at the pronouncement, every nerve in Cale's body flared with agony.

He shrieked with pain, fell to the floor, and writhed. Every beat of his heart sent agony along his veins. Each time he drew breath, razors sliced his lungs. He heard a voice in his head but it demanded too much.

Get up! Get up, Cale!

His skin felt as if it were aflame. Kesson stood over him, brandished his metallic holy symbol of Shar, and uttered the words to a spell.

Cale welcomed it. He wanted to die, for the pain to end.

I will take some of it, Cale, projected Magadon.

Cale felt an itch behind his eyes and the pain diminished. Outside the barrier of blades, he heard Magadon wail with the pain he had taken from Cale. Cale tried to focus, tried to stand.

Kesson stared down at him, hate in his eyes, words of power on his lips. Cale's limbs would not respond.

Behind Kesson, Riven jumped through the wall of blades, Weaveshear in hand. He landed on his feet, bleeding from a score of wounds but alive. Kesson must have sensed him, started to turn, but it was too late. Riven drove Weaveshear into the Divine One's back and out his chest. Blood sprayed Cale's face.

Kesson looked down at the blade, his black eyes wide.

Riven twisted it once and jerked it free.

Blood poured from Kesson's mouth. He staggered, looked down at Cale, and . . . smiled.

Cale tried to utter a warning to Riven but could manage only an incoherent shout. He rose to all fours as Kesson whirled around to Riven and spoke a couplet of arcane words. The Divine One finished and shouted, "Away!"

The magic of his spell augmented the shout to such volume and power that even with Kesson's back to him, Cale felt as if knives had been driven into his eardrums. The power in Kesson's voice cracked the floor, shattered several of Riven's teeth, shredded his clothing, and drove him to the floor, flat on his back. Somehow the magical stone about his head survived the onslaught. Riven did not move. Blood dripped from the sides of his mouth, his ears.

Kesson recovered himself and intoned a spell to close the hole in his abdomen.

Another impact shook the wall of stone. Another.

Cale willed his legs solid under him.

Kesson incanted another spell and black energy engulfed his hand. On the floor before him, Riven's hand twitched. Kesson bent and reached for Riven.

Before he could touch the assassin, two arrows, both glowing red with energy, streaked through the wall of blades and sank into Kesson's flesh. He stood upright, reaching around his wings to clutch at the arrows.

Do something, Cale! Magadon said.

Cale did. He rose and rushed Kesson, stumbling but determined. He took the root of one of Kesson's wings in his hand and shoved the Divine One past Riven and toward the spinning blades. Kesson shouted with surprise, tried to flap his wings, tried to bury his heels in the floor. Cale grunted, leaned into him, leaned into Magadon's arrows, and kept him moving.

Kesson shouted and Cale heard fear in it. The Divine One reached back blindly with his spell-empowered hand and touched Cale at the waist.

The spell cracked Cale's ribs and ankle, rent the skin of his legs. Pain blinded him but he held on and pushed. But he was weakening.

Kesson resisted, held his ground.

Cale was falling, failing.

"Kill him, godsdammit!" shouted Magadon from a hundred leagues away.

Three more arrows streaked through the wall of blades but they hit nothing.

Cale grunted, pushed, but he could not move Kesson. The Divine One began to incant another spell. Cale shouted in despair.

Riven appeared at his side and slammed his shoulder into Kesson's back. His added strength was enough. The Divine One lurched forward.

"Push this bastard!" Riven grunted. The assassin used his shoulder to drive Magadon's arrow deeper into Kesson's flesh and the Divine One exclaimed with pain, losing the thread of whatever spell he had intended to cast.

Kesson roared with frustration and fear as Riven and Cale together held him by the wings and levered him toward the blades. Kesson could not stop them. The two were greater than the one. Desperate, Kesson tried to fall to the ground to stop their advance but they held him on his feet.

Kesson screamed and held up his arms as if to brace himself against the blades.

The storm of steel sent his fingers flying, his hands, his forearms. Kesson howled with pain. Blood, bone, and skin showered the floor.

"Yes!" Magadon shouted. "Yes!"

Cale and Riven roared in answer to Kesson's screams and pushed him farther into the blades. He squirmed but they would not allow him to escape.

The blades chewed up Kesson's arms, face, chest, and legs. A shower of gore rained on Cale and Riven. Soon they each held only the stump of a wing.

Kesson Rel was dead, his remains cast about the floor in glistening scarlet lumps.

Abruptly the wings and gore on the floor dissolved, melted like ice into nothingness. Cale and Riven stepped back, breathing heavily. The wall of blades, too, vanished.

Another boom shook the wall. Cale heard stone crack. He and Riven stared at one another.

"Why is nothing happening?" Riven asked.

Cale shook his head. He had expected a rush of divine energy, an explosion of power, something, anything.

Instead, nothing.

"Where is it?" Magadon shouted. He moved across the chamber, holding the dead elf's bow in his hand. His face was drawn and pale from taking Cale's pain. "Where is it?"

Cale looked at the floor, at his hand.

"All this," Riven said. "For nothing?"

A series of thuds sounded against the stone. It held, but the giants were trying something new. It was only a matter of time before they got in.

"We have to leave," Cale said, and Riven nodded.

But first Cale had to fix his broken body. He wanted to order Magadon to rid them of the light, to let his flesh regenerate in the darkness, but he knew darkness would invite the undead shadows. Instead he cast a powerful healing spell on himself. He groaned as his bones rejoined and wounds closed. Riven did the same. The assassin moved a few paces and recovered Weaveshear. He returned it to Cale, hilt first. Kesson's blood was not on it.

"Doesn't fit me," Riven said.

Cale took it, sheathed it. "Seemed to fit you fine."

"We cannot leave, Cale," Magadon said, and Cale heard despair in his voice. "You promised me."

"I know, Mags. I—"

Near Magadon, the gnome woman audibly groaned.

Magadon whirled on her. "She is still alive. She can tell us what is happening."

Cale and Riven shared a look as another impact shook the

stone. Cale intoned the words to a spell that placed a second stone wall behind the first, doubling its width. He had bought them some time.

They moved to the gnome woman's side. She rolled over and her eyes opened.

"Sit up," Cale said. "Do only what we say or you die."

She sat up, wincing with pain. She wore a necklace of dried eyeballs around her neck. Her teeth were as black as her heart. Blood stained her shirt and leather jerkin. She looked around the chamber, eyes wide.

"You . . . you killed the Divine One?" she stammered.

"Not so divine anymore," Riven said with a sneer.

"How is that possible?" she asked, dazed. "How can that be?"

Cale loomed over her. "This can be difficult or easy, woman."

Her expression hardened and she stared defiance at Cale. "I will tell you nothing, Maskarran."

Cale put Weaveshear's tip to her throat. Shadows swirled from the blade, circled her neck like a garrote. She eyed Cale with hate and Cale saw the fear behind it. He nodded at Riven.

The assassin moved behind her, pulled her to her feet, and held her with a forearm around her throat.

Her breath came fast. She swallowed reflexively. "I will tell you nothing," she said. "Nothing."

Riven tightened his grip on her throat and she gagged. He put his mouth to her ear. "I promise you that you will."

The gnome blinked, struggled. She looked like nothing so much as a trapped rat.

"I can compel you with spells," Cale said. "You will eventually succumb."

A boom shook the wall. Another. Another. The gnome shook her head. "I will resist. You do not have time."

"Then I will compel you with sharp steel," Riven said, his voice low and dangerous. "And you will succumb sooner."

To that, the gnome said nothing, but her skin whitened. Cale feared she might faint.

Cale said, "We will have what we came for. One way or another."

"Leave her to me," Magadon said, his voice cold.

"Mags . . ." Cale began.

"It is my soul at stake!" Magadon snapped, his eyes flaring.

Cale could not argue the point.

"Can you do it?" Riven asked him.

Magadon stared at the gnome. "Mephistopheles did not take power, Riven. He took conscience."

Cale and Riven shared a look. Cale said, "Do it."

"You are going to like this," Riven said to the gnome, and released her.

Before she could run, a red glow flared around Magadon's head. The gnome stiffened and she froze. Her eyes went wide.

"No," she said, her voice hushed.

Magadon advanced on her.

Her fists clenched. She gritted her teeth. "I will tell you nothing," she hissed, and shook her head. Spit flew.

"No, but you will show me everything," Magadon said, and his voice sounded deeper. Cale was reminded of Mephistopheles's voice and almost called a stop to matters.

Magadon loomed over her. With his horns and his demonic flesh, he looked the way Mephistopheles had looked standing over Magadon on Cania. Red light flared around his head, brighter than before. Veins pulsed in his brow.

The gnome screamed.

"I see," Magadon said.

The gnome's mouth hung open, spit suspended between her teeth, eyes wide and vacant. She made no sound.

Magadon reached down and covered her brow with his palm. At his touch, her body spasmed and she whimpered.

Cale and Riven looked at one another with concern but neither moved to stop the mindmage. They needed the information.

Cale imagined Magadon boring into the gnome's memories, peeling her mind open layer by layer. It could not be pleasant.

Magadon spoke. "Kesson Rel was infused by the Shadowlord with a shard of his divine power."

Cale nodded. He knew as much.

"Later, he defied his god and drank of the Black Chalice. He was named heretic by his fellow priests and cast out. Kesson secretly abandoned the Shadowlord for Shar and took the name Volumvax. Shar prevented Mask from retaking what he had given and Kesson Rel avenged himself on his fellows by bringing first the Hall of Shadows, then all of Elgrin Fau to the Plane of Shadow to die."

Cale nodded again. He knew Kesson Rel's crimes, but hearing them spoken aloud reinforced the magnitude of the murders.

Magadon continued. "To accomplish his work, he bound a dragon to his service. To bind the dragon, he was forced to use some of the divine essence given him by Mask. Kesson meant it to be temporary, but Kesson's fellow priests sacrificed themselves to cage the divine essence within the dragon. The dragon's name was Furlinastis."

Riven and Cale looked at one another and cursed in unison.

"Kesson sought the dragon for millennia," Magadon said. "To kill him and recover what he had lost, but he could not locate the beast. As the centuries passed, Kesson grew weak from his lack. Soon he had power only on the Plane of Shadow, then only in the Adumbral Calyx, then only in his spire."

The gnome shrieked. The tendons and veins in her neck stood out like ropes under her skin.

Cale had heard enough. Kesson Rel did not have Mask's divine spark. Furlinastis did. They had been on the wrong hunt.

"Let her go, Mags. We've got what we need. The dragon is our prey, now. And we know where to find him."

Magadon held onto the gnome.

"There is more here yet, Cale," the mindmage said, his eyes hard. "It's deep, but I can get it."

Magadon's pupils disappeared altogether. His eyes went solid white, like those of Mephistopheles.

"Enough, Mags," Cale said.

Magadon seemed not to hear him. Creases and veins lined his brow. The gnome screamed again. Magadon smiled. He was taking pleasure in exerting his will over another.

"Enough, Mags," Cale said. "We have what we need. We are leaving."

Magadon did not stop. The gnome started to shake. The blood vessels in her eyes popped, drenching them in blood.

"Mags, enough!" Riven said. "Enough."

The assassin took Magadon by the shoulder and pulled him away from the gnome.

Magadon snarled, whirled on Riven. The assassin had a blade drawn and at Magadon's throat so fast it was a blur.

"Slow down, Mags," Riven said softly.

The rage left Magadon's eyes. His pupils returned.

"All right?" Cale asked him, and put a hand on his shoulder.

"Yes," Magadon answered. "I'm sorry, Riven."

Riven lowered his blade, nodded.

Magadon looked back on the gnome, her small form gibbering on the floor. He looked away, regret on his face.

Cale said, "Don't give in, Mags. I understand your fight."

"You cannot," Magadon said, and offered no further explanation.

Cale could think of nothing more to say.

Another boom shook the stone hemispheres he had created.

"Lower the light," he said, and pictured in his mind the hill outside Elgrin Fau.

The light dimmed and shadows formed.

Cale breathed easier and his flesh began to regenerate. He recited the words to a counterspell and unwound the magic that prevented magical transport from the room.

The moment he did, patches of shadow clotted all over the room and giants materialized, blades in hand and violence in their eyes. No longer held at bay by Magadon's light, undead shadows streaked in through the floors, ceiling, walls.

Cale ignored them all, pulled the shadows about himself and his comrades, and rode the darkness to Elgrin Fau, leaving the Adumbral Calyx behind.

CHAPTER ELEVEN

29 Uktar, the Year of Lightning Storms

Dawn's light showed distant smoke on the horizon. The faint stink of it hung in the air. Saerb was still a few leagues to the east. The smoke was to the northeast, not from Saerb, but from the direction of the Corrinthal estate. Abelar did not call for a Dawnmeet. He stared at the smoke, his heart and mind racing.

"It cannot have been Forrin. We would have seen signs of his forces."

"Agreed," Endren said, and Abelar heard the concern in his father's voice.

Regg said, "It could be nothing more than a brushfire."

Abelar nodded but the expanding pit in his stomach belied the gesture. It did not smell like a brushfire. And even if Forrin's main body had not yet reached Saerb, he knew that an advance force of scouts or raiders could have attacked the estate. Forrin had already shown his willingness to target civilians.

Abelar, Endren, and Regg stared at the smoke in silence for a time while the company geared up. Abelar's hand went to his holy symbol. He chose to believe the smoke came from something other than the Corrinthal estate. He did not think Lathander would have granted the miracle back in the village, would have returned his father to him, only to have Abelar fail to reach his son in time. But belief did not chase his fears.

"Mount up," he said to his father and Regg, then called Jiiris to him. Her green eyes mirrored his fears back at him. She understood what the smoke might mean. Everyone did. Abelar held onto his emotions and kept his voice level.

"Ride on to Saerb. We're ahead of Forrin's main force. Endren, Regg, Roen, and I will take two score men to investigate . . . the smoke."

She nodded, reached as if to touch his hand, but stopped just short.

"I would rather accompany you, Abelar."

He shook his head. "No. Take the company to Saerb and organize an evacuation. Regg's father will be at Oakhaven, and he is ill. Send men to secure his safety. Then send word to the nobility that we are to muster on the western shore of Lake Veladon. Make sure they know that my father rides with us, that he is calling the muster."

Jiiris nodded. "And from there?"

Endren put in, "Depends on our numbers. And Forrin's. Once our forces are assembled, we'll evaluate."

Abelar said, "We will meet you there. Be wary, Jiiris. There may be raiders afoot."

She lowered her gaze, nodded. "I am sorry, Abelar."

He refused to acknowledge the implication of her words.

"Stay in the light," he said to her.

She looked him in the eyes, firmed up. "And you, my lord."

The company said its farewells. The bulk of the men moved east to Saerb. Abelar, Endren, Regg, Roen, and a score more headed northeast toward the smoke, toward the Corrinthal estate, toward Elden.

They pushed their mounts into a gallop. Abelar tried to keep alert for any signs of raiders but he could not focus. The grass and the trees blurred in his vision.

The men spoke little, and the silence was telling. Abelar felt numb, dazed. With each of Swiftdawn's strides, he felt a little more of him shaken loose. He could not stop imagining one horrible end or another for his son. Tears wetted his cheeks and he gave Swiftdawn her head. She pulled away from the rest of the group. Abelar heard his companions calling after him but he ignored them. He had to see. He had to know.

And he had to be first.

The smell of smoke grew stronger as he dashed through the grasslands and woods that he knew well enough to navigate in his sleep. Clouds masked the sun. Abelar's mouth went dry as he neared a familiar rise that would allow him to see the estate. He slowed Swiftdawn, topped the rise, and saw the destruction below him.

"No," he said, and the tears started anew. He had expected it, but expecting it did nothing to prepare him for the sight of it.

He heeled Swiftdawn and she tore off down the rise and toward the estate.

The gates lay flattened on the ground, trampled underfoot. Dried blood spattered the gatehouse. Flames had consumed the manse and barracks. Both were little more than blackened skeletons of wood and stone. They still radiated heat. The village stood unmolested, but unoccupied and ghostly. The stables, too, remained, but they were empty of horses. Abelar halted Swiftdawn near the gatehouse. He saw no bodies.

Perhaps most of them had fled. Perhaps Elden was safe in Saerb even now.

"Hail!" he called. "Anyone!"

A murder of crows, startled by his shout, took flight from behind the manse. Their caws mocked his hopes. His heart climbed up his throat.

"Abelar!" Endren called from behind him.

The rest of his companions had reached the rise. They, too, saw the destruction, the crows.

"Wait, Abelar!"

His companions thundered down the rise and over the plains, but Abelar did not wait. He had to see. He whickered at Swiftdawn and she walked him around the ruins of the manse. Spots of churned earth dotted the grounds; blood stained the grass here and there.

His people had not fled. They had fought. And fallen.

He rounded the manse to see a pile of corpses heaped behind it. Dozens of them. Arms and legs jutted from the pile. Empty eyes stared out at Abelar. They had been cast into a pile like so much offal. Perhaps the raiders had thought to burn them but changed their minds.

Abelar felt lightheaded. He clutched at Swiftdawn's mane to keep from falling.

A few stubborn crows still worried at the corpses, poking at eyes, pulling at scraps of flesh.

Taken with a sudden rage, Abelar leaped off Swiftdawn, drew his sword, and ran at the birds. They cawed and took wing before he reached them, one of them with a grisly strip of flesh hanging from its beak.

Abelar stuck his blade in the earth and sank to his knees beside the bodies. He saw familiar faces among the dead—Erkin, Silla, Wrelldon, Mern, many others. He wanted to look away, fearing he would see Elden's face staring back at him, but the pile drew his gaze like a lodestone.

"How could you allow this?" he said, and meant both himself and Lathander. "How?"

Endren, Regg, Roen, and the rest of the men rode up.

"Name of the gods," Regg oathed.

Endren said nothing, merely stared, stricken.

Both dismounted and walked to Abelar's side. Regg put a hand on his shoulder, Endren a hand on the other.

"Forrin dies for this," Endren said softly. "By all the gods, he dies."

Abelar nodded. His grief left no room for anger, but Forrin *would* die for it. He leaned on his sword and rose to his feet.

"We separate them," he said to the men. "I want to see my son."

None of his men made eye contact. All nodded. Endren looked away.

As one, the men set about the grisly work of pulling apart the death-stiffened bodies. They grouped them into men, women, and children.

"Bastards," Endren said throughout. "Bastards."

The men took care to place the bodies in the sunlight and most murmured prayers to the Morninglord as they worked. Abelar did his share but he felt dead himself. His mind turned to everything he had not done with his son, everything he had never said.

"They are only hours dead," Roen said.

Abelar had arrived hours too late. Hours. He nodded.

Regg said, "Brend, examine the tracks at the gates. Learn what you can."

Brend, dark-haired and only a head taller than a dwarf, was the most proficient tracker in the company. He hurried off to the gates.

The men continued to disentangle the bodies. They called out the names of those they recognized. Abelar looked up sharply when Regg spoke Mriistin's name. The old priest had served the Corrinthals and Lathander for over two decades. Abelar had first learned of Lathander from Mriistin.

Shaking his head to clear it of memories, Abelar turned over a woman's body—Kaesa, Elden's nurse. Her brown eyes stared up at the sky. Blood stained her cloak and nightdress. He called out her name, his voice as dull and gray as the sky.

Endren looked up, eyes troubled, no doubt fearing Elden's name would soon follow. He and Regg moved to Abelar's side.

"Poor girl," Endren said.

"Aye," Regg said.

Despair sat heavy on Abelar's shoulders. Kaesa had been like an older sister to Elden. She had been like a daughter to Abelar. He lifted her from the earth, carried her over to the rest of the dead, and laid her gently on the earth. He returned to the place where he had found her.

"Help me," he said to Regg and Endren, and the three men searched the bodies for Elden. Abelar's heart pounded with trepidation. Soon they had identified all of the dead.

"He is not here," Endren said.

"Could he have escaped?" asked Regg, a touch of hope in his tone.

Abelar shook his head. Elden went nowhere without Kaesa. He looked at the burned manse, imagined his son dying in the flames. He could not bear it. Tears flowed anew.

Regg took him by the shoulder and held him up. "Abelar, he could have run away in fear. He is small. He could be hiding somewhere."

Endren seized on the possibility. "Yes. Search the grounds. The stag woods are his favorite."

Abelar said, "Call for him, Father. He will answer you if he is there."

Endren looked at him curiously. "He will answer you, too. Come."

Abelar shook his head. "I must do something else first. I will join you apace."

Regg tapped Endren on the shoulder. "Come. We ride."

Regg, Endren, and the men mounted up and Regg issued orders about where to search.

"Roen," Abelar called.

"Commander?"

"Hold a moment. I need something from you."

Roen looked a question at him but slid off his horse. Meanwhile, Regg, Endren, and the rest of the company galloped off.

"Elden is not in the stag woods, Roen," Abelar said.

The tall priest kept his face expressionless. "Nothing is impossible, Abelar."

"No, it's not," Abelar said. "Pray with me, Roen."

"Commander?"

Abelar's eyes welled but he did not care. "Pray with me. We are going to ask Lathander whether Elden lives. I will have the word from him. Now."

Roen's expression softened. He put a hand on Abelar's shoulder.

"I will pray with you, Abelar. But I am unable to cast so powerful a spell as will allow me to commune with Lathander. I—"

Abelar knocked his arm down and gripped him by the shoulders, more harshly than he intended. "I am not asking you to cast a spell, priest! I am asking you to pray with me to our god for my son."

Roen looked at him wide-eyed, nodded. "Of course. I am sorry. Of course."

Abelar removed his hands. Softly he said, "I'm sorry."

"It is nothing," Roen said. "Come. Let us pray."

Together, the two servants of Lathander kneeled in the grass, under a gray sky, in the shadow of ruins and death. While the men of Abelar's company scoured the grounds calling for Elden, Roen and Abelar clasped hands and prayed to their god. Abelar laid his shield in the grass beside him, the rose facing the sky. They recited the traditional prayer together. "Dawn dispels the night and births the world anew. Morninglord, light our way, show us wisdom, and in so doing allow us to be light to others."

Roen continued. "Let your light shine through the darkness of the deeds done here and illuminate the hearts of your servants. Your faithful follower Abelar Corrinthal would ask you about the fate of his son."

Abelar squeezed his eyes shut. Tears leaked between the lids and flowed down his cheeks, into his beard.

"Please give us a sign, Morninglord," Roen said. "Show us whether Elden Corrinthal is alive or . . . not."

Abelar, head bowed, felt as if he were awaiting an executioner's axe. He dreaded a sign, but he had to have one. If Lathander could send a miracle to a village to heal a plague, surely he could spare a sign for one of his faithful.

Nothing.

"Morninglord," Roen said. "Your faithful servant humbly requests some small token—"

"A sign," Abelar said, his voice too loud, his tone too demanding. He opened his eyes. "Give me a damned sign. I have dedicated my life to you and asked for nothing."

"Abelar . . ." Roen said.

"Is he alive?" Abelar slammed his fist on the face of his shield. "Is my son alive? Tell me!"

"Abelar Corrinthal," Roen said, and put a hand on his shoulder. "Times of crisis are a test of our faith."

"My son is not a plaything for tests!" Abelar shouted.

Roen merely looked at him, held him by the shoulder.

The priest's unwavering touch and steady voice calmed him. Abelar remembered his words to Denril at the Abbey of Dawn. He had condemned the Risen Sun heretics for wanting Lathander to change the world for them instead of changing it for themselves. His voice broke as he said to his god, "I am not asking you to do my work. Please, Morninglord. I am asking you to show me the way. Please, show me the way!"

Roen said, "It is not always clear . . ."

The clouds above them parted and sunbeams drenched Abelar's shield, lit up the battle-scarred rose enameled on it.

"Look, Abelar," Roen said, his voice hushed.

Hope pulled Abelar to his feet.

The rose flared and the scars of countless combats vanished. It was made anew.

"Blessed light," Roen breathed, staring in awe.

"He is alive," Abelar said, and looked to the sky, to the sun. "Where, Morninglord? Where?"

A peal of thunder rumbled the sky to the east.

"East," Abelar said.

Roen stood, speechless, his hand on the holy symbol at his throat. He shook his head. "I have never seen . . ."

Abelar held the priest by the shoulder with one hand and held his sword aloft with the other. He caused it to flare with white light, bright enough to summon his riders.

"To me!" he shouted. "Now, to me!"

He lifted his shield and kissed the rose as his men tore back to him at a gallop. They gathered around him, questions in their eyes. Abelar looked into the eyes of his father, his men.

"Lathander has shown me that my son lives."

"There is no question," Roen said, a touch of awe in his tone. "I saw it myself."

The men murmured, whispered supplications and thanks.

"The sun rises," Regg said, and the men all nodded.

Abelar searched their faces for Brend. "Brend, speak of what you learned."

"Four score," the tracker said. "Perhaps a hundred. All mounted. They rode—"

"East," Abelar finished, and sheathed his blade.

"The tracks are less than a day old, Commander," Brend said.

Abelar nodded. "Eighty of Forrin's men have Elden. They must. And they may have others. No doubt they intend to rendezvous with the rest of their army as it approaches Saerb."

He paced a circle amidst his men, holding the gaze of first one man, then another. "I intend to stop them."

Nods around.

"I intend to rescue my son."

He looked at the burned ruins, at the bodies, and his heart hardened. "And I intend to punish every one of those riders for the crimes they have committed here."

More nods, scattered, "Ayes."

"We are only a score of men."

"But we stand in the light," one said.

"Aye," echoed Regg, nodding approvingly at the young warrior. "That we do."

Abelar nodded. "I'd have your swords with me but I will not order it. Any man may ride for Saerb and meet up with the rest of our company. There is no shame in it."

"Bah," said Regg, and turned a circle on Firstlight. "All are with you."

Abelar looked into the faces of his men, took their measure. None looked away. None looked hesitant.

Pride and hope lightened him. Lathander had provided him countless blessings, none more important than the men and women who rode with him.

"Roen, I want you with me," he said. "But a priest must see to the fallen."

Roen nodded. "Driim, see that the dead are laid to rest."

Regg added, "Knest and Morrin, you are Driim's hands."

"There is honor in that work," Abelar said, and Driim, Knest, and Morrin nodded, though they looked crestfallen.

Abelar whistled for Swiftdawn. She came running and he climbed into the saddle.

"The rest of us ride," he said.

"Like the Hells are at our heels!" Regg shouted. "Ride!"

Trewe blew a clarion blast and the entire company thundered off under the light of the noon sun.

Cale, Magadon, and Riven materialized on the rise overlooking Elgrin Fau. They said nothing. The task before them was too big for words.

Below, the ruins crowded close to the shadow-shrouded earth. The light from the gate flashed its mockery into the darkness. Cale imagined the army of wraiths gathered around it, waiting for word from him.

"They will want to know he's dead," Riven said.

Cale nodded. "That will wait. First, the dragon."

"Now?"

"We wait a day," Cale answered. "No longer."

He remembered Magadon's expression as he had opened the mind of the gnome woman. He remembered the words Magadon had said to him days before—*I am falling, Cale, slipping away with every moment*. He remembered the black streaks in Magadon's mindblade. He could not waste time.

He held his holy symbol in hand and cast one healing spell after another on his comrades. By the time he finished, they were mostly hale.

"Eat," he said to them. "Rest. Tomorrow will be harder than today."

Riven chuckled at that.

They camped on a rise overlooking Elgrin Fau. The next day they would face Furlinastis.

Gobitran's head felt like it had been hit with a warhammer. Each beat of her heart sent a stab of pain from her temples to the crown of her skull. Her ears rang like war gongs. She opened her eyes, tried to sit up, but the room spun wildly. She swallowed and tried to keep down her last meal.

The shadow giants were already gone. None had stopped to help her. No wonder, considering the tortures she sometimes put them through.

They had left her for dead, and she would have been so but for the magical iron ring she wore that regenerated her flesh. The Divine One had given it to her.

The skin of her scalp still tingled. She felt still the echo of the half-fiend's violation of her will, of his mental fingers rooting through her mind, sifting through her knowledge, sorting through her memories.

She had never felt anything like it before, but she had fought, had kept her secret tucked away in the dark corner of a dark hole, just as the Divine One would have wished.

She sat up, endured the nausea, and wiped the drool from her mouth.

The shadows coalesced in the room and the Lord Sciagraph formed from the pitch. His presence dominated her vision. His deep voice filled her ears.

"You have done well, Gobitran. You have well served both me and the Lady of Loss."

She licked her lips and crawled forward to clutch at the hem of his leather robe. She inhaled its smell, his smell. "You are Shar's Shadow, Divine One, and I am your servant."

"You preserved the secret? The mindmage discovered nothing?"

She pressed his robe against her cheek and turned her head to look up into his dark face. His black eyes looked down on her, pierced her. She wondered why he did not already know the answer. Surely he had scried the events in the chamber.

"He and the Maskarrans learned only what you wished, Divine One. They destroyed your simulacrum and think you dead. They know that Furlinastis the Cursed holds what is rightfully yours."

"How did they respond to that revelation?"

Gobitran looked up, not understanding the question. "Lord Sciagraph?"

The Divine One grabbed her by her topknot and jerked her off the ground to face him. She winced at the pain but dared not protest. The Lord Sciagraph's smooth, impassive features belied the anger in his eyes.

"I have sought the dragon for millennia. You have assisted in this in recent centuries." He shook her by the topknot and she swung like a pendulum. "How did they respond to the dragon's name? Did they know it?"

She did not understand how he could know so little. Was he not the Divine One, Shar's Shadow, the Lord Sciagraph? She tried to nod but could not. "Yes, Lord Sciagraph. They knew the name. The one-eyed Maskarran cursed when I named the dragon. The tall one knew the dragon and where he was to be found. He knew. Scry them, Divine One. See where the dragon has hidden from you all these years. Kill him and take back what is yours."

The Lord Sciagraph's eyes grew thoughtful and he dropped her to the floor.

"I cannot scry them," he said softly. "The Shadowlord cloaks them, just as he cloaks Avnon Des and the dragon. They cannot be found. They are ghosts."

His fist clenched and Gobitran bowed her head in fear of his anger. He said, "I can only wait, confined to this spire." He shook his head and placed his palm over the adamantine and amethyst holy symbol he wore on a chain around his neck.

"The servants of the Shadowlord trapped a part of me in the dragon. The servants of the Shadowlord must free it now."

"Curse the Lurking Lord," Gobitran said.

"It is appropriate that matters stand thus, Gobitran," the Divine One said. "The Maskarran will serve me in ignorance and when they realize their folly, their despair will be sweet to the Lady."

"I hear her voice in my dreams of darkness," Gobitran said.

The Divine One lifted her to her feet.

"As do I, Gobitran. Come, we must prepare. The Shadowstorm is at hand. My imprisonment is nearly at an end."

Hurried boot steps in the hallway carried through the study door. Tamlin looked up from his desk.

A brisk knock sounded on the door and Thriistin's urgent voice called out, "Hulorn! Hulorn!"

"Enter," Tamlin said, and rose from his desk. His hands shook. He crossed them behind his back as the door to the study opened.

Thriistin stood in the archway, breathing heavily, his gray hair mussed, his shirt partially untucked.

"What is it?" Tamlin asked, alarmed.

Thriistin spoke between gasps. "You must come to the walls, my lord."

Tamlin found his own breath difficult to draw. "The walls?"

Thriistin nodded. "The Saerloonian army is arriving."

Tamlin's mouth went dry. "Arriving? So soon? How? We have received no word of a march, merely a marshal—"

The bell of the Tower of Song rang, repeated peals that did not signal the hour but instead signaled a citywide alarm. The huge gongs of Lliira's Temple of Holy Festivals joined it and kept time. Soon all of the bells, chimes, drums, and gongs of the city's temples sounded in unison. Tamlin's heartbeat pounded in his ears more loudly than all of them.

"You must see for yourself, my lord," Thriistin said. "Lord Rivalen is already about."

Mention of the Shadovar ambassador helped calm Tamlin. He took a deep breath, steeled himself. "Captain Onthul and Rorsin have been notified?" he asked Thriistin.

"Captain Onthul, yes," Thriistin answered. "Rorsin, I do not know."

"Send a messenger to him immediately. Where is Lord Rivalen now?"

"The Khyber Gate, my lord. At Rivalen's order, all refugees at the gate were granted entry and it is now sealed. A carriage awaits you outside the palace."

"Very good," Tamlin said, and managed to keep his voice calm. "Go, Thriistin."

The chamberlain bowed and scurried off. The moment Thriistin turned the corner of the hallway, Tamlin took a moment to quiet his heart and compose himself. When he had a grip on his emotions, he quietly and quickly spoke the words to a series of spells that warded him against harm. He went to his desk, collected his weapon belt and rapier, buckled it on.

As ready as he would get, he put on a brave face and walked the halls to the carriage. A few servants within the palace watched him pass. They asked no questions—word must have spread already—but he saw the fear on their faces.

He stepped out of the double doors of the palace just as the warning bells of Temple Avenue rang their last. A lacquered carriage awaited him in the circular cobblestone drive. The driver stood beside the open door, awaiting him.

Tamlin took a step forward and his legs went weak under him. He caught himself on the stone banister that lined the wide stairway. The driver pretended not to notice. Tamlin gathered himself and descended the stairs to the carriage.

"My lord," said the driver, and assisted him in.

He climbed inside, wondering what in the Nine Hells he would see when he reached the walls. The driver took his position on the bench, slapped the four-horse team with the reins, and the carriage lurched into motion.

The moment he cleared the palace grounds, he perceived the fear and tumult in the streets. Squads of armed Scepters and Helms bustled down the avenues toward the walls, strapping or pulling on helms, vambraces, and gauntlets as they went. Fearful residents hurried through the streets, heads down, as if braced against a storm. Shopkeepers gathered here and there before their storefronts, speaking with animated gestures to their neighbors. Wagons and carts sped recklessly down the thronged roads. Tamlin's driver showed little interest in slowing for pedestrians.

"Do not run anyone down!" Tamlin barked at him through the window.

The rattle of the wheels on the cobblestones muffled the driver's reply but he slowed the team. Uncertainty filled the eyes of those who stared into Tamlin's carriage as he passed.

Presently they reached the Khyber Gate. Armored men and women, all bearing crossbows and blades, dashed up the gatehouse stairs and took station along the wall beside their fellows. Sergeants barked orders at them, moved along the forming lines. Artillerists manned the four swivel-mounted ballistae above the gate. Tamlin eyed the gates. Despite the spells, despite the added bands of iron, they still looked fragile to him.

Tamlin spotted Prince Rivalen atop the wall, staring out at the field beyond. A second Shadovar, smaller in stature, stood beside him. The darkness swirled around both.

Some Scepters near Tamlin shouted, "The Hulorn is come!"

Tamlin nodded at his troops and tried to appear unafraid.

Rivalen and his Shadovar companion turned and saw him. Where Rivalen's eyes glowed golden, the second Shadovar's eyes glowed like iron. Rivalen raised a hand in greeting and Tamlin answered likewise. The shadows swirled around both Shadovar and in a blink they stood before Tamlin.

"Gods, man," Tamlin said, startled.

Scepters around him cursed with surprise.

Rivalen bowed slightly and gestured at his companion. "Hulorn, this is my younger brother, Brennus. I summoned him the moment I received word of the Saerloonians' arrival. Shadovar troops are not yet available, but they are on the way. Meanwhile, I thought some assistance better than none."

Brennus's iron-gray eyes fixed on Tamlin. "Greetings, Hulorn. My brother speaks highly of you."

Tamlin felt himself color. "Well met, Brennus Tanthul. Any assistance is welcome, especially that of the Tanthuls. Prince Rivalen has been an invaluable aid to me."

Rivalen inclined his head.

"So I have heard," Brennus said.

Two tiny, gray-skinned creatures with eyes the color of Brennus's stuck their bald heads out of Brennus's black cloak. With their leathery skin and blunt features, they looked carved from clay. Tamlin recognized them as homunculi, tiny constructs.

"Greetings, Hulorn," they said in unison, their voices annoyingly high pitched. "We also are Tanthuls."

"My homunculi," Brennus explained. The naked, sexless creatures climbed his cloak and took perch on his shoulders. "I dabble in such things."

"Things?" the homunculi asked angrily. They stuck their tongues out at Brennus.

Rivalen studied Tamlin. "You are warded. That is wise."

"Not well, though," Brennus observed, likewise eyeing Tamlin up and down.

"Well enough for now," Rivalen answered. "There is time yet."

Tamlin did not ask how Rivalen and Brennus could have sensed his wards. The spellcraft of the Shadovar no longer surprised him. He felt inadequate before them—as a leader, as a mage, as a man.

"Come," Brennus said. "You should see your enemy."

Tamlin nodded, started forward.

Rivalen put a hand on his shoulder. "If I may, Hulorn."

Tamlin understood, nodded.

The darkness coalesced around them and Tamlin felt a sickening lurch. When the darkness parted, he found himself standing atop the wall, flanked by the Shadovar Princes. He wobbled for a moment before finding his balance. What he saw caused him to wobble still more.

On the field outside, beyond the range of any of Selgaunt's weapons, an army gathered. Hundreds of men stood arranged around Saerloon's standard. Tamlin could not see the details of the pennons in the distance but he knew Saerloon's symbol well—a single human eye of white, surrounded by a black border, with a pupil made up of two tall, slim gray towers with a gold key between them.

As Tamlin watched, another score of men under Saerloon's colors materialized from nothingness. Then another score, another, then another. He looked to the Shadovar for an explanation.

"A teleportation circle," Brennus observed. "Powerful magics."

"Cadellin Firehands?" Rivalen asked.

Tamlin did not recognize the name and Brennus shrugged. His homunculi mimicked the gesture. He said, "Possible. But Lady Merelith has the resources of the churches of Mystra and Azuth at her disposal. She is using them well."

Tamlin knew that temples of the Magister and Goddess of Magic stood in Saerloon. Anger rose in him, fed by fear. "Our priests ring their bells and cower in their cloisters while Merelith's transport her entire army to our doorstep?"

"So it would seem," Brennus answered, the darkness clinging to him. "She has avoided the need to feed an army on the march and has taken Selgaunt by surprise."

"Why has she not teleported her army into the city?" Tamlin wondered aloud.

Brennus answered, "The risk of an errant teleport would be high, with the quarters so close. Assembling her forces would be impossible. They would have battle before all arrived. No, she is doing exactly as she should."

Tamlin eyed the Shadovar prince sidelong. "Let us not admire her too much."

Brennus chuckled, showing ornamental fangs like Rivalen's. "Be content that I do not."

Rivalen's eyes flared gold and he turned to Tamlin. "Hulorn, if you wish it, I can call upon priests who will fight. A handful only, but powerful. They are priests of Shar."

Tamlin stared at him, considering.

Rivalen said, "Your own priests will balk. Even your people may."

Tamlin looked out on the Saerloonian forces, and back at

his own meager defenses. Another two score Saerloonian troops appeared from nothingness and fell in with their fellows. He made up his mind.

"To the hells with Selgaunt's priests. And I will quell any concerns among the people. Call your priests, Prince Rivalen. We need all available assistance."

Rivalen and Brennus shared a look and the shadows about them coiled. Rivalen inclined his head. "Of course, Hulorn."

Together, the three men, surrounded by the soldiers of Selgaunt, watched their enemies gather. Another teleportation point opened, another. There was little the Selgauntans could do.

Saerloon's soldiers appeared a hundred men at a time. Tamlin spotted the standards of a few mercenary bands among their number. Soon there were thousands on the field. The low murmur of the assembling army gathered volume as its numbers grew.

"She has emptied Saerloon of fighting men," Tamlin said softly.

The Saerloonians arranged themselves into loose formations as they absorbed the steady influx of newcomers. Shouted orders carried over the plains. Frequent rat-a-tats of company drums echoed into the night. Horns sounded from distant corners. Standard bearers planted unit, company, and city standards into the earth. Men gathered around them. Thousands of hostile eyes fixed on Selgaunt, its walls, it soldiers. Tamlin watched it all with a growing sense of dread.

Meanwhile, Selgaunt's troops streamed to the walls from other areas of the city and took up their positions. The clink of armor, the thump of boots on stone, and the shouted orders of sergeants and captains sounded all around them. Barrels of pitch and oil were positioned strategically. Men placed ammunition on the ground near them, within ready reach.

Tamlin felt himself in the center of a maelstrom. He found Brennus's homunculi staring at him, smiling.

Brennus said, "Teleportation circles do not allow for the transport of siege engines."

The observation gave Tamlin hope until Rivalen said, "She is no fool. She has something else in mind to breach the walls. Spells."

Tamlin could not imagine spells powerful enough to breach Selgaunt's walls, but he was only a mediocre caster himself. "When will they come?" he asked softly.

Rivalen said, "We will have battle with the dawn. They must know you have Shadovar allies. Merelith knows our power is diminished by the light of day."

The homunculi on Brennus's shoulders sparred with one another as if they wielded blades. Brennus took no notice of them and said, "Agreed. They come with the morn."

The shadows around Rivalen swirled, brushed Tamlin. He found their touch cold but oddly comforting.

"Summon your wizards to the walls, Hulorn," Rivalen said. "I suspect we will need them soon. And I will send word to the temple in Shade Enclave. My priests will be at Selgaunt's disposal."

Tamlin felt a rush of gratitude. He knew that Selgaunt's only hope lay with the Shadovar.

"Thank you, Prince."

CHAPTER TWELVE

29 Uktar, the Year of Lightning Storms

Tamlin sent messengers racing along the walls and back into the city to summon the score of battle mages Selgaunt had at its disposal. None were powerful casters. The most powerful practitioners of the Art had left the city long ago.

Onthul soon appeared, his towering frame wrapped in mail, a sword at his belt. He took the stairs of the gatehouse at a run and reached the top of the wall. His bearded face showed no expression as he gazed out on the gathering Saerloonian army. He turned to Tamlin and the Princes and inclined his head.

"Hulorn. Princes."

"Captain Onthul," Tamlin said. "How do we stand?"

"Four companies secure the docks to repel any attack by the Saerloonian navy. Four more are in reserve, though two of them are militia. The rest of our forces will mass here. Rorsin Soargyl and a company of Helms are wheeling the trebuchets up even now. We will place them there." He pointed to the wide cobblestone plaza behind the Khyber Gate.

"They are slow to reload," Brennus observed.

Onthul nodded. "We will get off not more than one shot each as the Saerloonians advance. Two if the enemy is slow. We will endeavor to make those shots count. Other than that, the fight will be at the walls. I've stationed barrels of pitch and oil along the walls, but there is less than I'd wish."

"And the rest of the walls?" Tamlin asked.

"Those in uniform but too old or young to be of much use with a blade are stationed at intervals around. They are to sound an alert if they notice anything coming from another direction. The reserve forces can respond quickly, if needed."

Tamlin looked out on the Saerloonians, uncertain. He disliked leaving the rest of Selgaunt's wall so sparsely defended.

"If this is a feint, Captain . . ."

Onthul followed Tamlin's gaze out to the plains.

"If Merelith has thousands of men to spend on a feint, Hulorn, then we are all dead men already."

Tamlin could not deny it. "It is not a feint," he said, and trusted that it was true.

"The seaways are secure," Rivalen said to Onthul. "No naval assault will occur. Use your men at the docks for another purpose."

"My lord?" Onthul questioned.

Tamlin remembered that Rivalen had promised to use the kraken to prevent Saerloon from approaching by sea.

"Do it, Captain," Tamlin said.

Onthul nodded, saluted, took his leave, and issued orders. He moved among the men on the wall, thumping shoulders, offering advice and encouragement, mocking the Saerloonians. Tamlin admired his calmness.

Soon thereafter the creak and clank of the approaching trebuchets sounded from the road below. A cursing Rorsin Soargyl, three score sweating Helms, and four teams of underfed oxen wheeled the wooden siege engines up the road. The machines looked not entirely unlike the cranes used to unload ships at the docks. Tamlin had never seen them fired. Sembia had never seen significant warfare on its soil. Three wagons rumbled behind the engines. Tar-sealed casks of alchemical fire lay within.

The two artillerists, both gray haired but not stooped, walked before the column and directed the men in placing the trebuchets. Several Scepters and Helms moved to assist; others cleared out of the way.

With the weapons in rough position, two younger men in service to the artillerists—apprentices, Tamlin assumed—climbed the gatehouse stairs to the wall, eyed the terrain, the likely approach for Saerloon's forces, and shouted down directions and distances to the other two artillerists. Those two, in turn, issued instructions to Rorsin and his men, who maneuvered the trebuchets into final position, removed stones from the counterweights to adjust for range, slowly cranked the throwing arm back, and locked them down.

Scepters unloaded the barrels of alchemical fire and placed them near the lowered slings. The apprentices remained in position on the walls as spotters, while the artillerists on the ground made final inspections and took station. They nodded up at Tamlin. Tamlin nodded back.

When the city's war wizards arrived—a collection of men and women ranging in age from twenty winters to forty—Tamlin dispersed them among the men. Tamlin did not want them massed, lest they all be killed at a stroke.

Within the hour the Shadovar priests appeared. Six of them stepped out of the darkness with no warning near Rivalen, Tamlin, and Brennus. The Selgauntan soldiers nearby shouted and drew their blades. Others whirled and leveled crossbows.

"Hold," Rivalen said, his deep voice booming, shadows swirling.

Tamlin echoed Rivalen's words, though the priests' sudden appearance had startled even him. "Stay your blades. These are allies."

Each priest wore black plate armor and a full-faced helm. Their eyes were holes, invisible under the guards. Shadows clotted around them.

Shades, Tamlin realized.

On tarnished silver chains around their necks, each wore a disk of onyx bordered with tiny amethysts—Shar's holy symbol. Each also wore a black cloak trimmed in fur. All of them wore twin short swords at their belts. They threw up their face guards—Tamlin noted two women among them—and moved before Rivalen.

"Nightseer," a tall, dark-haired priestess said, and bowed.

"Variance," Rivalen said. He looked to Tamlin. "These are the priests and priestesses I promised, Hulorn."

Tamlin summoned his dignity and said, loud enough for his men to hear, "I extend welcome to you all. You have my gratitude and that of the city."

The priests and priestesses turned and acknowledged Tamlin with a tilt of their heads. Some of the soldiers nearby grumbled. Tamlin heard the word "Sharran" muttered several times.

He looked around at his soldiers and shouted, "Forget what you may have heard of Shar. They are lies. These men and women have come to Selgaunt willingly, to stand or fall at your side. They have answered a request from me to Prince Rivalen. He, and they, have my complete trust. And so should they have yours."

Few eyes held his. The grumbling ceased.

Onthul nodded a welcome at the priests as he moved among the men. "You heard the Hulorn. Mind your posts and be thankful at least some priests stand beside you."

Many nods answered Onthul's words, grudging agreement.

Satisfied, Tamlin looked to Rivalen. "I would prefer to spread them among the men, Prince."

"Well conceived," Rivalen said. He looked to Variance. "Disperse among the men. Help as you may. Battle comes with the sun."

She nodded and pulled down her faceguard. Shadows collected around the priests and priestesses and they disappeared, materializing here and there along the wall.

Saerloon's forces, too, continued to materialize from the darkness, appearing out of nothingness like shades themselves. They burned no torches. Only the moonlight lit their ranks, glittered off their helms and spear points. The influx of men soon stopped, but the number of men that had come was enough to cause Tamlin's heart to thump.

"Six thousand, I would wager," Brennus said matter-of-factly.

"Closer to seven," Rivalen said.

Except for an occasional cough, curse, or prayer, quiet ruled the walls of Selgaunt. All eyes stared out on the field, on the Saerloonians. Tamlin fought a rising sense of dread. Dawn was mere hours away.

As the false dawn lightened the sky, two carriages rumbled up to the gates, wheels clattering. The doors opened and a contingent of eight priests exited. Ansril Amhaddan, the fat High Songmaster of Milil, led the group, flanked by Aumraeya Ulmbrin, the High Priestess of Sune. Behind them stood representatives of the other major faiths of Selgaunt: Denier, Oghma, Lliira, Lathander, Tymora, and Waukeen. All of the priests and priestesses wore the formal vestments of their faith. They spoke to nearby soldiers and the soldiers pointed up at Tamlin. The priests' gazes fixed on him, on Rivalen, on Brennus. They did not wave in greeting.

Tamlin descended the stairs and met them on the road behind the Khyber Gate, in the shadow of the trebuchets. The men fell silent around him. He felt hundreds of eyes on him.

"What is this, Ansril?" Tamlin said.

Ansril answered in his smooth tenor. "Hulorn, we are here to vehemently protest the presence of the Shadovar priests."

"Sharran priests," spat Aumraeya, her attractive face twisted into a scowl.

Before Tamlin could respond, the darkness around him deepened and Rivalen appeared at his side. Brennus appeared in the next breath. A murmur went through the Selgauntan priests and the men nearby. Anger twisted the priests' expressions. Behind the anger, Tamlin saw fear.

Ansril and Aumraeya looked at Tamlin and studiously avoided eye contact with the Princes of Shade. "I will not discuss this with you in their presence," Ansril said to Tamlin.

The shadows around Rivalen churned. His words had an edge like a sword. "Mind your tone, priest."

Before Ansril could respond, Tamlin said, "You will discuss it in their presence or not at all. I requested that Prince Rivalen summon such aid as he could. The Sharran priests and priestesses are here at my invitation."

The priests behind Ansril and Aumraeya looked appalled.

"They are Sharrans," Ansril said, as if that settled the matter.

"They are," Tamlin acknowledged. "And?"

"Is that not enough?" Aumraeya asked, eyeing Rivalen with contempt.

Brennus's homunculi gestured obscenely at the Sunite priestess. She glared at them.

"It is not," Tamlin answered.

"We are here to assist in the defense of the city," Rivalen said.

"To what end, Sharran?" Aumraeya snapped. "What secrets hide in the dark hearts of you and your goddess? What do you really want here?"

Rivalen did not move, but he seemed to grow larger. The

shadows around him churned. As one, the priests of the entourage backed up a step, eyes wide, hands on holy symbols. "I will remind you all only once more to mind your tone."

Tamlin held up a hand. "That is enough. You have made your speech. I have heard it. Leave now."

"Desperate times are no excuse to ally with darkness, Hulorn," Ansril said, eyeing Rivalen and breathing heavily.

Tamlin lost patience. He stepped forward and glared into Ansril's face. He spoke in a voice loud enough for all nearby to hear. "Nor is politics an excuse for cowardice. The Sharrans you hold in such contempt are willing to fight and die beside the soldiers of this city. You are not. They man the walls while you cower in your temples. They stand shoulder to shoulder with our soldiers while you slink about in your carriage. You would not have even used the powers granted you by your gods to feed the people of this city had I not ordered it."

The soldiers around him nodded, mumbled agreement.

Ansril gulped. Aumraeya blanched.

"You mischaracterize us," she said. "We do not cower. Matters are complex. You, of all people, should understand that."

Tamlin could not keep the contempt from his voice. "I understand that you have failed me and this city. I understand that you are wasting my time while an army prepares to assault these walls."

Ansril said, "Hulorn, we have fellow priests in Ordulin, in Saerloon, in Urlamspyr. We cannot war against our brothers and sisters in faith. Surely you must—"

Tamlin cut him off. "Did you come here to fight, Ansril, or to explain why you will not? I have no time for the latter."

"Hulorn," Aumraeya said. "You are most—"

Tamlin could no longer bridle his tone. "Begone from here! Now! Before I have you arrested! I have heard all of the excuses I need to hear."

Aumraeya looked as if she had been struck. "Arrested?"

One of Brennus's homunculi chanted, "Arrested, arrested."

Ansril regarded the little creature, Brennus, Rivalen, and Tamlin. He stuttered, finally managed, "There is nothing more for us to say, I see. Come, Aumraeya."

The priests turned around and stalked back to their carriages. Tamlin watched them go, his anger unabated.

"Where is Vees Talendar, I wonder?" asked Rivalen casually.

Before Tamlin could consider the question, a drumbeat from the Saerloonian forces carried over the walls and reminded the men of their business.

"Back to work, lads!" shouted Onthul. "Nothing more to see. Back to it."

As the priests' carriages moved off, Brennus spoke softly to Rivalen and Tamlin. "Ansril or one of the other priests may do something foolish in their anger."

"We do not trust him," whispered the homunculi conspiratorially.

Rivalen met Tamlin's eyes and Tamlin saw in the Shadovar's expression that he did not trust Ansril either. Rivalen said, "Hulorn, he could communicate the composition of our forces to other priests of his faith outside of Selgaunt. Any of them could. If that information were passed to the overmistress or Lady Merelith, it could damage our cause."

Tamlin shook his head, trying to get his thoughts ordered. Too much was coming at him. He had meant the threat to arrest the priests as more bluster than promise. He said, "I do not think Ansril or any of the priests are traitors, Prince."

"I have seen it before," Rivalen said.

Brennus added, "You need not arrest them, merely put them under . . . observation in a controlled setting."

Tamlin pondered. Ansril was impulsive, and Aumraeya had been red-faced with anger. They could do something foolish. They might regret it afterward, but once done, it would not be something that could be undone. He made his decision, and summoned Onthul to him.

"Hulorn?"

Tamlin looked the tall guard captain in the eyes. "Send men to round up and detain the priests of the temples of Milil, Sune, Oghma, Deneir, Lathander, Tymora, Waukeen, and Lliira."

Onthul's eyes widened. "Imprison them, my lord?"

Tamlin shook his head, glanced at Brennus. "No. Detain them, lest one of them do something . . . rash. Hold them within my palace. Disarm them, but see that they are comfortable."

Rivalen said, "Tell them you are converting the palace to a battlefield hospital, Captain Onthul. Tell them you are consolidating the priests there to maximize their ability to heal the wounded."

Tamlin nodded. "But they are not to leave, Onthul. And the only spellcasting they are to do is in healing the wounded. Your men have the authority to enforce that edict with steel. Do you understand?"

Onthul did what soldiers did. He accepted his orders. "Yes, Hulorn."

"Trusted men only, Captain Onthul. Experienced men. This is a grave matter."

"Of course, my lord. I have a force in mind."

Tamlin patted his captain on the shoulder and Onthul moved off. When he was gone, Brennus said, "You have done the hard thing but the right thing, Hulorn."

Rivalen put a hand on his shoulder. "You have come far, Tamlin."

Tamlin nodded. He may have done the right thing, and he may have come far, but he still felt dirty.

"Something is happening!" a Scepter shouted from atop the walls.

"Here they come," Rivalen said.

Abelar drove Swiftdawn as hard as he dared. Her flanks heaved under him and sweat foamed her coat. Regg on Firstlight kept pace, but barely. The terrain flew past them in a blur. They stopped periodically to allow the horses a drink and to allow Brend to verify the tracks of the horsemen they pursued.

"They make no effort to hide their passage," Brend said, examining the ground. "I could track them from horseback at a full gallop. They are headed due west, riding hard."

Back to the main body of Forrin's troops, Abelar knew. If Abelar did not catch them soon, they would face not a raiding force, but an entire army.

"We ride harder," he said, and put his heels into Swiftdawn. She reared and tore off across the grasslands. The men followed.

Regg shouted at him over the beat of hooves. "They took Elden to draw us out, Abelar. Or to use against you as a negotiating tool in a forced peace. They will not harm him."

"The overmistress does not want peace," Abelar answered. "And she, or her niece, may want nothing more than to hurt my father and me by hurting Elden. I will not have it, Regg. I will not."

"Nor I," Regg answered.

Several hours later they spotted their prey ahead. The four score raiders rode in loose formation and crested a rise, perhaps half a league ahead of them. Abelar could not make out any details, but he knew Elden was among them. He had to be. Lathander had led him to his son. He said nothing to his men. All of them could see what he saw.

"We are riding out of the sun," Regg shouted to him over the thunder of hooves.

Abelar nodded. That they were.

They lost sight of Forrin's riders the moment the last of them rode over the rise. Abelar whispered to Swiftdawn to give him everything she could and she answered. Abelar knew they were closing the distance. Lathander would not have brought him so far for nothing.

When they topped the rise, he saw the eighty riders galloping east on the grasslands below them. But that was not all he saw. Not half a league ahead of the riders rode a handful of scouts, and behind them, stretching out in a long, dark column of steel and flesh, rode the main force of Malkur Forrin's army.

Abelar halted atop the rise and the rest of the men did the same. Swiftdawn snorted, flanks heaving. The rest of the horses gulped air and whinnied.

Endren unleashed a stream of epithets and Regg did the same.

Forrin's force rode in a line perhaps thirty riders wide. Supply wagons rumbled along in the rear. Shields, armor, and blades caught the setting sun and glinted orange. There were over a thousand men.

The raiders did not know they had been pursued but Forrin's scouts saw Abelar's force. A few pointed and three of them whirled their horses around and sped back to the main body. Another blew a signal on his trumpet while he awaited the approaching raiders—the raiders bearing Abelar's son.

Abelar unslung his shield, drew his blade.

The raiders met up with the scouts, swirled around them. Heads turned to look back on Abelar and his force. Abelar scanned the raiders, looking for Elden. He did not see him, but the riders were too distant for him to make out details.

"Do you see him, Regg? Father?"

Regg leaned forward in the saddle, shook his head.

"It is a blur to me at this distance," Endren said.

"Anyone?" Abelar shouted to his men.

All shook their heads but Roen, known for his sharp eyes. "I think I see him, Abelar. He is slumped in the saddle before another rider. I cannot be sure, but—"

"That is him," Abelar said, his heart on fire.

Trumpets sounded from Forrin's main force even before the retreating scouts reached it, and the entire formation halted. Two thousand eyes looked up at Abelar and his two score men. The raiding party galloped back to the main force and merged with it. The distance prevented Abelar from distinguishing one rider from the next.

"I cannot see him any more in that mix," Roen said.

"Why do they hesitate?" Regg asked.

"They're wondering if we have an army behind us," Endren said.

A breeze carried the faint sounds of shouted orders up the rise and the leading elements of Forrin's army shifted into a wider, looser formation, as if in preparation for a charge. Two hundred cavalry formed a broad line as their commanders moved among and along them, shouting orders. Meanwhile, the rest of Forrin's force slowed and started to arrange itself into a defensive crescent.

Abelar kept his eyes on the raiding party, but they melted into the main force. He could not tell where Elden might be. He looked for Forrin, assuming Elden would be taken to him but to no avail. He saw groups of men here and there that he assumed to be commanders, but he could not tell one from any other. He would not be able to find his son until he was in their midst.

"Line the men, Regg," Abelar said, and tightened the strap on his shield. Swiftdawn whinnied.

"Abelar?"

"Single rank. Tight spacing."

Regg looked away, back at Abelar, said softly, "Abelar . . ."

Abelar turned to look at his friend. "Line the men, Regg. Now. Tight spacing."

Regg stared at him for a moment and Abelar did not like the doubt he saw in his friend's eyes.

"We are forty men," Regg said, and nodded at Forrin's troops. "They are a thousand."

"You state the obvious."

"It seems I must. You will not see it."

Another clarion sounded from Forrin's force.

Anger gave Abelar's voice a hard edge. "I see it. But I also see Lathander's hand in it, just as clearly. It is as it was with the village and the plague. If we keep faith, he will deliver us. We will charge in, seize Elden, and ride out." He looked to Trewe. "Trewe, sound a blast."

Trewe dutifully put his trumpet to his lips.

"Hold, Trewe," Regg said, and held up a hand.

Swiftdawn snorted. Firstlight whinnied in answer.

Trewe hesitated.

Abelar stared at Regg, his anger building. "Are you countermanding my order?"

Below them, Forrin's forces sounded a trumpet blast. Regg did not look away from Abelar. Abelar did not look away from Regg.

"This is madness," Regg said. "Stop and think. You will kill us all. Endren, assist me."

Endren nodded, said, "Abelar, they are too many. For now. We can return to the muster at Lake Veladon. With an army—"

Abelar glared at his father. "They are not too many! There cannot be too many! My son is captive in there! My son!"

Endren's eyes softened. "I know. He is my grandson. I love him. But you are *my* son, Abelar, and they are too many."

Abelar could not believe his ears. First Regg, then his own father. Swiftdawn turned a circle, sensing his agitation.

"The men are with me. They will follow me."

"I know," Regg said softly. "That is why I cannot allow you to lead them down the rise."

"Then I will do it alone!"

Regg heeled Firstlight before Swiftdawn, blocking her. "You will not."

Abelar stared at his friend, a man who had saved his life, a man whose life he'd saved. His hand tightened on his sword hilt. Regg held his eyes, his jaw set.

"Move aside, Regg."

Below, two hundred of Forrin's cavalry started to trot toward them. The horses in Abelar's company, sensing battle, pawed the ground, snorted. The men drew their blades.

"They are with me," Abelar said. "Look."

Regg shook his head. "We go back to Lake Veladon, regroup."

Abelar stared at Regg and spoke in a low tone. "I will cut my way through you, Regg. For my son, I will do it."

Hurt flashed in Regg's eyes. He blinked but his jaw remained set. "You will regret those words when you reflect on them."

Abelar heeled Swiftdawn and she butted against Firstlight. The two horses, sisters, snapped at each other.

"Move aside, Regg." Abelar looked past his friend to Roen. "Roen, tight formation."

Forrin's forces started at a gallop.

Roen made no move to obey his order.

"You mean too much to the men," Regg said. "Too much to Sembia."

Abelar heard the truth of Regg's words but did not care. "Neither matters more to me than my son."

Regg nodded again. "I know that."

Abelar's eyes welled but he refused to let the tears fall. "Lathander did not bring me—us—all the way to this point only to turn back. He would not do that, Regg. He would not. Roen, ready the men, damn it!"

Tears in Regg's eyes answered those in Abelar's. "But he did, Abelar. I hope you will forgive him. And us."

He looked past Abelar and nodded.

Something hard slammed into the side of Abelar's head, just behind his ear. Pain and flashes of light exploded in his brain. He had a vague sense of falling, arms catching him. He thought he heard Elden crying, calling to him as everything went dark.

Forrin watched his cavalry under Enken ride after the small force of horsemen atop the rise.

Reht, Vors, and Norsim sat their horses near him. They had delivered the Corrinthal boy, who sat double on Norsim's horse. The boy's vacant gaze and slack mouth pronounced him as simple.

"Is that Corrinthal?" Reht asked, looking back to the rise. Something close to admiration colored his tone.

"We will know soon enough," Forrin said.

"Picked up our trail after we burned his estate," Norsim said.

Reht shook his head in disbelief. "Forty men hunting eighty and standing to face a thousand? It must be Abelar Corrinthal, from all I've heard."

"Come to get you, boy," Vors said, and smacked the Corrinthal boy in the side of the head.

The boy exclaimed in pain but made no response.

The horsemen atop the rise turned as one and rode out of sight.

"Not standing, after all," Forrin said, satisfied.

"There goes your father," Vors said to the Corrinthal boy. "Running away. He doesn't want you, boy."

Elden's eyes focused a bit. He looked up at the empty rise. "Papa?"

Vors laughed, showing his stained teeth. Reht's stare cut the war priest's mirth short and the glare each cast at the other told Forrin that something had passed between them.

"Sound the halt," Forrin said to one of the trumpeters near him. "Bring them back."

Forrin would not waste time chasing forty men. He wanted to get to Saerb and do what he had come to do. He had Corrinthal's boy, as the overmistress had instructed. If Corrinthal mustered an army to rescue his son, Forrin and his men would welcome it. Meanwhile, Saerb would burn.

"Are you sending the boy back to Ordulin?" Reht asked.

Forrin nodded. "Eventually."

Reht eyed Vors, then Forrin. "I will watch after him until then."

"No," Forrin answered. "You are going to lead the attack on Saerb."

Ordinarily, Forrin would have had Lorgan lead the assault,

but Lorgan was holding with his force to the south of Saerb, with orders to clean up anyone trying to flee. Strangely, Forrin had received no word from Lorgan recently.

"I will watch him, then," Vors said, and smiled maliciously at the boy.

Reht opened his mouth as if to protest, then appeared to think better of it.

"Keep him alive unless I say otherwise," Forrin said to Vors.

The war priest nodded. "Alive, yes."

"You'll answer for his treatment," Reht said.

"Answer to whom?" Vors said with a sneer. The war priest grabbed the boy roughly by the arm and pulled him from Norsim's horse and onto his own. The boy cried out and tears fell from his dull eyes.

"I want Papa."

"Shut your mouth," Vors said.

The boy whimpered and did exactly that.

"Commander," Reht said. "I would ask—"

Forrin cut Reht off. "The boy is no longer your concern. We hit Saerb tomorrow. You lead the assault. Burn it and kill anyone left in the city."

Vors licked his lips and chuckled at Reht. Reht's face remained expressionless.

"The men may balk," Reht said.

Forrin knew. "Tell them it is vengeance for Yhaunn."

Reht nodded.

Forrin said, "I do not care if there is an army. I do not care if they fight or surrender. Save anything of value and kill or burn the rest. The overmistress wants an example made. Make it."

Vors howled at the sky and Elden Corrinthal sobbed, his small body shaking, his hands buried in the horse's mane.

Reht glared at Vors a final time, saluted Forrin, and rode away.

CHAPTER THIRTEEN

30 Uktar, the Year of Lightning Storms

Rivalen and Brennus drew Tamlin into the darkness and transported him to the top of the walls. Dawn lightened the eastern horizon, casting the sky in red and orange. Tamlin looked out onto Saerloon's massed forces. They looked even more imposing in the growing light. Hundreds of standards flapped in the breeze. Thousands of spear points glinted in the sun. The Saerloonians stood arranged in a thick line, twenty ranks deep, a rectangle of flesh and steel.

Onthul paced among the men. "Here we go now, lads. Here we go."

The two armies regarded one another in eerie quiet. The wind stirred the drought-dried grass. To Tamlin's right, the waters of the Elzimmer glittered in the rising sun.

A small group of twelve men and women emerged

from the Saerloonian lines. They bore blades at their sides and wore no armor, not even helms.

"Spellcasters," Tamlin said.

Rivalen and Brennus nodded.

The Saerloonian wizards formed themselves into a large circle. All of them moved through a variety of complex gestures and incantations. Their spell chants carried over the plains. Tamlin could not make out the words.

"Protective spells," Brennus said. "And divinations."

Two of the wizards, both older and paunchier, stepped within the circle and intoned spells of their own. Their voices sounded the complex couplets of powerful spells. Energy gathered.

"A summoning," Brennus said.

"The battering rams, at last," said Rivalen, and Tamlin wondered at his meaning.

"Can we do nothing?" Tamlin asked.

"Not at this range," Brennus answered. "Best to wait and learn what comes."

The spells reached a crescendo and ceased. The Saerloonian drummers beat a slow, steady beat, then . . .

The earth rumbled, groaned. Outside the circle of wizards, ahead of the foremost lines of the army, the soil rippled, churned. Towering forms lurched from the rock and dirt in an explosion of grass and soil.

"Earth elementals," Rivalen said.

The Saerloonian army cheered and raised spears toward the sky as the huge creatures rose fully upright.

Composed mostly of soil and rock, with odd bits of sod and roots sticking from their forms, the elementals stood five or six times the height of a man. They stood on legs as thick as tree trunks, with arms the width of a man's waist. Misshapen heads perched atop uneven shoulders half as broad as their height. Their bellows sounded like a landslide.

"Dark and empty," Tamlin breathed. There were seven of them. Their heads were level with the top of Selgaunt's walls. He could well imagine what the creatures' powerful arms and rocky fists could do to the city's fortifications. And he had no illusions about what they could do to a man who stood in their way.

The two summoners within the circle of wizards gestured at Selgaunt. All seven elementals turned to face the city.

A nervous murmur ran through the city's defenders. Many of the militiamen rose and looked as though they might flee. The professional soldiers in the ranks ordered them down. Tamlin understood their fear. He tried to control his breathing.

"Trebuchet and crossbows as they come, lads," shouted Onthul, and he shook the trebuchet spotters to steel them. He stalked along the walls, nodding. "If they can walk, they can be knocked down. Steady, now. Steady."

"Ordinary crossbows are useless against such creatures," Brennus said softly.

His homunculi squeaked and darted into the safety of his cloak.

"What do we do?" Tamlin asked Rivalen.

Rivalen kept his eyes on the field. "The magic that holds them on our plane can be ended with a counterspell. It is not certain, but it can work. But they must be closer."

"They will be closer soon enough," Brennus said.

Tamlin shouted out so that his war wizards and the Sharran priests could hear him. "Counterspells on the elementals as they near. The magic will unbind them."

"*May* unbind them," Rivalen corrected.

Brennus pointed at the field. Despite daybreak, shadows swirled around his outstretched arm. "More to come, still."

The summoners moved through another series of spells and when they finished, a dozen towers of flame sprang into being amidst the earth elementals. The flames weaved and darted with obvious purpose.

"Fire elementals," Rivalen said.

Brennus said, "Merelith intends to tear down the walls and burn the city."

Tamlin said nothing, merely stared, heart pounding.

The fire elementals' tops reached only to the earth elementals' waists. Their forms ignited and consumed the grass near them, leaving nothing but charred earth. Black smoke and storms of glowing embers spun into the sky from each creature.

Tamlin had prepared the city for the possibility of flaming projectiles. Scores of men and women stood ready in various quarters of the city, armed with buckets, barrels of water, and shovels for hurling dirt. But he had not expected flaming creatures that could burn with purpose and intelligence.

"Onthul," Tamlin shouted to his captain. "Alert the bucketmen."

Onthul nodded, grabbed a messenger by the shoulder, issued him a series of curt orders, and sent him off.

One of the wizards forming the circle broke ranks and stepped near the fire elementals. He wore a red robe and his proximity to the fiery creatures appeared to do him no harm. The wizard moved through the gestures of a spell and when he finished, he and two of the elementals vanished.

The Selgauntans murmured, looked nervous questions at one another.

"Where did they go?" Tamlin asked. He was in water too deep, and he knew it.

A few moments later, the conjurer reappeared alone amidst the remaining elementals. He began to cast a spell.

A shout from the walls drew Tamlin's attention.

"Look! There!"

Men pointed back into the city. Tamlin turned to see the Hulorn's palace beginning to burn. One of the elementals that had vanished with the red-robed wizard moved methodically along its roof, leaving a trail of flame in its wake. Elsewhere, smoke rose from within the Noble District.

"He is teleporting the elementals into the city," Rivalen said.

Tamlin cursed. He knew weapons did little against fire elementals.

"Issger, Rheys," Tamlin shouted to two of his war wizards. "Put down those elementals."

The mages nodded, cast spells of flight, and launched through the air toward the palace.

"The fire elementals are a distraction," Brennus said.

"A good one," Tamlin snapped in irritation. "I cannot let the city burn."

A rumble from the field turned his attention back to the Saerloonian lines. All seven earth elementals lurched into motion and lumbered toward the walls. Their steps shook the earth and the sound of their approach was the rumble of an earthquake. Their motion flattened the grass, crushed trees, and left huge indentations in their wake. They started ponderously but gathered speed quickly, charging at the walls with such force that Tamlin could not believe the walls could withstand the impact.

A small inn, long abandoned, stood in their path and they crushed it underfoot, leaving little more than splintered timbers. Saerloonian drums beat time with their approach.

"Trebuchets, ready!" Onthul shouted, and the barrels of alchemical fire were loaded into the trebuchet slings. One of the spotters raised his hand, waiting until just the right moment to give the command to fire.

The walls vibrated under the approaching onslaught. The elementals closed the distance, raining dirt from their forms.

"Steady!" Onthul ordered, and crouched behind a battlement. "Steady!"

Halfway between the Saerloonian lines and Selgaunt's walls, before the spotter gave the order to fire, the earth elementals melted into the ground and merged with the soil. They left no trace of their presence.

Tamlin knew earth elementals could move through soil and rock the way men move through air.

Curses ran through the men. Selgauntans leaned over the walls to look down. Seeing nothing, they eyed one another with panic.

"Where are they?!" shouted some.

"They will come up under the walls!" said another.

"Hold your ground, men of Selgaunt," Onthul shouted. He stood and walked the walls, blade in hand. "Hold your ground."

Sergeants echoed his words and killed the rising panic. The men held their posts. Long, tense moments passed but the earth elementals did not reappear. The drumbeats from the Saerloonian army ceased.

"What in the Hells?" Tamlin asked.

Brennus intoned the words to a spell and gazed down on the earth before the walls as if he could see through it. "They are there," he said to Rivalen and Tamlin. "They are waiting."

"For what?" Tamlin asked.

"Our nerve is being tested," Brennus said.

Tamlin feared he would fail the test. He could hardly breathe.

Saerloonian drums began to beat anew, slowly at first, but gathering tempo.

The red-robed wizard incanted another spell and vanished from the field along with two more fire elementals. Eyes turned back to the city to see where the elementals would appear. A young soldier near Tamlin pointed up into the sky, toward the bay.

"There! Gods preserve us!"

Gasps and oaths sounded from all along the wall. Tamlin looked into the sky expecting to see fire elementals, but what he saw was much worse.

A huge green form bore down on the city from out of the sky. Even from his distance Tamlin could see the creature was enormous. Vermillion scales glittered in the sunlight. Huge, leathery wings stretched from its sinuous reptilian form. Terror went before the creature in a palpable wave. It roared and Tamlin's breath left him entirely.

"Merelith has a dragon," Brennus observed.

His homunculi cursed.

Cale, Riven, and Magadon awoke, ate in silence, and checked their gear.

"I think every arrow in this quiver is enchanted," Magadon said, examining the arrows he had taken from the elf woman in Kesson's spire. "I have never seen such craftsmanship. Look at these."

He held one up for Cale and Riven to see. To Cale, it looked like any other arrow.

Riven chuckled. "It's an arrow, Mags, not a woman. Don't get so attached to it you won't let it fly."

Magadon stuffed the missile back into the quiver. "You need not worry about that."

Cale figured they were as ready as they could be. "Link us, Mags. And see through my eyes."

Magadon, the circles under his eyes as dark as the shadowy air, nodded. A burst of orange light haloed his head and a faint hum sounded. Cale felt the tickle under his scalp, behind his eyes.

Done, Magadon projected.

"We play it as a feint and finish," Cale said.

Riven nodded. "Like old times."

Cale donned his mask and cast a series of spells in rapid succession. He warded himself, Riven, and Magadon against the dragon's life-stealing breath. He enchanted his armor, increased his strength and speed, and finally summoned unadulterated power directly from Mask. When the spell's energy filled him, the shadows around him deepened. He grew to twice his normal size, gained the strength of a giant. Riven watched him throughout.

"Put the same spell in the stone," Riven said to Cale, and withdrew from his belt pouch the small spell-storing stone he had taken from the Sojourner. He tossed it into the air before his face and it took up orbit around his head, whirring softly.

A year ago, Cale would not have considered sharing such

a spell with Riven. He had been too protective of his unique relationship with Mask. No longer. He and Riven were the First and Second, the Right and Left. They had killed Kesson Rel together. He cast the spell and Riven's stone absorbed the energy.

Come when I call, he said to them.

Riven held up his ringed finger. "We'll be there."

Magadon concentrated for a moment and a sheath of mental energy formed around his body. He took an arrow and nocked it in the bow he had taken from the elf in Kesson Rel's tower. The arrow's tip flared red as his mind charged it with power.

I will be watching, Magadon said, and Cale felt the tingle in his eyes that indicated Magadon was seeing what Cale saw.

Cale imagined Furlinastis's swamp in his mind, pulled the shadows about him, and rode them there. He materialized in the fetid shallow water of the swamp, Weaveshear in hand. Sickly, brownish fog floated around his knees. The stink of decay filled his nostrils. He heard none of the usual shrieks, howls, or buzzing of insects. The swamp was silent.

Furlinastis was near.

He tested the mindlink to ensure it was working at his unknown distance from his companions.

Mags, Riven?

Here, Riven answered.

Here, Magadon said. *And I see what you see.*

He's near, Cale said.

Shadows and fog walled him in on all sides. Stands of broad-leafed malformed trees jutted from the bog. Cale did not see the dragon. Furlinastis was as much shadow as Cale. He could be anywhere.

A hiss and the sound of a whispered incantation sounded from Cale's left. He chose a random stand of trees fifty paces away and stepped through the space between shadows. He materialized in the trees, but not before the spell took effect and stripped him of every ward and enhancement spell he had cast.

He cursed, shaped the shadows around him into illusory duplicates of himself that mimicked his every move. He looked back in the direction from which he had heard the dragon cast its dispelling incantation.

He saw nothing. His breath came fast.

The dragon's a spellcaster, he said to Magadon and Riven. *My wards are gone.*

Riven cursed. *Get clear, Cale. We'll rethink it.*

A soft splash from behind him whirled Cale around.

He had only a fraction of a heartbeat to process the sight of an onrushing mountain of scales, claws, teeth, and shadows before the dragon's gargantuan form buried him, his shadow duplicates, and the entirety of the copse of trees.

Tamlin fought his fear enough to utter the words to a weak spell as the dragon neared. He pointed his hand at the dragon and four bolts of orange energy streaked from his fingertips, hit the dragon's scales, and bounced off harmlessly. Bolts of lightning, a beam of gray energy, and a series of silver orbs streaked into the air on the heels of his spell but none seemed to harm the onrushing dragon.

Beside him, Brennus and Rivalen incanted spells of their own as the dragon closed. A black beam went forth from Rivalen's hand and hit the dragon in the chest. Several scales shattered and rained down on the city. The creature roared with anger and pain, beat its wings, but did not slow its approach. A green beam shot from Brennus's finger, hit the creature in the wing, but did no harm that Tamlin could see.

The men around them shouted, screamed, pointed, cowered. Onthul tried to maintain order, called for crossbows, but his commands went unheeded. The dragon angled itself lower, streaked directly for the walls. The Saerloonian drums beat so fast they sounded like one long, loud hum.

The fear that accompanied the dragon intensified and drove Tamlin to his knees. Some of the men cowered in their positions on the wall. Others jumped down in their terror and shattered legs and ankles. A few tried to run for the gatehouse, knocking others down, trampling them. The dragon roared.

"Disperse!" Rivalen shouted down at the men in the streets. "Get back! Spread out!"

Brennus and Rivalen began to cast again. The dragon roared, swooped over them, opened its mouth, and exhaled a thick cloud of green vapor. Rivalen and Brennus completed their spells. Tamlin felt a hand on him, felt his body shimmer into mist. The screams and shouts sounded far off. The walls around him appeared to be only gray shadows. Rivalen and Brennus stood beside him.

"The ethereal plane, Hulorn," Rivalen said. "The dragon's breath cannot affect us here."

Tamlin saw the shadows of men near him writhing in pain, clutching at their throats, digging fists into their eyes.

"Put an end to the conjurer bringing fire elementals into the city," Rivalen said to Brennus. "Then summon Yder."

"The earth elementals?" Brennus asked.

"Variance and the priests, as best they can."

Brennus nodded. "The dragon?"

"I will handle the dragon," Rivalen said, and his golden eyes flared. "Prepare yourself, Hulorn."

Sound and substance turned solid as Rivalen took them back across the planar barrier. Men lay about on the walls, the ground. Some screamed. Others gagged, vomited. Hundreds lay still. An acrid, stinging stink hung in the air. Tamlin's eyes watered.

Behind Tamlin, the city burned. Around him, fully a third of his men lay dead or incapacitated. As he watched, shadows clotted here and there on the walls and the Sharran priests stepped from the darkness.

"Variance!" Rivalen called to one of the Shadovar.

The darkness around Rivalen churned and the tall priestess appeared before him. She threw up her faceguard.

"Handle the earth elementals when they come, and protect the Hulorn," Rivalen said. "If he comes to harm, you answer to me."

She looked at Tamlin, at Rivalen. She nodded and lowered her faceguard. The shadows swirling around her brushed Tamlin.

"What are you going to do?" Tamlin asked Rivalen.

In the sky above, the dragon flew over the Saerloonian army and started to wheel around.

"Kill that green," Rivalen said. He jumped from the wall and took flight.

Meanwhile, Onthul's voice boomed over the chaos. The tall captain strode the battlements, rallying the men. His voice was a croak, whether from gas or shouting, Tamlin did not know.

"You can die fighting on your feet or crawling on your stomachs. How will you have it? Up and ready crossbows! Get on your damned feet!"

A few hundred of the reserve units rushed up from within the city. They looked at the carnage with wide eyes. Onthul shouted at them to take station on the walls and replace the fallen.

Out on the field, the red-robed wizard stood before the remaining fire elementals, preparing to teleport them into the city. Brennus watched him closely, hands ready, the words to a spell sitting just behind his lips. When the red-robed wizard disappeared with the fire elementals, Brennus hurriedly recited his spell and smiled. "I have him," he said to Tamlin. Darkness swirled around him and he disappeared.

With the fire elementals clear of the field, the Saerloonian trumpets sounded a march and the entire army lurched into motion.

"Trebuchets!" Onthul shouted.

The spotters, still alive, peeked over the wall and raised his hand. On the ground below, three of the four trebuchets remained manned. Replacements hurried in.

"You are a spellcaster?" Variance asked Tamlin. Her voice sounded stilted behind her faceguard.

Tamlin nodded.

"Can you cast counterspells?"

Again Tamlin nodded.

"Ready them," Variance said.

A rumble shook the walls and the earth elementals exploded out of the ground in bursts of rock and dirt. Their heads reached the top of the walls. Tamlin stared into the blank, blunt-featured face of the one nearest him. It did not seem to notice him.

The elementals bellowed, raised their arms to the sky, and smashed huge, rocky fists into the sides and tops of the walls. The impact shook Tamlin from his feet. The Khyber Gate rattled on its hinges. Dust, men, and rock flew into the sky. A thin crack opened along the wall near Tamlin. Another. Men shouted, screamed. Vats of oil shattered, soaked the walls, and burst into flame. Tamlin heard Onthul barking orders through the smoke and chaos. Crossbows twanged and bolts sank into the elementals by the dozen.

The Saerloonians shouted, moved double quick. The Selgauntan trebuchets fired and huge, sealed vats of alchemical fire arced into the sky. The impact would shatter the wooden vats and the viscous fluid would ignite upon contact with the air.

It would not be enough, Tamlin knew. He was watching Selgaunt fall. The siege of his city would not last months. It would last hours.

He decided to die fighting on his feet. He faced the nearest elemental and started to cast a counterspell. While he intoned the words, he saw the vats of alchemical fire hit the ground and explode in flame and heat. One landed short of the Saerloonians and lit the plains on fire, but three landed in the midst of the army and turned men to torches.

The huge elemental took notice of him. It bellowed, raised its fist high, to smash Tamlin or the wall or both. Tamlin completed his counterspell and his magic warred with the power of the summoner of the elemental.

And lost.

Tamlin stared, frozen, as the elemental's fist descended. Darkness gathered around him.

"Not here," Variance said, and transported him away before the elemental could crush him.

Brennus appeared in the center of a wide, cobblestone avenue. The red-robed wizard stood in the middle of the street, his back to Brennus, flanked by columns of living flame twice his height. The flames crackled but there was order to the sound, and Brennus knew it to be the elementals' language.

The few pedestrians on the street fled in panic. An underfed donkey tied to a hitching post bucked and kicked, terrified, but could not free itself. Its cries of fear rang down the street.

Behind Brennus, powerful impacts reverberated through the city. The attack on the walls had begun in earnest.

The wizard uttered a command, pointed to his right and left, and the elementals moved to nearby buildings and lit them aflame. Muffled screams sounded from within.

Brennus incanted the words to a spell that would prevent the wizard from teleporting. The wizard heard him, whirled. His eyes widened at the sight of Brennus.

"Incinerate him!" the wizard called to the elementals, and ran for the cover of a nearby wagon as he started to cast a spell of his own.

The elementals left off the buildings and raced toward Brennus like wildfire, leaving trails of flame in their wake.

Brennus ignored them, finished his spell, and fired a thin green beam from his outstretched finger. It hit the wizard in the side. The spell did not harm him, but a field of pale green flared around him. The wizard cursed and aborted his spell, knowing that he was prevented from using magical transport. He had intended to transport himself out of the city.

The elementals charged into Brennus and engulfed him. His world turned orange; the elementals' crackling voices sounded loud in his ears. His wards entirely shielded him and his homunculi from the heat and flame, but the protective spells would not last long under the elementals' onslaught.

He held out his hands and shouted the words to a counter-spell. His power engaged that of the summoner and overpowered it. The binding that held the elementals to the Prime Material Plane unwound and the creatures disappeared with a soft pop and a puff of smoke.

The wizard stared at him. He recognized that Brennus had overpowered his summonings with ease. He started backing away down the street, intoning a spell. Brennus walked after him, reciting the words to his own spell.

Heads poked out of windows.

"He banished the elementals!"

"He saved the city!"

"But what of the dragon?"

Brennus ignored the accolades. The summoner finished his spell, joined his thumbs, and blew on his hands. His spell amplified his breath, turned it frigid, and blasted it toward Brennus in a freezing sheet.

Brennus's body, infused with shadowstuff, resisted the magic of the spell and he endured the ice without harm. Completing his own spell, he pulled the summoner's palpable fear from his head and let the magic turn it against him in the form of an illusion.

Brennus did not see what form the illusion took, at least not clearly. He saw only a large shadowy form looming over the summoner. Its face suggested a muzzle; horns or large ears jutted from its head. The wizard collapsed to the ground on his knees, mouth open, eyes wide.

"Do not touch me!" he screamed to his fears.

Brennus's illusion reached out a muscular arm that ended in a pincer. It touched the summoner and he gasped, clutched his chest, and died. His fears blew away in the breeze.

Brennus walked over to the donkey. Its wild eyes rolled in its head and it backed off to the limit of its tether, but it was too exhausted to do anything more. Brennus reached out a shadow-shrouded hand, stroked its head. "There, now," he said.

His homunculi emerged from his robe and bit through the tether. The donkey turned and tore off down the street.

More and more heads poked out of windows and doors, all looking at him, back at the walls, up at the sky for the dragon. They wanted a savior and he had given them one. Rivalen would be pleased.

Through his ring, he reached out his mind for his brother Yder.

Come now, he said, and Yder returned a quick acknowledgement.

Brennus dared not transport himself blindly back to the walls, for fear he could materialize in a maelstrom. He did not know what damage the earth elementals had done. Using shadows as stepping stones, he worked his way back to the Khyber Gate.

The impact of Furlinastis's body drove Cale so deeply into the soft earth that the hole might as well have been a grave. The dragon's weight crushed him. His ribs shattered, his arm broke, his ankle. Pain lit a spark shower in his brain. He heard the dragon's roar, muffled by the mud that encased him.

Free us, said voices in his mind, and he knew them to be those of the souls trapped in the dragon's shadow shroud.

Cale? Magadon said, his voice tense. *Cale?*

He could not respond. He hung onto consciousness through force of will. Drawing on the darkness around him, he transported himself out from under the dragon. He appeared in another stand of twisted trees, a bowshot behind the dragon. Mud caked his cloak and trousers. He whispered the words to one of his most powerful healing spells and the magical energy reknit his bones. The shadowstuff in his flesh worked at the rest.

I am all right, he said to Magadon and Riven. He stood perfectly still and tried to control his breathing. His mind raced through his options.

Furlinastis reared back his long neck and cocked his head.

"I hear your heart, priest." He whirled his girth around with alarming rapidity. Shadows boiled around the dragon, faces formed, pleading with Cale.

"This is not as I would have it," the dragon said. "But one of us must die."

Cale did not bother to parse the meaning of the dragon's words. He invoked a spell that summoned a column of fire and immersed the dragon in flame. The spell appeared to cause no harm as the huge reptile roared and took flight out of the conflagration. The beat of his wings sent a gale of flames rushing across the swamp toward Cale. Trees and scrub shriveled in the heat. Cale ducked behind a tree and the firestorm did him no harm.

Airborne, the dragon pronounced a single eldritch word and the fog and shadows around Cale swirled, merged, and partly solidified. Cale could still breathe but could not see past his hands, and the fog resisted his movements as well as water. He knew what to expect next, even before he heard the beat of the dragon's wings above him and the inhalation of breath.

He frantically drew on the darkness to get him clear, but he was too slow. Furlinastis exhaled with a roar and the deadly, life-draining black vapor saturated the magical fog. Cale dived for a low spot in the earth but the fog stubbornly resisted his movements. The cold of the dragon's breath prickled his skin, entered his body through nose, ears, and mouth, and siphoned off much of his soul. He weakened; some of the power he used to cast spells drained away. He shouted with pain and rode the shadows to another stand of trees.

Riven's voice sounded in his head. *Cale?*

Cale could hardly breathe. *Soon,* he answered, and leaned on a tree to keep his feet. *Stand ready.*

Rivalen watched the huge green dragon wheel in a wide arc. Its scales glimmered like emeralds in the morning sun. The same sun felt like needles on Rivalen's exposed skin. With an effort of will, he dimmed the light around him and flew toward the dragon, cloaked in shadow.

Below him, he saw the Saerloonian forces advancing through trebuchet fire on the double quick. Behind he heard the elementals, the world-shaking crash of their fists on the city's walls.

The dragon completed its turn, saw him approaching, and roared. It spoke a series of arcane words, beat its wings, lowered its neck, and arrowed straight for him. The moment the great reptile flew within range, Rivalen intoned the words to a spell that pit his will against that of the dragon. He had used a similar spell to cow a kraken. Few could resist its power.

The moment he completed the spell, the arcane energy rebounded on him, shaped by the dragon. He had only a moment to process the event—the dragon must have cast a protective abjuration that rebounded spells back on their caster, or perhaps bore a ring imbued with that power.

The power of Rivalen's own will twisted back upon him, tried to make him subservient to the dragon. His own voice sounded in his head.

Remain still and do not resist.

Magic made the words a compulsion. He fought it but his body went slack. He stopped in mid air and hovered. The dragon beat its wings, loomed larger in his sight. He could not move.

Roaring, the dragon exhaled a cloud of corrosive green gas that engulfed Rivalen. The gas burned his skin, melted his clothes to his flesh, and sheathed him in agony. The gas did not dissipate, as Rivalen expected. Instead it clung to him, continued to burn, to melt his flesh. He screamed as skin sloughed from him and rained down on the plains below.

Pain focused his mind. He fought his way free of the will-dominating spell a moment before the dragon's enormous form careened unharmed through its own breath and crashed into him.

The impact shattered bone, drove him backward through the air. The dragon followed up and deftly snatched him in a claw. The creature squeezed him more tightly than a vise. Ribs cracked, snapped. The dragon's corrosive breath, clinging to Rivalen still, burned his flesh more. He groaned and fought to stay conscious as his shadowstuff-infused flesh, sheltered from the sun by the dragon's body, sought to regenerate some of its injuries. Unable to concentrate to cast a spell, he swung his blade weakly at the creature's underbelly but did not so much as scratch the scales. Luckily, the creature's long neck prevented it from bringing its fangs to bear while flying and holding him in a claw.

"Debts are owed, shade, your kind to mine," the dragon said. "You are the first to pay, but not the last."

Rivalen swallowed blood, fought through the haze of pain, and snarled an answer. "This debt is between only us, dragon. And you now owe me."

The dragon growled and squeezed him harder. Bones splintered and Rivalen screamed with agony. He gripped his consciousness with both hands, forced himself to concentrate, and spat the single word of a spell that would teleport him from the dragon's grasp. His pain-clouded brain imagined no end point for the spell except away from the dragon, and he appeared in open air three bowshots away.

The dragon roared at his escape, turned its head on its long neck to scan the sky. It spotted him and started to turn. Its awkwardness in flight gave Rivalen some time, a thirtycount perhaps.

The dragon's breath finally flowed off his skin and dissipated, though it had left his flesh raw, ragged, and slicked with blood. He held his holy symbol in sticky fingers and incanted the words to the most powerful healing spell he knew. The energy flooded him, healing most of the injuries wrought by the dragon. He winced as his bones and organs squirmed back into their proper positions and reknit.

The dragon roared again as it continued its turn. Rivalen presumed the reptile would renew the power of its spell-turning as it came, and he knew his options were limited. More than half his spells would be useless. He would have to disjoin the turning magic with one of his most powerful abjurations, or face the dragon with only indirect spells and his sword.

He would prepare for either option. The disjunction was uncertain and sometimes failed.

Speaking quickly, he incanted a series of spells that doubled his size and that of his sword, increased his strength, his endurance, and gave him supernatural speed. He hefted his enlarged blade in his hand. It did not seem an adequate weapon.

He attuned his communication ring to Brennus.

Where are Yder and Sakkors?

The answer came immediately.

Close.

Rivalen searched the sky in the direction of Selgaunt Bay but saw nothing other than smoke from the burning buildings in the city and rock dust from the walls.

Tamlin materialized with Variance on the avenue behind the Khyber Gate. The gate rattled on its hinges under an elemental's onslaught. The walls to the right and left of the gate cracked and shook under the fists of the huge creatures.

"Get me back up to the walls!" he said to Variance.

"That is no place for you," she answered.

Men dashed all around him, screaming, shouting. Several had dropped to one knee and fired their crossbows rapidly at the exposed heads of the elementals, which rose above the height of the wall. More of the men from the reserve units ran up to the walls, firing crossbows, shouting, adding to the chaos.

Tamlin heard Onthul's voice from somewhere above him on the walls, shouting orders. Lightning bolts and streaks of energy dotted the air as Selgaunt's mages unleashed spells on the elementals. Soldiers atop the walls shot crossbows and swung swords at any part of the elementals within reach.

The creatures shrugged them off and battered the walls, sometimes crushing a man. Bloody spatters stained the walls. Dozens of pulped corpses littered the ground. Cracks ran the length of the walls from top to bottom. Shards of stone rained down.

The elementals' assault on the walls and gate rang in Tamlin's ears. Boom after boom shook the walls, the earth.

"Counterspells only!" Variance shouted. "Cast!"

The priestess held her Sharran holy symbol and intoned the words to a counterspell. Tamlin interlaced his fingers and did the same.

Variance completed her spell. The elemental pounding on the Khyber Gate, fist raised for another blow, bellowed and dissolved into a pile of rock and dirt that showered the ground. Tamlin targeted another elemental and his magic again failed. He was no match for the summoner of the elementals.

"Dark!" he cursed.

Another elemental dissolved under the force of a counterspell. Another. A third, a fourth. Some of the soldiers near him, and those still on the walls, cheered. Tamlin did not know if the Sharrans were countering them or his own mages, and he did not care. From the other side of the wall, he heard Saerloonian horns. They sounded close.

"We need to—"

The ground before him erupted in a rain of cobblestones and

dirt, knocking him and Variance to the ground. An elemental rose out of the earth, its body coated in the cobblestones of Selgaunt's own streets, and blotted out the sun. It had dug under the wall.

Men screamed, shouted, ran. Others fired crossbows and charged with their swords. Variance pulled Tamlin to his feet.

Tamlin, unwilling to waste time on another counterspell, incanted the words to the first spell that came to mind. He pointed his hand and discharged a sizzling lightning bolt into the creature. The spell tore a divot in the creature's body, spraying rock and dirt. The elemental took no notice. Variance pulled Tamlin backward, away from the elemental, while she intoned another counterspell.

The elemental bellowed, lowered its shoulder, and charged the wall from the inside. Men scrambled out of its way as best they could. Several moved too slowly and the elemental crushed them underfoot in a spray of gore.

It hit the wall with a sound like thunder. The cracked wall surrendered at last and crumbled under the impact. The creature's momentum carried it through the breached wall. It stumbled on the rubble, bellowed, fell.

Variance completed her counterspell and the elemental crumbled into mud among the rubble of the wall. At almost the same moment, counterspells destroyed the remaining two earth elementals.

But it was all too late. The wall was breached.

Horns sounded from the field outside. The Saerloonians had an open road into the city.

"They are coming!" someone shouted.

Onthul's voice boomed over the burgeoning chaos. He stood his ground near the breach in the wall. "Gather here, before the breach! Tight formation! Hold here!"

Horns blared. Men ran through the dust-choked air. The cries of the wounded and dying sounded from all around. Tamlin had no idea how many men he still had under his command.

The Saerloonian horns blew another blast.

They were coming.

✧ ✧ ✧ ✧ ✧

Abelar returned to consciousness, slouched over Firstlight's saddle. His head ached but it paled beside the ache in his soul. Regg gripped him tightly and prevented him from falling off the horse.

Swiftdawn trotted beside him, riderless. She saw his open eyes and whinnied a greeting. Abelar did not respond. The rest of his company thundered around him. He felt no anger. Regg had done the right thing. He felt only loss.

"You are awake?" Regg said tentatively.

Abelar nodded once.

"I am sorry, Abelar. I hope you know that."

Abelar nodded again and watched the grass streak by, and watered it with his tears.

His god had failed him.

And Abelar had failed his son.

CHAPTER FOURTEEN

30 Uktar, the Year of Lightning Storms

The dragon completed its turn, beat its wings, and flew toward Rivalen. Twin streams of green smoke leaked from its nostrils. It roared, shouted an arcane word, and a coin-sized glowing orange sphere flew from its mouth, sped toward Rivalen, and blossomed into a cloud of flame and heat.

Rivalen's wards and the shadowstuff of his flesh allowed him to stand in the inferno unharmed. Flying backward as the dragon bore down on him, Rivalen answered the dragon's spell of fire with one of his own. He pointed his finger and summoned a curtain of violet flame directly in the dragon's path. The dragon, a clumsy flyer, could not avoid it and crashed right through it. It emerged trailing flames and smoke, roaring with pain and anger.

"Not warded against fire," Rivalen murmured.

Rivalen swooped upward and hard to his right, forcing the dragon to turn again to pursue. The dragon roared in frustration as Rivalen incanted the words to a powerful evocation. When he pronounced the last syllable, he held his hands out before him, fingers spread, and a hellstorm engulfed the dragon from head to tail. Curtains of flame immolated the creature. It roared, smoking, and twisted in the air to get clear of the flames.

Rivalen spared another glance out over the bay—nothing. Where was Yder?

Below him and across the plains, he watched an elemental burst through Selgaunt's walls. Dust and rock flew into the air. The Saerloonian army flowed toward the breach.

Rivalen cursed but could spare the city little attention. The dragon was coming. It turned and wheeled straight for him, incanting a spell as it came.

Rivalen intoned his own spell and turned his body and gear incorporeal, immune to the dragon's claws, fangs, and deadly breath. He became a living shadow. As ephemeral as the wind, he dived downward and hard left, forcing the dragon to bank to reach him.

Instead, the creature shouted an arcane word, vanished, and instantly materialized beside Rivalen.

The moment it appeared, Rivalen returned to his physical form. His wards ceased to function, his flying spell ceased, he returned to normal size and strength, and every magical item on his person was drained of power. A moment of surprise froze him, and that was all the dragon needed.

It grabbed him in a claw, crushed him enough to steal his breath and crack bones. Rivalen's shadow-infused flesh tried to regenerate while the dragon spiraled downward at alarming speed.

He understood its intent. It would crush him on impact, or would finish him on the ground with its fangs.

He had no wards to preserve him. No charms to protect him. The creature must have surrounded itself in a field of anti-magic, suppressing even Rivalen's ability to transport himself through the shadows. He tried to squirm free, failed. He swung his blade against the dragon's scales—futile. He twisted his head to look down, saw Selgaunt burning, its walls breached, saw the ground rushing up to crush him.

Only one solution leaped to mind. He could try to disjoin the anti-magic field. Only a disjunction could work against such a field.

Enduring the pain and focusing his mind, he intoned the elaborate couplets of the abjuration while the earth sped toward him.

The dragon held him close beneath it. If his spell failed, he would be pulped when the creature slammed into the earth.

The dragon's scales rippled as the creature tensed for impact. Rivalen focused his mind on his spell, only his spell, and pronounced the final couplet.

Power went forth from him. Motes of green energy sparkled all around the dragon as the magic of the disjunction tried to unravel the threads of magic that created the anti-magic field.

The earth filled his field of vision. Rivalen shouted, anticipating impact.

His spell disjoined the anti-magic field and all his suppressed spells, wards, and charms began to function again. He turned incorporeal as the dragon hit the earth so hard it sank four paces deep into the dry plain. Rivalen's incorporeal form sank harmlessly into the ground.

He felt a tingle in his mind as Brennus contacted him through his magical ring.

Rivalen?

Where is Yder?

I was unable to contact you for a time. I thought—

Where is Yder?

Look up, Brennus answered.

Rivalen floated through the dragon—his ability to see even in pitch darkness allowed him to view the dragon's huge lungs, its heart, bones—while the reptile, unaware that Rivalen had survived, stood and looked under its body for his corpse.

Above him, Sakkors descended out of the sun. The inverted mountaintop upon which the city floated blotted out the light and cast the plain in darkness. Clusters of barnacles discolored the rough underside of the floating chunk of rock. Darkness clung to the city, trailed from it like a fog. Newly constructed spires, towers, and buildings pointed accusingly at the sun. Rivalen saw the dome of a new temple to Shar and grinned.

A cloud of veserabs flew below and around the city. Their tubelike bodies undulated with each beat of their membranous wings. A shade armed with a long spear rode atop each, buckled to a specially made saddle.

The dragon looked up, saw the city, the veserabs, and roared. It noticed Rivalen and whirled on him, throwing up clods of dirt, and spat a cloud of corrosive gas.

Rivalen, incorporeal, stood unharmed in the midst of the churning acidic vapors. Few things could harm him in his ghostly form, but he could do little to harm the dragon. With the field of anti-magic disjoined, the creature's spell-turning ward would be functional. He would have to use his sword.

Yder is to hold the troops until I give the order, he said to Brennus. *And the bonded krinth are to order the Source to place all of its power in my sword. Now.*

Brennus did not bother to respond. Rivalen assumed his brother was communicating the orders to Yder.

The green vapors dissipated, leaving the plains pockmarked and dotted with curled grass and withered trees. The dragon, seeing Rivalen unharmed, snapped its jaws at him. Teeth half as long as Rivalen was tall closed on him, passed through him, and did no harm. The dragon roared its frustration.

Rivalen backed off, holding his blade at the ready. The dragon prowled after, as graceful as a cat.

A charge went through Rivalen's sword. Power gathered in it. It vibrated in his grasp. Shadows bled from it as more and more of the Source's power filled it. Rivalen shaped the growing power with his will, took the weapon in two hands.

The dragon, wary, backed away a step and pronounced an arcane word. Five glowing green bolts of energy streaked from the creature's mouth and slammed into Rivalen. His ghostly form did not protect him from the magical bolts and the impact burned his chest and drove him back a step.

He recovered and bounded forward. The sword hummed in his hands, charged by the Source with magic that would reach through planes, with magic baneful to dragons, with the power of an entire mythallar contained within it.

The dragon slashed at him with claws, bit at him with jaws. Rivalen did not attempt to dodge the blows and they passed through him. The dragon, perhaps sensing its danger, tensed and leaped into the air. Rivalen clutched the blade in both hands, leaped forward, and drove the blade hilt-deep into the dragon's chest as the creature took off.

The blade tore through scales as if they were leather and cut a furrow in the dragon's flesh that started in its chest and continued the entire length of its abdomen. When his sword stuck and could slice no farther, Rivalen pulled it free.

Steaming blood poured from the ghastly opening and soaked the grass, sizzling and smoking. The dragon gave a high-pitched roar of agony. Blood rained down as it frantically beat its wings and struggled to stay aloft. Rivalen flew upward with it, slashed crosswise, and opened another bloody tear in the dragon's underbelly.

The dragon roared, wings beating. It snapped at him in rage, but its bite passed through him without effect. Rivalen pressed the attack, chopping through scales and flesh in great sweeping arcs. The dragon screamed in frustration, pain, and finally, fear. Its blood soaked the plains. Its screams saturated the air. Rivalen closed, intent to finish the creature, but it glared at him, spat a magic word, and vanished.

Rivalen hurriedly recited the words to a spell that allowed him to see magically concealed creatures and to pierce illusions, and scanned the plain around him. Nothing. The dragon had fled.

Rivalen did not have time to revel in the victory. Selgaunt was falling.

Banish any remaining fire elementals, he sent to Brennus. *Have the Source retrieve its power from my blade and distribute it among Leevoth's men. Then meet me in the air over the walls.*

Elyril smiled. The Nightseer had looked directly at her with spell-augmented vision and seen nothing. She was shadow, spirit, invisible. She was Shar's weapon.

Thank you, Lady of Loss.

She laughed and the sound was like a breeze. She moved behind the Nightseer and stepped into his shadow. There she would lurk until he revealed to her the location of the rest of the book to be made whole.

Under Onthul's command, several hundred Selgauntan soldiers formed a line fifty or sixty men wide and twenty deep that spanned the breach in the wall. Rorsin raced around behind the line, gathering every crossbowman he could and putting them into a group behind the line to mass their fire.

Saerloonian trumpets bellowed.

The sky darkened and Tamlin looked up.

An inverted mountain floated above the plains and cast its shadow over the city. Thin spires and towers dotted its top. Creatures as large as ponies, with black, tube-shaped bodies and membranous wings, flew around the city's edges. Shade troops rode them. Shadows cloaked the entire city. Tamlin raised his fist and grinned at Variance.

"Stay close to me, Hulorn," she said.

Tamlin nodded.

Men pointed at the sky, cheered.

The Saerloonian trumpets blew anew and Onthul moved along the front of his men.

"They're still coming, lads! Ready now!"

Two lightning bolts shot through the breached wall and cut a swath through the Selgauntan ranks. Dozens of men fell, their bodies smoking. Other men stepped forward to fill the holes in the ranks.

Drums, trumpets, and a roar like an onrushing tide sounded as the Saerloonian army charged through the wall. They poured through the debris, blades high, standards flying.

"Fire!" Rorsin shouted, and a few hundred crossbow bolts winged into the Saerloonian army. Scores of men fell dead and their comrades trampled their corpses as they charged.

The men of Selgaunt met the charge with steel and sword. Metal crashed on metal. Men shouted, screamed, killed, and died. Bolts of magical energy flashed here and there on the battlefield as each side's wizards made their presence felt.

Above the plains the Shadovar city hovered. The flying creatures and their riders did not descend.

"Why are they waiting?" Tamlin shouted to Variance. "We need them now!"

The Saerloonian forces outnumbered his forces three or four to one.

"The Nightseer's purposes are his own," she answered. "They will come."

The Saerloonian forces surged forward. Blades rose and fell. The Selgauntan line buckled, broke in places. Saerloonians rushed through the openings. Selgaunt's men were crumbling as surely as the city's walls. The Saerloonians were too many.

Tamlin snarled, spotted a Saerloonian war mage hovering above the combat. The mage pointed a metal rod at Rorsin and the archers, and a cloud of black gas formed around them. Men fell to their knees, clutching their throats, dying. Others vomited and tried to stagger free.

"Counter that," Tamlin ordered Variance, and intoned the words to his own spell. When he finished, he put his fists together and a ray of white-hot energy streaked from him. It struck the Saerloonian mage in the face and neck as the man aimed his wand at another cluster of Selgauntan soldiers. The man pawed at his melting face, screaming, then fell out of the air, dead.

Meanwhile, Variance pointed her holy symbol at the killing black vapors and intoned a prayer to Shar. The power of her counterspell prevailed and the vapors dissipated.

Tamlin eyed Variance with envious eyes. "Shar is generous with the power she grants her faithful."

Variance threw up her faceguard and pointed to the sky.

"The Nightseer is returned. Only now will you see the true power that Shar grants."

Tamlin looked into the sky. Rivalen was streaking toward the walls, the shadows about him churning, giving him the appearance of an approaching storm.

❦　❦　❦　❦　❦

Furlinastis circled over the fog cloud, the tips of his huge wings brushing the treetops with each downbeat. He scanned the swamp nearby.

Cale knew he could not hide from the dragon for long, so he did not try. He stepped out from the shadows, showed himself, and intoned the words to a spell.

The dragon heard him and roared. Beating his wings with enough force to strip nearby trees of leaves, Furlinastis wheeled around and streaked toward Cale, mouth open, eyes hard.

Cale held his ground, pronounced the final word to his spell, and pointed his finger at a point ahead of the dragon. Where he pointed, a towering wall of translucent silver energy flashed into existence. The dragon's flight carried it into the wall head first and stopped it dead. The weight of the dragon's own momentum smashed it in a heap against the barrier and the impact sounded like a hundred war drums. The magical wall flared, buckled, and dissipated, but it had done its work. The dragon could do nothing but futilely flap its wings as it fell into the swamp and sent up a spray of foul water.

Cale wasted no time. He shadowstepped to the space near the wing joint on the dragon's back. The shadows that shrouded the dragon tugged at him.

The dragon is not at fault, First of Five, a voice in the shadows said to him.

Cale ignored it and said to Riven and Magadon, *Now! And bring light, Mags. Everything you have.*

He reversed his grip on his blade and drove Weaveshear through scales and deep into the dragon's wing joint. Black blood spurted around the blade. Furlinastis would not fly again soon.

The dragon roared and bucked, whirled its neck around to snap at Cale, but Cale dived from its back and rode the shadows away before the jaws could reach him.

He materialized in knee-deep water a long dagger's throw from the creature's flank. Magadon and Riven appeared before the dragon. A blazing ball of white light burned above Magadon's head and the mindmage's arrow, already nocked and drawn, glowed a brilliant crimson. Riven stood beside him, as tall as an ogre.

The dragon did not hesitate. It roared and expelled a cloud of deadly breath. The life-draining shadows engulfed Riven and Magadon but Cale's protective spells still warded his companions. They bounded out of the cloud, coughing but alive, Magadon's light still burning.

The mindmage stopped to fire his bow, and his charged arrow pierced the dragon's scales as if they were cloth. The missile hit the creature in the throat and sank to the fletching. Another followed, another. The dragon beat its wings, hissed in pain.

Riven sped forward, his magically enlarged sabers bleeding shadows. Furlinastis lashed out with a claw. Riven parried with one saber while he slashed at the dragon's exposed leg with the other. The blade ripped through scales, sliced tendon, and sent up a spray of blood.

The dragon reared back and spat a short couplet of arcane words. Instantly the mud around Cale's feet began to harden into rock. From their exclamation of surprise, he guessed the same thing was happening to Riven and Magadon. They would all be immobilized.

Cale responded instinctively and shadowstepped out of the mud and into the branches of a large tree. He saw Riven stick both his sabers in the hardening ground and do a handstand on their hilts to get his feet free of the mud until it hardened fully into rock. Magadon tried to pull himself free but was stuck fast.

Riven flipped to his feet and rushed forward on the hard earth, blades spinning. He leaped and parried a pair of claw attacks, got in close, and slashed twin gashes in the dragon's face when it darted its head down and tried to snap him in half. Furlinastis hissed, spun his body ninety degrees, and cracked his tail, as thick as an old oak, at Riven. It hit the assassin squarely in the side. The impact blew Riven's breath from his lungs and sent him careening into the water.

The dragon roared, lunged forward as if to finish Riven, and Cale struck. He chose a dark spot in the crook of the dragon's back where his long neck met his chest. Shadowstepping, he put his hands on the creature's scales and cast a spell that poured baleful energy into the dragon.

Scales cracked and blood seeped through the fissures. The dragon roared, spun around, and the abrupt motion sent Cale flying. Before he could interpose his blade, the dragon's jaws snapped closed on his thigh and jerked him into the air.

Cale screamed as the dragon shook him. His regenerative flesh could not keep up with the injuries and he felt his leg tearing away.

Magadon's calm but strained voice carried over the battlefield. "Give in to it," he said, and Cale did not know to whom or what Magadon was speaking.

Cale, upside down in the dragon's jaws, caught a glimpse of the mindmage. An ochre light haloed his entire body, and the veins in his brow, face, and bared arms stood out like lattice-work. The same ochre light formed around Furlinastis's head. The dragon's eyes—normally as black as onyx—turned as white as Magadon's.

The dragon dropped Cale and he hit the swamp in a heap. Adrenaline and his shadow flesh allowed him to endure the pain, and he leaned on his sword to climb to his feet.

Seemingly dazed, the dragon slowly lowered its head to eye level between Cale and Riven. The huge reptile extended its neck, exposing the smaller, softer, violet scales of its throat. The shadows around the creature swirled.

"Strike," Magadon said, his voice cracking. "The urge will not last for long."

Cale and Riven looked at each other in surprise.

"Strike!" Magadon said.

Cale and Riven lunged forward and struck as one. Weaves-hear opened a deep gash in the dragon's throat, just below its jaw. Riven's magically enlarged sabers slashed chasms so deep into the dragon's throat that he nearly beheaded the creature. Black blood gushed from the wounds, soaking them, flooding the swamp.

Furlinastis recovered his senses only in time to die. The dragon reared back, his head flopping grotesquely. He tried to roar but instead gave only a deep, bubbling gurgle through the gashes in his throat. He flapped his wings, shook, and collapsed into the swamp.

Magadon gasped and sagged. Cale and Riven stared at the enormous carcass in stunned silence. As they looked on, the shadow shroud around the dragon churned and darkened. Faces formed from the shadows and swirled in the darkness.

"Mags?" Cale said over his shoulder. The mindmage was weakened and remained stuck in the rock the dragon's spell had transformed.

"Finish it, Cale," Magadon said.

Cale took off his mask and clutched it in a fist. He held Weaveshear loosely in his other hand. "Kesson Rel," he called. His heart rattled his ribs; his breath came hard.

The faces vanished and several smaller shadows separated from the larger shroud. They formed a semi-circle before Cale and Riven and assumed humanoid forms, their outlines shifting like smoke. Hooded cloaks hid their hands and faces.

The one in the center threw back his hood to reveal the face of a man. Short black hair topped a high-browed, angular face adorned with a neat beard. The man looked into Cale's and Riven's faces.

I am Avnon Des the Seer. I was a servant and priest of the Shadowlord, as were all of those with me. You are the Chosen of the Shadowlord in this age.

Cale had no time for such nonsense. "We are taking back what Kesson Rel stole."

Avnon smiled softly. *What Kesson Rel took was given him, not stolen.*

Cale brandished Weaveshear. "I don't care. I want it. I want him."

The man smiled gently. *It is not ours to give.*

Behind the assembled priests, the rest of the shroud roiled and formed a towering, amorphous form roughly like a man. Wild eyes looked out of a chiseled face. Horns jutted from his brow. He was Volumvax, or the rest of Volumvax, and he was Kesson Rel.

Kesson Rel raised his arms to the shadowy sky and unleashed a shout of such combined rage and glee that it dwarfed even the dragon's roar.

In answer, flashes of green lightning crosscut the sky.

Cale and Riven shared a look and bounded past Avnon and his fellow priests, blades bare.

"Wait . . ." Avnon said.

"Low," Riven said.

"High," Cale answered, and shouted at Kesson. "Kesson Rel!"

Kesson took no notice of them.

Riven slashed low at Kesson's legs and Cale stabbed Weaveshear through his chest. Their blades passed through his shadowy form without contact.

Kesson turned his gaze to them and his mouth twisted with contempt. He looked up to the sky and thunder boomed. He vanished.

"No!" Magadon screamed.

CHAPTER FIFTEEN

30 Uktar, the Year of Lightning Storms

As Rivalen flew back toward Selgaunt, he intoned ward after ward, shielding himself from lightning, cold, fire, and projectiles. He surrounded himself in a translucent sphere of energy that would entirely block lesser spells.

Below him, dozens of Saerloonian soldiers lay dead on the smoking plains, burned by the alchemical fire thrown by the trebuchets. But the rest of the army straddled Selgaunt's toppled wall. Fully half the army fought within the city, while the rest waited for the way to clear for them so they could push through.

Saerloonian soldiers in the rear ranks spotted him as he approached, pointed. A hail of crossbow bolts and a storm of magical energy greeted his arrival. His wards and the shadowstuff in his flesh repelled all of it.

He hovered, pointed an open palm at each side of

the breach in the wall, and recited arcane words while cross-bow bolts bounced off his flesh and spells lit the air. When he finished casting, a wall of gray stone materialized from nothingness and spanned the breach. Rivalen's magic melded to the wall, sealing off Selgaunt and cutting the Saerloonian army in half.

He followed up immediately with one of his most powerful necromantic spells. Choosing one of the fat Saerloonian wizards he had seen summoning the earth elementals earlier, he recited the incantation. A wave of gray magical energy went forth from his hands, to the Saerloonian wizard, and outward from the wizard in a circle twenty paces in diameter. His spell pulled every drop of liquid from every Saerloonian in the sphere. Pink fluid burst from noses, eyes, ears, groin, and pooled on the ground to form a macabre pond. Men screamed, but only for a moment before their desiccated corpses splashed to the ground in their own fluids. Hundreds died in the span of three breaths. Rivalen offered their death shrieks to Shar. Shouts of fear and anger rose from the army.

Leevoth and his soldiers are to assist the Selgauntans within the city, he sent to Brennus. *No krinth. Join me here for sport, if you wish. But hurry.*

Hurry? Brennus said. *There are thousands of Saerloonians.*

Not for long, Rivalen answered.

A ball of flame exploded around him, soaking him in fire. His wards shielded him. He spotted the mage who had cast it and incanted his own spell. A green beam shot from his finger, struck the gray-robed mage in the chest, and reduced him to dust.

More crossbow bolts thumped off his flesh. Two bolts, presumably enchanted, sunk into his thigh and shoulder. He grunted with pain while his regenerative flesh pushed them out and healed the wounds.

He flew down just above the army. More bolts slammed into him. Three sank into his limbs. He endured the pain, let it fuel his burgeoning anger. Upturned faces stared at him with eyes full of fear, anger, awe. He looked down on them and intoned the words to a spell that would infuse him with unholy power. The shadows swirled around him as energy gathered. Some among the Saerloonians broke and ran.

When Rivalen completed the spell, he landed in their midst, profane words lined up behind his teeth. Swords and axes chopped at him. Men shouted, tried to pin his arms. The shadows swarmed around him to deflect warriors and weapons. A few blade thrusts penetrated his defenses and cut his skin but he did not care. He was about Shar's work.

He unleashed the words, turning a circle as he shouted his blasphemous phrase.

Every Saerloonian around him to a distance of twenty paces—seven score soldiers, perhaps eight—withered, screamed, and died. Rivalen was surrounded by corpses.

Another two or three score Saerloonians stopped short and stared at gray, vaguely formed phantasms that materialized out of the air before them. Rivalen had seen the spell often enough. The men saw their darkest fears, and a touch from the illusion would kill them.

Brennus, Rivalen said, and looked up. His brother floated in the air above him, his gray eyes hard. His homunculi looked out of his robe to leer at the death below.

High above Brennus, Sakkors floated into position over Selgaunt's walls. The veserabs with their shade riders began to spiral down. Leevoth and the shade troops would follow.

Some sport remains yet, I see, Brennus answered.

The Saerloonians affected by Brennus's spell shrieked, cowered. The phantasms reached for them, touched them, and all but two fell dead.

The Saerloonian army on Rivalen's side of Selgaunt's walls broke and started to run.

A conjured wall trapped the Saerloonians within the city and divided their army in half, and they fought with increasing desperation. The battle spilled into the open area behind the Khyber Gate. The combat grew disorganized. Pockets of ten and twenty men fought here and there. Crossbow bolts winged over the combat. Shouts and screams sounded from every direction. Saerloonian and Selgauntan commanders shouted orders but most went unheeded as the soldiers on both sides swung blades and axes at any enemy within reach. The dead and dying littered the streets.

Tamlin fired bolts of magical energy at any Saerloonian commander or mage he could mark. Variance pulled him beside the frame of the unmanned trebuchet and cloaked them both in darkness.

"I will not cower while the city falls!" he said to her.

She nodded up at the sky. "It will not fall."

Tamlin looked up to see the Shadovar enclave float directly over the wall and cast its shadow over the battlefield. For a moment, combat ceased. A hush fell and all eyes looked up.

The batlike creatures flitting about the flying city spiraled downward. Pockets of darkness formed on the battlefield. Soldiers on both sides backed away warily.

"It is over," Variance said, and sheathed her short swords.

Shadovar troops materialized and stepped from the pitch. They bore blades crafted of glistening black metal, and wore armor forged of the same. Shadows curled around them. The Saerloonians did not even have time to shout in surprise before the Shadovar began to kill. Their black blades cut flesh and steel with equal facility. Two hundred Saerloonians died in three breaths.

Shouts erupted anew, the ring of metal, battle cries, the screams of the wounded and dying. Tamlin watched, awed, as the Shadovar troops disappeared into the shadows only to reappear ten paces away, often behind a Saerloonian soldier to run him through. The combat was no longer a battle. It was a slaughter.

"Thank Shar for this," he murmured. "She has saved the city."

Variance looked at him and smiled. "Indeed."

Cale cursed and whirled around to the shadow priests, all of whom had turned to watch them. Cale stalked up to Avnon and pointed Weaveshear at his chest. "Where did he go?"

Back to himself, to make whole what was sundered. The Shadowlord's power is Kesson's until it is taken from him. All we could do was contain it.

Riven shook his head in disbelief.

Cale looked past Avnon to Magadon, who stood with his head bowed, shoulders hunched.

"How do I take it from him, priest?"

There is only one way. Kill him.

"We did kill him," Cale said.

"No. He lives. And now he is stronger than before."

Magadon cursed softly, but there was no heat in it, only despair.

"Dark, Cale," Riven said. "A duplicate. We were duped."

Cale could not believe it. The duplicate of Kesson Rel had almost killed them. If the real Kesson were stronger . . .

"But why?" Riven asked.

Cale remembered what Magadon had learned from the gnome. "He could not leave his spire. We did his work for him."

"And now he's free?" Riven asked.

Cale nodded. "So it would seem."

He did not relish the thought of battling Kesson Rel again. He slowed his racing mind. "Tell us everything, Avnon Des."

Our time is limited, Avnon said. *We should have died millennia ago. Hear me, then. Kesson Rel was the first Chosen of the Shadowlord. In him the Dusklord invested some of his own power, his own divinity. Kesson became a god but the power drove him mad. We tried to stop him but he forced our temple onto this plane and used the soulbound shadow dragon to murder us one by one. Through a vision the Shadowlord told me our fate. We could not stop Kesson but we could make our deaths meaningful by using our own souls to trap the divine spark he had been forced to use to bind the dragon to his will. This we did, though it cost the dragon dearly.*

Avnon looked to the dragon's carcass and shook his head. *I do not know what occurred with Kesson after that.*

Cale did, at least part of it. "He abandoned Mask for Shar and avenged himself on Elgrin Fau. He brought the entire city to the Plane of Shadow. Everyone in it died in darkness."

Avnon looked up, shock and pain in his expression. His fellow priests shuffled on their feet, murmured in distress to one another.

"The City of Silver? Lost?"

Cale nodded. "I'm sorry."

"What was the point of it all?" Riven asked. "Mask had a plan millennia in the making and now things are right back where they started. Kesson Rel is not only alive, but whole."

Avnon looked Riven and Cale in the face. *Things are not back where they started. You are here. That was the point. We were waiting for you. The Shadowlord was waiting for you.*

Cale looked at Riven and both looked back to Avnon.

"We are going to kill Kesson Rel."

I know.

"Then what happens?" Cale asked.

I do not know, Avnon said. *But I envy you.*

"Don't," Cale said.

Avnon smiled. His form started to blur at the edges, then to fade.

Farewell, First and Second.

Avnon and his fellow priests dissipated into the surrounding shadowstuff.

Cale and Riven stood in silence for a moment, then turned away from the dragon's carcass and walked back to their friend.

Softly, Cale asked, "Mags, what did you do to the dragon?"

Magadon stared at him, his eyes troubled. "It's dead. That is what we wanted. What does it matter what I did?"

"It matters."

Magadon's expression went from troubled to that of a man about to confess a transgression. He looked away. "I . . . magnified the self-destructive urge in its mind."

"Magnified?" Cale asked. "What does that mean?"

Magadon spoke softly. "Everyone carries a seed of self-loathing, Cale. For some, it's quite powerful. So it was with Furlinastis. It is easy to twist that into a suicidal impulse. "

"Dark," Riven said.

Cale agreed. The power unnerved him. That Magadon would use it unnerved him more.

He looked at the dragon's carcass, the hole of its open neck a black tunnel. He felt a certain pity for the dragon, even kinship. Avnon Des had said the dragon had been unwillingly bound by Kesson Rel. Despite its immense power, the creature had been a tool of fate, caught up in one of Mask's schemes. It had despised itself in consequence. Cale understood the feeling well. He looked back to Magadon, held his mask in hand, and incanted the words to a spell that turned the rock back into mud. Cale helped pull the mindmage free.

"Are you all right, Mags?" He meant more than the words alone expressed.

Magadon seemed to understand. "I am nearly spent, Cale."

"Hang on," Cale said, and Magadon nodded.

"What now?" Riven asked.

Cale answered, "The Wayrock."

Riven smiled and said, "There's nothing at the Wayrock. We've been in Hell and the darkest hole in the Plane of Shadow, Cale. I need a drink and two women. Or a woman and two drinks. I'll decide on the way, but there are neither at the Wayrock. Mags, you can join me. Cale's a monk."

Cale chuckled, despite it all. "When did you get funny?"

"I am not making a jest."

Cale smiled. "Use your ring. I'll follow after."

Riven grew serious and a question formed on his brow. "Follow?"

"Yes." Cale nodded at the dragon.

Riven shook his head. "Cale . . ."

"It's the right thing."

Furlinastis had spent almost his entire existence bound to serve others, whether Kesson Rel, Avnon Des, or Mask. The dragon had hated his existence as a result, and Cale, Riven, and Magadon had used that self-hate to kill him. Servants of Mask had stolen the dragon's life. Cale was going to give it back.

Riven studied him, looked to the dragon, and sighed in surrender. "Let's move, Mags." To Cale, he said, "See you soon."

Cale nodded. "See you soon."

Cale donned his mask. Sound had returned to the swamp—howls, shrieks, and the buzzing of insects. Cale splashed through the water until he stood before the dragon. The horns that jutted from the reptile's head were as tall as Cale; the teeth were swords.

Cale took a deep breath and hoped he was doing the right thing.

He placed both hands on the dragon's head—the scales felt as smooth as a polished shield—and incanted the words to a spell that revivified the recently dead. Power gathered as he intoned first one couplet, then another, another. When the magic reached its apex, he felt the doors between worlds open.

"Return, Furlinastis," he shouted, and his voice carried over and through the planes of existence. "If you wish it."

The buzzes, howls, and clicks went dead around him, as if the swamp were holding its breath. Silent moments passed.

A hum sounded, gradually gathering volume. Streamers of

shadow formed in the air and wrapped themselves around the dragon's neck, merged with his flesh, and repaired the gash. Cale took his hands from the reptile's head, put one on Weaveshear's hilt, and backed up a step.

Furlinastis's chest expanded sharply as he inhaled a great gasp of air. His dark eyes opened, looked upon Cale, narrowed. He opened his mouth in a roar that hit Cale like a gale. The dragon lurched to his feet, spraying water, flapped his wings once.

For a moment, man and dragon simply regarded one another.

"Why have you done this?" Furlinastis asked at last, his voice low and sibilant. Before Cale could answer, the dragon added, "I will never again serve another. Not even in payment for this."

Cale nodded and explained it like a Sembian. "This is compensation, dragon. The Shadowlord took too much from you."

The dragon considered that. "And from you, too, perhaps?"

Cale cocked his head in acknowledgement. "I am his willing instrument. You never were. Now you are free."

A hiss escaped the dragon's mouth. Cale took it as one of pleasure. Twin streams of shadow spiraled out of his nostrils.

Cale had done what he wanted. He drew the darkness about him. "Farewell, Furlinastis."

The dragon watched him through slitted eyes. As the shadows around Cale deepened, the dragon said, "One service, First of Five. Freely given. If you call in darkness, I will hear."

With that, the dragon launched itself into the dark sky, roaring with pleasure.

Cale smiled and imagined the Wayrock in his mind.

He needed to rethink things. An enormous task lay ahead of them. They had to find a way to murder a god.

Abelar saw the world through a gray haze. His company cut south and west for Lake Veladon and rode for hours, half a day. He felt thick, numb. Again and again in his mind he replayed the moments he had shared with his son. He could think of nothing else. He ate, drank, responded in single words to Regg's inquiries, and sat atop Swiftdawn. But he felt nothing.

The afternoon of the next day, they reached Lake Veladon. Shrubs and scattered willows bordered its edge and the waters glittered in the sunlight. Men, women, children, horses, wagons, carts, and tents dotted the shore. Abelar put the number of fighting men at only several hundred. Not enough to engage Forrin; not enough to rescue his son.

Eyes watched them approach. Armed and armored men rode forth to greet them, as did Jiiris and the rest of Abelar's company. Greetings and news were exchanged. Abelar greeted no one and cared nothing for news.

"I am going to surrender myself to Mirabeta," he said to Regg, and heard the dullness in his own voice. He swung out of Swiftdawn's saddle.

Regg, too, dismounted, as did Endren and the rest of the men and women.

"You cannot," Regg said.

Endren put a hand on Abelar's shoulder. "She will not honor a bargain with you. You know this."

Abelar did know it. He found it hard to breathe. He found it pointless to breathe.

"I cannot stand idle while my son suffers." He wanted to die, to crawl alone into a dark place and find oblivion.

"You do not know that he is suffering," Endren said.

But Abelar did know it. They all knew it.

Regg patted him on the shoulder. "You did all you could, Abelar. We have not given up."

Abelar looked at Regg and brandished his shield, the shield adorned with Lathander's rose. Heat rose in him, gave his voice an edge. "But Lathander did not do all he could. I dedicated my life to him, Regg. Did he do enough? Do you think he did?"

Regg held Abelar's gaze for only a moment before he looked away.

Anger rooted in Abelar's gut, rushed up his throat. He voiced an inarticulate roar of despair and anger. Hundreds of eyes turned to look at him. He ignored them all, turned, and ran toward the lake. Regg, Endren, and Roen raced after him, calling his name. He charged into the water, sinking to his ankles in the muddy bottom, and flung his shield far out into the lake. It caught the light as it spun, hit the water, and sank into darkness. He jerked the holy symbol from around his neck, spat on it, and cast it into the water, too. "I will never forgive you!" he shouted to his god. "Never!"

Endren, Regg, and Roen waded into the water and stood beside him in silence. The setting sun cast the lake in fire. It was beautiful and Abelar hated it. Having shed shield and symbol, he found it hard to stand. Only his anger kept him upright.

Regg put an arm around him, steered him back toward shore. Men, women, and children had assembled there, and all of Abelar's company. Abelar could not look them in the face. Hands patted his shoulder as he passed. Jiiris brushed his hand with hers.

He shook his head, bereft. "I need to be alone," he said to Regg.

Regg nodded, ordered one of the men to get Abelar a tent. While they waited, a shout captured their attention.

"Smoke!"

Eyes turned north, where clouds of black smoke billowed into the sky.

"Saerb is burning!"

Word spread through the camp. Women cried, children sobbed, men shook their fists and cursed Forrin and the over-mistress. Abelar felt almost nothing. He walked to his tent and collapsed. He emerged later to find that Regg, Roen, and Jiiris had taken station outside.

"Stragglers have been arriving from Saerb throughout the day," Roen said.

"They got out before Forrin arrived," Regg said. "Our rout

of his southern force made that possible, Abelar. Without us, they'd have been killed on the road as would everyone here with us now."

Abelar nodded.

"Are you all right?" Jiiris asked, and her green eyes showed concern.

"No."

His father was taking stock of the fighting men and women who had gathered for the muster, planning their next steps. Abelar did not disrupt him. He walked to the shore of the lake and sat down alone. He whispered farewell to his god as the sun set and darkness fell.

As the night bloomed, he made up his mind. He would not surrender his son to Forrin and the overmistress. Not until he had done absolutely everything he could. He could not look to the light to rescue Elden, so he would look to the darkness.

He stood, walked purposefully through the camp until he found Roen. The priest of Lathander sat with a dozen other men of Abelar's company around a fire. They had pulled a dozen silvergills from the lake. The fish cooked over the flames.

"Commander?" Roen asked, and stood.

"I need you to find Nayan."

Roen looked confused.

"The shadowwalker who rescued my father."

Roen's eyes flashed recognition. "Why?"

"Because he can find Erevis Cale. And if Erevis Cale can pull my father out of the Hole, he can pull my son out of Forrin's camp."

"Abelar . . ."

"Do it," Abelar said, and grabbed Roen roughly by the shoulders. He regretted the gesture immediately and released the priest. "Please do it, Roen. Any way you can. I need them here. Now."

Roen looked at the men around the fire, back at Abelar, nodded. "Of course, Abelar."

❦ ❦ ❦ ❦ ❦

Corpses and rubble from the wall littered Selgaunt's streets. A floating Shadovar city cast its shadow over the battlefield. Shadovar and Selgauntan troops stood shoulder to shoulder amid the carnage. Coughs and the cries of the wounded sounded loud in the dusty air. Variance stood beside Tamlin, taking in the scene. Other priests and priestesses of the Lady of Loss stood among the victors.

Tamlin found the entire scene surreal. He had been certain his city would fall. Shar and the Shadovar had saved it. "It is quiet now," he said, and immediately thought the words stupid.

Variance nodded.

Rivalen and Brennus appeared over the walls, cloaked in shadows and power. The Shadovar troops hailed them with raised blades. The Selgauntans, too, raised their weapons and cheered.

The two Princes of Shade descended to stand before Tamlin and Variance. Shadows curled lazily around the brothers.

Rivalen's face, bruised around one eye and with a deep gash down one cheek, healed before Tamlin's eyes. The Prince seemed not to notice.

Brennus's homunculi emerged from his cloak, gazed about tentatively, and grinned when they saw the battle had ended.

"You are both well?" Tamlin asked.

Both nodded.

"And you?" Rivalen asked him, though he looked at Variance.

"Fine," Tamlin answered. "The rest of the Saerloonian army?"

Rivalen made a dismissive gesture. "Destroyed or fled. We will want to arrange a detail to dispose of their bodies. The dragon, too, has fled."

"Gods, man," Tamlin breathed. He was standing before two men of inordinate power. He envied them. "I scarcely know what to say, Prince. Or how to thank you and your men."

Rivalen inclined his head. "Thanks are unnecessary. I am a man of my word, Hulorn. We are . . . allies."

"You are that, and we are that."

"This war is not yet over," Brennus said.

"Agreed," Tamlin said. They had defeated part of Mirabeta's army, but much of it still remained.

"We should discuss next steps," Rivalen said.

"Next steps?" Tamlin asked.

Rivalen looked to Variance. "See to the wounded, Dark Sister."

"Yes, Nightseer," she said, nodded at Tamlin, and vanished into the shadows.

"There are provisions and accommodations on Sakkors," Brennus said. The homunculi rubbed their stomachs and licked their lips.

"So that is Sakkors," Tamlin said, eyeing the floating mountaintop hanging in the air above his city.

Brennus said, "Our troops will garrison there, of course, but there is ample space for more. The city was recently rebuilt. Selgaunt is overcrowded, some of its people could temporarily relocate . . ."

"This, too, you would share with us?" Tamlin asked.

Brennus's homunculi gave bows and Brennus said, "As my brother said, we are allies, Hulorn."

Tamlin was glad of it. He would not want to be an enemy of the Princes or Shade Enclave. He turned to face Rivalen. "Shar saved Selgaunt through you and your men. I will be candid and tell you that I wish to know more of her. Everything there is to know, Prince Rivalen."

Rivalen's eyes flashed and he regarded Tamlin for a moment. The shadows around him swirled. "I believe you, Hulorn."

Onthul appeared before them. Scratches covered his face. Rips marred his tabard and dents marked his breastplate. A piece of torn fabric bound a wound on his forearm. Dust caked his beard. Tamlin almost embraced the old war dog.

"My lords," he said to Tamlin and the Princes, and bowed. "We have more than three hundred Saerloonian prisoners, Hulorn."

"They can be imprisoned on Sakkors until you decide their fate," Rivalen said to Tamlin.

Tamlin nodded. "Very good. Gather them, Captain Onthul. The Shadovar will transport them."

Onthul nodded. "Shall I send for the priests held in the palace so that they may assist with the wounded?"

Tamlin looked out on the battlefield, at Variance and her fellow priests and priestesses moving among Selgaunt's wounded, healing them. "Are the Sharrans unable to do what needs to be done?"

Onthul looked at the battlefield, back at Tamlin. "The Sharrans appear to have matters in hand, Hulorn."

"Good. Then leave the priests where they are. Their disposition remains . . . under consideration."

Onthul saluted and started to walk away.

"Captain," Tamlin called.

Onthul turned, eyebrows raised in a question.

"You served Selgaunt well today, Captain."

Onthul smiled, nodded, and walked off, barking orders.

"Let us retire to discuss matters, Hulorn," Rivalen said.

"Yes," said Tamlin.

CHAPTER SIXTEEN

1 Nightal, the Year of Lightning Storms

Tamlin paced the study in Stormweather Tower. He ran his fingertips over the spines of his father's books. He had read almost none of them.

"Vees Talendar a traitor?" he said to Rivalen. "That cannot be, Prince. I've known him for years. He has been indispensable to me."

Rivalen stood in the center of the study, near the chessboard, arms crossed. He advanced a black pawn. "You wished to know all, Hulorn. This is all. Will you hear the rest?"

Tamlin's stomach fluttered but he nodded.

"Recall my mention of renegade, heretical elements within the Sharran church. Vees Talendar is not a priest of Siamorphe, as he purports, but a priest of Shar."

Tamlin gave a start. "Shar? Like you?"

"Shar," Rivalen nodded. "But not like me. I learned of

this months ago but kept it from you to earn Talendar's confidence and learn more of his plans. Talendar leads a group of like-minded worshipers. All of them are heretics, Hulorn. All of them are guilty of dark deeds in which innocents suffered."

Tamlin swallowed, looked out of the window onto Storm-weather's night-shrouded grounds. He could not believe what he was hearing.

Rivalen continued. "The temple of Siamorphe is a carefully constructed disguise, long in planning. The true temple is below it. It is a temple to Shar, dedicated by heretics. I have seen it."

Tamlin could think of no words. He merely shook his head.

"There is more still," Rivalen said.

"Isn't that enough?" Tamlin said bitterly.

Shadows swirled about the Prince and his eyes glowed in the darkness. His expression showed sympathy. "I know this must be hard to hear. I regret having to tell you these things. But we are at war and cannot have a traitor in our midst."

Tamlin held his goblet in the air between his lips and the tabletop. "Traitor. The word does not fit. Traitor?"

Rivalen nodded.

Tamlin set the goblet down untouched.

"And now I enter into the realm of speculation," Rivalen said. "But here are my thoughts. I believe Vees Talendar told the overmistress and Lady Merelith of the alliance between Shade Enclave and Selgaunt. I believe Vees Talendar then encouraged the other priesthoods in the city to take a neutral stance in the conflict. Some of them may be in league with him."

"If he is a Sharran, as you say . . ." Tamlin said.

"They would not know that. They believe him a worshiper of Siamorphe."

Tamlin's head swam. He tried to make sense of Vees's treachery, replayed in his mind their many meetings and dis-cussions over the past year. Vees had been secretive, prohibiting anyone from entering the temple of Siamorphe, disappearing for days at a time.

"Why would he do this?" Tamlin asked.

"We discussed the nature of men once before, Tamlin. Is that not reason enough? Perhaps he still harbors ill will due to the conflict between his family and yours. In the end, I believe he wished to see Selgaunt fall and for you and me to die. I suspect he had arranged with Merelith and the overmistress to become the new Hulorn. At the same time, by eliminating me, he would kill Shar's high priest and move a step closer to his heresy becoming accepted in the church. Perhaps he thought to become a high priest himself. Why else would he not have fought beside us at the walls?"

Tamlin picked up the wine goblet and drank it empty in a single gulp. He refilled it, his mind racing. Everything Rivalen said made sense. Anger and shame warmed Tamlin's cheeks. He had been played for a fool. He thought of how disappointed his father would have been with him, how smug Erevis Cale would have been, and his anger grew. He looked to Rivalen.

"These are accusations. I need proof before I authorize steps."

Rivalen crossed the room and stared down at Tamlin. "I will give you proof. This moment. Stay near me and remain silent."

The darkness deepened around them until Tamlin could not see. His stomach fluttered as the shadows moved them elsewhere. He heard a voice, Vees's voice, chanting as the darkness parted.

"Love is a lie," Vees said. "Only hate endures. Light is blinding. Only in darkness do we see clearly."

Rivalen and Tamlin stood in the back of a vaulted, windowless chamber. Wooden pews arranged before them faced a black altar draped with a purple and black altar cloth. Vees Talendar, dressed in black robes, knelt before the altar, chanting. He held in his hands a black disc ringed in purple—Shar's symbol.

Coming face to face with Vees's treachery lit Tamlin's anger. He exhaled in a hiss.

Vees stopped chanting of a sudden and started to rise and turn.

Rivalen surrounded them in darkness and whisked them back

to the study in Stormweather Tower. When the shadows parted, Tamlin slammed a fist on the side table. The impact tipped his wine goblet and the red fluid pooled on the table and dripped to the floor.

Vees had lied to him, betrayed him, betrayed the city.

"He must be held to account," Tamlin said.

"He must be punished," Rivalen said, and the shadows about him swirled.

"I will have him arrested."

Rivalen put a hand on his shoulder. The strength in the Prince's hand surprised Tamlin. The shadows around Rivalen churned, touched Tamlin.

"He is a heretic. I would ask that you allow me to see him punished in accordance with church doctrine."

"What does doctrine demand?" Tamlin asked, though he knew the answer.

Rivalen did not blanch. "Death."

Tamlin stared into Rivalen's golden eyes. His breath came short and shallow. He hesitated, then remembered Rivalen's words—*Squeamishness is seldom rewarded in war*. His heart raced but his anger burned.

"His family will not stand for it."

The shadows around Rivalen roiled and he took on a sly look. "Vees Talendar died in combat with the Saerloonian army. I saw it. His body was crushed nearly beyond recognition in the rubble of the wall. He will be buried in a mass grave with the others who fell, assuming his body can be recovered at all."

Tamlin looked into Rivalen's eyes and considered. If Vees had been in seclusion since the battle began, as it appeared he had, the claim could hold up. And if it did not, the threat of revealing a Talendar son as a heretical Sharran would keep a scandal from erupting. He took a deep breath, nodded. "I saw the same thing."

Rivalen did not smile, but his eyes showed approval. "You have grown in our time together."

Tamlin nodded, pleased with Rivalen's praise. He *had* grown.

"I wonder," Rivalen said softly, "whether you are willing to take the final steps?"

Tamlin looked up, a question in his eyes.

"You have seen what Shar offers and have expressed a desire to know more. I have seen in your face that you wish, even, to become one of us?" Rivalen held up his hands and the shadows swirled around his flesh.

Tamlin did not bother to deny it. He had seen shades do what ordinary men could never hope to do.

"All of that is possible," Rivalen said. "But you must demonstrate your commitment to Shar, to me, to yourself. May I be candid?"

Tamlin tried to speak but his mouth was dry. He nodded.

"Too long you have tried to do things halfway, to compromise, to equivocate, to hedge. This, perhaps, is a lesson you learned from your father. I understand well a father's effect on his son."

Tamlin did not respond, but knew that Rivalen was correct. Thamalon had always been a negotiator, a conciliator. Tamlin, too, had always sought a middle path. It had been easiest.

Rivalen continued. "Shar will not stand for such and neither will I. A new world was born today, Tamlin. Your decision here, now, will determine what role you have in it."

Tamlin thought of his mother, his sister, his father, brother, Cale. They would never understand what he had seen, faced, been through. But he decided that he did not need them to. And that decision freed him, for the first time in his life.

"You know my mind, Prince. You know what I want."

Rivalen smiled, showing his fangs. "Then it falls to you to administer punishment to Vees Talendar. In so doing, you will help me reclaim the temple he has desecrated with his heresy. In so doing, you will earn the favor of the Lady of Loss. Are you prepared to do this?"

Tamlin felt mildly lightheaded. He tried to swallow but could not. He was sweating. He felt as if he were standing at the edge of a cliff. Rivalen's eyes burned into him. He thought of all the times he had stood in the study, facing not a Prince of Shade but the disapproving eyes of his father. He thought of the times he had overheard his father confiding to Erevis Cale his disappointment with Tamlin.

He was done trying to satisfy others. He would satisfy himself. He looked from the top of the cliff, eyes open, and stepped off.

"No more compromises, Prince," he said.

Rivalen nodded. "Have you ever taken a man's life before?"

Tamlin cleared his throat. "Yes. But not like this."

Rivalen nodded. "There is no shame in that. Ready yourself. I will prepare matters."

Rivalen returned to his quarters, pleased. He saw potential in Tamlin and hoped the boy would not fail him. He would regard it as unfortunate if he needed to kill him.

He sat on the lush divan before the fireplace. The ambient light of the city's streets filtered in through the windows. Long shadows stretched across the chamber. The darkness embraced him.

On the floor near the divan sat the warded chest that held *The Leaves of One Night*. Rivalen had turned the chest invisible, but his magically enhanced vision saw invisible objects as clearly as visible ones. He pulled the chest before him, spoke the series of passwords that allowed him to bypass the wards, and opened the lid.

Tendrils of shadows snaked into the air. Sussurant, indecipherable whispers filled the chamber for a moment.

Within the chest lay the holy book. Rivalen intoned another series of passwords, reached within, and withdrew it. The moment he touched it, a cacophony of voices sounded in his mind, whispers, shouts, screams, mutterings. He knew they pronounced secrets from ages past, present, and future, but he could not make sense of the words.

The silver characters on the book's frigid cover shifted under his touch, squirmed like worms beneath his fingertips. He held the book on his lap for a time, running his fingers over the pages and losing himself in its utterings. Variance had once told him that listening to the voices too long made the listener mad. Rivalen knew better. Listening to the voices made the hearer wise.

His mind drifted, floated. He thought of the mother he had murdered, his coin collection, his father, his brothers, he thought of the centuries he had spent in darkness. He considered the role of the goddess in his life and saw that the thread of her plots sewed together every moment of his existence from birth to present. It was her voice that spoke to him through the book. He could not understand the divine tongue in which she spoke, but he knew it spoke of a plan to return existence to the perfect, unmarred nothingness of pre-creation.

He focused on the present, on the role he had played and would play in effecting his goddess's will. Events had transpired much as he had hoped. He had only a single frayed end to burn off.

He took his hand from the book—instantly missing the voices—and touched the holy symbol he wore around his neck. He should not take the next step without an augury.

Softly intoning the words to a spell that allowed him communion with Shar, he expanded his consciousness. He found himself floating in emptiness. Insignificant. Alone.

A presence manifested and the emptiness had purpose, consciousness.

The power of Shar's mind, the frigid cold of the void tugged at him. He slipped toward it. Oblivion beckoned. He resisted its call and sent Shar his question.

Vees Talendar, Lady?

The void spoke with a woman's voice and its power stripped him bare.

The Dark Brother has served his purpose, as all do. Even you.

The words made Rivalen uneasy. *I would know more, Lady. Knowledge would allow me to serve you better.*

You know what you need to know, and are ignorant of those things of which you should be ignorant. Proceed as you have planned, content in your knowledge and in your ignorance.

Rivalen dared not dispute the matter.

Thank you, Lady, he said, and cut off the spell. He returned to his body, shaking, gasping, cold. He swallowed and grounded himself back in the world by clutching the divan, feeling the floor under his feet. His flesh bled shadows, and they swirled around him torpidly. He felt at sea. He knew much, but not all. Whatever Shar had planned, Rivalen was but a part of it.

He took a moment to compose himself, then activated the magical ring on his finger and reached out for Vees Talendar.

Nightseer? Vees asked.

Summon the members of your congregation and meet me in the temple, Dark Brother. I have news from the Lady of Loss.

Yes, Nightseer.

Rivalen cut off the connection, returned the book to its chest, and reset his wards. A shadow stretched across the chest. Rivalen turned, expecting to see someone, but there was nothing. He attributed the sensation to an aftereffect of his communion.

He stood, drew the shadows about him, and transported himself to the secret temple of Shar. He had to prepare matters for Talendar and Tamlin.

Elyril watched Rivalen draw the darkness about him and disappear. Excitement made her giddy. She had seen *The Leaves of One Night,* the rest of the book to be made whole, had heard its whispers in her mind. She had seen the Nightseer commune with Shar and had felt the Lady's presence in the room.

Elyril willed her body corporeal and moved across the chamber to the invisible chest. Her burned and withered flesh felt constraining. She felt heavy in her skin, uncomfortable, but she endured it for a time. Her incorporeal form was her true form. The flesh she had worn for decades—the flesh that had been withered by the Nightseer's spell and transformed in fire—had been only the mask she wore until Shar had revealed to her the truth of the Shadowstorm.

She knelt before the invisible chest, holding her holy symbol between the unfeeling stubs of her fingers. Her shriveled lips pronounced the supplication without grace. "In the darkness of the night, we hear the whisper of the void."

The shadows in the room shrouded her like a lover. She took it as a sign. She imagined Volumvax's touch would feel much the same.

She pronounced the words that allowed her to see invisible items and the chest appeared to her. With careful precision she repeated the words she'd heard the Nightseer use to dispel the protective wards on the chest. She held her breath, unlatched it, and threw it open.

Whispers filled the air, indecipherable utterances that hinted at madness, despair, and darkness. Elyril looked into the chest and there saw the book. The otherwise ever-changing silver characters on the book's black cover stilled. She read aloud the words written there, words written centuries before for her, and only her, to see. "Night comes. A storm of shadows is its herald."

The cover dissolved into a stinking black mist and dissipated into the air. The pages of *The Leaves of One Night* lay exposed, naked.

She took out the rest of the book to be made whole, the book gifted her by Shar herself in the guise of the guardsman, Phraig, the book she had pulled from the fire of her own transformation. It trembled in her grasp like a living thing. Its cover flew open and the pages flipped until they reached the gap in the text, the void that wanted filling.

She echoed the words of the Nightseer and discharged the wards cast on *The Leaves of One Night*. She lifted it gently from the chest—whispers sounded in her mind—and placed it atop the other book.

The darkness in the room deepened. The books bound themselves one to the other.

The whispers in her mind intensified, rose in triumph. She clutched her head and gritted her teeth. The voices, thousands of them, spoke at once in a babble of tongues, tones, dialects. She could not bear it for long. She wanted to scream for silence, to demand that they speak so she could understand—

The voices fell silent.

Elyril, sweating, gasping, stared at the book.

A single voice sounded in her head, a woman's voice so heavy with power that it stole Elyril's breath.

Summon the Shadowstorm, Dark Sister.

The book slammed shut.

Elyril stared at it, awed. Its words were an elaborate lie. But in the spaces between its words lay the truth of the ritual.

She picked up the book and dropped her ring, the ring the Nightseer had given her, the ring that had triggered her transformation, into the Nightseer's chest.

"Know my secret now, Nightseer."

She turned herself and the book incorporeal. She rose through the ceiling of the Nightseer's quarters and up into the moonless sky, where she shouted her joy into the darkness.

She would do her goddess's bidding and complete the ritual. She would sit at the side of the Lord Sciagraph as he ruled a world covered in darkness.

She laughed when she realized that the Nightseer would soon know that the Lady of Loss kept secrets even from him.

Cale materialized in darkness on the lowered drawbridge that led into the temple of Mask on the Wayrock. Faerûn's stars shone in the sky above him. The night clung to him. The smell of clean sea air filled his nostrils and he inhaled deeply. The soft rush of the distant surf sounded in his ears.

Riven's two small dogs tore out of the archway and charged Cale, tails wagging. Cale kneeled and patted their flanks, pleased to see them. They licked his hands, put their forepaws on his arm and tried to lick his face. The shadows that coiled about him seemed not to trouble them.

He stood and looked to his right, to the hill where he and Riven had buried Jak. He nodded at the little man's grave. He thought Jak would have been pleased with Cale's resurrection of the dragon.

"Come on, girls," he said to the dogs. "Inside."

The dogs sped ahead of him and he followed them into the temple of his god. He smiled when he thought that Mask had been able to fill his temple with only two men and two dogs.

He found Riven, Nayan, and Magadon awaiting him in the foyer. Riven's dogs circled their master. Riven patted them absently.

"What is it?" Cale asked.

"All went well with the dragon?" Riven asked.

"As well as it could," Cale said.

"You should have left him dead," Magadon said.

"You don't mean that, Mags. The dragon was not a willing vessel."

Magadon stared at him. "I mean it. You just don't like that I mean it."

Cale felt a flash of anger but stifled it. He remembered Magadon's mindblade, its yellow light polluted by black streaks. Magadon, too, was not a willing vessel.

Nayan disrupted the awkwardness. He said, "A priest in service to Abelar Corrinthal has been seeking you. He contacted me through a sending. I have ignored it until now."

"Abelar Corrinthal?" Cale asked, surprised.

Nayan nodded. "We returned Endren to him. He knew of me in that way. He purported to be your ally."

Cale would not have called Abelar an ally, though he had reached an understanding with the man.

"Who is Endren?" Magadon asked. "What does he have to do with matters?"

"Endren is a Sembian nobleman," Cale said. "Abelar is his son and a servant of Lathander. They're enemies of the overmistress."

Magadon's face showed no recognition, or perhaps it was apathy.

"Sembia is at war, Mags," Cale explained. "Or at least it was. I met Abelar on the road out of Selgaunt. He and his men stopped an attack on the Hulorn. They probably saved my life, too. I owe him."

"You owe me," Magadon said.

Cale held his calm with difficulty. "I know."

"What does Abelar want with you?" Riven asked.

Cale looked to Nayan and the shadowwalker shook his head. "The sending asked only for you to attend him," Nayan said.

"Perhaps he needs assistance with the war?" Cale said.

"That is not our fight," Magadon said.

"Maybe the Uskevren boy is in trouble," Riven said. "Rivalen Tanthul had him under his sway."

Magadon looked to Riven. "Rivalen Tanthul?"

Riven's eye narrowed. "Your fight now, eh?"

"I asked you a question," Magadon said, and advanced on Riven.

Riven's mouth hardened. "Take a step back, Mags. Do it now, and get your mouth under control."

"I want Rivalen Tanthul dead for what he did to me."

"That's both of us, then," Riven answered. "Step back."

Magadon did and turned to Cale. "Take me to Rivalen, Cale."

"No."

Cale's word brought Magadon up short. "No? I owe him."

Cale nodded. "As do I. As does Riven. But Rivalen Tanthul is no more our fight than is Sembia's civil war. Not now, at least."

Magadon's brow furrowed, his colorless eyes narrowed.

"We have other concerns," Cale said soothingly. "You need some time, Mags. You've been through a lot. We all have."

"Time is the last thing I need," Magadon said softly, and looked away. "Or have."

"Nayan, get him some food and a place to rest," Cale said. "He's had it harder than Riven and I."

The easterner nodded and beckoned Magadon into the temple. Magadon sighed, nodded, and followed Nayan.

"Mags," Cale called after.

The mindmage turned. He looked ten years older than he had when Cale had first met him. "Kesson Rel is the priority, Mags. Trust me."

Magadon nodded. "I do. I am sorry about my . . . tone."

"You're not yourself."

"No," Magadon said. "I am not."

He turned and Nayan led him off. Cale and Riven shared a look. "He's fading," Riven said.

Cale nodded.

"But you are going to answer this Abelar Corrinthal's call anyway."

Cale nodded again. "I'm indebted to him. And I've got enough debts outstanding. Time to start closing them out."

"I will come with you."

Cale shook his head. "This is my problem. You stay with Mags. I'll return quickly and we'll hunt Kesson Rel."

"He may be hunting us, Cale. You think of that? You think that duplicate was there by chance? He arranged it all."

Cale nodded. Riven was right.

"If he comes for us, he needs to find you and me together. Mags is safe in the temple. Not even Kesson Rel can scry here. No one can. Nayan can watch over him. I am with you," Riven said.

"Riven . . ."

The assassin cut him off. "I've got debts to pay, too, Cale. I am with you."

Cale stared into Riven's one good eye. "Well enough. I will find Abelar with a divination and we go."

"Now?"

"Now."

Cale's spell located Abelar quickly. The servant of Lathander had taken no steps to ward himself. He resided in an encampment along the shore of a small lake. Fires burned here and there in the camp. Hollow-eyed men, women, and children gathered around the fires, hovered near the tents.

Refugees, Cale figured, as he drew the shadows to himself and transported there with Riven.

They materialized before a group of seven armed men seated near a fire. The men leaped to their feet and exclaimed in surprise, but none drew blades.

Cale held up his hands, still leaking shadows. "We are friends and are here to see Abelar Corrinthal."

"He has answered," one of the men said.

A man as tall as Cale stepped forward. He wore a holy symbol on a chain around his throat—Lathander's sun. His long brown hair hung loose to his shoulders.

"I am Roen. You can only be Erevis Cale. Well met. My sending found you. Thank you for coming."

Old men, women, and children, perhaps attracted by the commotion of Cale's sudden appearance, hovered at the edge of the firelight. They eyed Cale and Riven warily. They looked dirty, underfed, fearful.

"All is well here," Roen called to them. "These men are allies."

The refugees nodded, some of the children even smiled.

"I will take you to Abelar," Roen said, and led them to a

nearby canvas tent. "Abelar, the sending is answered."

Cale heard motion within and the tent flap flew open. Abelar Corrinthal stepped out and Cale scarcely recognized him. Dark circles stained the skin under his eyes. Lines of worry creased his brow. His red-rimmed eyes pronounced how little he had slept.

"Thank you for coming, Erevis," Abelar said. He eyed Riven appraisingly and without judgment.

"Why did you send for me?" Cale asked.

Despite his forlorn appearance, Abelar held Cale's eyes with the same calm intensity he had when first they'd met. "My father told me that you got him out of the Hole, that you can walk the shadows like roads. Is that so?"

Cale nodded and the shadows around him swirled. "Yes. That is so."

Voices behind Cale and Riven murmured. Abelar's men had followed them to the tent. Abelar nodded and took a deep breath, like he was leaping into deep water. "I thank you for that. But now . . . I need to ask your assistance again."

"Abelar, Sembia's civil war is not—"

Abelar's face twisted in grief. "To the Hells with Sembia. They took my son, Erevis. My four-year-old son."

"What? Who?"

"Malkur Forrin. His soldiers. They burned my estate and took my son to get at me. We pursued but . . . could not save him. I failed. Lathander failed. I need your help."

Before Cale could answer, Riven said, "They took a boy to get at you?"

Cale heard brewing anger in the assassin's tone.

Abelar nodded, his eyes filled with tears. "My son was born without his full wits. He will not understand what is happening to him. He has never been away from our estate. I cannot bear the thought of . . ."

He bowed his head and tried to compose himself. Roen stepped forward and put a hand on Abelar's shoulder.

"Forrin's army numbers over a thousand," Roen said. "We saw it for ourselves."

"Where did they take the boy?" Riven asked.

Abelar looked up, first to Riven, then to Cale, his eyes hopeful. "Their camp. He is in the midst of their army still, I presume. It is much to ask, I know, but I thought if you could pull my father from the Hole, you could . . ."

He trailed off, staring at Cale, at Riven.

Cale's thoughts turned to Jak, to Aril, and he did not hesitate. "We will help you get him back."

"Tonight," Riven said with a nod. "Steps over a line, taking a boy. Someone pays for that. In blood."

The men around them murmured approvingly.

Abelar stared at them with gratitude, nodded. "You are what I'd hoped. But not what I'd expected."

"Nor I," added Roen.

Riven chuckled.

"We bring him back here?" Cale said. "To you?"

Abelar looked surprised by the question, as if he had not considered it. His expression went from hopeful to troubled to pained. He shook his head. "No . . . no. Bring my son back here to my father. I . . . do not want him to see me this way."

"What way is that?" Riven asked.

Abelar looked down at his palms as if they were covered in stains. He looked at Riven and Cale. "I have to get something out of me before I see him. Do you understand what I am saying?"

"It doesn't come out," Riven said softly, and Abelar blanched.

"Abelar," Roen said, "The Morninglord is . . ."

"You want Forrin to pay," Cale said. "Where do you want him?"

Abelar's eyes focused, burned. "The ruins of Fairhaven, my estate. Can you take me there, or should I ride?"

"I can take you there. At dawn?"

"No," Abelar said, and a cloud passed over his face. "Before dawn. This is nothing to be done under the light of the sun. Well enough?"

"Well enough. Gather your gear. We go now."

They waited while Abelar donned his armor, belted on his blade, and explained matters to his men.

"Your shield?" Cale asked.

Abelar glanced at the still lake, its surface reflecting the stars and Selûne's light, and shook his head. "I do not use it anymore."

Cale decided to ask nothing more. "Fairhaven, you said?"

"Aye."

"I will return shortly," Cale said to Riven. He focused his mind on the name and opened his consciousness. The name alone was enough to provide a beacon for his power. He shrouded himself and Abelar in darkness, felt the corresponding darkness in Fairhaven, and took them there.

The smell of smoke still hung in the air. The shadows parted to reveal the charred skeleton of a once grand estate, burned nearly to the ground. Outbuildings, too, had been set aflame and reduced to heaps of blackened wood. Only the stables and a small village had been spared the flames. A breeze whistled the ruins.

They stood in the midst of dozens of graves marked with river stones. The turned earth showed them to be freshly dug.

"Dark," Cale oathed, and shadows swirled around him.

"They murdered everyone," Abelar said, and the coldness in his tone reminded Cale of Riven. Small wonder he had not wanted to see his boy before doing what needed to be done. "Children. Women. The old. Forrin ordered it, the same way he ordered the burning of Saerb."

Cale stood in respectful silence for a moment. "I should begin the process of finding your son. I need his name."

Abelar's expression softened. "His name is Elden. He is a good son."

Cale and Abelar clasped hands. "You can tell him so yourself. Elden comes home tonight. Then I'll bring you Forrin."

Abelar's expression hardened. "I will be waiting."

Cale stared into his face. "What Riven said . . . he's right,

Abelar. There's no stepping back from some things once you've started down the path."

"I know."

Cale was not sure Abelar did know, but did not feel it his place to lecture the man further. He gathered the shadows to him, knowing there would be another murder in Fairhaven before the sun again showed its face.

Cale materialized in the camp beside Riven and wasted no time. "The boy first," he said, and started for Abelar's tent.

"The boy first," Riven agreed, falling into step beside him.

A bearded man in plate armor stood outside Abelar's tent. He bore a shield enameled with the rose of Lathander. Cale recognized him as Regg, Abelar's lieutenant. They stopped before him.

"He's gone?" Regg asked.

"He'll be back. He needs to do something first."

Regg nodded, his expression troubled. "I know what he needs to do. It's deserved, but . . ." He looked up at Cale. "Is there anything I can do to help?"

Cale shook his head.

"Thank you for your aid," Regg said, and stepped aside.

Cale and Riven ducked into the tent and found it furnished with only a few blankets, a bucket, and a tree stump for a table. Cale pulled shadows into the air before his face and thickened them into a circular clot that looked like a hole in the world. He focused his mind and cast his scrying spell. "Elden Corrinthal," he said.

The circle of shadows spun lazily, took on a reflective gloss. Dim flickers of light flashed deep within it. Cale felt the magic of his spell reach through the shadow lens and across Faerûn. He pushed through any resistance he encountered, using his will as a weapon.

An image formed in the lens.

A small form lay trussed on the ground within what looked like a field tent. Ropes bound the boy at wrist and ankles. Dirt and blood stained his shirt. Bruises discolored his small face. His eyes were closed, nearly swollen shut. Cale feared him dead until he noticed the slight rise and fall of his chest. He was sleeping, or unconscious.

"He's been beaten," Cale said. "Badly."

A low hiss slipped Riven's lips.

Cale forced the magic of his spell to change perspective, to show Elden from another angle and give them a glimpse of the interior of the tent.

A hulking figure with long black hair sat with his back to a large wooden travel chest. His shield and a double-headed battle-axe lay on the ground beside him. He slept in his breastplate, with one hand on the axe's haft. Furs and wool blankets piled elsewhere on the floor. A short spear and a second battle-axe lay propped near the tent flap.

"You get the boy," Riven said. "Then silence the tent with a spell and leave me."

Cale studied Riven's face, his ruined eye. There was no mercy in that eye.

"Well enough," he said. "Ready?"

Riven sheathed his sabers. "Ready."

Cale pulled the shadows about them, felt the corresponding darkness in the distant tent, and took them there.

They stepped from the shadows to the sounds of snores from the long-haired axeman and whimpers from the sleeping boy.

Riven knelt and put his left hand on the boy's head. Shadows leaked from Riven's hand, coalesced around the boy's bruises. Most of them faded and the swelling around his eyes lessened.

Elden winced, cried out in his sleep, curled up into himself. Cale whispered a healing spell of his own and gently placed his right hand on Elden's shoulder. The bruises on his face faded entirely and the boy murmured, muttered something inaudible, and inhaled a deep breath.

Riven and Cale shared a hard look. Riven used handcant to communicate to Cale. *I'll wake him,* he said, nodding at the sleeping man. *He gets to see what's coming.*

Cale nodded, leaned in close to Elden, and whispered in his ear, "You are safe. I will take you to your grandfather."

Elden said nothing, but his small body started to shake. Cale and Riven might have healed the physical wounds, but the boy's scars ran deeper than the flesh.

Cale's anger burned. Any man who beat a boy deserved what he got. He signaled Riven in handcant, the gestures curt and cutting. *Make it hurt.*

Riven nodded, his gaze as hard as adamantine. The assassin prowled across the tent, his hands empty of weapons.

Cale readied his spell of silence.

Riven kicked the axeman's foot and said, "On your feet. Time to die."

Cale cast his spell as the axeman's eyes snapped open and his hand tightened around his weapon.

Sound died, but Cale had already heard the emotionless tone of Riven's voice and it told Cale all he needed to know. The assassin was working. And the tent was no place for a boy. He pulled the shadows about himself and Elden and rode them back to the camp at Lake Veladon.

Years of training and hundreds of combats had sharpened Riven's skills to a sharp edge. Controlled rage honed them to a razor. He stepped backward and drew a throwing knife as the lumbering man jumped to his feet, axe in hand.

Riven hurled the small blade at the man and it tore a gash in his forearm. He screamed in silence and dropped the axe. Blood streamed down his wrist and hand and onto the tent floor.

Riven showed the man his empty hands and beckoned him forward.

The big man understood his meaning. His mouth twisted in a silent roar and he charged Riven, head down and arms out. He outweighed Riven by twenty stones, maybe thirty, but Riven did not back off. Instead, he stepped forward into the man's charge and combined a jump with a sharp right knee.

The man's jaw broke from the impact and his charge ended on the spot. He fell to all fours, wobbling, senseless, bleeding from arm and mouth and spitting teeth.

Riven kicked him in the side of the head and he fell flat to the ground. Straddling him, Riven turned him over roughly. The man's eyes tried to focus. Riven punched him in the face, shattering his nose in a spray of blood and snot. The man screamed silently, tried to roll away, but Riven held him fast. He punched him again, again, again, and again. Soon the man's face was a shattered mess of blood and bruises, and Riven's knuckles were sore and nicked.

Riven knelt over him and stared into his eyes, one of which was clouded with blood from broken vessels. He shook the big man's head by the hair until the eyes focused.

"This is what it feels like to be beaten," he said with a snarl, though Cale's spell swallowed the sound.

The man's mouth moved but Riven could not read his bloody, broken lips. He did not care. The man had nothing to say that Riven cared to hear.

Riven normally killed with efficiency, but he had occasionally provided services for a patron who wanted a target to suffer. Riven had never enjoyed it, but he'd done it.

He would enjoy it now.

He stepped away from the stunned man and walked across the tent. He retrieved the metal-tipped spear and returned.

Drooling blood, the man stared up at him and moved his head slowly from side to side.

Riven cuffed him about the face, used another of his knives to cut the straps of the man's breastplate. He tore it off and threw it to the side. He searched the man to ensure he bore no healing potions. He didn't.

Riven stood and put the point of the spear on the man's gut.

The man was senseless. Riven would not have it.

With his free hand he pulled shadows from the dark air, twined them about his fingers, and put his darkness-adorned hand on the man's shoulder. He let healing magic flow through him. He did not need to speak to generate healing energy, so Cale's spell did not thwart him.

Some of the bruises and cuts on the man's face closed, as did the slash in his forearm. Riven waited for the man's eyes to clear. When they did, he stared into the man's face and drove the spear through his gut. The man's mouth opened in a silent scream of agony that continued as Riven leaned on the spear's haft and sank it half an arm's length into the dirt. Blood poured from the wound.

Wailing and squirming, the man pulled at the spear haft but his strength was already failing him. He pawed at the wooden shaft futilely. He glared at Riven through his pain, cursed him, spat at him.

Riven sneered.

Cale's spell would prevent anyone from hearing the man's screams. Riven had seen men die of gut wounds before. The man would be dead within a hundredcount but every moment would be agonizing. The man who beat a witless boy would die swimming in his own blood, in his own shit, in excruciating pain.

He deserved worse.

Staring without sympathy into the pain-wracked eyes of the dying man, Riven pictured the camp at Lake Veladon in his mind, triggered the magic of his ring, and transported himself there.

CHAPTER SEVENTEEN

1 Nightal, the Year of Lightning Storms

Cale carried the limp boy through the camp. Eyes followed him, then a crowd of men, women, and children. He had two score refugees in his wake by the time he put Elden into Endren's arms. The elder Corrinthal, too shocked to speak, cradled the boy as if he were a babe and cried. Elden stiffened at first.

"Granfah?" the boy said in a tiny voice.

"Yes," Endren said through his tears. "Yes. It's grandfather."

Elden wrapped his arms around his grandfather's neck, buried his face in his beard. Sobs shook his small frame. "He hurt Bowny," the boy said, and sobbed.

"Shh," Endren said, and caressed the boy's back. "Shh. It is all over and you are safe. You are safe." Endren looked past Elden to Cale and said, "I owe you whatever you ask, whenever you ask it."

"No need. It is rare that I get to do something like this."

Endren looked puzzled.

Cale shook his head, "Nevermind."

Endren's eyes showed sympathy, appreciation, concern. Cale could not bear it. He turned to go back to Abelar's tent and found himself facing a crowd. Gratitude filled their eyes. An approving murmur ran through them.

"There is light even in darkness," someone said.

Regg emerged from the crowd, stalked toward Cale with purpose, and wrapped him in an embrace. The shadows around Cale swirled but did not hold Regg at bay. "You stand in the light," Regg said, and released him.

"I hope not," Cale said, but smiled. "And now I have other work."

Regg nodded and backed away.

Cale pulled on the shadows and rode them back to Abelar's tent. For a moment, he wondered after Riven's well-being, but decided the assassin could take care of himself.

Willing the darkness in the tent to deepen, Cale stood in the center of the pitch and repeated the words to his scrying spell. He formed the lens from shadow and reached through it for Malkur Forrin. The power of his spell, of his will, grasped Forrin's name and reached across Faerûn.

Unlike the boy, Forrin was warded. Cale could feel resistance. Dark shadows clouded the scrying lens. He focused his mind, his power, and tried to push through.

The lens went dark. Cale cursed, cast the spell anew, failed again. His frustration grew. He recalled the broken boy he had just returned to his grandfather, a boy taken and beaten on Forrin's orders. He thought of the graves at Fairhaven, of the broken look in Abelar's eyes.

Instead of using Forrin's name as the focus of his spell, he used Abelar's hate for Forrin. Again and again he cast the spell and finally he broke through.

The lens cleared and brightened. He saw Forrin, awake,

standing alone in a field tent, strapping on his breastplate. Glowballs lit the tent brightly, more than necessary to illuminate the tent. He must have feared an attack by the Shadovar.

Cale gave a hard smile. Glowballs would not save Malkur Forrin.

Cale watched as the mercenary general donned his armor, strapped on his blade, adjusted his tabard. Cale waited, the shadows swirling around him. He needed only a single shadow.

Forrin walked across the tent and as he did, his body blocked the light from one of the glowballs, casting his shadow on the ground.

Cale pounced. He rode the shadows across Faerûn to appear directly in Forrin's shadow. The general, perhaps sensing a rush of wind from the air displaced by Cale's arrival, shouted, started to whirl around and draw his blade. "I am attacked!" Forrin called.

Cale grabbed Forrin by the wrist, wrenched his arm behind him, and drove the general into the ground. The dirt muffled Forrin's shout of pain.

Shouts and clinks of armor sounded from outside the tent. Cale willed the glowballs to dim and they answered his command. Shadows cloaked the tent, cloaked Cale. He jerked a dagger from his belt and put it to Forrin's throat. The mercenary snarled but did not move.

"What do you want?" Forrin asked.

"You," Cale answered.

The tent flap flew open and three armored soldiers in green tabards rushed in, blades bare. They seemed surprised to find the tent dark.

"Stop where you stand," Cale said, and they did.

"Release him," one of the men ordered, and another bolted out of the tent and shouted an alarm.

"He is coming with me," Cale said, and gave Forrin's arm another twist. "And if any of you try to find him, I will come for you. Nowhere is safe from me. Do you understand? Nowhere."

The darkness around him churned and the soldiers charged. Cale imagined Fairhaven in his mind and used the darkness to move there.

The shouts of the soldiers faded. The pair materialized in the midst of the ruins. Cale jerked Forrin to his feet, still holding his arm behind him. Forrin struggled but he was no match for Cale, made strong by darkness.

"Will you kill me now, shade?" Forrin said over his shoulder. "Did you bring me all the way out here just to do what you could have done back in the camp?"

Cale shoved him away. Forrin staggered, fell, but jumped to his feet and drew his blade.

"It would be better for you if it were me."

Forrin hesitated, looked uncertain at that. "Who, then?"

From behind Cale, Abelar called, "Leave now, Erevis. This is for him and me. What of Elden?"

Forrin looked past Cale, seeking the source of the voice.

"With Endren," Cale said. He looked to Forrin. "Die poorly." He pulled the darkness about him and rode it away. He materialized on the rooftop of the stables to find Riven already there.

"The boy?" Riven asked.

"Safe with his grandfather. The man who beat him?"

"Not safe," Riven answered.

"How did you know where to find me?" Cale asked.

"I always know where to find you, Cale."

Cale looked at Riven but Riven only stared down at Forrin.

"What are we doing?" Riven asked.

Cale answered, "We're watching."

Riven turned his eye to him. "He told you to leave."

Cale nodded. "It's only justice if there's a witness."

"Justice isn't what he's after, Cale."

Cale had not considered that.

Abelar stood in the ruins of his estate. He recalled the pile of bodies he had found there. Forrin stood where Abelar's servants, family, and friends had been murdered. The smell of death still lingered, as did the smell of burnt wood. He stared across the compound and looked not at Forrin's flesh but into his soul. He saw guilt there, not merely for what the mercenary had done to Elden, but for a multitude of evils. Abelar did not stand in Lathander's grace, but he still could see that Forrin's soul radiated a foul purple light the color of an old bruise.

Forrin paced a circle. He stared across the empty yard, seeking his foe in the darkness. "Show yourself," he called. The mercenary eyed the ruins, the nearby graves.

Abelar stared at him in silence, letting his anger build. Ordinarily he would have prayed to Lathander and asked for the Morninglord to guide his hand and mind. But he would not pray, not now. Faith would not be his guide.

Forrin hefted his blade. "Your pet shade is gone," he taunted. "Are you afraid now?"

Abelar detected no nervousness in his tone. That was well.

Forrin continued. "It is just you and me, now. I have nowhere to run. Come, show yourself."

Abelar concentrated on his magical sword, held it above his head, and set the blade aglow. The area around the estate lit up.

Forrin blinked in the sudden illumination and backed up a step. He was an insect and Abelar had just flipped over his rock.

Through squinting eyes, Forrin focused his gaze on Abelar. His expression showed recognition. "Abelar Corrinthal. I should have guessed."

Abelar strode forth, blade and anger blazing. "Then perhaps you can guess what comes next," Abelar said, his voice as hard as stone. "Look about you. This is where your men murdered my people. This is where your men abducted my son. All on your orders. This is where you will be punished for it."

Forrin assumed a defensive stance and his eyes narrowed. "You are out of your depths here, boy. I killed twenty men ere you were born. I've killed scores since. Reconsider."

Abelar did not slow his step. He walked across the grass toward Forrin.

Forrin licked his lips. "You think your god makes you strong, boy?"

"There is no god here," Abelar answered. "This is between you and me."

Forrin stared, his eyes dark. "It always is."

Abelar had killed many men, all of them evil, but had never felt such hate for another man as he felt at that moment. Righteous hate. He picked up his pace.

Forrin swung his blade in a slow pattern, readying himself.

"You caused my son pain," Abelar said.

Forrin's blade went still and he raised an eyebrow, as if puzzled by the remark. "We're at war, boy. I did what I had to. I would do it again."

"Not after today," Abelar said. He took his blade in a two-handed grip and charged.

Forrin squared his feet and held his sword high.

Abelar closed the distance in ten strides and opened with a quick thrust to the abdomen. Forrin lurched to the side and answered with a reverse crosscut for Abelar's throat. Abelar ducked it and bulled forward, slamming his shoulder into Forrin's chest. The breath went out of the mercenary and he staggered backward.

Abelar did not fight with grace. He fought with efficiency. He followed up, unleashing an overhand slash that would have split Forrin's skull had he not gotten his blade up to parry. Abelar grabbed a fistful of Forrin's shirt; Forrin grabbed a fistful of Abelar's. They turned a circle, nose to nose.

"There are consequences for the life you've lived, Forrin," Abelar said. "There are always consequences."

Forrin snarled and spat into Abelar's face. Abelar shoved him away. Eyeing each other, appraising, they paced a circle around one another.

"Your boy cried from the moment we brought him into camp," Forrin said.

Abelar gritted his teeth but did not take the bait. "I am looking at a dead man."

"So you say," said Forrin, grinning through his scars. He feigned a relaxed posture then abruptly lunged forward, blade leveled at Abelar's chest.

Abelar knocked the mercenary's blade toward the ground with his gauntlet. Forrin's momentum carried him forward and Abelar lashed out at the mercenary's back. The blade bit through armor and Forrin roared. The mercenary answered with a wild, blind defensive swing that caught Abelar on the forearm. The blow did not penetrate Abelar's mail but left his arm numb for moments.

Abelar shook it out, then bounded forward, unleashing a flurry of slashes. Forrin retreated, desperately parrying, answering with his own stabs and slashes where he could. Abelar locked Forrin's blade low and right, got in close, and put an elbow into the side of the mercenary's head. Forrin's helmet flew off and he staggered, but managed to answer with a glancing punch to Abelar's cheek.

Still stunned, Forrin clumsily jerked his blade free of Abelar's blade lock and swung a crosscut at Abelar's torso. The slash hit Abelar in the ribs but his armor turned the steel. Abelar stabbed low and his blade cut through Forrin's armor and bit deep into his thigh.

The mercenary roared with pain, somehow kept his feet, and launched a desperate two-handed overhead slash at Abelar's head. Abelar lurched aside but could not dodge the blow entirely. It struck his left shoulder and split the links of his mail. Pain shot down his arm. Warm blood followed it. He did not allow the pain to slow him. He kicked his boot into the wound in Forrin's thigh. While Forrin screamed and tried to bring his blade to bear, Abelar slashed the mercenary's leg again. Steel grated against bone and Forrin collapsed.

Abelar ignored the pain in his arm and loosed a blinding series of hammering overhead slashes into Forrin's blade. He could have killed Forrin any time, but he wanted and needed to pound the mercenary. With each slash he whispered a word, an incantation, an imprecation.

"Consequences."

One after the other, the blows pounded down. Forrin parried desperately but each of Abelar's blows drove his blade down more. Abelar's arms were numb; Forrin's had to be filled with lead.

"I submit," the mercenary said. "Enough."

Abelar ignored the words and continued to rain down blows. "Consequences." His blade rang off Forrin's.

Fear crept into Forrin's eyes. "Damn you, Corrinthal!" he shouted.

"Consequences," Abelar said, and let loose another blow. Another.

Forrin parried them but his blade shook in his hands. He screamed in helpless rage.

"Consequences," Abelar said.

"Enough! Enough!"

Abelar didn't stop, couldn't stop, wouldn't stop.

"Consequences."

In desperation, Forrin lunged forward and stabbed at Abelar's abdomen. Abelar knocked the blade to the side and stomped on Forrin's arm. He heard the bone snap. Forrin screamed, collapsed on the ground again. Blood from his wounded leg soaked the earth under him.

Abelar stood over him, blade held high, his breath coming hard.

Cale saw what was about to happen and knew exactly what it would cost Abelar. He cursed, stood, and started to pull the shadows around him.

Riven's hand closed on his arm. "No, Cale."

Cale did not take his eyes from Abelar.

"He won't be able to live with himself if he does it."

Riven shook his head. "He won't be able to live with himself if he doesn't. You saw his son."

Cale hesitated. "A bad choice."

Riven nodded. "But that's how the world works."

Cale did know it. Being able to live with yourself and keeping your soul clean weren't always the same thing. And when it came to it, a man had to choose one or the other.

"He's different from us, Riven."

Cale did not need to look at Riven to know he wore his familiar sneer. Riven said, "No, he's not."

And Cale knew Riven was right.

Cale let the shadows dissipate. He would watch. Abelar had to make his own choice.

Abelar stood over Forrin. The mercenary rolled onto his back, bleeding, a knot the size of a pommel ball rising on his temple.

"I surrender to you, Corrinthal," he said with a pained grimace. "I surrender. The overmistress will pay for my safe return. Use me to negotiate a peace."

Abelar stared into Forrin's eyes. His thoughts turned to his son and blackened. He tightened his grip on his blade.

Forrin must have seen it. "Lathander will punish you if you do it, Corrinthal. You know that."

"I already told you," Abelar said, "there's just you and me here."

With that, Abelar reversed his grip and drove his blade through Forrin's heart, pinning him to the earth. The mercenary's eyes bulged, his legs thrashed.

Abelar twisted the blade. "That is for my son."

He twisted it again. "That is for my friends and my servants."

He twisted it once again and Forrin screamed, gasped, writhed. "And that is for Saerb."

Abelar leaned down, palms on his pommel, and stared into

the mercenary's eyes. "There are *always* consequences, Forrin. Die with that knowledge."

Forrin said nothing, merely gagged on his own blood and took a tencount to die. When he expired, Abelar withdrew his blade and wiped it clean on Forrin's tabard.

As he sheathed it, he said softly, "Consequences for both of us."

Cale swept Riven up in the shadows and transported them to Abelar's side. Abelar did not look at them. He stared down at Forrin, his face unreadable. The mercenary's dead eyes stared up at the lightening sky.

"You saw?" Abelar asked.

Cale and Riven nodded.

"Your son is safe," Cale said.

Abelar nodded, looked to the west. Tears filled his eyes. "It's not out of me," he said.

"It never will be," Riven said. "Live with it."

Abelar eyed Riven and seemed about to speak. Cale cut him off. "We should go. I need darkness to do what I do."

Abelar smiled without mirth and looked to Riven. "Me, too, it appears."

"You did the right thing here," Riven said, and nudged Forrin's body with his toe.

"No," Abelar said. "Not the right thing, but the only thing."

"Fair enough," Riven said.

Abelar looked to Cale and said, "Please take me to my son."

Rivalen, garbed in a black cloak and blacker shadows, awaited Tamlin in the dark alley beside Siamorphe's temple. Tamlin had come alone. He wore a hooded cloak to disguise himself. His heart was racing. His breath came fast.

The shadows around Rivalen spiraled lazily from his flesh. "Are you prepared, Hulorn?"

Tamlin gulped to wet his mouth, nodded. "Where is Vees?"

"He is within. As are his fellow conspirators."

Tamlin froze. "Conspirators? We discussed only Vees."

Rivalen put a fatherly hand on Tamlin's shoulder. The shadows coiled around Tamlin's face. "I know, Tamlin. But all of them are guilty. All of them conspired against you and the city. All of them would have quietly taken positions of power as you hung on the overmistress's gallows."

Tamlin heard truth in Rivalen's tone. Still, he hesitated. Rivalen must have seen it. He said, "We have trusted each other, Hulorn. Continue in that. You wish to approach Shar? You wish to meld with the shadows, to transform your vulgar flesh into something lasting?"

Tamlin nodded. He did. He envied everything Cale was, everything Rivalen was. He wanted it.

"Then you must be Shar's instrument tonight. Now."

Tamlin stared into Rivalen's golden eyes and found his nerve. He nodded. "I'm ready."

Rivalen turned, spoke an arcane word before the alley wall, and a cunningly disguised secret door swung open. He led Tamlin inside. They descended a narrow flight of stairs until they reached a small room. A single candle provided light. Shadows danced on the gray walls. Black cloaks with purple piping hung from pegs on the wall.

"Don the cloak and throw up the hood. The Lady does not want to see your face. She wants to know your soul."

Tamlin exchanged the cloak with his own and threw up the hood. Rivalen did the same. To his surprise, Tamlin's legs felt sturdy under him.

"What occurs within Shar's temples is a secret known only to the worshipers who participate. To breach that confidence is to incur the Lady's wrath. Do you understand?"

Tamlin nodded. His heart beat faster. "I do."

"After you have served as the Lady's instrument this night, you will return to your quarters and pray to the Lady of Loss. You will offer to her a secret known only to you. This will be your Own Secret, thenceforth known only to you and the Lady and never shared with others. This will bind you to her. Do you understand?"

Tamlin nodded. He sweated under the robe. "I do."

Rivalen reached into a pocket and withdrew a thin dagger. Amethysts adorned its crosspiece and pommel. "Take this."

Tamlin stared at the blade. Rivalen held it forth and did not move. The shadows about the Prince roiled. A single strand of darkness emerged from Rivalen's flesh and coiled around the blade.

Tamlin took it. The shadows felt warm against his flesh; the blade felt cool.

Rivalen turned and opened a door. A candlelit worship hall loomed beyond. "If you walk through this door, there is no turning back. If you enter and do not do what you are here to do, I will kill you rather than let you leave."

Tamlin looked up sharply, took a step back.

"It would give me no pleasure to do so, but I would have no choice. I am not forgiving in matters of faith. Look into yourself and determine if you are willing to shed blood to have what you wish. Are you?"

Tamlin looked at the doorway, the worship hall, Rivalen. He thought of his family, his friends. They all seemed very far away. But his desires were close. He knew what he wanted. He knew there was only one way to get it. "I am."

A voice from inside sent Tamlin's heart to racing.

"Tamlin?" Vees called, his voice muffled. "Is that you? Thank the gods. Tamlin! Get me out of here. The Prince is mad."

Rivalen raised his hand and Vees fell silent.

Tamlin felt Rivalen's gaze on him, his burning golden eyes. He was studying him, measuring his reaction to Vees's voice.

Tamlin nodded and stepped through the doorway. Rivalen put a hand on his shoulder and followed. "In the darkness of night, we hear the whisper of the void," Rivalen said.

Whispers sounded in Tamlin's ears. He could not make out words, but he knew they represented a promise of power. "I hear whispers," Tamlin said, his voice hushed.

"Heed its voice," Rivalen said.

Six men and women knelt, facing the black altar. Vees was among them. Ropes of shadow bound their hands behind their backs and bound their ankles together. All were nude. All looked upon Tamlin and Rivalen with terror in their wide eyes. They shook their heads, and their mouths opened to plead, but they made no sound. Rivalen must have had them magically silenced. He had allowed Vees to be heard only to test Tamlin.

Tamlin had never felt such power. "Let me hear them."

Rivalen looked at him and nodded. He raised a hand and the silencing magic ended. Tears, wails, and shouts for mercy blended together into a chorus of despair. Tamlin heard Vees's voice among the rest. "Deuce, don't do it! It's me, Vees. Deuce, please!"

"Their despair and regret we offer to you, Lady of Loss," Rivalen intoned.

He moved behind the heretics. Tamlin followed, his breath coming fast, his body tingling, weak.

All six of the heretics struggled against their bonds but to no avail. They pleaded for mercy.

"Do not, Deuce. I am your friend," Vees said.

Tamlin felt outside himself, felt embraced and nurtured by the darkness of the hall. He moved behind Vees but did not see his onetime friend. Memories flashed through his mind: his mother, Tazi, Talbot, all with love in their eyes, but love colored by disappointment, even pity. Other faces flashed, too: his father, with the ever-present stare of disapproval and the frequent, disappointed shake of his head; Mister Cale, shrouded in shadows, with the faint look of contempt and distaste in his eyes; a lifetime of faces that regarded him as a buffoon, a ne'er do well, an unaccomplished fop.

Tamlin had spent his adult life trying to efface those looks. He could do it now, at a stroke.

"Choose your path, Hulorn," Rivalen said.

Tamlin looked to the Prince and saw in his eyes no judgment, no disappointment, no quiet dislike. He saw in Rivalen a friend and mentor.

The Prince nodded and the shadows about him reached out to touch Tamlin.

Tamlin nodded.

Vees screamed. "Please, Tamlin! No! Whatever he told you is a lie! Don't, Deuce!"

Tamlin raised the blade high and drove it downward into Vees's back, into his father, into Cale, into the man he had been his entire life.

Cradling the book, hearing the voice of her goddess, Elyril flew high above Selgaunt. She decided that she would summon the Shadowstorm in the city in which she had murdered her parents and first sworn herself to the Lady of Loss. She intoned the words to a spell and the magic transported her high above Ordulin.

Lights and glowballs lit the capital's streets. A sea of tents dotted the plains around the city. Even at the late hour, soldiers milled through the camp.

Elyril thought the entire city looked like a lesion. She would excise it, and as eternal darkness fell, she would stand beside Volumvax the Divine One, Shar's Shadow, the Lord Sciagraph.

She was giddy, lightheaded with expectation, more elated than she had ever been from minddust.

The voice of the book fell silent but it began to pulse in her hands like a living thing, like a heart. Shadows coiled around it, around her.

Elyril opened its cover and looked not to the words, but to the words between the words. She gave voice to the empty spaces.

She did not understand the full meaning of the words but she spoke them with vigor. As she read, understanding dawned. Elyril was part of a plan that reached across time and worlds. Even the coming cataclysm of the Shadowstorm was but a single step in Shar's plan that had millennia still to unfold. Shar had been plotting since the cosmic war with her sister, Selûne, had wrought creation from the pristine emptiness of oblivion. Shar would return to the peace of nothingness and all of existence would return with her.

Power gathered as Elyril moved through the book, pronounced the words, summoned the shadows. As she incanted, the pages from which she read dissipated into nothingness. The book was consuming itself, turning to nothingness, as she moved through the ritual.

Below her, the lights in Ordulin dimmed more and more as she progressed. The sky above her darkened. Clouds as thick and black as any thunderhead she had ever seen gathered. Wind picked up, roared in her ears. Her voice gained volume until she was shouting Shar's words into the night sky.

On the darkened streets and in the darkened camp far below her, groups of people started to gather. They pointed at the gathering clouds, the whipping wind. They looked tiny, insignificant.

And they were.

Her voice boomed across the heavens. Darkness blotted out the moon, the stars. Elyril exalted in the ritual, laughed as she cast the spell. She voiced the last words and her voice was a scream.

The wind died. Silence fell. Darkness reigned. Eldritch currents of green fire flared in the air.

Elyril could not breathe in her excitement. She awaited the coming of Volumvax the Divine One, the advent of the Shadowstorm.

A crack that sounded like the breaking of the world shook the heavens. A green line formed an arc in the sky over Ordulin and split the darkness in two. The line expanded, wider, wider, until it formed a door as large as the city.

Voices from the city below carried up into the sky. Elyril heard fear in them.

Another crack sounded and shadows and power boiled out of the doorway in a rushing wave.

Elyril could not avoid the onrush of power. She grinned as the wave struck her, turned her to flesh, drew the breath from her body, and drove her like an arrowshot toward the ground. As she plummeted toward the earth, she heard Ordulin's citizens scream as one and knew their terror and despair were sweet to the Lady.

She hit the ground outside the city walls and the impact shattered bones. Pain lit her body on fire. Her flesh changed to shadow, to flesh, back to shadow. Her eyes stared upward, fixed on the ever-growing rift in the sky, a rift between Faerûn and the Adumbral Calyx.

More and more of the Calyx poured through the glowing green tear and fell onto Ordulin like a black tide. Darkness swirled over the ground like fog, saturated the air, shrouded the city, assimilated Faerûn with the Calyx. Panicked screams carried through the shadows, distant and delightful. Thunder rumbled and green lightning split the sky.

The grass and trees of the plains wilted around Elyril, twisted, transformed into horrid mockeries of their normal shapes. Animals emerged from their dens, metamorphing into caricatures of themselves as they breathed the transformative darkness.

The Shadowstorm had come.

Mirabeta raced toward a balcony of her tallhouse. The servants and men-at-arms thronged the halls, panic in their eyes. "What is happening? What is happening? Are we under attack?" she screamed at everyone and no one.

They answered only with screams of terror.

"Obey me! I am the overmistress!"

No one even slowed.

Wearing a nightdress, she pushed open a door and stepped out on the balcony. The wind whipped at her and what she saw drained her of breath.

Darkness cloaked the city, swirled through the air like a fog of pitch. Screams from every quarter cut through the night. She looked up to see a glowing green portal in the sky as large as Ordulin itself. Shadows thronged the air.

At first she thought perhaps the Shadovar had attacked, but this was bigger than that. She thought she heard a voice in the wind, giggling. "Elyril?"

She realized she was suddenly cold. She looked down to see the fog of darkness clinging to her skin, her clothes. Her heart leaped in her chest. She tried to brush it away but it clung to her hands, to her face. She screamed as its cold sank further into her flesh, her bones. "Get off! Get off! Get it off!"

The cold stole her energy and her speech slurred. Exhausted, she collapsed to the balcony while more and more of the fog embraced her. Her dreams of empire faded away and her life went with them.

Elyril laughed through her pain as she listened to Ordulin die. She looked to the city and saw guards falling from the walls, soldiers stepping out of their tents to collapse, die, and rise anew as shadows. Perhaps some of the citizens would escape, or perhaps none would. Tens of thousands died in darkness in a moment's time.

A shriek sounded from the sky and an army of undead shadows from the Calyx boiled through the rift in a black cloud, hundreds, thousands. The transformed dead of Ordulin rose into the sky to meet them. Shadow giants materialized in the darkness, their pale flesh and towering forms one with the dark.

Elyril's laughter turned to a cough and she spat blood.

A shadow formed in the rift, as black as pitch, backlit by the green light. She recognized it as her lord, Volumvax the Divine One. His presence filled her mind, awed her, put her at peace. He had come for her at last. He would make her whole and she would take her place at his side.

She called to him, lifted a shattered arm to beckon him to her.

He paid her no heed as he stepped through the rift and flew down to Ordulin, borne earthward on a cloud of shadows.

The screams in the city ceased. Volumvax perched on the wall and held his arms aloft. Swirling darkness and red-eyed shadows surrounded him. He laughed and the sound shook the heavens.

Elyril realized at once that he was not coming for her. He had betrayed her. She wept, railed, cursed. The darkness around her mirrored her mood. She had been used.

She lay on her back, her dying body somewhere between shadow and flesh. Spasms of pain wracked her. Green lightning split the lightless sky. She reached for her invisible holy symbol, brushed it with her fingertips.

"The Shadowstorm is come," she mouthed, and imagined her aunt's terror as the night came for her. That, at least, brought her pleasure. She giggled, but it gave way to a cough. She rolled onto her side and spat a gob of black phlegm and blood.

She found herself staring at a pair of sandaled feet, female feet with the palest, most flawless skin Elyril had ever beheld. She knew instantly who stood before her, and she buried her face in the earth.

"Lady," she mouthed.

She wanted to ask why she had been misled, why should would not rule at Volumvax's side, but she choked on the words.

"Your bitterness is sweet," the Lady said. "Look upon me, now."

The goddess's voice was emotionless, devoid of anything recognizably human other than the words. And it held such power that Elyril felt as if a mountain had fallen onto her back. She feared to obey, but she feared more to disobey. She rolled over and lay flat on her back.

A form stood over her, a black-haired woman with skin as pale as alabaster and eyes as dark and deep as the shadows that filled the sky and air.

No, it was the shadow of a woman as tall as the sky that loomed over her. Stars blinked in her form, ancient and dim, and the power she contained threatened to break the world.

Elyril fought to breathe. Her heart pounded and her body changed from shadow to ruined flesh with each beat. Her vision blurred as tears filled her eyes.

She struggled to speak. "It is too much, Lady. Too much."

"It has only just begun," Shar answered. "Your part is done. You have served, priestess, and I am come."

Elyril's body shook at her goddess's praise, slight though it was. Shar regarded her with frigid eyes, and Elyril's body shook under the goddess's regard.

"Am I mad, Lady?" she asked, fearing the answer. "Is this real?"

Shar raised a finger to her lips.

"Shh. It is a secret."

She smiled but Elyril had never before seen a colder expression. Shar reached down for Elyril and frigid, unforgiving fingers as old as creation closed Elyril's eyes.

She felt a flash of exquisite agony, followed by revelation, then emptiness, emptiness forever.

I sit at the table in the temple, awaiting Cale and Riven's return. The shadowwalkers observe me but say little. Darkness clings to them, crowds around them.

But darkness is in me. And it is growing.

Words come out of my mouth before I can consider their meaning. Vile words. Feelings that would make a demon blanch well up from some dark place in my soul. The urge to do violence, to kill, is powerful. I try to focus it on Rivalen, on Kesson Rel, but the impulse longs to be expressed indiscriminately.

To kill what is growing in me, we must kill a god.

I do not know if it can be done. I see doubt in Cale's eyes. He fears for me.

"We must go for a time," says Nayan, the leader of the shadowwalkers.

I nod. I do not wish them to leave, but I cannot bring myself to ask them to stay.

Without a word, they disappear into the twilight. I think of the words my father spoke into my ear on Cania: *One of you must die, the shade or you, ere this is done. How will you have it?*

I take Riven's knife in my hand, and lay it across my wrist. It would be simple, a single cut. But I cannot. I do not know if it is man or fiend that urges suicide. I drive the blade into the table.

Tears wet my face. I am an observer watching myself sink into evil.

The fiend laughs at my weakness.

I push him down—for now—but know that I cannot do so much longer.

LISA SMEDMAN

The *New York Times* best-selling author of *Extinction* follows up on the War of the Spider Queen with a new trilogy that brings the Chosen of Lolth out of the Demonweb Pits and on a bloody rampage across Faerûn.

THE LADY PENITENT

BOOK I

SACRIFICE OF THE WIDOW

Halisstra Melarn has been a priestess of Lolth, a repentant follower of Eilistraee, and a would-be killer of gods, but now she's been transformed into the monstrous Lady Penitent, and those she once called friends will feel the sting of her venom.

BOOK II

STORM OF THE DEAD

As the followers of Eilistraee fall one by one to Halisstra's wrath, Lolth turns her attention to the other gods.

September 2007

BOOK III

ASCENDANCY OF THE LAST

The dark elves of Faerûn must finally choose between a goddess that offers redemption and peace, or a goddess that demands sacrifice and blood. We know what a human would choose, but what about a drow?

June 2008